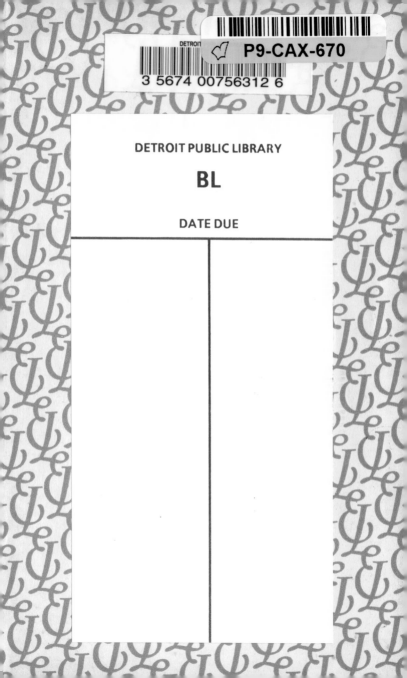

EVERYMAN'S LIBRARY

920

FICTION

Everyman, I will go with thee, and be thy guide,
In thy most need to go by thy side

PIERRE LOTI was the pseudonym of Louis
Marie Julien Viaud, who was born at Roche-
fort on 14th January 1850. He entered the
navy in 1867, became lieutenant in 1881 and
captain in 1906, and was transferred to the
reserve in 1910. Died at Hendaye on 10th
June 1923.

PIERRE LOTI
ICELAND FISHERMAN

TRANSLATED BY
W. P. BAINES

LONDON   J. M. DENT & SONS LTD
NEW YORK   E. P. DUTTON & CO INC

INTRODUCTORY NOTE

Pêcheur d'Islande, in English *Iceland Fisherman*, was Pierre Loti's seventh book, and the story that established his greater fame as a novelist and story-teller. He had been a sailor serving in the French navy many years when he wrote it, and his intimate understanding of the sea in all its moods, its northern and wintry aspects and its summer calms, was never turned to finer effect. His Breton strain aided in the interpretation of the characters who were like his hero Yann, both sturdy and wayward, or like the girl Gaud, simple and complex by turns. Those who know the Breton coast and its 'Sept Isles' and their azure setting, or its bleak moors and rocky coasts will recognize the truth of his scene-painting. His Paimpol and his Porseven become alive and real in his tale-teller's page. The touch of Celtic fatalism in the story may be traced to his temperamental reactions and the same early influences.

Here and there possibly an ultra modern reader may question his use of the idyllic note and his frequent dropping into the minor key. But that too was typical of the man and his narrative method, for he could be gay and melancholy, with equal instinct; and he could not resist at the end of all a cadence that is almost too affectionately turned. When the final summing up of Pierre Loti as a French novelist comes to be made, it will be to the books in which his Breton and his seafaring early memories give fictive reality to the writing that the old Censor, Time, will turn—and in that earlier cycle of stories *Iceland Fisherman* will hold a sure place.

ERNEST RHYS.

SELECT BIBLIOGRAPHY

WORKS. *Aziyadé* (published anonymously), 1879; *Le Mariage de Loti*, 1882 (issued first in the *Nouvelle Revue* in 1880 as *Rarahu*); *Le Roman d'un Spahi*, 1881; *Fleurs d'Ennui*, 1882; *Mon Frère Yves*, 1883; *Les Trois Dames de la Kasbah*, 1884; *Pêcheur d'Islande*, 1886; *Propos d'Exil*, 1887; *Madame Chrysanthème*, 1887; *Japoneries d'Automne*, 1889; *Au Maroc*, 1889; *Le Roman d'un Enfant*, 1890; *Le Livre de la Pitié et de la Mort*, 1891; *Fantôme d'Orient*, 1891; *L'Exilée*, 1893; *Jérusalem*, 1895; *Le Désert*, 1895; *La Galilée*, 1895; *Ramuntcho*, 1897; *Matelot*, 1898; *Figures et Choses qui passaient*, 1898; *Reflets sur la Sombre Route*, 1899; *Les Derniers Jours de Pékin*, 1902; *L'Inde*, 1903; *Vers Ispahan*, 1904; *La Troisième Jeunesse de Madame Prune*, 1905; *Les Désenchantées*, 1906; *La Morte de Philae*, 1909; *Le Château de la Belle-aux-bois-dormant*, 1910; *Un Pèlerin d'Angkor*, 1912; *La Turquie agonisante*, 1913; *La Hyène enragée*, 1916; *L'Horreur allemande*, 1918; *Prime Jeunesse*, 1919; *La Mort de Notre Chère France en Orient*, 1920; *Suprême Vision d'Orient*, 1921; *Un Jeune Officier pauvre*, 1923.

Loti also did a little dramatization, including versions of *Pêcheur d'Islande* and *Madame Chrysanthème*, and a play written in collaboration with Judith Gautier called *La Fille du Ciel*. His two best-known miscellaneous works are the *Discours de Reception de Pierre Loti à la Séance de l'Académie Française*, 1892, and *L'Outrage des Barbares*, 1917, translated into English by Madox Hueffer. A collected edition of his works was published in eleven vols., 1893–1911.

BIOGRAPHY AND CRITICISM. Frédéric Mallet, *Pierre Loti: son Œuvre*, 1923; E. B. F. D'Auvergne, *Pierre Loti*, 1926; C. Farrère, *P. Loti, quand je l'ai connu*, 1927; R. Lefèvre, *La Vie inquiète de P. Loti*, 1934; F. A. Chassériau, *Souvenirs sur P. Loti*, 1937.

CONTENTS

PART I

An Iceland girl struggles to become important to a young fisherman who is "married to the sea".

CHAPTER I

THERE were five of them, mighty-shouldered fellows, round a table drinking, in a gloomy sort of room which smelt of brine and the sea. The den, for so it might be described, was too low for men of their stature, and tapered towards one end, like the interior of a great hollow sea-gull; it rocked gently, giving out a monotonous plaint, with a slowness of sleep.

Outside, no doubt, was the sea and the night, but there was little or no indication of this within: a single opening cut in the roof was closed by a wooden lid, and the light came from an old hanging lamp which swung slowly.

There was a fire in a stove; their wet clothes were drying, shedding a vapour of steam which mingled with the smoke from their clay pipes.

Their massive table occupied the whole of the room, conforming exactly to its shape, and there remained just room to get round in order to sit on the shallow lockers fixed to the oaken walls. Large beams passed above them, almost touching their heads; and, behind their backs, sleeping berths, which seemed to have been hollowed out of the thickness of the timber, opened like the niches of a vault for the dead. All the woodwork was massive and defaced, impregnated with dampness and sea salt; worn, polished by the rubbings of their hands.

They had been drinking wine and cider out of their bowls, and the joy of physical well-being brightened

3

their faces which were open and honest. And they remained now round the table, talking of women and marriage.

Against a panel at the end of the room a Holy Virgin in faïence was fixed on a little shelf, in a place of honour. She was rather ancient, the patron saint of these sailors, and coloured with an art still crude. But personages in faïence last much longer than real men and women; and her red and blue robe still produced the effect of a little something very bright amid all the sombre greys of that poor wooden house. She had heard, doubtless, more than one heartfelt prayer, in hours of distress and peril; at her feet someone had nailed two bunches of artificial flowers and a rosary.

These five men were clothed all alike: a thick jersey of blue wool fitting tight to the body and disappearing inside the waistband of their trousers; on the head, the kind of helmet of tarred canvas which is called a sou'wester (from the name of the wind which in our hemisphere brings the rains).

They were of divers ages. The captain might have been forty; three others, between twenty-five and thirty; the last, whom they called Sylvestre or Lurlu, was no more than seventeen. He was already a man in stature and strength; a dark beard, very fine and very curly, covered his cheeks; but he had kept his boyish eyes—grey-blue eyes, which were extremely gentle and quite innocent.

Very close to one another, for want of space, they seemed to be enjoying a great sense of ease, talking thus in their dark little room.

Outside, no doubt, was the sea and the night, the infinite desolation of dark and profound waters. A brass watch, hanging on the wall, marked the hour of eleven—eleven at night, doubtless; and against the wooden roof could be heard the pattering of rain.

They were discussing very merrily among themselves these questions of marriage, but without saying anything that was indecent. Simply projects for those who were still unmarried, or, maybe, droll stories of things that had happened in their villages during wedding festivities. True that sometimes they uttered, with an honest laugh, an allusion a little too frank to the pleasure of love. But love, as men so tempered understand it, is always a healthy thing, and in its very crudity remains almost chaste.

Sylvestre, however, was a little restless, on account of another called Jean (a name which the Bretons pronounce Yann), who had not come.

Where, in fact, was this Yann; still at work above? Why had he not come down to take a share in this feast?

'It's nearly midnight, too,' said the captain.

And, standing upright, he raised with his head the wooden lid, in order to call, through the opening, this fellow Yann. A very strange light fell then from above.

'Yann! Yann! Eh! You man there!'

The *man* replied roughly from without.

And through this lid, half opened for a minute, the pale light which entered was almost like the light of day. 'Nearly midnight'—and yet the light seemed to be sunlight, a sort of crepuscular light transmitted from afar by mysterious mirrors.

The opening closed, darkness returned, the little pendent lamp resumed its yellow glare, and one heard the *man*, in huge clogs, descending a wooden ladder.

He entered, obliged to bend double like a great bear, for he was almost a giant. And, at the outset, he made a grimace and held his nose on account of the acrid odour of the brine.

He exceeded by rather too much the ordinary proportions of men, especially in the breadth of his shoulders, which were as square as a cross-bar; when he faced you, the muscles of his shoulders, outlined under his blue jersey, formed, as it were, two balls at the top of his arms. He had large brown eyes, very mobile, at once shy and proud in expression.

Sylvestre, passing his arms round this Yann, hugged him affectionately, as children do; he was betrothed to his sister, and treated him as an elder brother. The other allowed himself to be caressed with the air of a spoilt lion, responding by a good-humoured smile, which showed his white teeth.

His teeth, which had more room in which to arrange themselves than is the case with other men, had little spaces between them, and seemed quite small. His fair moustache was rather short, although it was never cut; it was curled very closely in two little symmetrical rolls above his lips, which were thin and beautifully shaped; and then, at the two ends, it spread out in disorder on either side of the deep-set corners of his mouth. The rest of his beard was clipped close, and his ruddy cheeks had preserved a fresh bloom, like that of fruits which no one has touched.

The glasses were refilled when Yann had sat down, and they called the shipboy to refill the pipes and light them.

This lighting of the pipes enabled him to smoke a little himself. He was a sturdy lad, round-faced, a distant cousin of all these sailors, who were all more or less related to one another; apart from his work, which was hard enough, he was the spoilt child of the ship. Yann gave him to drink out of his glass, and then he was sent to bed.

Afterwards they took up again the great topic of marriage.

'And you, Yann,' asked Sylvestre, 'when are you going to get married?'

'Aren't you ashamed,' said the captain, 'a great fellow like you, at twenty-seven, to be still unmarried? What must the girls think when they see you!'

He shrugged his formidable shoulders with a gesture that was full of disdain for women, and replied:

'I marry in the night; at other times, I marry when the opportunity offers; it all depends.'

Yann had just finished his five years' service in the navy, and it was there, as a gunner in the fleet, that he had learnt to speak French and to entertain sceptical notions. And he began to tell of his most recent 'marriage,' which, it appeared, had lasted a fortnight.

It was at Nantes, with a singing-girl. One night, going ashore, he had entered, a little the worse for drink, an alcazar. At the door was a woman selling enormous bouquets at twenty francs apiece. He had bought one, without knowing very well what he was going to do with it, and then, as soon as he got in, he had thrown it full in the face of the singer on the stage—partly in rough homage, partly in mockery of the painted doll, who seemed to him too 'made up.' The girl fell from the blow; afterwards, she had worshipped him for nearly three weeks.

'She even,' he said, 'when I was going away, made me a present of this gold watch.'

And, so that they might see it, he threw it on the table, as if it were a contemptible plaything.

This was related in homely words and with characteristic imagery. Nevertheless, this commonplace of civilized life was sadly out of tune among these primitive men, with the great silence of the sea which was felt to be around them; with the luminous midnight, glimpsed a short while before through the opening above, which had brought the notion of the dying summers of the Pole.

And, especially, these ways of Yann pained and surprised Sylvestre. He was a wholly innocent lad, brought up in the respect of the sacraments by an old grandmother, the widow of a fisherman of the village of Ploubazlanec. When quite little he used to go daily with her to recite the rosary on his knees at the grave of his mother. From this same cemetery, situated on the cliff, he could see in the distance the grey waters of the Channel, where his father had disappeared some time before in a shipwreck. As they were poor, his grandmother and he, it had been necessary for him at a very early age to join in the fishing, and his childhood had been passed on the open sea. He used still to say his prayers every night, and his eyes had preserved a religious candour. He, too, was good-looking, and, after Yann, the best set-up of those on board. His gentle voice and childlike intonations contrasted a little with his tall figure and dark beard; he had grown up very quickly, and he felt almost embarrassed at having become all at once so big and tall. He hoped soon to marry Yann's sister, but he had never yet responded to the advances of any woman.

On board they possessed but three sleeping-berths —one for two—in which they slept in turn, dividing the night between them.

When they had finished their fête—celebrated in

honour of the Assumption of the Virgin, their patron saint—it was a little after midnight. Three of them curled themselves up to sleep in the dark little niches that resembled sepulchres, and the three others climbed up on deck to resume the interrupted labour of the fishing; they were Yann, Sylvestre, and one of their country, called Guillaume.

Outside it was quite light, eternally light.

But it was a pale, pale light, which resembled nothing; it cast on things what might have been reflections of a dead sun. Around them began at once an immense void which was without colour, and, apart from the planks of their boat, everything seemed diaphanous, impalpable, chimerical.

The eye scarcely perceived that which was no doubt the sea; what they saw at first had the aspect of a kind of trembling mirror which had no image to reflect; as it stretched away it seemed to become a plain of vapour, and then nothing at all; it had neither horizon nor contours.

The damp freshness of the air was more intense, more penetrating, than real cold; and, as they breathed, they savoured very strongly the taste of salt. It was quite calm and the rain had ceased; above, shapeless and colourless clouds seemed to contain this latent light which remained inexplicable; one saw clearly, while being conscious, nevertheless, of the night, and all the palenesses of things were of no colour that can be named.

The three men who were standing there had lived since their boyhood on these frigid seas, in the midst of their phantasmagorias, which are as vague and confused as visions. All this changing infinitude they had been used to see play around their narrow house of planks, and their eyes had become as much accustomed to it as those of the great birds of the high sea.

The boat rocked slowly where it lay, giving out unceasingly its same plaint, as monotonous as a song of Brittany repeated in a dream by a man asleep. Yann and Sylvestre had prepared their hooks and lines very quickly, while the other opened a barrel of salt, and, sharpening his large knife, sat down behind them to wait.

He had not to wait long. Scarcely had they cast their lines into this cold and tranquil water than they brought them back again, weighted with heavy fish, which glistened with the shining grey of steel.

And still, and still, the live cod allowed themselves to be caught; it was rapid and incessant, this silent fishing. The other gutted with his large knife, flattened, salted and counted, and all the time the soused fish which was to make their fortune on their return was piling up behind them, streaming and fresh.

The hours passed monotonous, and, in the great empty regions round about, slowly the light changed; it seemed now more real. What had been a wan twilight, a sort of evening of hyperborean summer, had become, without the intermedium of night, something like a dawn, which the multitudinous mirrors of the sea reflected in hazy trails of ruddy light. . . .

'Really, you know, you ought to marry, Yann,' said Sylvestre suddenly, speaking very seriously this time, his eyes upon the water. (It seemed as if he knew that there was a certain someone in Brittany who had fallen captive to the brown eyes of his brother but felt rather shy in broaching so serious a matter.)

'I! . . . Oh, yes; one of these days I shall marry' —and he smiled, this fellow Yann, disdainful still, rolling his lively eyes—'but not with any of the girls of the country. No, my marriage will be with the sea, and I invite you all, here as you stand, to the ball which I shall give. . . .'

They went on with their fishing, for there was no time to lose in conversation; they were in the midst of an immense population of fish, of a migrating shoal, which for two days now had passed without ceasing.

They had all worked through the preceding night, and caught in thirty hours more than a thousand very large cod; and their arms were tired, and their spirit drowsy. Only their body kept vigil and continued mechanically the movement of the fishing, while, for minutes at a time, their mind was wrapt in sleep. But this air of the wide sea which they were breathing was pure as in the first days of the world, and so vivifying that, in spite of their weariness, they felt their lungs dilated and their cheeks aglow.

The light of morning—the real light—had come at last; as in the days of Genesis, it had separated itself from the darkness, which seemed now to be heaped on the horizon and to rest there in a solid mass; and, seeing it there so clearly, one perceived unmistakably now that one had issued from the night—that the preceding light had been indeterminate and strange, like that of dreams.

In the heavy overcast sky there were breaks here and there, like openings in a dome, through which came wide beams of the colour of ruddy silver.

The lower clouds were arranged in a belt of intense shadow, making a circle round the waters, filling the distances with indistinctness and gloom. They gave the illusion of an enclosed space, of a limit; it was as if they were curtains drawn over the infinite, as if they were veils stretched out to hide some too gigantic mysteries which might have troubled the imagination

of men. On this morning, around the little assemblage of planks which carried Yann and Sylvestre,
the changing world without had assumed an aspect
of immense calm; it had turned itself into a kind of
sanctuary, and the sheaves of rays which entered
through the openings of the temple vault were prolonged in reflections on the still water as on a marble
parvise. And then, gradually, in the distance another
chimera took shape in the growing light; a kind of
rosy figuring, very high; a promontory of gloomy
Iceland. . . .

The marriage of Yann with the sea . . . Sylvestre
had pondered it in his mind, as he continued to fish,
not daring to speak of it again. It grieved him to
hear the sacrament of marriage turned thus into
mockery by his elder brother; and, what was more,
it made him afraid, for he was superstitious.

He had thought for so long of this marriage of
Yann! He had dreamt that it would be with Gaud
Mével—a fair-haired girl of Paimpol—and that he
would have the happiness of being present at the
wedding feast before he departed for his service at
sea, before that five years' exile, with its doubtful
return, the inevitable approach of which began
already to weigh upon his heart. . . .

Four o'clock in the morning. The others, who had
remained to sleep below, came up, all three, to relieve
them. Still a little drowsy, breathing deeply of the
fresh, cold air, they had fastened their long sea-boots
as they ascended, and they screwed up their eyes,
dazzled at first by all these reflections of pale light.

Then Yann and Sylvestre made a hasty breakfast
of biscuits; after having broken them by hammering,
they began to crunch them in very noisy fashion,
laughing to find them so hard.   They were very merry

again at the prospect of going down to sleep, of being cosily warm in their little berths, and, with arms round one another's waist, they moved off towards the hatchway, traipsing to the tune of an old song.

Before disappearing down this hole, they stopped to play with a certain Turk, the boat's dog, a Newfoundland puppy, which had enormous paws, still clumsy and babyish. They teased him with their hands, while he mouthed them like a wolf and ended by hurting them. Then Yann, with a frown of anger in his expressive eyes, pushed him off rather violently, so that he rolled over and howled.

He was good-hearted, this Yann, but his nature had remained a little wild; and when the physical part of him was alone in play a gentle caress was often, with him, very near to an angry blow.

CHAPTER II

THEIR boat was called the *Marie*, Captain Guermeur. It used to go every year to take a part in the dangerous sea-fishing in those cold regions where the summers are nightless.

It was very old, like the faïence Virgin, its patroness. Its thick sides, ribbed with oak, were roughened, wrinkled, impregnated with moisture and brine; but sound withal, and strong, exhaling the quickening savour of tar. At rest, it had a clumsy air, with its massive framing, but when a stiff breeze blew from the west it recovered its lightsome vigour, as the gulls do when the wind awakens them. Then it had a way of its own of rising to the wave and of rebounding, more nimbly than many a younger boat, fashioned with modern fineness.

As to its crew, the six men and the boy, they were 'Icelanders,' a valiant race of mariners which is bred especially in the country round Paimpol and Tréguier, and is dedicated from father to son to this particular kind of fishing.

They had scarcely ever seen a French summer.

At the end of every winter they received, with the other fishermen, in the harbour of Paimpol, the benediction of those about to depart. For this day of festival, a kind of altar, always the same, was constructed on the quay; it was in the form of a rocky grotto, and, within it, among trophies of anchors, oars, and nets, was enthroned, gentle and impressive, the Virgin, patroness of mariners, come for their sake out of her church, gazing always, from generation to generation, with her same lifeless eyes, on the fortunate for whom the season was going to be prosperous —and on the others, those who would not return.

The Blessed Sacrament, followed by a slow-moving procession of wives and mothers, sweethearts and sisters, made the round of the harbour, where all the boats of the Icelanders, gaily beflagged, saluted as it passed. The priest, stopping before each of them, said the words and made the gestures of blessing.

Afterwards they all departed, like a fleet, leaving the country almost empty of husbands, lovers, and sons. As they moved off, the crews sang together, with full, resonant voices, the hymns of Mary Star-of-the-Sea.

And every year there was the same ceremonial of departure, every year there were the same adieux.

Afterwards, began again the life of the ocean, the isolation, with three or four rough companions, on this floating house of wood, amid the cold waters of the hyperborean sea.

Until now, they had returned—the Virgin Star-of-the-Sea had protected this boat which bore her name.

The end of August was the time of their return. But the *Marie* followed the custom of many of the Icelanders, which is simply to call at Paimpol, and then to proceed to the Gulf of Gascony, where their catch sells well, and to the sandy, salt-marshed islands where they buy the salt for their next voyage.

In these ports of the south, which the sun still warms, the sturdy crews run loose for a few days, avid of pleasure, intoxicated by this remnant of summer, by this warmer air—by the earth and by the women.

And then, with the first mists of autumn, they would return to their hearths, at Paimpol or in the little scattered cottages of the country of Goëlo, to busy themselves for a while with domestic matters, and with love, with marriages, and births. Almost always they found there little newcomers, conceived the winter before, who had been waiting for godparents in order to receive the sacrament of baptism —there is need of many children in the families of these fishermen, whom Iceland devours.

CHAPTER III

AT Paimpol, on a fine evening of this same year, a Sunday evening in June, two women were busily occupied in writing a letter.

They were sitting before a large window which was open and of which the sill, of old and massive granite, bore a row of flower-pots.

Bent over their table, both seemed young; one wore a coif extremely large, in the fashion of former days; the other, quite a small coif, of the new form adopted by the women of Paimpol—two fond ones, one would have said, composing together a tender message for some handsome Icelander.

She who dictated—the one in the large coif—raised her head, casting about for ideas. And, wonderful to tell, she was old, very old, in spite of her youthful figure, seen thus from behind, beneath her little brown shawl. Quite, quite old: a worthy grandmother, of at least seventy years. Still comely, nevertheless, and fresh-looking, with the rosy cheeks which some old people have the gift of preserving. Her coif, very low on the forehead and on the top of the head, was composed of two or three cornets in muslin, which seemed to escape one from the other and fell on the nape of her neck. Her venerable face was meetly framed in all this whiteness and in these folds which had a religious aspect. Her eyes, very kindly, were full of an honest worthiness. She had no trace of teeth, none at all, and, when she smiled, you saw in

their place her round gums, which had a little air of
youth.   In spite of her chin which, as she was accustomed to say, was pointed like a sabot, her profile
was not too much marred by her years; one could see
still that it must have been as regular and pure as
that of the saints of the church.

She gazed out of the window, trying to think what
more she could tell to amuse her grandson.

Truly, there did not exist elsewhere, in all the
country round Paimpol, such another old woman as
she for finding entertaining things to say about one,
or about another, or about nothing at all.   In this
letter there were already three or four priceless stories
—but without the least malice, for there was nothing
of evil in her soul.

The other, seeing that the well of ideas had dried up,
began carefully to write the address: 'To Monsieur
Moan, Sylvestre, on board the *Marie*, Captain Guermeur, in the waters of Iceland, by Reikiavik.'

Having done that she raised her head and asked:

'Is that all, Grannie Moan?'

She was quite young, this one, adorably young, a
face of twenty years.   Very fair, a rare colouring in
this part of Brittany, where the people are dark; very
fair, with eyes of gridelin and lashes almost black.
Her eyebrows, fair like her hair, were, as it were,
retouched in the middle with a line of deeper, more
reddish colour, which gave an expression of vigour
and will.   Her profile, a little short, was very noble,
the nose prolonging the line of the forehead with an
absolute straightness, as in the faces of the Greeks.
A deep dimple, sunk beneath her lower lip, accentuated deliciously the line of the lip, and, every now
and then, when preoccupied with a thought, she bit
her lip with her white upper teeth, which made

little trails of deeper pink course beneath the fine skin. In all her slim person there was something proud, something, too, a little serious, which came to her from the hardy mariners of Iceland, her ancestors. In her eyes was an expression at once obstinate and gentle.

Her coif was in the form of a shell; it came down low on the forehead, fitting tight almost like a band, and was then caught up on either side, exposing the thick plaits of hair rolled snail-like above the ears— a fashion of hairdressing handed down from very ancient times, which still gives an old-time air to the women of Paimpol.

One felt that she had been brought up differently from this poor old woman to whom she gave the name of grandmother, but who, in fact, was only a distant relation, fallen upon evil days.

She was the daughter of M. Mével, a sometime Icelander, a little bit of a pirate, too, who had enriched himself by dangerous enterprises on the sea.

This seemly room in which the letter had just been written was hers: a new bed of the fashion used in the great cities, with muslin curtains edged with lace; and, on the thick walls, a light-coloured paper, which accentuated the irregularities of the granite. On the ceiling a coating of whitewash covered the great beams which bore witness to the antiquity of the dwelling—it was a typical home of the comfortable middle-class. And the windows overlooked the old grey square of Paimpol, where the markets were held and the pardons.

'Is that all, Grannie Yvonne? Have you anything more to tell him?'

'No, my child; but just ask him, if you will, to remember me to the boy Gaos.'

The boy Gaos! . . . That is to say, Yann . . .
The proud, fair girl became very red as she wrote
that name.

As soon as she had made this addition in a flowing
hand at the bottom of the page, she got up, averting
her head, as if she wanted to see something very
interesting that was happening in the square.

Standing, she was rather tall: her figure was
moulded like that of a fashionable lady of the town
in a tight-fitting bodice which was without fold or
crease.   In spite of her coif she had an air of breeding.
Even her hands, without having that excessive
etiolated smallness which has become a beauty by
convention, were shapely and white, having done no
rough work.

It is true that she had begun by being a little Gaud
who ran barefoot in the water, having no mother,
going almost uncared for during the seasons of fishing
which her father passed in Iceland; pretty, rosy-
cheeked, dishevelled, wilful, headstrong, waxing
vigorous in the strong keen breezes of the Channel.
In those days she had her home with this poor
grannie Moan, who entrusted little Sylvestre to her
during her days of hard work for the good folk of
Paimpol.

And she had the adoration of a little mother for
this other little one, scarce eighteen months younger
than herself, who had been placed in her care; as dark
as she was fair, as submissive and affectionate as she
was lively and capricious.

She looked back on this beginning of her life, as one
whose head was in no wise turned by riches and the
attractions of the big cities; it returned to her mind
as a far-off dream of wild freedom, as a memory of a
shadowy and mysterious time when the sands of the

sea-shore were somehow more spacious, when certainly the cliffs were more gigantic. . . .

When she was about five or six years old, still very early days for her, her father having made money by buying and selling ships' cargoes, she was taken by him to Saint Brieuc, and later to Paris. Then, from little Gaud she had become a *Mademoiselle Marguerite*, tall, thoughtful, serious-looking. Still left a good deal to herself in a different kind of freedom from that of the Breton sea-shore, she had retained the self-willed nature of her childhood. What she knew of the things of life had been learnt quite by chance, without any sort of discrimination; but an excessive, innate dignity had served her for safeguard. Now and then she took on an air of boldness, saying straight out to people things which surprised by their frankness; and her brave, clear eyes were not always lowered before those of young men; but they were such honest eyes and so indifferent that it was scarcely possible that any one should misunderstand them; it was clear that one had to deal with a sensible girl whose heart was as pure as her complexion.

In the great cities her clothes had changed more than herself. Although she had retained her coif, which the Breton women are loth to lay aside, she had quickly learnt to dress herself in another fashion. And this young body of the little fisher-girl, formerly so untrammelled, in developing, in taking on the plenitude of those graceful contours which had germinated in the wind of the sea, had been made slender at the waist by the long corsets of fashion.

Every year, with her father, she used to return to Brittany—in the summer only like the fair bathers— renewing for a few days her memories of earlier days, and her name of Gaud (which in Breton means

Marguerite); a little curious, perhaps, to see these
Icelanders of whom she heard so much, but who were
never there, and of whom every year some few more
were missing from the muster; hearing everywhere
talk of this Iceland which appeared to her as a
distant abyss—and where now was he whom she
loved. . . .

And, then, one fine day, she had been brought
back for good to the country of the fishermen, by a
whim of her father's, who had wished to end his days
there, and to live in well-to-do retirement on the
square of Paimpol.

The good old grandmother, poor and neat, got up
to go with an expression of thanks, as soon as the
letter had been read over and the envelope sealed.
She lived some distance away, on the border of the
district of Ploubazlanec, in a hamlet of the coast,
still in the same cottage where she was born, where
she had had her sons and her grandsons.

As she passed through the town she answered a
great many people who greeted her.   She was one of
the old inhabitants of the country, the remnant of a
valiant and esteemed family.

By a miracle of method and care she contrived to
appear almost well-dressed, in poor mended clothes
which scarcely any longer held together. Always
that little brown shawl of the Paimpol women, which
was her best wear and on which had fallen for more
than sixty years the muslin cornets of her large coif:
the shawl she had worn at her marriage, once upon a
time blue, dyed for the wedding of her son, Pierre,
and since that time kept carefully for Sundays and
looking still quite presentable.

She had continued to carry herself very straight

when she walked, not a bit like an old woman; and truly, in spite of that chin which asserted itself a little too much, it was impossible not to admit that she was charming to look upon.

She was greatly respected, as might be seen even from the greetings which people gave her.

On her way she passed before the house of an old admirer of hers, who formerly had been an aspirant for her hand. He was a carpenter by trade, an octogenarian now, who used to sit all day at his door, leaving to the young, his sons, the work at the bench. He had never consoled himself, so people said, for her refusal of him, both in first and in second marriage; but with age his disappointment had turned into a kind of comical rancour, half-malignant, and he used always to call out to her:

'Well, old lady, when are they going to send for me to come and measure you? . . .'

She thanked him and said she had not yet decided to have that particular dress made for her. The fact is that this old fellow, in his rather heavy pleasantry, was speaking of a certain dress made of spruce wood which is the last of this world's habiliments.

'Very well, then, when you wish; but don't hesitate, my dear, you know. . . .'

He had already made this same little joke a hundred times. And to-day she was not in the mood to smile at it; for she felt more weary than usual, more broken by her life of incessant toil—and she thought of her beloved grandson, her last, who, on his return from Iceland, was going away for his service in the Navy. Five years . . . Going away to China, perhaps, to war! . . . Would she still be here, when he returned? An anguish seized her at the thought. . . . No, decidedly, she was not so cheerful as she looked, this poor old soul; and presently her face contracted painfully as if she were about to weep.

It was possible, then, nay, it was certain, that they were going soon to take him from her, her last grandson. . . . Alas! to die, perhaps, all alone, without having seen him again. . . . Steps had indeed been taken (by some worthy people in the town whom she knew) to prevent his departure, on the plea that he was the support of a grandmother almost indigent who soon would be past working. They had not been successful—on account of the other, Jean Moan, the deserter, an elder brother of Sylvestre, of whom one no longer spoke in the family, but who existed nevertheless somewhere in America, debarring his younger brother from the benefit of military exemption. And a further objection was that she had a small pension as the widow of a sailor. It was not considered that she was poor enough.

When she was back in her home she prayed for a long time for all her dead ones, sons and grandsons: afterwards she prayed also, with an ardent hope, for her little Sylvestre; and then she tried to sleep, thinking of that wooden dress, her heart pitifully wrung to feel herself so old at the moment of this departure. . . .

The other, she who was young, remained sitting at her window, watching on the granite of the walls the yellow reflections of the setting sun, and, in the sky, the eddying of the dark swallows. Paimpol was always very dead, even on a Sunday, during these long evenings of May; some young women, who had no men now to pay them court, walked about two by two, three by three, dreaming of the gallants of Iceland. . . .

'. . . Remember me to the boy Gaos . . .' It had greatly troubled her to write that phrase, and that name which, now, was never out of her mind.

She often passed her evenings at this window, like a little lady. Her father did not care for her to go about with the other girls of her age, who, formerly, had been her equals. And besides, when, coming out of his café, he took a stroll, smoking his pipe, with other old sailors like himself, it pleased him to see, above, at her window, framed in granite, behind the pots of flowers, his daughter installed in his prosperous-looking house.

The boy Gaos! . . . She looked in spite of herself in the direction of the sea, which could not be seen, but was felt to be there, quite close, at the bottom of these narrow little streets by which the boatmen ascended. And her thoughts travelled on into the infinities of this alluring thing, which fascinates and which devours; her thoughts travelled on until they reached the distant polar seas, where sailed the *Marie, Captain Guermeur*.

What a strange fellow this boy Gaos was! . . . Fleeing, elusive now, after having come forward in a way at once so bold and so charming.

.   .   .   .   .

Afterwards, in her long reverie, she went over again the recollections of her return to Brittany in the preceding year.

One morning in December, after travelling through the night, the train from Paris had dropped them, her father and her, at Guincamp, in the misty, whitish half-light of a cold dawn. She had been seized then by an impression previously unknown: this old little town, which she had never passed through except in summer, she no longer recognized it; she experienced something like the sensation of plunging into the distant times of the past. This silence, after Paris! This tranquil current of life of people of another world, going about their little affairs in the mist! These old houses of sombre granite, darkened by damp and what remained of the night. All these Breton things —which charmed her now that she loved Yann—had impressed her that morning with a desolating sadness. Here and there a busy housewife, up betimes, had already opened her door, and, as she passed, she looked into these old, open-hearthed interiors, where were sitting, in attitudes of quietude, old coifed grandams who had just got up. As soon as it became a little brighter, she had gone into the church to say her prayers. And how immense and gloomy it had seemed to her, this magnificent nave—and different from the churches of Paris—with its rough pillars worn at the base by the centuries, its savour of cavern, of old age, of saltpetre! In a deep recess, behind some columns, a candle was burning and a woman was on her knees before it, no doubt making a vow; the light of this slender little flame was lost in the indistinct emptiness of the vaults. . . . She had rediscovered there suddenly, in herself, the trace of a sentiment she had quite forgotten: that sort of sadness and awe which she had experienced formerly, while still a child, when she was taken to the early mass on winter mornings in the church at Paimpol.

And yet, very surely, she had no regret for the Paris which she had left, although there were there many beautiful and interesting things. In the first place she found herself almost cramped there, she who had in her veins the blood of the sea-rovers.

And, then, she felt she was a stranger there and out of place: the Parisiennes, they were women whose slim bodies had at the hips an artificial camber, who affected a manner of their own of walking, of fluttering in whaleboned sheathes: she had too much intelligence ever to try to copy these things closely. With her coifs, ordered every year from the maker in Paimpol, she was ill at ease in the streets of Paris, not realizing that, if people turned round so much to look at her, it was because she was charming to look upon.

There were some of these Parisiennes, indeed, whose bearing had a distinction which attracted her, but she knew that these were unapproachable. And the others, those of a lower order, who would have been pleased to make her acquaintance, she kept them disdainfully at a distance, not deeming them worthy. And so she had lived without friends, almost without other society than that of her father, often busy and preoccupied. She did not regret this life of exile and solitude.

But, all the same, on this day of arrival, she had been surprised in a painful way by the roughness of this Brittany, seen now in mid-winter. And the thought that it would be necessary to drive for four or five hours more, to penetrate much further still into this mournful country in order to reach Paimpol, had weighed on her like an oppression.

All the afternoon of this same grey day they had, in fact, travelled, her father and she, in a crazy, old little diligence, open to all the winds of heaven; passing, as darkness fell, through forlorn villages, under ghosts of trees which seemed to ooze the mist in fine little drops. And presently it had been necessary to light the lamps, and then they could see nothing—except two tracks of green Bengal-fire

which seemed to run ahead of the horses on each side,
and which were the lights of these two lamps thrown
on the interminable hedges of the road. How came
it that this verdure should suddenly be so green, in
December? . . . Surprised at first, she leant over so
that she might see better, and then she seemed to
understand and to remember: the gorse, the ever-
green gorse of the lanes and cliffs, which never withers
in this country of Paimpol. At the same time a
warmer breeze began to blow, which also she thought
she recognized, and which smelt of the sea. . . .

Towards the end of the journey she had been quite
awakened and interested by this reflection which
had come to her:

'Why, since we are now in winter I shall see, this
time, the handsome fishermen of Iceland.'

In December they should be there, home, all of
them, the brothers, the sweethearts, the lovers, the
cousins, of whom her friends, large and small, had
spoken so much, on each of her summer visits, during
their walks together in the evening. And this idea
had filled her mind while her feet were freezing in the
immobility of the little diligence.

And, in fact, she had seen them . . . and now she
had lost her heart to one of them. . . .

CHAPTER IV

THE first time she saw him, saw this fellow Yann, was on the day following her arrival, at the pardon of the Icelanders, which is held on the 8th of December, the Feast of our Lady of Good-Tidings, patroness of fishermen—shortly after the procession, while the sombre streets were still hung with white draperies, on which had been fastened ivy and holly, winter foliage and winter flowers.

At this pardon the rejoicing was heavy and a little barbarous, under a mournful sky. A rejoicing without merriment, made up in the main of recklessness and defiance: of physical strength and alcohol; on which weighed, less disguised here than elsewhere, the universal menace of death.

Paimpol was agog with noise, ringing of bells and chanting of priests. Coarse and monotonous songs in the taverns; old sea chaunties, old ballads come from the sea, come from Heaven knows where, from the deep night of time. Groups of sailors linked arm in arm, zig-zagging in the streets, partly from the habit of rolling, partly from incipient intoxication, casting on the women glances a little too appreciative after the long continence of the sea. Groups of maidens in the white coifs of nuns, their bosoms full and fluttering, their young eyes filled with the desires of a whole summer. Old granite houses enclosing this human swarming; old roofs bearing witness to their struggles of many centuries against the west wind, against the fogs, the rains, against all that comes from the sea; bearing witness, too, to the living stories they had sheltered, to dead and gone deeds of daring and love.

And a sentiment of religion, an impression of the past, hung over all this, with a respect for the ancient cult, for the protecting symbols, for the Virgin, white and immaculate. By the side of the taverns, the church, its flight of steps littered with foliage, thrown open in the form of a wide sombre bay, with its odour of incense, with its candles seen in the obscurity within, and its ex-voto of sailors suspended everywhere from the sacred vault. By the side of the maidens bright with thoughts of love, the fiancées of sailors who had disappeared, the widows of men shipwrecked, issuing from the little chapel of the dead, in their long shawls of mourning, in their little glazed coifs; their eyes on the ground, silent, passing in the midst of this noise of life, like a dark warning. And hard by the sea, always the sea, the great nurse and the great devourer of these vigorous generations, stirring itself, too, making its noise, taking its part in the festival . . .

Of all these things together Gaud received a confused impression. Excited and laughing, but with heart strangely moved, she felt a kind of anguish seize her at the thought that this country now was become hers for always. On the square, where there were games and mountebank shows, she walked about with her friends who pointed out to her by name, on right and left, the young men of Paimpol and of Ploubazlanec. Before some singers of ballads, a group of these Icelanders had stopped, their backs turned to them. And, at first, struck by one of them who had the stature of a giant and shoulders almost too broad, she had said simply, even with a shade of mockery:

'Look at that one, how tall he is!'

There was almost this of undermeaning in her phrase:

'For her who marries him, what an encumbrance in the house, a husband of that size!'

He had turned round as if he had heard her, and from head to foot he had enveloped her in a rapid glance which seemed to say:

'Who is this who wears the coif of Paimpol and is so elegant and whom I have never seen before?'

And then he had lowered his eyes very quickly, out of politeness, and had seemed to be very occupied again with the singers, not letting any more be seen of his head than his dark hair, which was rather long and very curly behind, on his neck.

She had asked without hesitation the names of a number of others, but she had not dared to ask his. That fine profile seen for a brief moment; that proud and rather shy regard; those brown pupils lightly flicked with fawn, moving very rapidly on the bluish opal of his eyes, had impressed her and intimidated her also.

He was, in fact, that 'boy Gaos,' whom she had heard spoken of so often, at the Moans, as a great friend of Sylvestre; on the evening of this same pardon, Sylvestre and he, walking arm in arm, had met her with her father, and had stopped to exchange greetings. . . .

. . . And little Sylvestre had immediately become for her again a kind of brother. Cousins as they were, they had continued to address each other by their Christian names—it is true she had hesitated at first, before this great fellow of seventeen who already had a dark beard; but as his eyes were the same honest, gentle eyes of his childhood she had quickly got to

know him again well enough to imagine that she had
never lost sight of him.   When he came into Paimpol,
she made him stay to dinner in the evening: it meant
nothing, and he ate very heartily, for he was on rather
short commons at home. . . .

If the truth must be told, Yann had not been very
gallant to her at this first presentation—at the turning
of a little grey street bestrewn with green branches.
He had done no more than raise his hat to her, with a
gesture which, though graceful enough, was almost
shy; and then having looked her over with that same
rapid glance of his, he had turned his eyes in another
direction, appearing to be a little irked by this
meeting, and to be impatient to proceed on his way.
A strong west wind, which had risen during the
procession, had littered the street with branches of
box-tree and spread over the sky a curtain of dark
grey. . . . Gaud, in her reverie of recollection, saw
all that again very clearly: the mournful oncoming of
night at the close of the pardon; all the white draperies
decked with flowers which twisted in the wind along
the walls; the noisy groups of Icelanders, children
of the wind and the tempest, singing as they entered
the taverns to take shelter there against the impending
rain; and above all this tall fellow, standing before
her, his head turned away, looking bored and rather
annoyed at having met her. What a profound
change had taken place in her since that time! . . .

And what a difference between the noise of that
close of a day of festival and the peacefulness now!
How silent and empty was this same Paimpol this
evening, during the long May twilight which held her
at her window, alone, thoughtful, and enamoured! . . .

CHAPTER V

THE second time they saw each other was at a wedding. This 'boy Gaos' had been named to give her his arm. At first she imagined that she was annoyed about it: to walk in procession through the street with this young man whom every one would look at on account of his height, and who, besides, would probably not know what to say to her on the way! . . . And, then, he intimidated her, did this Yann, there was no doubt about it, with his large, untamed air.

At the hour appointed, when all were assembled for the procession, Yann had not appeared. Time passed and still he did not come; and already it was being suggested that they should wait for him no longer. Then she had realized that it was for him alone that she had attired herself; that with any other of these young men, no matter whom, the feast, the walk would be for her spoilt and without pleasure. . . .

At last he had arrived, in festive attire also, excusing himself without embarrassment to the parents of the bride. It appeared that a large shoal of fish, which had been quite unexpected, had been signalled from England as being due to pass towards evening, a little off-shore from Aurigny; and all the boats in Ploubazlanec had been got under sail in haste. Excitement in the villages, women seeking their husbands in the taverns, pushing them to make them run; lending a hand themselves to hoist the sails; helping in the manœuvring; in short, a regular 'all hands on deck' in the countryside.

Amid all these people who gathered round him, he

related this with an extreme ease; with gestures of his own, rolling his eyes, and with a charming smile which disclosed his glistening teeth.   The better to express the haste with which the boats were made ready, he interjected every now and then in the midst of his phrases a certain prolonged little 'Hoo,' very comical, which is a sailor's cry giving an impression of speed and resembling the whistling noise of the wind.   He himself had been obliged to find a substitute in a great hurry and to get him accepted by the owner of the boat to whom he had engaged himself for the winter.   Hence his lateness; and through his unwillingness to miss the wedding he had sacrificed his share in the catch.

These motives had been perfectly understood by the fishermen who heard him, and none of them dreamt of finding fault with him for his delay—for is it not well known that, in life, everything is more or less dependent on the unforeseen chances of the sea, more or less subject to the changes of the weather and to the mysterious migrations of fish?   The other Icelanders who were there regretted only that they had not received the notice early enough to profit, like the men of Ploubazlanec, by this good fortune which was about to pass in the offing.

It was too late now, and, since ill-luck would have it so, there was nothing to do but to offer an arm to the girls.   Outside the violins began their music, and the procession set off gaily.

At first he had uttered nothing but aimless, complimentary things, such as one says at a wedding to a girl whom one scarcely knows.   Among these wedding couples, they alone were strangers to each other; in fact, in the procession there were only cousins and betrothed couples, with perhaps some pairs of lovers too; for in this district of Paimpol one falls deep in love at the time of the return from Iceland. (But it is an honest love, and ends in marriage.)

But in the evening, when the dancing was on, the conversation between them having turned again to the shoal of fish, he said suddenly, looking full into her eyes, this unexpected thing:

'You are the only one in Paimpol—and even in the world—who could have made me miss this expedition; there is no one else, I can tell you that, Mademoiselle Gaud, for whom I would have missed my share in the fishing. . . .'

Astonished at first that this fisherman should dare to speak to her thus, to her who had come to this ball a little as a queen, and then thrilled deliciously, she had ended by saying:

'Thank you, Monsieur Yann, and I, too, I prefer to be with you rather than with any other.'

That had been all. But, from that moment until the end of the dancing, they had fallen to talking together in a different way, with voices lower and gentler. . . .

The dancing went on to the tune of a hurdy-gurdy, to the strains of a violin, the same couples nearly always together. When he returned to claim her, after dancing, out of politeness, with someone else, they exchanged a smile as of old friends meeting, and continued their conversation of before, which had become quite intimate. Simply, Yann told her of his life as a fisherman, his labours, his earnings, the struggle his parents had formerly had to bring up the fourteen little Gaoses, of whom he was the eldest brother—now they were freed from anxiety, mainly on account of a derelict which their father had come across in the Channel, the sale of which had brought

them ten thousand francs, part of which had to be
rendered to the State; in this way they had been
enabled to build an upper story to their house—which
was at the extremity of the district of Ploubazlanec,
on the land's edge, in the hamlet of Pors-Even, over-
looking the Channel, with a very fine view.

'It was a hard calling,' he told her, 'this Iceland
fishing: to leave, as they had to leave, in the month
of February, for such a country, where it was so cold
and gloomy, where the sea was so rough. . . .'

Gaud, who recalled it as if it had been a thing of
yesterday, went over in her memory, as she watched
the May night descend on Paimpol, all their conversation at the ball. If he had had no thought of
marriage, why had he acquainted her with all these
details of his existence, which she had listened to a
little as a fiancée might. He had not the air of a
commonplace youth fond of communicating his affairs
to all and sundry. . . .

'And yet the calling is not so bad, after all,' he had
said, 'and for myself, I would not change it. Some
years, it is eight hundred francs; others, twelve
hundred, that I receive on our return and that I hand
over to my mother.'

'That you hand over to your mother, Monsieur
Yann?'

'Surely, yes, all of it, always. Amongst us Icelanders it is the custom, Mademoiselle Gaud' (he
said this as if it were a thing very fitting and natural).
'I, for example, you would not think it, I have scarcely
ever any money. On Sunday, my mother gives me
a little when I come to Paimpol. For everything it
is the same. Thus, this year my father made me get
these new clothes, without which I should never have
dared to come to the wedding. Oh, I assure you, I

would not have come to give you my arm in the clothes I wore last year.'

For her, accustomed to see the men of Paris, they were not very smart, perhaps, these new clothes of Yann's, this very short jacket, open on a rather old-fashioned waistcoat; but the figure which they moulded was irreproachably handsome, and somehow the dancer had a distinguished air in spite of all.

He gazed, smiling, straight into her eyes every time he said anything to her, to see what she thought of it. And how simple and honest his gaze was, while he recounted all this so that she might be forewarned that he was not rich!

She also smiled at him, looking always straight into his eyes, saying very little, but listening with all her soul, ever more surprised and more attracted towards him. What a mixture he was, of rough strength and winning childlikeness! His deep voice, which with others was brusque and decided, became, when he spoke to her, more and more tender and caressing; for her alone he could make it vibrate with an extreme softness, like the muted music of stringed instruments.

And how singular and unexpected it was to learn that this tall young man with his devil-may-care airs, his formidable aspect, should still be treated in his home as if he were a child, and should find it quite natural: having roamed the world, tasted all its adventures, all its dangers, and preserving for his parents this respectful, this absolute submission.

She compared him with others, with three or four coxcombs of Paris, clerks, scribblers, or what not, who had pursued her with their attentions, for the sake of her money. And this simple fisherman seemed to her what she had known of most worth, at the same time that he was the most handsome.

In order to place herself more within his reach she
had told him that, in her home, also, circumstances
had not always been as rosy as they were at present;
that her father had begun by being an Iceland fisherman, and held the Icelanders in high esteem; that she
herself remembered having run barefoot when she
was quite small—on the shore—after the death of
her mother.

Oh! that wonderful night of the ball; that delightful night, decisive and unique in her life—it was
already almost distant, since it dated from December,
and it was now May. And all the gallant dancers
were fishing now far away, scattered over the sea of
Iceland—seeing clear there, in the pale sunlight, in
their immense loneliness, while darkness settled
peacefully on the land of Brittany.

Gaud remained at her window. The square of
Paimpol, almost entirely enclosed on all sides by its
old houses, became more and more mournful with the
night; there was scarcely a sound to be heard anywhere. Above the houses, the still luminous void of
the sky seemed to become hollow, to lift, to separate
itself more from terrestrial things—which now, in
this twilight hour, were all ranged in a single dark
silhouette of gables and old roofs. Every now and
then a door was shut or a window; some old sailor,
with rolling gait, issued from a tavern, and made his
way along the gloomy little streets; and presently
some belated damsels returned from their walk with
bouquets of May flowers. One, who knew Gaud, in
bidding her good night, held high towards her with
outstretched arm a sheaf of hawthorn as though to
let her smell it; in the transparent darkness the light
tufts of the little white flowers could still be more or
less distinguished. There was, besides, another soft

perfume which had ascended from the gardens and the courtyards, that of the honeysuckle blooming on the granite of the walls—and also a vague savour of seaweed which came from the harbour. The last bats glided through the air, in silent flight, like the beasts of dreams.

Gaud had passed many evenings at this window, looking out on the melancholy square, dreaming of the Icelanders who had departed, and always of this same ball. . . .

. . . It became very warm towards the end of the wedding festival and the heads of many of the dancers began to swim. She recalled how she had seen him, dancing with others, with wives and maids of whom he must have been more or less the lover; she recalled his half-disdainful condescension in answering to their appeals. . . . How different he was with them! . . .

He was an excellent dancer, straight as a forest oak, and turning with a grace at once light and dignified, his head thrown slightly back. His brown hair, which was long and curly, fell a little over his forehead, and stirred in the wind of the dance. Gaud, who was rather tall, felt it brush against her coif when he bent towards her in order to hold her more firmly in the quick waltzes.

From time to time he indicated to her with a sign his little sister Marie and Sylvestre, the affianced pair, who were dancing together. He smiled, very good-humouredly at sight of them, so young, so reserved with each other, so ceremonious, looking so shy as they said to each other, very low, things which, no doubt, were very pleasing. He would not have permitted that it should be otherwise, no doubt; but, none the less, it amused him, rakish and venturous as he had become, to find them so simple; he exchanged

with Gaud smiles of intimate understanding which
said: 'How quaint and sweet they are, *our* little
brother and sister! . . .'

There was a great deal of embracing at the close of
the night: kisses of cousins, kisses of betrothed, kisses
of lovers, which retained nevertheless a seemly air of
frankness and modesty, kisses of mouth on mouth,
given there in the sight of all. But he, Yann, had
not kissed her; none would have ventured so far with
the daughter of Mons. Mével; he had done no more
than press her a little more closely against his heart,
during the concluding dances, and she, confident, had
not resisted, nay, had clung to him rather, yielding
with all her soul. In this sudden whirl, profound,
delightful, which drew her body and soul towards
him, her senses of twenty years counted, no doubt, for
something, but it was in her heart that the movement
had begun.

'Have you seen how she looks at him, the bold-
faced minx!' said two or three fair damsels, with eyes
chastely lowered under blond or dark eyebrows, who
had among the dancers one lover at least, if not two.
And it was true that she looked at him; but she had
this excuse, that he was the first and the only man to
whom she had ever given attention in her life.

As they separated in the frosty dawn, when the
party broke up, they had said good-bye to each other
in a special way, as two lovers might who were going
to meet again on the following day. And then, on
her way home, she had crossed this same square, with
her father, conscious of no fatigue, feeling alert and
joyous, ravished by the mere act of breathing, loving
the chill mist outside and the mournful dawn finding
everything delightful, everything gracious.

. . . The May night had fallen some time now;

one by one the windows had all been closed, with
little creakings of their bolts. But Gaud was still
there, leaving hers open. The last rare passers-by,
discerning in the darkness the white shape of her coif,
must have said: 'There is a girl who, one may bet, is
dreaming of her lover.' And it was true. She was
dreaming there—but with half a mind to weep; her
little white teeth were biting her lips, unmaking
continually the dimple which emphasized the contour of her fresh mouth. And her eyes remained
fixed in the darkness, looking at nothing that was
real. . . .

But, after this ball, why had he not returned?
What was the meaning of this change in him? Met
by chance, he seemed to shun her, turning away
his eyes, the movements of which were always so
rapid.

She had often spoken of it to Sylvestre, but he
understood no more than she.

'But nevertheless it is with him that you ought to
marry, Gaud,' he said, 'if your father will permit it,
for you will not find in the countryside another who
is his equal. In the first place I can tell you that he is
very steady, without seeming to be so; it is very rarely
that he gets tipsy. It is true he is a little headstrong
sometimes, but at bottom he is quite gentle. You
cannot realize how good he is. And as a sailor! At
every fishing season the captains contend among
themselves for his services.'

The permission of her father she was quite sure of
obtaining, for she had never been crossed in her
wishes. Nor did it matter to her that he was not
rich. For a sailor such as he it would need but a
small advance payment to enable him to follow for
six months the coasting trade course, and he would

become a captain to whom any of the shipowners
would be willing to entrust his vessels.

And it did not matter to her either that he was
something of a giant; to be too strong may become a
defect in a woman, but in a man it does not detract
at all from his beauty.

Without committing herself she had made inquiries
of the girls of the district who might be trusted to
know all the gossip of love; none had knowledge of
any engagement of his; without appearing to be more
attached to one than another, he went hither and
thither, to Lézardrieux as well as to Paimpol, with
the fair creatures who were enamoured of him.

One Sunday evening, very late, she had seen him
pass beneath her window, escorting, his arm about
her waist, a certain Jeannie Caroff, who was pretty,
undoubtedly, but whose reputation was very doubtful. That, indeed, had hurt her cruelly.

She had been assured also that he was very violent;
that one evening, when he was drunk, in a certain
tavern in Paimpol where the Icelanders were wont to
hold their feasts, he had hurled a large marble table
through a door which had been closed against him. . . .

But all this she forgave him: one knows what sailors
are sometimes, when the fit takes them. . . . But if
his heart was good, why had he come to seek her out,
she who was fancy-free, only to leave her afterwards:
what need had he to gaze at her a whole night long,
with that bright smile which seemed so frank, what
need to lower his voice to impart confidences as to
a betrothed? Now she was incapable of giving her
affections to another, incapable of changing. In this
same country, many years ago, when she was quite a
child, they had been used to say of her that she was a
wilful mite, obstinate in her ideas as no other; and so

she was still. Become in these days a fine little
lady, rather serious and proud of bearing, whom no
one had fashioned, she remained in essence the same.

After this ball the winter had been passed in the
expectation of seeing him again, and he had not even
come to say good-bye before his departure for Iceland.
Now that he was no longer there nothing existed for
her: the flagging time seemed to drag on very slowly
—towards the return of the autumn for which she had
formed her projects for reaching an understanding
and settling the matter once and for all. . . .

. . . Eleven by the Town Hall clock—with that
peculiar sonority which bells assume during the calm
nights of spring.

In Paimpol eleven o'clock is very late; and Gaud
closed her window and lit her lamp in order to go to
bed. . . .

Perhaps, after all, with Yann, it was only shyness;
or, since he too was proud, was it the fear of being
refused, thinking her too rich? . . . She had already
wanted to ask him this herself, quite simply; and it
was Sylvestre who judged that it could not be done,
that it would not be well for a young girl to appear so
bold. In Paimpol people were already criticizing
her manner and her dress. . . .

. . . She undressed with the absent-minded slowness of a maid bemused: first her muslin coif, then her
dress of fashion, fitting in the manner of the towns,
which she threw at hazard over a chair.

And afterwards the long corsets, which made folk
talk, for the Parisian air they gave her. Then her
figure, free once more, became more perfect; being
no longer compressed, nor too narrowed at the waist,
it resumed its natural lines, which were full and
gracious as those of marble statues. As she moved

they changed their aspects, and each one of her poses was exquisite to behold.

Her little lamp, which was burning alone at this late hour, illumined with a certain mystery her shoulders and her breast, her admirable form which no eye had ever gazed on, and which no eye now would ever gaze on, which would wither without ever having been seen, since Yann did not wish to make it his own. . . .

She knew that her face was pretty, but she was quite unconscious of the beauty of her body. For that matter, in this region of Brittany, among the daughters of these Iceland fishermen, this beauty is a kind of natural attribute; it is scarcely noticed, and even the least modest among them, so far from making a parade of it, would feel a shame to let it be seen. It is the over-civilized people of the towns who attach so much importance to these things that they mould them and paint them. . . .

She began to undo the snail-like coils of hair above her ears, and the two plaits fell down her back like two sleepy serpents. She gathered them up in the form of a crown on the top of her head—more convenient so for sleeping—and then with her straight profile she resembled a Roman virgin.

But her arms remained raised, and, biting her lip still, she continued to toy with her fair tresses, much as a child, its thoughts elsewhere, might torment a casual plaything; afterwards, letting them fall again, she began very quickly to undo them in a spirit of play, to shake them out, and soon they covered her to her waist, and she had the appearance of a druidess of the forest.

And then, sleep having come in spite of love and in spite of the inclination to weep, she threw herself suddenly into her bed, hiding her face in the silky mass of her hair, which was spread out now like a veil. . . .

In her cottage in Ploubazlanec Grandmother Moan, who was on the other and darker slope of life, had ended also by falling asleep, the frigid sleep of the old, thinking of her grandson and of death.

And, at this same hour, on board the *Marie*—on the northern sea which this evening was moving restlessly—Yann and Sylvestre, the two beloved ones, were singing to themselves, as merrily they went on with their fishing in the unending light of day. . . .

CHAPTER VI

•　　•　　•　　•　　•

ABOUT a month later—in June.

Around Iceland the weather was of that rare sort which sailors call a 'white calm'; that is to say, there was no stir in the air; it was as if all the breezes were exhausted, finished.

The sky was covered with an immense whitish veil, which darkened in the distance, towards the horizon, turned to leaden grey, to the dull colour of pewter. And, below, the inert waters gave out a pale glare, which wearied the eyes and created an impression of cold.

And on this particular day there were waterings, nothing but changing waterings which played over the surface of the sea; blurrings of the lightest sort, such as one may make by breathing on a mirror. The whole gleaming expanse seemed covered with a net-work of vague designs which intermingled and lost their shape, very quickly effaced, very fugitive.

Eternal evening or eternal morning, it was impossible to tell: a sun which no longer indicated any hour remained in position always, presiding over this splendour of dead things; it was itself only another blur, almost without shape, enlarged so that it looked immense by a troubled halo.

Yann and Sylvestre, as they fished side by side, were singing *Jean François de Nantes*, a song which never ends—amusing themselves by its very monotony, and looking at each other out of the corner of their eye to laugh at the kind of childish drollery with which they continued the couplets indefinitely, seeking each time to infuse into them a new humour. Their cheeks were ruddy from the salty freshness of the atmosphere; the air they breathed was vivifying and virgin; they filled their lungs with it, at the very source of all vigour and of all existence.

And yet the aspect around them was of a kind of non-life, of a world dead or not yet created: the light gave no heat; things remained motionless and as if frozen for ever, under the gaze of this sort of great spectral eye which was the sun.

The *Marie* cast on this expanse a shadow which was very long, like the shadows of evening, and which looked green, amid these polished surfaces reflecting the whiteness of the sky; and in all that shadowed part which gave no reflection one could distinguish by transparency what was happening under the water: innumerable fish, myriads and myriads, all alike, gliding noiselessly in the same direction, as if they had a goal in their perpetual journeying. They were the cod which were executing their evolutions together, all lengthwise in the same direction, strictly parallel, making an effect of grey hatchings, and agitated unceasingly with a rapid quivering, which gave an air of fluidity to this mass of silent lives. Sometimes, with a sudden stroke of the tail, they all turned together, showing the gleam of their silvered bellies and then the same stroke of tail, the same turn were propagated through the entire shoal in slow undulations, as if thousands of metal blades had given, under water, each a little flash.

The sun, already very low, was sinking: it was clear, therefore, that it was evening. As it descended into the leaden-coloured zone which rested on the sea

it became yellow, and its circle became more clearly
defined, looked more real. It was possible to fix it
with your eyes, as one may the moon.

It gave light still; but one would have said that it
was no great distance away; it seemed that if one but
went in a boat as far as the edge of the horizon, one
would encounter there this large mournful balloon,
floating in the air some few feet above the water.

The fishing was proceeding busily enough; looking
into the still water one could see very clearly the
manner of it; the cod coming to bite, with a gluttonous
movement; then shaking themselves a little, at the
nip of the hook, as if to tighten the grip on their
muzzle. And from minute to minute, rapidly, with
both hands, the fishermen hauled in their lines—
throwing the beast to him whose business it was to
gut it and flatten it.

The little fleet of the Paimpol men was scattered
over this tranquil mirror, animating this desert.
Here and there appeared the distant little sails, spread
for form's sake, for there was no breath of air, and
very white, outlined clearly against the greyness of
the horizon.

And on this day the occupation of the Iceland fisherman seemed a very peaceful one, a very easy one—a
ladylike occupation.

·   ·   ·   ·   ·

Jean-François de Nantes;
Jean-François,
Jean-François!

They sang on, the two great children.

And Yann gave little thought to his fine looks and
distinguished bearing. Nevertheless, he unbent only

with Sylvestre, singing or playing only with him; with the others, on the contrary, he was reserved, and inclined to be proud and solemn—very kindly, none the less, when one had need of him, always good-humoured and obliging when he was not irritated.

And they continued to sing this one same song; the two others, a few yards away, sang a different song, another melody compact of somnolence, of health and vague melancholy.

They were kept busy and time passed quickly.

Below, in the cabin, there was still a fire, smouldering at the bottom of the iron stove, and the cover of the hatchway was kept shut to produce an illusion of night for those who wanted to sleep. They needed little air in their slumbers, and men less robust, men bred in towns, would have wanted more. But when the deep chest has been filled throughout the day, directly from the infinite atmosphere, it sleeps itself in turn afterwards, and scarcely any longer stirs; then one can snuggle down in any little hole that offers, as the beasts do.

After their spell of fishing they turned in at will, at any time they pleased, the hour being of no account in this continual daylight. And always they slept soundly, without moving, without dreaming, a sleep of complete repose.

When, by chance, their thoughts turned to women, then, no doubt, the sleepers stirred: as they told themselves that in six weeks the fishing would be over, and that soon they would possess new mistresses, or maybe old ones loved already, they opened wide their eyes.

But that happened rarely; and when it did more often than not the thoughts were honest thoughts· of wives, sweethearts, sisters, relatives. . . . In the

habit of continence the senses also slept—for long
periods at a time.

.   .   .   .   .

Jean-François de Nantes;
Jean-François,
Jean-François!

They were looking now, on the far background of
their grey horizon, at something scarcely perceptible.
A long column of smoke, ascending from the waters
like a microscopic tail, of a different grey, a very
slightly deeper grey than that of the sky. With their
eyes used to probing the depths, they had quickly
perceived it.

'A steamer!'

'It seems to me,' said the captain, looking at it
narrowly, 'it seems to me it's a warship—the cruiser
going its round. . . .'

This faint smoke was bringing to the fishermen news
of France, and, amongst others, a certain letter from
an old grandmother, written by the hand of a fair girl.

It came on slowly; presently one saw its dark hull—
it was the cruiser, sure enough, which was making a
tour of the western fiords.

At the same time a light breeze which had sprung
up, stimulating to breathe, began to marble in places
the surface of the dead waters; it traced on the gleaming mirror designs of a blue-green, which were prolonged in trails, spreading out like fans, or ramifying
in the form of madrepores; and this happened very
quickly with a light rustling; it was a sign of awakening, presaging the end of this immense torpor. And
the sky, freed of its veil, became clear; the vapours
fallen on the horizon were heaped there in accumu-
lations of grey wads, forming, as it were, soft walls
round the sea. The two limitless glasses, between

which the fishermen were—that above and that below
—took on once more their deep transparency, as if
someone had wiped away the mists which had
tarnished them. The weather was changing, but in a
sudden fashion which boded no good.

And from different points of the sea, from different
sides of this expanse, came the fishing boats: all the
French fishing boats, which roamed these latitudes,
Bretons and Normans, Boulogne boats, and Dunkirk
boats. Like birds rallying to a call, they assembled
at the coming of the cruiser; they appeared even from
the empty corners of the horizon, and their little
greyish wings could be seen on every side. They
peopled the pale desert.

Not drifting slowly any more, they had spread
their sails to the new fresh breeze and gained speed
as they approached.

Iceland, in the distance, had appeared also, as if it,
too, had wished to draw near; it showed more and
more clearly its tall mountains of bare rock—which
have never been illumined except from the side, from
below, and as if grudgingly. It was continued, even,
by another Iceland similar in colour which took shape
gradually—but this other Iceland was chimerical,
and its mountains, more gigantic than their real
counterpart, were only a condensation of vapours.
And the sun, still low and languishing, incapable of
climbing, showed itself through this illusory isle in
such wise that it appeared as if it were suspended in
front of it, having for human eye an incomprehensible
aspect. It had no longer a halo and its round disk,
which had taken on again a sharply defined contour,
seemed rather some poor planet, yellow, dying, which
had come to a halt there irresolutely, in the middle
of chaos.

The cruiser, which had stopped, was surrounded
now by this pleiad of Icelanders. From all these boats
smaller boats put off, little nutshells, taking to the
cruiser rough-looking men with long beards, in
accoutrements that smacked of savagery.

They all had some request to make, a little in the
manner of children, remedies for minor wounds,
renewals, provisions, letters.

Others came from their captains to be put in irons,
in expiation of some refractoriness; as they had all
served in the Navy, they found the thing quite
natural. And when the narrow spar-deck of the
cruiser was encumbered with four or five of these great
fellows lying with pinioned feet, the old boatswain,
who had padlocked them, said to them: 'Lie skew-
wise, my lads, so that folk may pass,' which they did
obediently, with a smile.

There were many letters this time for the Icelanders. Amongst others, two for the *Marie, Captain
Guermeur*, one to *Monsieur Gaos, Yann*, the second to
Monsieur Moan, Sylvestre, the latter having come by
way of Denmark to Reikiavik, where the cruiser had
collected it.

The postman, diving into his sailcloth bag, delivered
them over, having difficulty often in reading the
addresses which had not all been written by very
practised hands.

And the captain said:

'Hurry up, hurry up, the glass is falling.'

He was a little concerned to see all these nutshells
loosed upon the sea, and so many fishermen assembled
in this very doubtful region.

Yann and Sylvestre were used to reading their
letters together.

This time it was by the light of the midnight sun which remained still high above the horizon, with its same aspect of a dead star.

Sitting together, apart from the rest, in a corner of the deck, each with an arm round the other's shoulders, they read very slowly, as if to let these tidings of home sink in better.

In Yann's letter, Sylvestre found news of Marie Gaos, his little betrothed. In Sylvestre's, Yann read the droll stories of old Grandmother Moan, who had not her equal for amusing the absent; and then the last paragraph which concerned him: 'Remember me to the boy Gaos.'

And when the letters were read Sylvestre shyly showed his to his big friend, to try to make him appreciate the hand which had written it.

'Look, is it not a beautiful handwriting, Yann?'

But Yann, who knew very well whose girlish hand it was, turned away his head and shrugged his shoulders, as much as to say that he was getting tired of hearing of this Gaud.

Then Sylvestre carefully folded the despised little letter, put it back into its envelope, and slipped it beneath his jersey against his heart, saying quite sadly to himself:

'I 'm afraid it 's hopeless, they will never marry. . . . But what can have turned him against her in this way? . . .'

The cruiser's bell sounded midnight. And still they remained there, sitting side by side, thinking of their homeland, of their dear ones, of a thousand things, in a dream. . . .

And now this eternal sun, which had dipped its rim slightly in the waters, began slowly to rise.

It was morning. . . .

PART II

CHAPTER I

. . . It had changed its aspect, also, and its colour, the sun of Iceland, and it opened this new day by a sinister morning. Completely rid of its veil, it gave out great rays which traversed the sky in jets, announcing impending storms.

It had been too fine in the last few days and a change was due. The wind blew on this assembly of boats, as if it felt the need of scattering them, of ridding the sea of them; and they began to disperse, to flee like a routed army—simply before this menace written in the air, about which there could be no mistake.

And it steadily increased in strength, until men and ships alike shivered at it.

The waves, still small, began to chase one another, to group themselves. They had been marbled at first with a white foam which spread over them in slaver; but presently, with a sound of crackling, they gave out a smoke of spray; one would have said that the sea was boiling, that it was burning—and the shrill noise of it all augmented from minute to minute.

There was no thought now for the fishing, but only for the management of the boats. The lines had been hauled in long before. All were hurrying to get away, some to seek a shelter in the fiords, striving to arrive in time; others, preparing to pass the southern point of Iceland, deeming it the safer course to take to the open sea and have free space in which to sail before

the wind. They still saw one another a little; here
and there, in the hollows of the waves, sails rose up,
poor little things, wet, weary, fugitive—but keeping
upright nevertheless, like those children's toys of
pith of elder-wood which one may lay flat by blowing
on them, but which always raise themselves again.

The great shag of clouds which had condensed on
the western horizon with the aspect of an island began
to break up at the top and the tatters coursed across
the sky. It seemed inexhaustible, this shag: the wind
stretched it, extended it, unravelled it, making issue
from it an indefinite succession of dark curtains, which
it outspread over the clear yellow sky, become now
livid in its cold depths.

And still the wind increased, agitating everything.

The cruiser had made off towards the shelters of
Iceland, the fishermen remained alone on this agitated
sea, which now had an angry air and a dreadful colour.
They made haste in their preparations for foul weather.
The distance between them increased. Soon they
were lost from sight of one another.

The waves, curling in volutes, continued to chase
one another, to unite, to join forces in order to
become still higher, and, between them, the hollows
deepened.

In a few hours all was ploughed up, convulsed in
this region which on the preceding evening had been
so calm, and, in place of the silence of before, one was
deafened with noise. Very quickly the scene had
changed, and all now was agitation, unconscious,
useless. What was the object of it all? . . . What
a mystery of blind destruction! . . .

The clouds were completing their unfolding, coming
always from the west, overlaying one another, hurrying, swift obscuring everything. There remained

now only a few yellow openings, by which the sun sent down its last rays in sheaves. And the water, greenish now, was veined more and more with white slaver.

By midday the *Marie* had assumed completely her foul-weather trim; with closed hatches and reefed sails, she bounded supple and light; amid the disorder that was commencing she had the air of playing as play the porpoises whom storms amuse. With only her foresail spread she ran before the wind, according to the nautical expression which describes this particular trim.

Above, the heavens had become completely over-cast, a closed, oppressive vault—with darker shadings spread over it in shapeless smudges; the impression was almost of an immobile dome, and it was necessary to look close to realize that on the contrary it was in a very whirl of movement: great grey sheets, hastening to pass, and replaced without ceasing by others which came from below the horizon; funereal tapestries unwinding as if from an inexhaustible roll. . . .

She ran before the wind, the *Marie*, ever more quickly—and the wind ran, too—before I know not what mysterious and terrible power. The wind, the sea, the *Marie*, the clouds, all were seized with the same madness of flight and speed in the same direc-tion. That which ran ahead the fastest was the wind; then the great heavings of the water, more lumbering, slower, followed after it; then the *Marie*, dragged in the universal movement. The waves pursued her, with their pale crests, which rolled on in a perpetual crashing, and she—continually overtaken, continually outstripped—escaped them, none the less, thanks to a wake she skilfully left behind her, an eddy on which their fury broke.

And in this movement of flight the chief sensation was an illusion of lightness; without any difficulty, without an effort, one felt oneself leap. When the *Marie* rose on the waves she rose without a shock as if the wind had lifted her, and her descent afterwards was like a sliding, causing those internal qualms one has in the simulated fallings of the switchback or in the imaginary descents of dreams. She slid backwards, as it were, the racing mountains slipping away from under her to continue their course, and then she was plunged again in one of those deep troughs which raced in their turn; without taking hurt she touched the dreadful bottom of them, in a shower of spray which did not even wet her, but which sped on like everything else; which sped on and vanished ahead of her like smoke, like an intangible nothing. . . .

At the bottom of these troughs there was a deeper gloom, and as each wave passed one saw behind another coming on; another larger still which rose up quite green by transparency, with furious writhings, with volutes that threatened to close, with an air of saying: 'Now I have got you, now I will engulf you.'

But no; it raised you merely, as with a lifting of a shoulder one might raise a feather; and, almost gently, you felt it passing under you, with its rustling foam, its roar as of a cascade.

And so it went on continuously. But getting worse all the time. The waves followed one another, becoming ever more enormous, in long chains of mountains, the valleys of which began to cause fear. And all this madness of movement became faster, under a sky that grew darker and darker, amid a noise that swelled until it became a roar.

It was very heavy weather indeed, and it was necessary to keep watch. But, then, there was so

much free space before them, space in which to run!
And it happened also that this year the *Marie* had
spent the season in the most western part of the
Iceland fisheries; so that this headlong flight towards
the coast was so much way made in their voyage home.

Yann and Sylvestre were at the helm lashed by the
waist. They were singing again the song of *Jean-
François de Nantes*; drunk with movement and speed,
they sang at the top of their voices, laughing to find
they could not hear each other amid all this unloosing
of noise, turning round in their high spirits, to sing
against the wind, and losing breath for their pains.

'Hallo, there! you youngsters, do you find it stuffy
up there?' Guermeur asked them, putting his bearded
face through the half-opened hatchway, like a devil
ready to leap out of his box.

No, there was no lack of air on deck, that was
certain!

They were not afraid, having a very exact notion
of what was manageable, having confidence in the
solidity of their boat, in the strength of their arms.
And also in the protection of the faïence Virgin who,
during forty years of voyages to Iceland, had so often
danced this same disagreeable dance, forever smiling
between her bouquets of artificial flowers. . . .

Jean-François de Nantes;
Jean-François,
Jean-François!

In general they could see but a short distance
around them: some hundreds of yards away everything seemed to end in monstrous waves whose pale
crests stood erect, shutting out the view. One
seemed always to be in the middle of a restricted
scene, which, nevertheless, was perpetually changing;
and, in addition, things were drowned in this kind of

watery smoke, which scudded like a cloud, with an extreme swiftness, over all the surface of the sea.

But, from time to time, a rift appeared in the north-west, from which a sudden shift of wind would come; then, a glancing light arrived from the horizon; a trailing reflection, making the dome of the sky seem darker, shed itself on the white agitated crests. And this rift was sad to see; these glimpsed distances, these vistas oppressed the heart the more in that they made you realize only too well that there was the same chaos everywhere, the same fury—even beyond the great empty horizon, and infinitely beyond that again: the terror had no limits, and one was alone in the midst of it.

A gigantic clamour issued from things like an apocalyptic prelude sounding the alarm of the end of the world. And thousands of voices could be distinguished in it; from above came whistling voices and deep voices, which seemed almost distant because they were immense: that was the wind, the mighty soul of this disorder, the invisible power directing the whole commotion. It was terrifying enough; but there were other noises, closer, more material, carrying a more imminent menace of destruction, which the tormented water gave out, spluttering as if on burning coals.

And still the storm waxed fiercer.

And, in spite of their close trim, the sea began to cover them, to 'eat' them as they said: first, the spray lashing from behind, then water in masses, hurled with smashing force. The waves rose higher still, more madly high, and the higher they rose the more jagged they became; one saw large greenish tatters of them, rags of falling water, which the wind scattered everywhere. Some of them fell in heavy masses on the

deck, with a smacking sound, and then the *Marie*
shook in her whole being as if in pain. Now one
could distinguish nothing, on account of all this white
scattering foam; when the blasts roared more fiercely,
one saw it rushing in thicker clouds—like the dust of
the roads in summer.   A heavy rain, which had begun,
fell slantwise also, almost horizontally, and these
things together whistled, whipped, hurt like blows of
a lash.

They remained both at the helm, bound and holding
firm, clothed in their oilskins, which were tough and
glistening as the skins of sharks; they had tied them
tight at the neck, by tarred laces, and tight at the
wrists and ankles, so as to keep the water out; and
everything streamed over them, who bowed their
backs when it fell too thick, buttressing themselves
well, so as not to be borne completely over.   The
skin of their cheeks burnt, and at every minute they
caught their breath.   After each great mass of water
had fallen they looked at each other—and smiled to
see the salt amassed in their beards.

In time, nevertheless, it became an extreme weariness, this fury which did not abate, which remained
always at its same exasperated paroxysm.   The rage
of men, the rage of beasts, exhausts itself and quickly
subsides; one has perforce to suffer long the rage of
inanimate things which is without cause and without
aim, mysterious as life and as death.

Jean-François de Nantes;
Jean-François,
Jean-François!

Through their lips, which had become white, the re-
frain of the old song passed still, but like an aphonous
thing, continued from time to time unconsciously.
The excess of movement and noise had made them

drunk; it was in vain that they were young, their smiles grimaced on their teeth which chattered in their trembling from the cold; their eyes, half-closed under burning, flickering eyelids, remained fixed in a grim atony. Lashed to the helm like two marble buttresses, they made, with their cramped, blue fingers, the efforts that were necessary, almost without thinking, by simple habit of the muscles. With streaming hair, and contracted mouths, they had become strange, and in them reappeared a whole background of primitive savagery.

They could see no longer! They knew only that they were still there, side by side. At the moments of greatest danger, every time that behind them the new mountain of water rose up, overhanging, clamorous, horrible, dashing against their boat with a mighty thud, one of their hands moved involuntarily in the sign of the cross. They no longer thought of anything, not of Gaud, not of any woman, nor of any marriage. It was lasting too long and they were past all thinking; their intoxication of noise, of weariness, of cold, obscured everything in their heads. They were now only two pillars of stiff flesh who kept the helm; only two vigorous beasts clinging there by instinct so that they should not die.

CHAPTER II

. . . It was in Brittany, in the latter part of September, on a day already cool. Gaud was making her way alone over the barren moor of Ploubazlanec in the direction of Pors-Even.

Nearly a month before the Iceland boats had returned—save two which had disappeared in that June storm. But the *Marie* having held fast, Yann and all those of the ship's company were at home, peacefully.

Gaud was very perturbed at the idea that she was bound for Yann's home.

Once only had she seen him since the return from Iceland; it was when they had gone, all together, to bid good-bye to poor little Sylvestre, on his departure for service. (They had accompanied him as far as the diligence, Sylvestre weeping a little, his old grandmother weeping much, and he had gone to join the depot at Brest.) Yann, who had also come to embrace his little friend, had seemed to avert his eyes when she looked at him, and, as there were many people round the diligence—other conscripts who were departing also, and relatives assembled to bid them good-bye—they had no opportunity of speaking to each other.

And so she had taken at last a great resolution, and, a little fearful, was on her way now to the home of the Gaoses.

Her father had formerly had some common interests

with Yann (affairs of that complicated sort which, among fishermen, as among peasants, seem never to end), and owed him some hundred francs in respect of the sale of a boat which had just been completed.

'You ought,' she had said, 'to let me take him this money, father. In the first place, I should be very pleased to see Marie Gaos; and, then, I have never been so far into Ploubazlanec, and it would interest me to make the long tramp.'

In her heart she had an anxious curiosity to see this family of Yann's, into which one day perhaps she would enter, to see his home, his village.

In a last conversation, Sylvestre, before departing, had explained to her in his fashion the unmannerliness of his friend:

'You know, Gaud, it's because he is made like that: he doesn't want to marry any one. It's an idea he has got into his head. He loves only the sea, and one day, even, in a jest, he told us he had promised himself to the sea in marriage.'

And so she pardoned him his little ways and, treasuring always in her memory his kind, frank smile of the night of the ball, continued to cherish hope.

If she met him there, in his home, she would not say anything to him on any account; she would not have dreamt of doing anything so forward. But, perhaps, he, seeing her again in the familiarity of his home, perhaps he would speak. . . .

CHAPTER III

SHE had been walking for an hour, alert, agitated, breathing the wholesome breeze from the sea.

There were large calvaries planted at the cross-roads.

From time to time she passed through sailors' villages, little hamlets which are beaten the year through by the wind and have the colour of rocks. In one, where the lane narrowed suddenly between sad-looking walls, between high thatched roofs, pointed like Celtic huts, an inn sign made her smile: 'The Chinese Ciderhouse'; someone had painted two ape-like personages in green and red robes, with pigtails, drinking cider. No doubt a fancy of some old sailor man returned from foreign parts. . . . As she passed she looked at everything; people who are very preoccupied by the object of their journey are always more interested than others in the thousand and one details of the road.

The little village was far behind her now, and, as she advanced over this lost promontory of Breton land, the trees became rarer about her, the country more forlorn.

The ground was undulating, rocky, and from all the heights could be seen the open sea. There were no hills at all now; nothing but the bare sandy moor with its green furze and, here and there, the crucifixes, outlining against the sky their spreading arms, giving to all this country the appearance of an immense place of justice.

At a cross-way, protected by one of these enormous Christs, she hesitated between two roads which
disappeared between banks of thorn.

A little girl, coming up in the nick of time, relieved
her from her embarrassment:

'Good morning, Mademoiselle Gaud!'

It was a little Gaos girl, a little sister of Yann.
After she had embraced her she asked her if her
parents were at home.

'Daddy and mummy, yes. All except my brother
Yann,' said the little one, without any malice, 'who
has gone to Loguivy; but I think he will be back
before long.'

He was not there! Again this perverse fate which
kept him at a distance from her, everywhere and
always. She was strongly inclined to postpone her
visit until another time. But this child, who had
seen her on the road, who would surely tell . . .
What would they think of that at Pors-Even? She
decided, therefore, to continue her journey, dawdling
as much as possible in order to give him time to
return.

In measure, as she drew near to Yann's village, to
this point remote and lost, things became wilder still
and more desolate. This great air of the sea, which
makes men more vigorous, also makes the plants
lower, shorter, stunts them, flattens them on the
unkindly soil. In the lane there were seaweeds which
trailed over the ground, foliage of a foreign sort,
indicating that another world was close by. They
shed in the air their salty odour.

Gaud met a few passers-by, men of the sea, whom
one saw at a great distance in this bare country, outlining themselves in a kind of magnified way, against
the high and distant line of the waters. Pilots or

fishermen, they seemed always to have their eyes on the far distance, to be keeping vigil over the sea; as she passed them, they gave her good day. Bronzed faces, very masculine and decided, under a sailor's bonnet.

Time did not pass, and now she was at a loss to know what to do to prolong her journey; the people she passed wondered to see her walking so slowly.

What was Yann doing at Loguivy? Running after the girls, perhaps. . . .

Ah, if she had known how little he bothered his head about them, these fair charmers! At any time, when the mood seized him, he had, as a rule, but to present himself to make a conquest. The little ladies of Paimpol, as the old Icelander song says, are somewhat lavish of their favours, and could not be expected to resist so handsome a suitor. No, quite simply, he had gone to give an order to a certain basket-maker in the village, who alone in the country round had the true art of weaving lobster-traps. His head at that moment was very free from love.

She reached a chapel, which she had seen from a distance on a hill. It was a chapel all in grey. Very small and very old; in the midst of the arid surroundings, a cluster of trees, grey also and already leafless, served it for tresses, tresses tossed all on the same side, as by a hand which had been passed there.

And this hand was the same as made founder the boats of the fishermen, the eternal hand of the west wind, which bends back, in the direction of the waves and the swell, the twisted branches of the shore. They had grown slantwise and dishevelled, the old trees, bowing their backs under the age-long pressure of this same hand.

Gaud was now almost at her journey's end, for this
was the chapel of Pors-Even.   She stopped, therefore,
to gain a little more time.

A low crumbling wall made a boundary round an
enclosure containing crosses.   And everything was of
the same colour, the chapel, the trees, and the tombs;
the whole place seemed uniformly weather-beaten,
gnawed by the wind from the sea; an identical greyish
lichen, with pale sulphur-yellow patches, covered the
stones, the gnarled branches, and the granite saints
who stood in the niches of the wall.

On one of these wooden crosses a name was inscribed
in large letters: 'Gaos—Gaos, Joël, eighty years.'

Ah, yes, the grandfather; she knew that.   The sea
had not wanted him, had not wanted this old sailor.
To be sure, many relatives of Yann must be sleeping
in this enclosure; it was natural, and she ought to
have expected it; nevertheless, this name read on
this tomb made a painful impression on her.

To pass yet another minute or two she entered to
say a prayer under the ancient porch, which was very
small, and worn, and coated with lime-wash.   And
then she stopped short, with a more marked contrac-
tion of the heart.

Gaos!   The same name again, graven on one of the
memorial plaques, such as are placed to preserve the
memory of those who die at sea.

She read the inscription:

In memory of
GAOS, JEAN-LOUIS,
Aged 24 years, sailor on board the
Marguerite, who disappeared in Ice-
land on the 3rd of August 1877.
May he rest in peace!

Iceland—always Iceland!—All about, at this

entrance to the chapel, were nailed other wooden plaques, with the names of dead mariners. It was the corner of the shipwrecked sons of Pors-Even, and she regretted she had entered, seized by a dark presentiment.

At Paimpol, in the church, she had seen similar inscriptions; but here, in this village, it was smaller, ruder, wilder, this empty tomb of the Iceland fishermen. On either side was a granite seat for the widows, for the mothers: and this low place, irregular as a grotto, was protected by a very ancient statue of the Virgin, painted over in red, with large, unfriendly eyes, which resembled Cybele, the primitive goddess of the world.

Gaos, again!

In memory of

GAOS, FRANÇOIS,

Husband of Anne-Marie Le Goaster, Captain on board the *Paimpolais*, lost in Iceland between the 1st and 3rd of April 1877, with the twenty-three men of his crew.

May they rest in peace!

And, below, two cross-bones, under a dark skull with green eyes, a painting crude and grotesque, savouring still of the barbarism of an earlier age.

Gaos! The name was everywhere!

Another Gaos, called Yves, 'swept overboard and lost in the neighbourhood of Norden Fiord in Iceland, at the age of twenty-two years.' The plaque seemed to have been there for many years. He must have been quite forgotten, this Yves. . . .

As she read, there came to her for this Yann yearnings of great tenderness, which were charged also

with despair. Never, oh, never, would he be hers!
How could she dispute him with the sea, which had
claimed so many other Gaoses, ancestors, brothers,
who must have been so like him in many ways.

She entered the chapel, already dark, the light
scarcely penetrating through the low windows in the
thick walls. And there, her heart full of tears which
wanted to flow, she knelt down to pray before the
large statues of saints, surrounded with common
flowers, whose heads almost touched the vault.
Outside, the wind which had risen began to groan,
as though bringing to this Breton land the plaint of
young men dead.

The evening was approaching: it was necessary,
therefore, to make up her mind to pay her visit and
acquit herself of her commission.

She took to the road again, and, having made
inquiries in the village, she found the house of the
Gaoses, which backed against a high cliff; a dozen or
so granite steps led up to it.

Trembling a little at the idea that Yann might
have returned, she crossed the little garden in which
chrysanthemums and speedwell were growing.

On entering she said that she had brought the
money realized by the sale of the boat, and she was
asked, very politely, to sit down and await the return
of the father, who would sign the receipt for her.
Among the people who were there she looked for
Yann, but did not see him.

There was an air of business in the house. On a
large, very white table, they were already cutting out,
from a piece of new cotton cloth, the garments called
oilskins, for the next Iceland season.

'For you see, Mademoiselle Gaud, they must each
have two changes complete for the trip.'

They explained to her how they would afterwards dye them and wax them, these garbs of suffering. And while they described these things to her, she surveyed attentively this dwelling of the Gaoses.

It was laid out in the traditional manner of Breton cottages; a large fireplace occupied the back, and press beds were ranged on either side. But it had not the gloom nor the melancholy of those labourers' dwellings, which stand always half-buried by the roadside; it was bright and clean, as is usual with the homes of sailor-men.

Several little Gaoses were there, boys and girls, all the brothers or sisters of Yann—not counting the two grown-up men at sea; and, in addition, a fair little girl, pathetic-looking and neat, who was like none of the others.

'One we adopted last year,' explained the mother; 'not that we hadn't enough already; but what could we do, Mademoiselle Gaud! Her father was on the *Maria-Dieu-t'aime*, which was lost in Iceland last season, as you know—and, amongst the neighbours, they divided the five children who were left, and this one has fallen to us.'

Hearing that they were talking of her the little adopted one lowered her head and smiled, as she hid herself behind little Laumec Gaos, who was her special friend.

There was an air of comfort everywhere about the house, and the ruddy cheeks of all these children glowed with eager health.

They were at pains to show Gaud every attention —as a young lady whose visit was an honour to the family. They led her by a staircase of new white wood, up to the first floor room, which was the glory

of the dwelling.   She remembered well the history of
the construction of this upper story; it followed the
finding of a derelict ship in the Channel by the elder
Gaos and his cousin the pilot; on the night of the ball
Yann had told her all about it.

This room of the derelict was pretty and cheerful
in its new whiteness; there were two beds in it, beds
of the modern type, with curtains of pink chintz;
a large table in the middle.   From the window one
saw all Paimpol, all the roadstead, with the Iceland
boats beyond, at anchor—and the channel by which
they went to sea.

She did not dare to ask, but she would have greatly
liked to know where Yann slept; evidently, when he
was quite small he must have slept below, in one of
those old press beds.   But now, perhaps, it was here,
between these pretty pink curtains.   And she would
have dearly loved to know the details of his life.
Especially to know how he passed the long winter
evenings. . . .

. . . A rather heavy step on the stairs made her
tremble.

No, it was not Yann, but a man who resembled
him in spite of his white hair, who had almost his tall
stature, and who was as erect as he: the elder Gaos
returned from his fishing.

After having saluted her and inquired the object
of her visit, he signed the receipt for her.   It took
him rather long, for his hand, as he said, was no
longer steady.   Nevertheless, he did not accept the
hundred francs as a final payment, in full settlement
for the sale of the boat, but only as a payment on
account; he would talk it over with M. Mével.   And
Gaud, to whom the money signified little, smiled a
scarcely perceptible smile: so then the story was not

yet finished; very quickly she caught at the wild hope; at any rate, it meant that she would still have business with the Gaoses.

They were almost apologetic in the house about Yann's absence, as if they would have found it more seemly that all the family should be assembled to receive her. The elder Gaos had perhaps guessed, with his old sailor's shrewdness, that his son was not indifferent to this fair heiress, for he was rather insistent in his references to him:

'It 's very odd,' he said, 'he is never out so late. He went to Loguivy, Mademoiselle Gaud, to buy some lobster-traps; as you know, that is our chief fishing in the winter.'

She, inattentive, prolonged her visit, although she knew that she was staying too long; her heart ached at the thought that she would not see him.

'A sober fellow like him, what can he be doing? He is not in a tavern, that is certain; we have not that to fear with our son. . . . I don't say that once in a way, on a Sunday perhaps, with old friends . . . You know, Mademoiselle Gaud, what sailors are. . . . And, bless my soul, when a man is young, you know, why should he deny himself altogether? . . . But the thing is very rare with him, he 's a steady fellow, we can speak as to that.'

And now darkness was falling: the oilskins were being folded up, work was suspended. The little Gaoses, and their little adopted sister, sitting on benches, snuggled close to one another, subdued by this grey hour of the evening, and looked at Gaud, as who should say:

'What is she staying for; why doesn't she go?'

And, in the fireplace, the fire began to burn red in the falling twilight.

'You must stay and have supper with us, Mademoiselle Gaud.'

Oh, no; she could not do that; the blood rushed suddenly to her face at the thought of having stayed so long. She got up and said good-bye.

Yann's father had got up also to accompany her to the end of the road, to the farther side of a certain lonely valley, where aged trees made the way dark.

While they walked side by side she felt herself moved by a feeling of respect for him and of tenderness; she wanted to speak to him as to a father, in impulses which came to her: but the words died away in her throat, and she said nothing.

They walked on, in the cold wind of the evening which savoured of the sea, passing here and there, on the bare plain, cottages already shut up for the night, very gloomy, under the hump-backed roofs, poor nests in which the fishermen were hidden; passing crucifixes, and furze, and stones.

How remote it was, this Pors-Even, and how late she had stayed there!

From time to time they met people returning from Paimpol and Loguivy; as she watched the silhouettes approach she thought each time of Yann; but it was easy to recognize him in the distance, and she was quickly undeceived. Her feet caught in long brown plants, intertwined like coils of hair, which were seaweeds trailing over the ground.

At the cross of Plouëzoch she said good-bye to the old man, begging him to return. The lights of Paimpol were already visible, and there was no longer any reason to be afraid.

And so it was finished for this time. . . . And who could tell now when she would see Yann. . . .

She might have found pretexts enough for returning

to Pors-Even; but she would have had too forward an air in repeating the visit.   She would have to be more courageous and prouder.   If only Sylvestre, her little confidant, had been here still, she could have charged him, perhaps, to seek out Yann on her behalf and endeavour to ascertain his intentions.   But he had gone away, and it would be years before he returned.

CHAPTER IV

'I MARRY?' said Yann to his parents that same evening; 'I marry? And, bless my soul, why should I? Shall I ever be so happy as here with you; nothing to worry about, no one to wrangle with, and a good supper piping hot every evening, when I return from the sea. . . . Oh! I know very well that you are thinking of her who came to see you to-day. But, in the first place, a girl so rich as she, how should she care about poor folk like us? It doesn't seem reasonable to me. And, anyhow, neither with her nor any one else. I have thought it out well, and my mind is made up. I will not marry.'

They looked at one another in silence, the two old Gaoses, profoundly disappointed; for, after they had talked it over together, they had formed a very sure belief that this young girl would not refuse their handsome Yann. But they did not attempt to press the matter, knowing how useless it would be. His mother, in particular, bowed her head and said not another word. She respected the wishes of this son, of this eldest son, who ranked almost as the head of the house; although he was always very gentle and very considerate with her, more submissive even than a child in the little things of life, he had for long now been his absolute master in things that mattered, brushing aside all pressure with a calmly stern independence.

He never stayed up late, being used, like the other fishermen, to rise before daybreak. And after supper, at eight o'clock sharp, having given a last look of satisfaction at the traps he had brought from Loguivy, at his new nets, he began to undress, his mind, to all appearance, completely at ease; then he went upstairs to bed, to the bed with the pink chintz curtains, which he shared with his little brother Laumec.

CHAPTER V

. . . For the past fortnight Sylvestre, Gaud's little confidant, had been in the depot at Brest—very much out of his element, but very steady; wearing with a swagger his open blue collar and his red pompomed bonnet; a rather proud and very handsome sailor, with his rolling gait and tall figure; at bottom regretting still his fond old grandmother and remaining the innocent lad of old.

On one evening only had he got tipsy—with the lads of his native district; it was a custom, and they had returned to their quarters, the whole band of them, arm in arm, and singing at the top of their voices.

One Sunday, also, he had gone to the theatre, and sat in the gallery. The play was one of those thrilling dramas at which the sailors, exasperated against the villain, greet him with hootings which they utter in unison, making a noise like the deep roar of the west wind. What he noticed most was that it was very warm, that there was a lack of air and room: an attempt to remove his overcoat brought him a rebuke from the officer in charge. And he had ended by falling asleep.

As he was returning to the barracks after midnight he had come upon some women, no longer in their first youth, without covering on their heads, who were strolling up and down the footpath.

'Good night, dear,' they said in deep, hoarse voices.

He had understood at once what they wanted, not being by any means so simple as one might have thought. But the memory, evoked immediately, of his old grandmother and of Marie Gaos had caused him to pass them by contemptuously, surveying them from the height of his beauty and his youth with a smile of childlike mockery. He had surprised them, even, for they were not used to such reserve in a sailor.

'Did you see him! . . . Take care, run, my boy; run quickly, or else you 'll be eaten!'

And the noise of the very vile things they shouted after him had been drowned in the vague hum which filled the streets on this Sunday night.

He lived in Brest as in Iceland, as at sea, a life of continence. But the others did not make fun of him, because he was very strong, and strength is a thing which sailors respect.

CHAPTER VI

ONE day he was called to the office of his company;
he was told that he had been named for China, for
the Formosa Squadron! . . .

He had half expected for some time past that this
would happen, having heard said by those who read
the newspapers that the war in that part of the world
showed no sign of finishing. On account of the
urgency of the departure it was intimated to him also
that it would not be possible to allow him the leave
to say good-bye, usually given to those about to make
a voyage: in five days he would have to pack his
kit-bag and be off.

He was assailed by very conflicting emotions: first,
the delight of a long voyage, the lure of the unknown,
the thrill of war; and then the pain of leave-taking,
with the vague fear that he might never return.

A thousand things whirled in his head. There was
a great commotion around him, in the barrack rooms,
where many others had just been named also for this
same China squadron.

And quickly he wrote to his poor old grandmother,
quickly, in pencil, sitting on the floor, wrapt in an
agitated reverie, amid the coming and going and the
clamour of all these young men who, like him, were
about to depart.

CHAPTER VII

'SHE is a little ancient, his lady-love!' said the others, two days afterwards, as they smiled behind him: 'all the same, they seem to be getting on very well.'

They were amused to see him, for the first time, walking in the streets of Recouvrance with a woman on his arm, like everybody else, bending towards her with a tender air, saying things to her which seemed to be very winning.

A little person, whose figure was alert enough— seen from behind—a skirt rather short, to be sure, for the fashion of the day; a little brown shawl, and a large Paimpol coif.

She also, hanging on his arm, turned towards him, and gazed tenderly at him.

'She is a little ancient, his lady-love!'

They said that, the others, without any great malice, seeing quite well that it was a fond old grandmother, come from the country.

. . . Come in haste, seized with a dreadful fear, at the news of the departure of her grandson—for this war in China had already cost the district of Paimpol many a sailor.

Having gathered together all her poor little savings, and packed in a pasteboard case her best Sunday dress and a second coif, she had set off to embrace him at least once more.

She had gone straight to the barracks to ask for him, and at first the adjutant of his company had refused to let him out.

'If you want to make an application, my good woman, you must address yourself to the captain; that is he over there.'

And straightway she had gone to him. He, the captain, allowed himself to be touched.

'Send Moan to change,' he said.

And Moan, three steps at a time, had gone up to change into his holiday wear—while the old woman, to amuse him, as always, made behind the adjutant's back an inimitable little grimace, with a curtsey.

When he reappeared, this grandson of hers, very *décolleté* in his outdoor rig, she had been astonished to find him so handsome: his dark beard, which a barber had trimmed for him, was pointed in the fashion affected that year by sailors, the frills of his open shirt were neatly gauffered, and his bonnet had long floating ribbons terminated by golden anchors.

For a moment she had imagined she saw her son Pierre, who, twenty years before, had also been a topman in the Navy, and the memory of this distant past already grown so remote, of all her dear ones dead, had cast a fleeting shadow of sadness over the present hour.

But it was a sadness quickly effaced. They had set off arm in arm, in the joy of being together; and it was then that, taking her for his lady-love, his companions had judged her 'a little ancient.'

She had taken him to dinner, for a little spree, in a tavern kept by some Paimpol people, which had been recommended to her as not being too dear. Afterwards, still arm in arm, they had gone into Brest, to look at the shops. And there was nothing so amusing as the mirth-provoking tales she found to tell her grandson—in the Breton of Paimpol which the passers-by could not understand.

CHAPTER VIII

SHE had remained three days with him, three days of holiday, over which hung an *afterwards* gloomy indeed; they might have been called three days of grace.

And at last it had been necessary to leave, to return to Ploubazlanec. In the first place she had reached the end of her slender financial resources. And, secondly, Sylvestre was to embark on the day but one following, and the sailors are always confined rigorously to their quarters on the day before departure (a custom which at first sight seems a little barbarous, but which is a necessary precaution against deserting which they have a tendency to do when on the point of leaving for a voyage).

Oh, this last day! In vain had she tried, in vain had she sought in her head to find further amusing things to tell her grandson; she could think of none; and now there were tears which would not be denied, sobs which at every moment rose to her throat. Hanging on his arm, she gave him a thousand and one recommendations, which made him in turn inclined to weep. And they had ended by going into a church to pray together.

It was by the evening train that she went away. To save money they had repaired to the station on foot; he carrying her pasteboard case and supporting her with his strong arm on which she leant with all her weight. She was very, very tired, the poor old soul; she could do no more, after the heavy strain of the past three or four days. With back bowed under her brown shawl, having no longer strength to bear herself erect, there was nothing now of youthfulness in her figure, and she was conscious of all the overwhelming weight of her seventy-six years. At the thought that her visit was over, that in a few minutes more she would have to leave him, her heart was wrung in a piteous manner. And it was to China that he was going, to far-off China, to the place of slaughter! She had him with her still; she clung to him still with her poor worn hands. . . . And, nevertheless, he was going away; not all her will, nor all her tears, nor all her aged despair could avail one whit to keep him! . . .

Encumbered with her ticket, her basket of provisions, her mittens, agitated, trembling, she gave him some last words of advice to which he replied in a low voice by a little submissive 'yes,' his head bent tenderly towards her, looking at her with his gentle eyes, with a small-boy air.

'Now, then, old lady, you must make up your mind if you want to go!'

The engine whistled. Seized with the fear of missing the train, she took her pasteboard case from him—then let it fall to the ground in order to hang on his neck in a last embrace.

Many people looked at them in the station, but no one now was inclined to smile. Pushed by the porters, exhausted, bewildered, she threw herself into the first compartment that offered, the door of which was shut brusquely on her heels; while he, with the nimbleness of a sailor, made a birdlike sweep in order to reach the barrier outside, in time to see the train pass.

A shrill blast of the whistle, a noisy rattling of wheels—and the old grandmother passed. He, against the barrier, waved with a youthful grace his beribboned bonnet, and she, leaning out of the window of her third-class carriage, signalled with her handkerchief, so that she might be better recognized. As long as she could, as long as she distinguished the blue-black figure which still was her grandson, she followed him with her eyes, throwing him with all her soul that always uncertain 'au revoir,' which one says to sailors when they are going away.

Look at him well, poor old woman, at your little Sylvestre; until the last moment keep your eyes on that diminishing silhouette, which is effacing itself in the distance for ever. . . .

And when she could see him no longer she fell back in her seat, heedless of the rumpling of her pretty coif, sobbing bitterly, in an anguish of death. . . .

And he made his way back slowly, head bowed, with tears rolling down his cheeks. The autumn night had fallen, the lights were lit everywhere, the sailors' festival was beginning. Heedless of everything, he passed through Brest, then across the bridge at Recouvrance, returning to his quarters.

'Good night, dear,' might be heard already in the husky voices of the ladies who had commenced their evening strolling up and down the footpaths.

He rolled himself in his hammock, and wept alone, scarcely sleeping until the morning.

CHAPTER IX

.   .   .   .   .

. . . HE had put to sea, borne very quickly over unknown waters, much bluer than those of Iceland.

The ship which was carrying him to the Far East had orders to hasten, to stop nowhere.

He felt already that he had travelled a great distance on account of the speed they made, which was incessant, unvarying, without intermission, almost heedless either of the wind or the sea. Being a topman he lived in his crow's-nest, perched like a bird, aloof from the soldiers crowded on the deck, from the crush below.

They had stopped twice on the coast of Tunis to take on more Zouaves and mules; from afar he had perceived white towns on the sands and mountains. He had even come down from his top to look curiously at some very dark men, draped in white veils, who had come in boats selling fruit: the others had told him they were Bedouins.

The heat and the sunshine, which persisted still in spite of the autumn season, gave him an impression of an extreme foreignness.

One day they reached a town called Port Said. All the flags of Europe floated above it at the top of long staffs, giving it the air of a festive Babel, and glistening sands surrounded it like a sea. They had anchored there alongside the quay, almost in the middle of the long streets of wooden houses. Never, since their departure, had he seen so clearly and so closely the outside world, and this movement, this profusion of ships, interested him greatly.

With a continual noise of whistles and steam sirens all these ships engulfed themselves in a kind of long canal, narrow as a ditch, which disappeared in a silvery line across the infinitude of the sands. From the height of his top he saw them make their way as in a procession to lose themselves in the plain.

On the quay circulated every kind of costume; men in robes of every colour, busy, shouting, in the great bustle of the transit. And in the evening, with the diabolical whistlings of the engines, was mingled the confused racket of numerous orchestras, playing noisy tunes, as if to soothe the poignant regrets of all these passing exiles.

On the following day, as soon as the sun rose, they, too, had entered the narrow ribbon of water which stretched across the sands, followed by a queue of boats of different countries. It had lasted for two days, this promenade in file across the desert; then another sea had opened before them, and they had run for the offing again.

They were steaming at full speed still; this warmer sea had red marblings on its surface, and sometimes the churned water in their wake had the colour of blood. He lived almost all the time in his top, singing softly to himself *Jean-François de Nantes*, to remind himself of his brother Yann, of Iceland, of the good times past.

Sometimes, in the background of distances full of mirage, he would see appear some mountain of an extraordinary colour. Those who steered the ship knew, no doubt, in spite of the distance and the vagueness, these advanced capes of continents, which are, as it were, the eternal guiding points on the great

highways of the sea.   But, when one is a topman, one
is borne along as a chattel, without knowing anything,
ignorant of distances and measurements on the
expanse which never ends.

Sylvestre had only the notion of a dismaying
distance which increased continually; but his notion
of this was very clear, as he watched from on high the
ship's wake, noisy, rapid, for ever vanishing behind
them; as he remembered how long this speed had
lasted without ever slackening either by day or night.

Below, on deck, the crowd—the men huddled
together in the shade of the tents—panted in the
overpowering heat.   The water, the air, the light had
assumed a mournful, crushing splendour; and the
eternal festival of these things had a kind of irony for
mortal men, for our ephemeral existences.

Once, in his top, he was very interested by clouds of
little birds, of an unknown species, which threw
themselves on the ship like a whirling cloud of black
dust.   They allowed themselves to be picked up and
stroked, being utterly exhausted. Every topman
had one of them on his shoulders.

But presently the more weary of them began to die.

They died in thousands, on the yards, in the
portholes, these tiny things, in the glare of the
terrible sun of the Red Sea.

They had come from beyond the great deserts,
driven by a wind of tempest.   In fear of falling into
the infinite blue which was all about they had flung
themselves in a last despairing effort on this passing
ship.   Far away, in the background of some distant
region of Libya, their kind had multiplied in exuberant
loves; had multiplied beyond measure, until there were
too many of them; and then the blind mother, Mother
Nature, blind and heartless, had swept away with a

breath this excess of little birds, with the same impassiveness as if they had been a generation of men.

And they died, all of them, on the burning ironwork of the ship: the deck was strewn with their little bodies, which yesterday had palpitated with life, and song, and love. . . . Little black rags, with moistened feathers, Sylvestre and the topmen picked them up, spreading out in their hands, with an air of commiseration, the fine bluish wings, and then swept them with brooms into the great nothingness of the sea. . . .

Afterwards a swarm of locusts passed, daughters of those of Moses, and the ship was covered with them.

And then for many days they sailed in an unchanging blue, in which there was no longer any living thing—save, sometimes, for the flying fish, which skimmed the water in their flight. . . .

CHAPTER X

. . . RAIN in torrents under a dark, lowering sky—
it was India. Sylvestre had just set foot on shore,
chance having caused him to be chosen to complete
the crew of a whaleboat.

Through the thickness of the foliage the warm rain
descended on him, and he looked around him at
things new and strange. All was magnificently
green; the leaves of the trees were fashioned like
gigantic plumes, and the people he passed had large
velvety eyes, which seemed to be closing under the
weight of their lids. The wind which brought the
rain smelt of musk and flowers.

There were women who beckoned him; they
reminded him of the 'good night, dear!' heard so
many times in Brest. But, in this enchanted land,
their appeal was disturbing and sent a thrill through
his flesh. Their shapely bosoms swelled under the
transparent muslins, which draped them; they were
tawny and polished like bronze.

Still holding back, but fascinated, nevertheless, he
was beginning slowly to follow them.

. . . But there came a little nautical whistle,
modulated in birdlike trills, which recalled him
suddenly to the whaleboat, which was about to
put off.

And so he said good-bye to the beauties of India;
and when the evening found him once more out at
sea he was still as virgin as a babe.

After a new week of blue sea the ship stopped at

another country of rain and verdure. A cloud of little yellow men, with strange cries, immediately invaded the ship, carrying coal in baskets.

'Are we already in China, then?' asked Sylvestre, seeing that they all had ape-like faces and pigtails.

But they told him no; he must have a little patience. This was only Singapore. He climbed back to his top, to avoid the black dust which the wind blew about, while coal from thousands of little baskets was being heaped feverishly in the bunkers.

And then one day they reached a place called Tourane, where they found a certain warship called the *Circe*, at anchor, keeping a blockade. This was the ship for which he had known for some time past that he was destined, and he was transferred to it with his kit-bag.

He met there some men from his homeland, and even two Icelanders, who, at the moment, were gunners.

In the evenings of these still warm and tranquil days, when they had nothing to do, they foregathered on the deck, isolated from the rest, to make together a little Brittany of memories.

He had to pass five months of inaction and exile in this mournful bay, before the longed-for moment arrived when he went forth to battle.

CHAPTER XI

. . . . .

PAIMPOL—the last day of February—the eve of the departure of the fishermen for Iceland.

Gaud was standing against the door of her room, motionless and very pale.

And the reason was that Yann was below, talking to her father. She had seen him come and she could hear indistinctly the sound of his voice.

They had not met once during the whole of the winter. It was as if a fatality had kept them always apart.

After her journey to Pors-Even she had built some hope on the pardon of the Icelanders, at which there are many opportunities of meeting and talking, in the groups that gather in the evening on the Square. But, from the morning of that feast-day, the streets being already hung with white, decorated with green garlands, a dismal rain had fallen in torrents, driven from the west by a blustering wind; at Paimpol the sky had never been so dark. 'The Ploubazlanec folk will not come,' said the girls sadly, whose lovers lived in that district. And, as a matter of fact, they had not come, or, if they came, had disappeared at once into the taverns. No procession, no promenade, and she, her heart more oppressed than usual, had remained throughout the evening at her window, listening to the water dripping from the roofs, and the noisy songs which ascended from the interior of the taverns.

For some days past she had foreseen this visit of Yann's, shrewdly guessing that, in connection with this outstanding matter of the sale of the boat, the elder Gaos, who did not like coming to Paimpol, would send his son. And so she had made up her mind that she would go to him, a thing which commonly girls did not do, that she would speak to him in order to reach a clear understanding. She would reproach him for having troubled her and then abandoned her, in the manner of men who are without honour. Waywardness, shyness, attachment to the calling of the sea, or fear of being refused . . . if these obstacles, which Sylvestre had mentioned, were the only ones, perhaps they might be removed, who knows! after a frank discussion such as theirs would be. And then, perhaps, that engaging smile of his would reappear to settle everything—that same smile which had so surprised and charmed her the previous winter, on a certain night spent wholly dancing in his arms. And this hope gave her courage, filled her with an eager impatience.

From a distance all appears so easy, so simple to say and do.

And, as chance would have it, this visit of Yann's fell at an hour she herself would have chosen: she was sure that her father, sitting smoking as he would be, would not disturb himself to see him off the premises; in the passage, therefore, where they would be alone, she would be able at last to have her straight talk with him.

But now, the longed-for moment come, her boldness seemed to her extreme. The mere idea of meeting him, of seeing him face to face at the foot of these stairs, made her tremble. Her heart beat as if it would burst. . . .

. . . And to think that, at any moment, the door below might open—with the little creaking noise she knew so well—to give him passage!

No, decidedly no, she would never dare; rather would she pine in waiting and die of grief than attempt such a thing. And already she had taken some steps to return to the seclusion of her room, to sit there and work.

But she stopped again, hesitating, bewildered, remembering that to-morrow was the day of departure for Iceland, and that this opportunity of seeing him was unique. It would be necessary, if she let it pass, to begin over again those months of solitude and waiting, to languish for his return, to lose another whole summer of her life. . . .

Below, the door opened! Yann came out! Suddenly resolved, she ran down the staircase and reaching the bottom planted herself trembling before him.

'Monsieur Yann, I want to speak to you, if you please.'

'To me! Mademoiselle Gaud?' he said, lowering his voice, his hat in his hand.

He looked at her in a shy sort of way, his eyes questioning, his head thrown back, stern in expression, looking even as if he were wondering whether he would so much as stop. With one foot forward, in readiness for escape, he leaned his broad shoulders against the wall, as if to increase his distance from her in this narrow passage in which he found himself caught.

Nonplussed at this, she remembered nothing of what she had prepared to say to him; she had not foreseen that he might put this affront upon her of leaving without having heard her.

He averted his eyes and looked out into the street. His cheeks had become very red, a rush of blood made his face burn, and his mobile nostrils dilated at each respiration, following the movements of his heart, like those of bulls.

She continued with an effort:

'On the night of the ball, when we were together you said good-bye to me in a way one does not say it to people to whom one is indifferent. . . . Monsieur Yann, have you forgotten? . . . What have I done to you? . . .'

. . . The blustering west wind, coming from the street, rushed into the passage, stirring Yann's hair, and the wings of Gaud's coif, and making a door bang furiously behind them. It was not a comfortable place in which to talk of grave matters. After the first sentences, strangled in her throat, Gaud remained silent, her head swimming, unable any more to think. They had moved towards the street door, he seeking always to escape.

Outside, the wind was blowing with a great roar, and the sky was dark. Through the open door a lurid and mournful light fell full on their faces. A neighbour opposite watched them: 'What can they have to say to each other, those two, in the passage there, with airs so troubled? What is happening at the Mévels?'

'No, Mademoiselle Gaud,' said he at last, breaking away with the facility of a wild beast. 'Already I have heard that people in the neighbourhood are talking about us. . . . No, Mademoiselle Gaud. . . . You are rich, we are not people of the same class. I am not the kind of man you want coming to your house. . . .'

And he went away. . . .

And so all was over, over for ever. And she had not said anything of what she wanted to say, in this interview which had only succeeded in making her appear in his eyes as a brazen-faced minx. . . . What sort of a man was he, this Yann, with his contempt for women, his contempt for money, his contempt for everything! . . .

She remained rooted to the spot, seeing things swim about her in a sort of vertigo.

And then an idea, more intolerable than all, came to her in a flash: some comrades of Yann's, Icelanders were walking up and down outside waiting for him! If he should tell them what had happened, make a jest of it, how utterly odious this affront would be! She ran up quickly to her room to watch them through the curtains. . . .

In front of the house she saw, indeed, the group of men; but they were simply looking at the sky, which was becoming darker and darker, and making forecasts of the rain which was threatening:

'It's only a shower; let us go in and drink until it's over.'

And then they made merry, out loud, about Jeannie Caroff and other frail beauties; but none of them turned to look at her window.

They were all in high spirits, except Yann, who did not speak or smile, but remained serious and saddened. He did not go in to drink with the others, and without taking any more notice of them or of the rain which was now falling, walking slowly through the downpour in the manner of one absorbed in thought, he crossed the Square, in the direction of Ploubazlanec. . . .

Then she forgave him everything, and a feeling of

hopeless tenderness took the place of the bitter contempt which at first had filled her heart.

She sat down, her head in her hands. What was she to do now?

Oh! if he had but listened to her only for a minute; or, better, if he could come to her there, alone with her in this room, where they might talk in peace, all might perhaps come right yet.

She loved him enough to dare to avow it to him to his face. She would say to him: 'You came to me when I had not sought you: now I am yours with all my heart, if you want me. You see I do not fear to become the wife of a fisherman, although, among the young men of Paimpol, I would only have to choose if I wanted one of them for a husband; but I love you, because, in spite of all, I think you better than all the others: I am fairly well provided for, I know I am good-looking; although I have lived in cities I swear to you that I am a sensible girl, and have never done anything of which I am ashamed; then, since I love you so much, why will you not take me?'

. . . But all this would never be expressed, never spoken except in dream: it was too late. Yann would never hear it. To attempt to speak to him a second time. . . . Oh, no! What kind of creature would he take her for then! . . . She would rather die.

And to-morrow they would all depart for Iceland!

Alone, in her pretty room, where the wan daylight of February entered, cold, seated at hazard on one of the chairs ranged along the wall, it seemed to her that the world was tumbling, with things present and things to come, into a mournful, awful void, which had just opened everywhere about her.

She would fain have been released from life, have been lying peacefully in her grave, so that she might suffer no more. . . . But, in her heart, she forgave him, and no hatred was mixed with the despairing love she had for him. . . .

CHAPTER XII

•   •   •   •   •

THE sea, the grey sea.

On the unmarked highway which leads the fishermen, every summer, to Iceland, Yann had been running now for a day.

The preceding day, when they had set out to the singing of the old canticles, a south wind was blowing and all the boats, covered with sails, had been dispersed like sea-gulls.

Then the wind had become softer, and their progress slackened; banks of mist travelled level with the waters.

Yann was perhaps more silent than usual. He grumbled at the calm weather, and seemed to have need of movement, to drive from his mind some obsession; there was nothing to be done, however, except to glide tranquilly in the midst of tranquil things; except to breathe and go on living. Looking round one saw only grey depths; listening, one heard only silence. . . . Suddenly a dull noise, scarcely perceptible, but unusual, which came from below with a sensation of scraping, as in a carriage when the brakes are applied to the wheels! And the *Marie*, ceasing her progress, remained motionless. . . .

Stranded! Where, and on what? Some bank off the English coast probably. For they had seen nothing since the evening before, with these curtaining mists.

The men bestirred themselves and rushed about, and their excited movements contrasted with this sudden fixed tranquillity of their ship. But the *Marie* had stopped and would not budge. In the midst of this immensity of fluid things, which, in this sluggish weather, seemed not even to have consistency, she had been seized by I know not what resistant and immovable thing which was concealed beneath the waters; she was held fast there, and was in danger perhaps of perishing.

Who has not seen an unfortunate bird, a luckless fly, caught in birdlime?

At first one notices scarcely any difference; their aspect is not changed. It is necessary to know that they are held fast from below and in danger of never extricating themselves.

It is when they struggle afterwards that the sticky substance begins to soil their wings, their head, and that, little by little, they assume the pitiful air of a beast in distress which is about to die.

So it was with the *Marie*; at first nothing much seemed to have happened; she stood firm, leaning over a little, perhaps, but it was broad daylight and the weather was fine and calm; only those who knew would have been anxious, would have understood that the position was serious.

The captain almost moved one to pity: it was his fault for not paying sufficient attention to the position of the boat. He waved his hands in the air, saying: 'My God! My God!' in a tone of despair.

Quite near them, in a break in the mist, appeared a promontory of land which they did not recognize; but it was hidden again almost immediately, and they saw it no more.

There was not a sail in sight, not a sign of smoke.

And, for the moment, they almost preferred it so; they had no desire to see the English rescuers who come forcibly to get you out of your difficulties in their own fashion, and against whom you have to defend yourself as against pirates.

They strove hard, all of them, changing, over-turning the stowage. Turk, their dog, although he did not fear the movements of the sea, was very distressed also by the incident: these noises beneath them, these heavy jars when the swell passed, and then these immobilities, he understood very well that all this was not natural and cowered in corners, his tail between his legs.

Afterwards they lowered boats to drop the anchors, and tried to haul off, uniting all their forces on ropes —a rude manœuvre which endured for ten solid hours —and, when evening came, the poor boat, which in the morning had been so neat and trim, was already cutting a melancholy figure, drenched, dirty, in complete disarray. It had struggled, shaken itself in every possible way, and still it remained where it was, rooted like a dead boat.

.   .   .   .   .

Night came on, the wind rose, and the swell grew higher; things were looking ill when, suddenly, at about six o'clock, the boat extricated itself and moved off, breaking the ropes which they had left to keep her steady. . . . Then one saw the men running like madmen from fore to aft crying:

'We are floating!'

And they were indeed floating; but how can one express the joy that this mere fact of floating gave them, to feel that they were moving, that they had become once more a thing light and living, instead of the beginning of a wreck, which just now they had been! . . .

And, by this same token, the melancholy of Yann had disappeared too.   Buoyed up like his boat, cured by the healthy weariness of his arms, he had recovered his careless air, shaken off his memories.

The following morning, when they had finished hauling in the anchors, he continued his way to his cold Iceland, his heart to all appearance as free as in his boyhood's days.

CHAPTER XIII

THE post from France was being distributed on board
the *Circe*, in the roadstead of Ha-Long, at the other
side of the earth.   In the midst of a packed group of
sailors the postman was calling out in a loud voice
the names of the fortunate ones for whom there were
letters.   It was in the evening, in the gun-room, with
all jostlîng one another round a lantern.

'Moan, Sylvestre!' There was one for him, one
which bore indeed the Paimpol date-stamp—but
which was not in Gaud's handwriting.   What did
that mean?   And from whom could it be?

Having turned it over and over he opened it in
trepidation:

> Ploubazlanec,
> *5th March*, 1884.

MY DEAR GRANDSON,

It was from his dear old grannie right enough, and
he breathed more freely.   She had even added at the
foot her large signature learnt by heart and all
tremulous and scholarlike: 'Widow Moan.'

Widow Moan.   He pressed the letter to his lips,
with an impulsive movement, and kissed the poor
name as if it had been some holy amulet.   For the
letter arrived at a supreme moment of his life:
to-morrow morning, as soon as daylight came, he
was to depart for the seat of war.

It was in the middle of April; Bac-Ninh and Hong-Hoa had just been taken. No operations on a large scale were imminent in this Tonkin—the reinforcements which were arriving were, however, insufficient—and they were mustering from the ships, therefore, all the men that could be spared in order to complete the companies of marines already landed. And Sylvestre, who had for long languished in cruisings and the monotony of the blockade, had just been nominated with a number of others to fill the gaps in the ranks.

It was true that at this time there was talk of peace; but something told them, nevertheless, that they would be landed in time to see a little fighting. Having packed their kit-bags, completed their preparations, and bidden their adieux, they had aired themselves all the evening among their colleagues who were remaining behind, feeling very important and proud before these latter; each in his own fashion manifested his feelings on departure, some of them grave, and rather thoughtful; others expanding in fulsome words.

Sylvestre was rather silent and kept to himself his impatience of waiting; only, when any one caught his eye, his satisfied little smile said clearly: 'Yes, I am one of them, and it's to-morrow morning.' War, battle, he had yet but an incomplete idea of what they meant, but they fascinated him, nevertheless, for he came of a valiant race.

Uneasy about Gaud on account of this unfamiliar handwriting, he tried to get near a lantern in order that he might be able to read. And it was difficult in the midst of these half-naked men who crowded there, to read also, in the suffocating heat of the gun-room.

Right at the beginning of the letter, as he had anticipated, Grandmother Yvonne explained why she had been obliged to have recourse to the unpractised hand of an old neighbour:

MY DEAR GRANDSON,

I have not asked your cousin to write for me this time because she is in great distress. Her father died suddenly two days ago. And it seems that all his fortune has been eaten up in some unfortunate speculations he had made this winter in Paris. The house and the furniture are going to be sold. It is a great surprise to every one in the country. I think, my dear boy, that this will greatly grieve you, as it has me.

The boy Gaos asks to be remembered to you. He has renewed his engagement with Captain Guermeur, still on the *Marie*, and the departure for Iceland took place rather early this year. They set sail on the 1st of this month, two days before the great misfortune happened to poor Gaud, and they do not yet know of it.

But I am afraid, my dear boy, that now it is all over, and that we shall never see them married; for, as things are, she will have to work to gain a living. . . .

. . . He was thunderstruck; this bad news had spoilt for him all the joy of going into battle. . . .

PART III

CHAPTER I

. . . . .

IN the air, the whistling of a bullet! . . . Sylvestre stops short, and listens. . . .

It is on a limitless plain, green with the tender velvety greenness of spring. The sky is overcast, throwing a weight on the shoulders.

There are six of them, six armed sailors reconnoitring amid the growing rice fields, in a muddy lane.

Again! . . . That same noise in the silence of the air! . . . A shrill, high-pitched noise, a kind of prolonged *zipp*, giving a very good impression of the cruel devilish little thing passing there, very straight, very swift, carrying with it the menace of imminent death.

It was the first time in his life that Sylvestre had heard this particular kind of music. These bullets that travel towards you have a different sound from those you dispatch yourself: the noise of the report, coming from a distance, is attenuated so that you scarcely hear it, and you can distinguish better this thin humming of metal, which passes in a rapid trail, grazing your ears. . . .

And *zipp* again, and *zipp !* It was raining bullets now. Quite near the sailors, who had stopped short, they buried themselves in the sodden soil of the rice field, each with a little click as of hail, dry and rapid, and a slight splashing of water.

III

They looked at one another, smiling as at a comically played farce, and said:

'Chinamen!' (Annamites, Tonkinese, Black-flags, for these sailors, were all of the same Chinese family.)

But it is impossible to describe the contempt, the old mocking rancour, the zest for battle, which they contrived to put in their manner of announcing them: 'The Chinamen!'

Two or three more bullets whistled, lower in flight, these; they saw them ricochet, like grasshoppers in the grass. It had lasted less than a minute, this rain of lead, and now it had stopped. Over the wide, green plain, absolute silence reigned again, and nowhere was there any sign of living thing.

They were all still standing, eyes alert, scenting the wind, trying to find out whence the bullets had come.

From beyond, doubtless, from that cluster of bamboos, which made in the plain a little isle of plumes, and behind which appeared, half-hidden, some horned roofs. They advanced towards it running; in the sodden earth of the rice field, their feet sank and slithered; Sylvestre, thanks to his longer and more nimble legs, was foremost in the race.

Nothing whistled any longer; it seemed that they must have been dreaming. . . .

And as in every country of the world certain things are always and eternally the same—the grey of overcast skies, the tender colour of meadows in spring—you might have imagined yourself in the fields of France, and that these stout youths were running gaily there in some quite other game than that of death.

But, as they drew near, these bamboos revealed more clearly the exotic fineness of their foliage, these village roofs accentuated the strangeness of their curves, and some yellow men, who had been in ambush behind, advanced to take stock of them, their flat faces contracted with malice and fear. . . . Then suddenly they rushed forward with a cry, spreading out in a long line, irregular, but determined enough and dangerous.

'The Chinamen!' said the sailors again, and their smile had the same valiancy as before.

But, none the less, they realized now that the enemy was in force, in too great force. And one of them, looking round, discovered others coming from behind, emerging from among the foliage. . . .

. . . . .

In this hour, on this day, little Sylvestre bore himself very gallantly; his old grandmother would have been proud to see him!

His appearance had changed in these last few days. His face was bronzed; his voice had taken on a new note; and he was now as if in his proper element. In a moment of supreme indecision the sailors, raked by bullets, had almost begun a movement of retreat which would have meant death for all of them, but Sylvestre had continued to advance; holding his rifle by the muzzle he had confronted a whole group, laying about him to right and left, with sweeping blows, which knocked out several of his foes. And, thanks to him, the encounter took a new turn: the panic, the bewilderment, that indescribable moral thing, which is the deciding factor in these little battles of outposts, had passed to the side of the Chinese: it was they who began to fall back.

. . . It was over now, they were fleeing. And the six sailors, having recharged their quick-firing rifles, slaughtered them at their ease; there were red puddles in the grass, foundered bodies, heads which oozed out their brains in the water of the rice field.

They fled cowering, keeping close to the ground, flattening themselves like leopards. And Sylvestre pursued them, already twice wounded—a spear thrust in his thigh, and a deep gash in his arm—but feeling nothing but the intoxication of the fight, that unreasoned intoxication which comes from vigorous blood, which gives a superb courage to the ordinary man, which made the heroes of old.

One, whom he was pursuing, turned and faced him in an impulse of desperate terror. Sylvestre stopped, smiling, contemptuous, sublime, to let him fire, and then, seeing the direction of his aim, threw himself a little to the left. But in the movement of pulling the trigger the barrel of the rifle deviated by accident in the same direction. Sylvestre felt a commotion in his chest, and realizing what it was, in a moment of thought, although yet he had suffered no pain, he turned round to the other sailors who were following, and tried to say to them, in the consecrated phrase of the old soldier: 'I think I've got my ticket!' In the deep breaths he took, as a result of his running, to fill his lungs with air, he felt the air enter also by a hole in his right breast, with a horrible little noise, as in a wheezy bellows. At the same time his mouth became full of blood, while a sharp pain smote him in the side, a pain which increased very, very quickly, until it became a thing atrocious, unspeakable.

He swung round two or three times, his head swimming with vertigo, in an effort to get his breath in the midst of this red liquid, the flood of which choked him —and then, heavily, he sank down in the mud.

CHAPTER II

·   ·   ·   ·   ·

ABOUT fifteen days afterwards, when the sky had
already become more overcast at the approach of the
rainy season, and the heat pressed more heavily on
this yellow Tonkin, Sylvestre, who had been brought
back to Hanoi, was conveyed to the roadstead of
Ha-Long, and put on board a hospital ship which
was returning to France.

For many days he had been borne on divers
stretchers, with short periods of waiting in ambu-
lances. They had done what they could for him;
but in the unfavourable conditions to which he was
subjected his chest had become filled with water, on
the wounded side, and the air entered still, gurgling,
by the hole which had not yet closed.

He had been awarded the military medal, and this
had given him a moment's joy.

But he was no longer the warrior of old, quick and
decided in movement, curt and vibrant in speech.
All that had fallen from him in the course of his long
suffering, in the weakness resulting from fever. He
had become a child again, and was very homesick.
He scarcely spoke, answering only in a weak voice
that had scarcely any sound at all. To feel so ill, and
to be so far, so very far away; to think that so many
days, so many weary days, must pass before he could
reach home—would he ever live so long, with his well-
nigh exhausted strength? . . . This notion of terrifying remoteness was a thing which obsessed him
unceasingly; which oppressed him on awakening—
when, after a few hours of appeasement, he came

back once more to the horrible smarting of his
wounds, to the morning fever, and the little wheezing
noise of his punctured chest. And so he had begged
to be put on board, whatever the risk might be.

He was very heavy to carry in his stretcher, and,
without meaning it, they gave him some cruel jars in
getting him on board.

On the transport, which was about to depart, they
put him in one of the little iron beds, aligned in
hospital fashion, and he began again in the opposite
direction his long voyage across the seas. But, this
time, instead of living like a bird in the wind of the
tops, he was in the closeness of below decks, amid the
exhalations of medicines, of wounds, and of illness.

During the first few days the joy of being on his
way home had made him a little brighter. He was
able to raise himself on the bed with the help of
pillows, and now and then he asked for his box. His
sailor's box was the little deal casket, bought at
Paimpol, in which he kept his treasures; in it were
the letters from his Grandmother Yvonne, those from
Yann, and those from Gaud, a copybook, in which he
had transcribed some sailors' songs, and a volume of
Confucius in Chinese, picked up by chance in a pillage,
in which, on the blank side of the leaves, he had
written the simple journal of his campaign.

Nevertheless, his condition did not improve, and
after the first week the doctors began to fear that he
would not pull through.

. . . Near the Equator now, in the excessive heat
of a time of storm. The transport sped on, shaking
the beds, the wounded, and the sick; sped on without
slackening speed, through a sea rough and tormented
as at the change of the monsoons.

Since the departure from Ha-Long more than one

of them had died and had been cast into the deep water on this highway to France; many of the little beds were rid already of their poor contents.

And on this particular day, in the moving hospital, the weather was very bad; it had been necessary, on account of the swell, to close the iron lids of the portholes, and this rendered more horrible the suffocating sickroom.

He was growing worse; the end was near. Lying always on his punctured side he compressed it with both hands, with all the strength that remained to him, in order to immobilize the water, the liquid decomposition in his right lung, and to try to breathe only with the other. But this other, also, had gradually become affected by contact, and the last agony had begun.

All sorts of visions of his homeland haunted his dying brain; in the hot darkness faces loved and faces loathed came and leant over him; he was in a perpetual state of hallucination, in which the scene changed from Brittany to Iceland, from Iceland to Brittany.

In the morning he had asked for the priest, and the priest, who was an old man used to seeing sailors die, had been surprised to find, under this envelope so virile, the purity of a little child.

He craved air and more air; but there was none anywhere; the wind-sails no longer gave any; the sick-berth attendant, who fanned him continuously with a flowered Chinese fan, did no more than waft on him an unwholesome reek, dead air which had been breathed already a hundred times and which the lungs did not want.

Sometimes he was seized with a desperate rage to get out of his bed, where he felt so surely the approach

of death; to seek the pure air outside, to try to win
back life. . . . Oh, the others, who moved about the
shrouds, who lived in the tops! . . . But all the effort
he made to get up ended in nothing more than a feeble
raising of his head and neck—something like those
incomplete movements that one makes in sleep.
Alas! he could not; he fell back into the same hollows
of his disordered bed, held fast there now by death;
and each time, after the fatigue of his effort, he lost
consciousness for a time of everything.

To humour him they opened a porthole at last,
although it was still dangerous, for the sea was not
yet calm enough. It was in the evening, at about
six o'clock. And when the iron shutter was raised
there entered only light, dazzling red light. The
setting sun appeared on the horizon with an extreme
splendour, in a break in the overcast sky; its blinding
light moved about with the rolling of the ship, illu-
mining this hospital in a vacillating way, as if someone were swinging a torch.

A last vision distressed him greatly; his old grandmother, passing along a road, very quickly, with an
expression of heartbreaking anxiety; the rain fell on
her from dark and funereal clouds; she was on her
way to Paimpol, summoned to the office of the naval
authority to be informed that he was dead.

He was struggling now in his death agony. They
sponged from the corners of his mouth the water and
blood which came up from his chest in gushes, during
his contortions of suffering. And the magnificent
sun was shining still; at its setting one might have
thought that a whole world was on fire and that the
clouds were charged with blood; through the open
porthole a broad shaft of red fire entered and fell on
Sylvestre's bed, making a nimbus round him.

. . . And at this same moment this same sun
showed itself in far-off Brittany, where midday was
about to sound. Identically the same sun and at
precisely the same moment of its endless duration;
riding higher in a bluish sky, it illumined with a soft
white light old Grand'mère Yvonne, who was sitting
sewing at her door.

In Iceland, where it was still morning, it appeared
also, at this same moment of death. Paler still, it
might have seemed that it came to show itself there
only by some *tour de force* of obliqueness. It shone
mournfully in a fiord where the *Marie* drifted, and its
sky was this time of that hyperborean purity which
awakens ideas of cooled planets which have no longer
an atmosphere. With its frozen clearness, it accentuated the details of that chaos of stones which is
Iceland: this whole country, seen from the *Marie*,
seemed a patchwork in one same plane standing
somehow upright. Yann, who was there, illumined
rather strangely, he also, was fishing in his usual way,
in the midst of these lunar aspects.

. . . At the moment when this trail of red fire,
which had entered by the ship's porthole, was extinguished, when the equatorial sun disappeared totally
in the golden waters, the eyes of the dying grandson
flickered, turned up towards his forehead as if about
to disappear into his head. And then they lowered
over them the long-lashed eyelids—and Sylvestre
became very calm and beautiful, like a recumbent
marble. . . .

CHAPTER III

. . . I cannot forbear also from telling of the burial of Sylvestre, of which I myself had charge, in the island of Singapore.   We had thrown overboard many others in the China Sea during the first days of the voyage; but as this unwholesome land was quite near us, it was decided to keep him a few hours longer and bury him there.

It was in the morning, very early, on account of the terrible sun.   In the launch on which he was carried ashore his body was covered with the French flag.   The great strange town was still asleep when we drew alongside.   A little wagon, sent by the Consul, was waiting on the quay; we put Sylvestre on it, with the wooden cross which had been made for him on board: the paint on it was still wet, for it had been necessary to make haste, and the white letters of his name ran on the dark background.

We passed through this Babel as the sun was rising.   And it was passing strange to find there, scarcely two paces from the unclean Chinese swarming, the calm of a French church.   Under this high, white nave, where I was alone with my sailors, the *Dies Iræ* sung by a missionary priest resounded like a sweet magical incantation.   Through the open doors we saw things which resembled enchanted gardens, verdure most admirable, palms immense; the wind shook the tall blossoming trees; and there was a rain of petals, carmine red, which fell almost in the church.

Afterwards, we proceeded to the cemetery which was some distance away. Our little escort of sailors was a very modest one; the coffin was covered still with the flag of France. We had to pass through a Chinese quarter, a teeming yellow population; then through unhealthy Indian suburbs, where every type of Asiatic face gazed at us with wondering eyes as we passed.

And then the open country, already burning; shady roads where fluttered admirable butterflies with wings of blue velvet. A great abundance of flowers, of palm-trees; all the splendours of equatorial luxuriance. At last, the cemetery: mandarin tombs, with multi-coloured inscriptions, dragons and monsters; astonishing foliage, strange and unknown plants. The spot where we laid him resembled a corner of an Indian garden.

On his grave we placed the little wooden cross which had been hastily made during the night:

SYLVESTRE MOAN

Aged Nineteen Years

And we left him there, in haste to get away on account of the sun which was gradually climbing, turning round for a last look at him, under his wonderful trees, under his wealth of blossom.

CHAPTER IV

THE transport continued its voyage across the Indian
Ocean. Below, in the floating hospital, there were
still cooped-up miseries. On deck one saw only
carelessness, health, and youth. Around, on the sea,
a veritable festival of pure air and sunshine.

In this fine weather of the trade winds the sailors,
lying in the shade of the sails, amused themselves
with their parrakeets, in teaching them to fly. (In
this Singapore, which they had just left, all kinds of
tame beasts are sold to the passing sailor.)

They had all chosen baby parrakeets, with little
infantine airs on their bird's faces, still without a tail,
but already green, admirably green. Their papas
and their mamas had been green; and they, too,
therefore, quite small as they were, had inherited
unconsciously this same colour; placed on the spotless
deck of the ship, they resembled very fresh leaves
fallen from a tropical tree.

Sometimes they made a little muster of them, and
then they observed one another drolly; they would
turn their necks in every direction, as if to examine
one another under different aspects. They walked
in halting fashion, with comical little flutterings,
suddenly setting off at a great rate, as if hastening
for I know not what fatherland; and there were many
of them that came a cropper.

And the monkeys, too, learnt to do tricks, and that
was another source of amusement. There were some

of these little beasts of whom the owners were very fond, who were embraced with rapture, and who cuddled themselves against the hard chests of their masters with the doting eyes of women, half grotesque, half touching.

On the stroke of three o'clock the quartermasters brought on deck two canvas sacks, sealed with large seals of red wax, and marked with Sylvestre's name; and they proceeded to sell by auction—as the regulations require in the case of the dead—all his clothes, all his worldly possessions. And the sailors, with alacrity, grouped themselves round; on board a hospital ship these sales of kit are common enough, and there is little or no sentiment about them. And, moreover, in this boat Sylvestre was comparatively unknown. His oilskin-slops, his shirts, his blue-striped vests, were handled, turned over, and finally purchased for any sort of price, the buyers amusing themselves in outbidding one another.

Came the turn of the little sacred box, which was valued at fifty sous. The letters and the military medal had been taken out for transmission to the dead man's family; but there remained the copybook of songs, the book of Confucius, and the thread, the buttons, the needles, all the little things placed there by the foresight of his grand'mère Yvonne for mending and sewing.

Afterwards, the quartermasters who exhibited the articles for sale brought out two little Buddhas, picked up in a pagoda and intended for Gaud; they were of so comical a shape that a great laugh went up when they were shown as the last lot. But if these sailor-men laughed, it was not from want of heart, but rather out of mere thoughtlessness.

Finally, the sacks themselves were sold, and the

purchaser at once set to work to erase the name inscribed on them and to substitute his own.

Afterwards the spotless deck was carefully swept in order to remove the dust and odds and ends of thread left from the unpacking.

And the sailors went back gaily to amuse themselves with their parrakeets and monkeys.

CHAPTER V

•   •   •   •   •

ONE day, in the first half of June, as old Yvonne was re-entering her home, her neighbours told her that someone had been inquiring for her on behalf of the superintendent of the Naval Record Office.

It was something concerning her grandson, no doubt; but that did not cause her any uneasiness.   In the families of sailors there is often business to do at the Record Office, and she, who was a sailor's daughter, wife, mother, and grandmother, had known this office for nearly sixty years.

It was probably about her allotment; perhaps there was a little allowance from the *Circe* to be drawn, on presentation of her authority card.   Knowing what is due to a superintendent, she smartened herself up, put on her best dress and a white coif, and set off as the clock was striking two.

Trotting along the cliff paths, with rather quick little steps, she made her way towards Paimpol, a little anxious now, on reflection, because it was two months since she had had a letter.

She passed her old admirer, sitting at his door, much enfeebled by the cold of the past winter:

'Hallo? . . . When you like, you know; you must not hesitate, my dear! . . .' (He had still in mind that wooden robe about which it pleased him to tease her.)

The gay June weather smiled everywhere about

her.   On the stony hills there was still only the low-growing, yellow-flowered furze; but as one descended into the valleys sheltered from the wind of the sea, one found immediately beautiful new verdure, hedges of blossoming thorn, full-growing, sweet-smelling grass.   But she scarcely saw all this, she, so old, on whom the fugitive seasons, short now as days, had so accumulated. . . .

Around crumbling, dark-walled hamlets, there were rose-trees, carnations, gillyflowers, and, even on the high roofs of thatch and moss, a thousand little flowers which attracted the first white butterflies.

This spring was almost loveless in this country of the Icelanders.   The handsome proud-bred girls, whom one saw dreaming at the doors, seemed to be seeing, with their eyes blue and their eyes brown, things a great distance off, far beyond all visible objects.   The young men, to whom their melancholies and their desires went out, were at their fishing in Iceland, on the hyperborean sea. . . .

But it was spring-time, none the less, warm, suave, troubling, with light dronings of flies, perfumes of growing plants.

And all this, which has no heart, continued to smile at this old grandmother who was walking as fast as she could on her way to learn of the death of her last grandson.   She was drawing near to the terrible moment when this thing, which had happened so far away on the China Sea, was going to be announced to her; she was making the sinister journey which Sylvestre, at the moment of dying, had foreseen, and which had wrung from him the last tears of his agony: his kind old grand'mère, summoned to the Record Office at Paimpol to be told that he was dead!   He had seen her very clearly, passing along this road, going very quickly, very straight, in her little brown shawl, with her umbrella and her large coif. And this apparition had made him raise himself, had made him writhe in excruciating anguish, while the enormous red sun of the equator, which was setting magnificently, entered by the porthole of the hospital to watch him die.

Only, in his last vision, he had pictured this tramp of the poor old woman under a rainy sky, whereas, on the contrary, it was in the mocking brightness of a spring day. . . .

As she drew near Paimpol she became more uneasy, and began to walk more quickly even than before.

And now she is in the grey town, in the little granite streets on which the sunlight pours, giving goodday to other old women, her contemporaries, sitting at their windows. Puzzled at seeing her, they said:

'Where is she going like that so quickly, in her Sunday clothes, on a weekday?'

The superintendent of the Record Office was out. A very ugly little being, about fifteen years of age, who was his clerk, was sitting in the office. Being too misshapen to make a fisherman, he had been given some schooling, and now passed his days on this same chair, in false black sleeves, driving his pen.

With an air of importance, when she had told him her name, he got up and took a number of stamped documents out of a pigeon-hole.

There were many of them, many documents. . . . What did that mean? Certificates, papers bearing seals, a sailor's pay-book yellowed by the sea, all these having, as it were, an odour of death. . . .

He spread them out before the poor old woman, who began to tremble and to see dimly. For she

had recognized two of the letters which Gaud had
written to her grandson, and which were there
unopened. . . . And this same thing had happened
twenty years before, when her son Pierre died: his
letters had been returned from China to the office of
the superintendent who had remitted them to her. . .

He read out now, in an important voice: 'Moan,
Jean-Marie Sylvestre, enrolled at Paimpol, folio 213,
registered number 2091, deceased on board the
Bien-Hoa, the 14th. . . .'

'What? What has happened to him, my good
sir?'

'Deceased! . . . He is deceased,' he replied.

No doubt, he was not intentionally cruel, this little
clerk; if he said this thing in this brutal way it was
rather through want of judgment, through the unin-
telligence of an incomplete and stunted being. And,
seeing that she did not understand the fine phrase he
used, he repeated it in Breton:

'Marw éo! . . .'

Marw éo! . . . (He is dead. . . .)

She repeated it after him, with the tremulousness
of old age, like a poor cracked echo giving back an
indifferent phrase.

It was what she had half guessed, but the confirmation only made her tremble; now that it was certain it
scarcely seemed to affect her. In the first place her
faculty of suffering was really a little blunted, by
reason of age, especially since this last winter. She
no longer reacted at once to grief. And, secondly,
something, for the moment, turned topsy-turvy in
her head, and she confused this death with others
that had gone before; she had lost so many, so many
sons! . . . It needed a moment for her to realize
that this was her last, so fondly cherished, he to whom

all her prayers related, in whom were centred all her
life, all her expectation, all her thoughts, all those
poor thoughts already blurred by the sombre approach
of second childhood. . . .

She felt ashamed also to show her despair before
this little gentleman, whom she regarded with a kind
of horror: was that the way in which to announce to
a grandmother the death of her grandson! . . . She
remained standing before his desk, rigid, twisting the
fringe of her brown shawl with her poor old hands,
chapped from washing.

And how far away her home seemed to her! . . .
Just Heaven! What a journey she had to make, and
to make decently, before she could reach the little
thatched shelter where she longed to take refuge—
like a wounded beast which hides itself in its hole
to die. And that was another reason why she
forced herself not to think, not yet to realize, scared
above all by the length of the road that lay before
her.

She was given a money order to enable her to draw,
as next of kin, the thirty francs realized by the sale of
Sylvestre's kit, and also the letters, the certificates,
and the box containing the military medal.

Clumsily she took these things with fingers which
remained open, passing them from one hand to
the other, not seeming to think of putting them in
her pocket.

She passed out of Paimpol like an automaton,
looking at no one, her body bowed a little as if she
were about to fall, a throbbing of blood in her ears,
and hastening, straining, like some poor machine
already worn-out, which one would have driven at
full speed for the last time, heedless whether the
springs would break or not.

At the end of the second mile she was bent nearly double, utterly exhausted; every now and then her sabot struck against a stone which sent a sharp pain through her head. And she pressed on to hide herself in her home, in fear of falling and having to be carried. . . .

CHAPTER VI

'Look at old Yvonne! She's tipsy!' She had fallen and the little urchins of the street were following her. It happened just as she was entering the commune of Ploubazlanec, where there is a number of houses along the road. Nevertheless, she had had strength enough to pick herself up, and, limpingly, with the help of her stick, she was pressing on.

'Look at old Yvonne! She's tipsy!'

And the brazen-faced little people came and peered into her face, laughing. Her coif was all askew.

There were some of these children who were not evil at heart—and when they had seen her close, seen her grimace of senile despair, they turned away saddened and silent, not daring to say another word.

Once in her home, with the door closed, she uttered a cry of despair which almost choked her, and sank down in a corner, her head against the wall. Her coif had fallen over her eyes; she threw it on the ground—her poor white coif of which hitherto she had taken such care. Her Sunday dress, her only presentable one, was all soiled, and a slim wisp of hair, of a yellow white, issued from her headband, completing a picture of tragic poverty. . . .

CHAPTER VII

GAUD, coming to inquire after her, found her so, uncoifed, her arms hanging limp, her head against the wall, with a grimace and a plaintive '*hi, hi, hi!*' as of a small child. She was scarcely able to weep; grand'mères, when they grow too old, have no more tears in their dried-up eyes.

'My grandson is dead!'

And she threw on Gaud's knees the letters, the papers, the medal.

Gaud, glancing hastily at these things, saw that it was true, and knelt down to pray.

They remained there together, almost mute, these two women, as long as the June twilight lasted—and it lasts long in Brittany, and in Iceland it does not end. In the fireplace the cricket, little herald of happiness, made, all heedless, his shrill music. And the yellow light of the evening entered by the skylight, into this cottage of the Moans, all of whom the sea had taken, who were now an extinct family. . . .

At last Gaud said:

'I will come, my dear grand'mère, and live with you; I will bring my bed which they have left me, and I will nurse you and look after you; you shall nôt be all alone. . . .'

She wept for her little friend, Sylvestre, but in her grief she was distracted by the thought of another— of him who had departed for the fishing.

They would have to let Yann know that Sylvestre was dead; in fact, the *Chasers* must soon be leaving.

Would he so much as weep for him? . . . Perhaps he would, for he loved him well. . . . And in the midst of her own tears she thought much of that. Sometimes waxing indignant against his hardness, sometimes softening at her recollection of him, on account of this grief which he was about to suffer too, and which was, as it were, a bond between them—in sum, he filled her heart. . . .

CHAPTER VIII

. . . On a pale evening of August the letter which
announced to Yann the death of his brother arrived
at last on board the *Marie* in the Iceland sea. It
was after a hard day's toil, at a moment of excessive
fatigue, when he was about to go below for supper
and sleep. His eyes heavy with slumber, he read it
below, in the gloomy cabin, by the yellow light of the
little lamp; and, in the first minute, he also remained
insensible, stupefied, like someone who does not
properly understand. Very reserved, out of pride,
in regard to all which concerned his heart, he hid the
letter in his blue jersey, against his chest, as sailors
do, without saying a word.

But he felt he had not the courage to sit down to
supper with the others; and so, disdaining even to
tell them why, he flung himself on his bed, and
immediately went to sleep.

Presently he dreamt of Sylvestre dead, that he was
present at his burial. . . .

As midnight drew near—being then in that state
peculiar to sailors who are conscious of the hour in
their sleep, and feel the approach of the moment when
they will be awakened for their watch—he was still
watching this burial.   And he said to himself:

'I am dreaming; fortunately they are coming to
awaken me, and all this will vanish.'

But when a rude hand was placed on him and a
voice said: 'Gaos! Get up! It's your turn!' he
heard on his chest a light rustle of paper—a sinister

little sound, affirming the reality of the death—
'Ah! yes, the letter! . . . It was true, then!' And
the impression now was more poignant, more cruel,
and, as he sat up quickly in his sudden awakening, he
struck his broad forehead against the beams.

Then he dressed himself, and opened the hatchway
to go and take his post above for the fishing. . . .

•

CHAPTER IX

WHEN Yann came on deck he looked all round him, with eyes newly awakened from sleep, at the great familiar circle of the sea.

And on this particular night what he saw was immensity presented in its most astonishingly simple aspects, neutral in tint, giving an impression only of depth.

This horizon, which marked no precise region of the earth, nor even any particular geological period, must have had this same appearance so many times since the beginning of time, that in looking at it one seemed verily to be seeing nothing—nothing but the eternity of things which *are*, and have no choice but to continue *to be*.

It was not absolutely dark. There was a feeble illumination, a kind of residue of light, which came from nowhere. There was noise, a kind of habitual murmur, an aimless plaint. There was greyness, a hazy kind of greyness, which disappeared as one looked more closely. The sea during its mysterious repose and slumber disguised itself under subtle tints which are without a name.

Above were diffuse clouds. They had assumed shapes of sorts, since things can scarcely be without; in the darkness they were merged one with another so as almost to form merely one immense veil.

But at one point of the sky, very low, near the water, they made a kind of marbling more distinct, although very distant; a loose sort of design, as if traced by a distracted hand; at once fortuitous, not intended to be seen, and fugitive, about to die. And this alone, in all this ensemble, seemed to signify something; one would have said that all the melancholy, unseizable meaning of this nothingness was inscribed there; and the eyes ended by fixing themselves upon it involuntarily.

Yann, as gradually his mobile pupils became accustomed to the darkness outside, looked more and more at this unique marbling in the sky; it had the shape of someone sinking down with outstretched arms. And now that he had once detected this resemblance it seemed to him that it was really a human shade, magnified, made gigantic by force of distance.

And then, in his imagination, where inexpressible dreams and primitive beliefs floated together, this mournful shade, foundered on the edge of this tenebrous sky, mingled little by little with the memory of his dead brother, as if it had been a last manifestation of him.

He was used to these strange associations of images, such as are formed especially at the beginning of life in the heads of children. . . . But words, vague though they be, are yet too precise to express these things; it needs that uncertain language which is spoken sometimes in dreams, and of which on awakening one retains only enigmatical fragments which have no longer any meaning.

As he contemplated this cloud he felt himself seized by a sadness, profound, agonized, full of the unknown and of mystery, which chilled his soul; much better than before, he understood now that his poor little brother would never be seen again, never, never; grief which had been long in penetrating the

robust and hard envelope of his heart entered now
until it overflowed. He saw once more the kindly
face of Sylvestre, his honest boyish eyes; at the
thought of embracing him something like a veil fell
suddenly from beneath his eyelids, in spite of himself
—and for a moment he did not realize what it was,
never having wept since manhood came to him. But
tears began to flow, big, streaming tears, down his
cheeks; and sobs shook his deep chest.

He continued to fish very busily, losing no time
and speaking no word, and the other two who heard
him in the silence feigned not to notice, lest they
might irritate him, knowing how reserved and proud
he was.

. . . To his way of thinking death was the end of
everything. . . .

He was wont, out of respect, to associate himself
with the prayers which are said in the family circle
for those deceased; but he did not believe in the
immortality of the soul.

In the talks these sailors had together this view of
his was the one commonly accepted; the thought was
echoed, in a brief, assured way, as if it were beyond
argument; but this did not prevent them from being
vaguely apprehensive of ghosts, vaguely fearful of
graveyards, completely confident in the efficacy of
the statues and pictures which protected them, and,
above all, innately respectful towards the sanctified
ground which lies around the churches.

And so Yann dreaded for himself a grave in the
wide ocean, as if that represented a more complete
annihilation—and the thought that Sylvestre was
buried yonder, in that distant land on the other side
of the earth, made his grief more hopeless, more
gloomy.

With his disdain of others he wept without any constraint or shame, as if he had been alone.

. . . Outside, the emptiness was slowly whitening, although it was scarcely two o'clock; and as it whitened it seemed to expand, expand, to become more limitless, to hollow itself out in a more dismaying manner.   With this kind of dawn that was breaking, eyes opened wider and the awakened spirit conceived better the immensity of the distances: the limits of visible space receded more and more in an unending perspective.

The light was very pale, but it was growing: it seemed that it came in little spurts, in light pulsings; these eternal things seemed as if they were illumined by transparency, as if white-flamed lamps had been raised one by one behind the shapeless grey clouds— raised discreetly, with mysterious precautions, for fear of disturbing the mournful repose of the sea.

Below the horizon the great white lamp which was the sun was dragging itself feebly along before making above the waters its slow and cold promenade, commenced in the earliest hour of the morning. . . .

On this day there were nowhere the rosy tones of dawn; all remained pale and sad.   And on board the *Marie* was a man who wept, the tall, broad-shouldered Yann. . . .

These tears of his wayward brother, and this more than melancholy of the world without, were the mourning apparel used for the poor little humble hero in these seas of Iceland where he had spent the half of his life. . . .

When broad day came Yann wiped his eyes brusquely with the sleeve of his woollen jersey, and wept no more.   That was over.   He seemed completely absorbed by the labour of the fishing, by the

monotonous succession of things real and present,
as if he had no longer any other thought.

And, as it happened, the lines were very fruitful,
and arms had almost more than they could do.

Around the fishermen, in the immense distances,
the scene had changed. The great unfolding of
infinity, the great spectacle of the morning was over,
and now the distances seemed, on the contrary, to
draw in, to close upon them. How came they to
think but an hour or so ago that the sea was so
limitless? The horizon now was quite near, and it
seemed even that there was a want of space. The
void became filled with tenuous floating veils, some
vaguer than mist, others with contours almost visible
and, as it were, fringed. They fell softly in a great
silence, like white muslins having no weight; but they
descended from all sides at once, imprisonment within
them was completed very quickly, and it produced a
sense of oppression to see the air they breathed
thus encumbered.

It was the beginning of the first fog of August.
In a few minutes the shroud was uniformly dense,
impenetrable; about the *Marie* one could now distinguish nothing but a damp paleness diffused with
light, in which even the masting of the ship seemed
to lose itself.

'This is it, right enough; the vile fog!' said the men.

They had known for long this inevitable companion
of the second period of the fishing; but it was also
the beginning of the end of the Iceland season, the
time when one turned homewards to Brittany.

It was deposited in fine glistening drops in their
beards; it made their browned skin shine with moisture. Those who looked at one another from end to
end of the boat saw one another dimly, like phantoms;

by way of contrast, objects very near showed up more crudely under this pale, whitish light. One took care not to breathe with the mouth open; a sensation of cold and damp penetrated the lungs.

At the same time the fishing proceeded with ever-increasing rapidity, and they no longer spoke, so busy were they with the lines; at every moment came the sound of heavy fish falling on the ship, striking the planks with the noise of a whip; they writhed furiously, beating their tails against the wood of the deck; everything was bespattered with sea-water, and the fine silvery scales which they scattered in their struggles. The sailor who was gutting them with his huge knife, in his precipitation, cut his fingers, and his red blood mingled with the brine.

CHAPTER X

THEY remained, this time, ten days on end, caught in the thick fog, without seeing anything. The fishing continued to be good and, with so much activity, they were not bored. From time to time, at regular intervals, one of them blew a horn which gave out a sound like the bellowing of a wild beast.

Sometimes, from without, from the depth of the white fog, another bellowing replied from a distance to their call. Then the look-out became sharper. If the cry came nearer, every ear on board was strained in the direction of this unknown neighbour, whom, no doubt, they would never see, and whose presence there was nevertheless a danger. They questioned who it might be; it became an occupation, an association and, in their curiosity, eyes strove to pierce the impalpable white muslins which remained stretched everywhere in the air.

Then it would sheer off, the bellowings of the horn would die away in the dull distance; and they would be alone once more in the silence, in the midst of this infinity of immobile vapours.

Everything was impregnated with water; everything streamed with salt and brine. The cold became more penetrating; the sun loitered in its slow crawl below the horizon; there were now real nights of one or two hours, the grey fall of which was sinister and glacial.

Every morning they took soundings to ascertain the depth of the water, in fear lest the *Marie* should have drifted too close to the island of Iceland. But all the lines of the ship, threaded end to end, did not reach to the bottom of the sea; they were, therefore, still in the open sea and in good deep waters.

The life was rude and healthy; this keener cold augmented the comfort of the evening, the impression of snug shelter which they experienced in the cabin of massive oak when they descended to sup or sleep.

During the day these men, who were more cloistered than monks, spoke little among themselves. Each, holding his line, would remain for hours and hours at his same invariable post, the arms alone occupied in the incessant labour of the fishing. They were separated from one another by only three or four yards, and they ended by no longer seeing one another.

This colour of the fog, this white obscurity, threw a spell over the spirit. As they fished they sang to themselves some native air, but very softly for fear of scaring the fish. Thoughts took shape more slowly and less often; they seemed to be distended, to be prolonged in duration in order to fill the time without leaving voids, without leaving intervals of non-being. There was no longer any idea of women, because it was already cold; but they dreamed of incoherent or marvellous things, as in sleep, and the weft of these dreams was as little solid as a mist.

This foggy month of August usually closed thus each year, in a sad and tranquil manner, the Iceland season. Otherwise there was always the same plenitude of physical life, swelling the lungs and hardening the muscles of the sailors.

Yann had quickly recovered his habitual demeanour, as if his great grief had not persisted: vigilant and alert, prompt in seamanship and in the fishing, easy in movement as one who has no care; for the rest,

communicative in his hours only—which were rare—
and carrying his head as high as ever with his air at
once indifferent and dominating.

In the evening at supper, in the defaced room protected by the faïence Virgin, when they were sitting
round the table, their large knives in their hands,
before a plateful of good, hot food, it would happen
that he would laugh, as formerly, at the droll things
which the others said.

In himself, perhaps, he thought a little of this
Gaud, whom Sylvestre, no doubt, had given him for
wife in the last poor thoughts of his agony—and who
now was become a penniless girl, without a friend in
the world. . . .

And perhaps, also, nay, almost surely, his grief for
this brother remained still in the depth of his heart. . . .

But this heart of Yann was an untrodden region,
difficult to govern, little known, where things happened which did not show themselves on the outside.

CHAPTER XI

ONE morning, at about three o'clock, while they were dreaming peacefully beneath their shroud of fog, they heard what seemed the sound of voices the tone of which struck them as strange and unfamiliar. They looked at one another, those who were on deck, with an interrogating glance:

'Who was that who spoke?'

Nobody; nobody had said a word.

And, as a matter of fact, the sounds had seemed to come from the exterior void.

Thereupon, he who had charge of the horn and had neglected to use it since the evening before hurriedly seized it, and blew with all his might, sending out the long bellow of alarm.

That alone was enough to cause a thrill of fear in this silence. And then, as if out of contrariness an apparition had been evoked by this vibrant bagpipe sound, a huge unexpected thing outlined itself in grey, loomed up menacing, very tall and very close to them: masts and yards and cordage, the outline of a ship which had taken shape in the air, everywhere at once and altogether like those fearsome phantasmagorias which, by a single shaft of light, are created on an outspread sheet. And other men appeared on it, almost touching them, leaning over the rail, looking at them, with straining eyes, in an awakening of surprise and horror. . . .

They threw themselves on to oars, on to reserve masts, on to gaff-hooks—on to anything they could find in the booms which was long and solid—and thrust them out in order to keep at a distance this thing and these visitors that were approaching them. And the others, too, scared in turn, pushed out towards them enormous poles to keep them off.

But there was only a very light creaking in the yards above their heads, and the rigging, for a moment caught, disengaged itself at once without any damage; the shock, very slight in this calm, was scarcely noticeable; it had been so feeble even that really it seemed that this other ship had no solidity, that it was a thing soft, almost without weight.

And then the tension relaxed; the men began to laugh; there was mutual recognition.

'Ho, there!   The *Marie*!'

'Hi!   Gaos, Laumec, Guermeur!'

The apparition was the *Reine-Berthe*, Captain Larvoër, also of Paimpol; these sailors were from villages in the neighbourhood; that tall fellow there, with the black beard, showing his teeth as he laughed, was Kerjegou, a native of Ploudaniel; and the others came from Plounès or Plounérin.

'Say, there, why didn't you sound your horn, you band of savages?' asked Larvoër of the *Reine-Berthe*.

'What's that?   And why didn't you, band of pirates and sea-scum, poisonous fish of the sea? . . .'

'Oh! us. . . . That's different; *we are forbidden to make a noise.*' (He made this answer with an air of suggesting some dark mystery; with a droll smile, which, later on, often recurred to the minds of those on the *Marie*, and gave them seriously to think.)

And then, as if he had said too much, he finished by this pleasantry:

'This fellow here has broken our horn by blowing it so hard.'

And he pointed to a sailor with a Triton-like face,

who was all neck and chest, over-broad, short in the legs, with I know not what of grotesque and disquieting in his misshapen strength.

And while they were looking at one another, waiting until some breeze or some current in the water beneath should choose to move one of them more quickly than the other, to separate the boats, they engaged in conversation. All leaning to port, keeping one another at a respectful distance with their long wooden poles, as besieged men might with their pikes, they spoke of the affairs of their homeland, of the last letters received by the *Chasers*, of their old parents, and of their wives. ·

'Mine,' said Kerjégou, 'mine tells me she has just had the little one we were expecting; that means that we have a dozen now.'

Another had had twins; and a third announced the marriage of the fair Jeannie Caroff—a girl well known to the Icelanders—with a certain rich old invalid of the commune of Plourivo.

They saw one another as through white gauze, and it seemed also that their voices were changed; they sounded somehow smothered and distant.

But Yann was not able to remove his eyes from one of these fishermen, a little man already old whom he was sure he had never seen anywhere before, and who, nevertheless, had greeted him at once with: 'Hallo! Yann, my fine fellow!' as if he had known him intimately: he had the irritating ugliness of a monkey, with a monkey's malicious blinking of his piercing eyes.

'They tell me also,' said again Larvoër of the *Reine-Berthe*, 'they tell me also that the grandson of old Yvonne Moan, of Ploubazlanec, is dead; he was serving his term in the Navy, as you know, in the China squadron; a very great pity!'

Hearing this the others of the *Marie* turned towards Yann to see if he already knew of this misfortune.

'Yes,' he said, in a low voice, his air indifferent and aloof, 'it was in the last letter I had from my father.'

They all looked at him, in the curiosity they had of his grief, and this irritated him.

The conversation passed hastily, through the pale mist, while the minutes of their strange interview sped quickly by.

'My wife tells me at the same time,' continued Larvoër, 'that the daughter of M. Mével has left the town to live at Ploubazlanec, and look after old Grand'mère Moan, her great aunt; she has started to work now, for people by the day, in order to make a living. For that matter, I have always thought she was a brave and high-hearted girl, in spite of her lady-like airs and her finery.'

Then, once more, they looked at Yann, thus completing his displeasure, and a red flush mounted to his cheeks beneath the golden tan.

With this appreciation of Gaud came to an end the interview with these men of the *Reine-Berthe*, whom no living soul was ever to see again. For the last minute or so their faces had seemed already to be more shadowy, for the ships were drifting apart, and, all at once, those of the *Marie* found that there was no longer anything to push, no longer anything at the end of their long wooden poles; all their spars, oars, or masts, or yard-arms, moved gropingly about the void, and then fell heavily, one after another, into the sea like long dead arms. They hauled in, therefore, these useless defences; the *Reine-Berthe*, plunged again in the deep fog, had disappeared suddenly all at once, as disappears the picture on a transparent film behind which the lamp has been blown out. They tried to hail her, but no answer came to their calls—only a kind of mocking clamour from many voices, ending in a groan which made them look at one another with surprise. . . .

This *Reine-Berthe* did not return with the other Icelanders and, as those on the *Samuel-Azénide* had encountered in a fiord what was indubitably wreckage (her stern crowning and a portion of her keel), she was given up as lost; in October the names of all her crew were inscribed in the church on dark slabs.

Moreover, from the time of this last apparition, the date of which had been noted by the crew of the *Marie*, until the period of the return, there had been no dangerously bad weather on the Iceland sea, while, on the contrary, three weeks before, a westerly gale had carried away many sailors, and two ships. They remembered then the smile of Larvoër, and, in putting all these things together, they made many conjectures. Yann, more than once, at night, saw again the sailor with the monkey-like blink, and some of the crew of the *Marie* asked themselves fearfully whether, on that morning, they had not spoken with ghosts.

CHAPTER XII

THE summer advanced and, at the end of August, at the same time as the first morning mists, the Icelanders returned.

For three months now the two abandoned ones had lived together at Ploubazlanec, in the cottage of the Moans; Gaud had taken the place of a daughter in this poor nest of dead sailors. She had brought thither all that had been left to her after the sale of her father's house; her pretty modern bed, her pretty frocks of divers colours. She had made for herself a new black dress of a more simple fashion, and wore, like old Yvonne, a mourning coif of thick muslin ornamented only with tucks. Every day she did needlework in the homes of the rich people of the town, and returned at night, not concerning herself on the road with any lover, remaining still a little proud, and still surrounded with the respect due to a little lady: as they wished her good evening, the lads, as formerly, raised their hand to their caps.

In the long twilight of the summer evenings she used to return from Paimpol, following the long cliff road, breathing the fresh sea air which brings repose. Her work with the needle had not had time to deform her—as others who live for ever bent to one side over their work—and, as she looked at the sea, she straightened the slim supple figure that was hers by right of race; as she looked at the sea, as she looked at the wide ocean, in the far background of which was Yann. . . .

This same road led to his home. . . . Continuing
it a little, towards a certain region more stony and
more swept by the wind, one would reach the hamlet
of Pors-Even, where the trees, covered with grey
moss, grow quite small among the rocks and bend
down in the direction of the west wind. She would
never go there again, no doubt, to this Pors-Even,
although it was less than a league away; but once in
her life she had been there, and that had sufficed to
leave a charm on all the road; Yann, too, must often
pass along it, and, from her door, she would be able
to follow him going and coming over the bare plain,
through the short furze. And so she loved all this
region of Ploubazlanec; she was almost happy that
fate had stranded her there; in any other part of the
country she would not have been able to continue
to live.

In this season of late August there comes a kind of
listlessness as of a warmer clime which spreads north-
wards from the south; the evenings are luminous,
there are reflections of the potent sun of other parts
which succeed in penetrating as far as the Breton Sea.
Very often the air is clear and calm, without sign of
a cloud.

In the hours when Gaud was used to make her way
home things were already beginning to become confused in the gathering dusk, to merge and form silhouettes. Here and there a cluster of furze, standing
on a hill between two rocks, would show like a
ruffled plume; a group of twisted trees would form a
dark mass in a valley, or may be, elsewhere, some
straw-thatched hamlet would upraise above the plain
a little hunchbacked outline. At the crossways the
old Christs, which kept guard over the countryside,
spread out their dark arms on the calvaries, like real

men crucified, and in the distance the Channel stood
out clearly as a great yellow mirror under a sky
which was already obscured in its lower part, already
tenebrous towards the horizon.   And in this country
even this calm, even this fine weather was melancholy;
there remained, in spite of all, a sense of disquiet
brooding over things; an anxiety borne in from the
sea, to which so many existences had been entrusted,
and of which the eternal menace was only slumbering.

To Gaud, dreaming on her way, the long homeward
walk in the wide, free air never seemed long enough.
She loved the salty savour of the sandy shore, the
sweet perfume of certain flowers which grew on the
cliffs among the meagre thorn.   Had it not been for
the old Yvonne who was awaiting her at home, she
would willingly have loitered in these furze-bordered
paths, in the manner of those fair damsels who like
to dream, on summer evenings, in the parks.

As she traversed this country there came to her
also recollections of her early childhood; but how
effaced they were now, how remote, how diminished
by her love!   In spite of all it still pleased her to
consider this Yann as a sort of fiancé—an elusive,
disdainful, unmannerly fiancé, who would never
really be hers; but one to whom she persisted in
remaining faithful in spirit, without confiding her
secret to any one.   For the moment she was glad to
know that he was in Iceland; there, at least, the sea
held him in its deep cloisters, and he could not give
himself to another. . . .

It is true that one of these days he would return;
but this return also she envisaged now with more
calm than formerly.   Instinctively she knew that her
poverty would not serve as cause to increase his
disdain—for he was not as other men.   And, more-

over, the death of little Sylvestre was a thing that must clearly bring them together. On his arrival he could not fail to come to see the grandmother of his friend; and she had decided that she would be present at this visit, for it seemed to her that this would show no want of dignity; without appearing to remember anything, she would talk to him as to someone whom she had known for a long time; she would speak to him affectionately, even as to a brother of Sylvestre, striving always to preserve a natural air. And who knows? It was, perhaps, not impossible that he should come to regard her as a sister, now that she was going to be so lonely in the world; that she should be able to count on his friendship; nay, even she might ask that much of him, if she did it in such a way that he would not think there was any suggestion of marriage. She judged him unmannerly only, obstinate in his ideas of independence, but kind, frank, and capable of understanding well the good things which come straight from the heart.

How would he feel when he found her there, poor, in this cottage almost in ruin? . . . Poor, indeed! For old Grand'mère Moan, not being strong enough now to go out to her daily washing, had nothing more than her widow's pension; it is true she ate very little now, and that both were able to manage to live without asking help from any one. . . .

Darkness had always fallen by the time she got home; before entering, it was necessary to descend a little, on worn rocks, the cottage being situated below the Ploubazlanec road, in the portion of the ground which slopes downward to the shore. It was almost hidden under its thick, warped roof of brown straw, which resembled the back of some enormous dead beast weighed down by its heavy coat. Its walls had the dull colour and the ruggedness of rocks, with mosses and scurvy-grass forming little green tufts. One ascended the three warped steps of the threshold, and opened the interior latch of the door by means of a piece of thick cord which issued from a hole.   Facing you, as you entered, was the little window, pierced as if in the thickness of a rampart and opening on the sea from which came a last pale yellow light.   In the wide fireplace burnt some odorous twigs of pine and beech which old Yvonne had gathered in her walks along the roads.   She herself was sitting there, super-intending their little supper; in the cottage she wore a headband only, in order to save her coifs; her profile, pretty still, was outlined against the red light of the fire.   She raised towards Gaud eyes which had once been brown, but now had taken on a faded colour, turning to blue, and which were troubled, wavering, bewildered from old age.   Every time she said the self-same thing:

'Goodness me, my girl, how late you are to-night.'

'But no, grand'mère,' Gaud, who was used to her, would reply gently.   'It is the same time as usual.'

'Ah! . . . It seems to me, my girl, it seems to me that it is later than usual.'

They supped on a table which had become almost shapeless from long use, but was still as thick as the trunk of an oak.   And the cricket never failed to recommence for them his little silvery-noted song.

One side of the cottage was occupied by roughly carved woodwork, which now was all worm-eaten; opened, it gave access to sets of shelves on which many generations of fishermen had been conceived, had slept, and on which the aged mothers of them all had died.

From the blackened beams of the roof hung very

old household utensils, bunches of herbs, wooden spoons, smoked bacon; also old nets which had slept there since the shipwreck of the last of the Moan sons, and the meshes of which the rats used to gnaw in the night.

Gaud's bed, installed in a corner with its white muslin curtains, seemed a thing elegant and new, garnishing a Celtic hut.

There was a photograph of Sylvestre in sailor's clothes, in a frame, hung on the granite of the wall. His grandmother had attached to it his military medal, with one of those pairs of anchors in red cloth which sailors wear on the right sleeve, and which had been his; Gaud had bought also at Paimpol one of those memorial crowns, in black and white beads, with which in Brittany people encircle the portraits of the dead. It was his little mausoleum, all that he had to consecrate his memory, in his native Breton land. . . .

On these summer evenings they used not to stay up late, in order to economize light; but when the weather was fine they would sit for a while on a stone bench in front of the house, and watch the people who passed along the road a little above their heads.

Afterwards old Yvonne would retire to her little press-bed, and Gaud to her pretty modern one; there, she would soon fall asleep, tired by her hard work and her long walk, and dreaming of the return of the Icelanders as a sensible girl might, resolute, without worrying overmuch. . . .

CHAPTER XIII

BUT one day, at Paimpol, hearing it said that the
Marie had just arrived, she felt herself seized with a
kind of fever. All her calm of waiting had deserted
her; hurriedly finishing her work, without knowing
why, she started for home earlier than usual—and,
on the road, as she was hastening, she saw him in the
distance coming towards her.

Her legs trembled so that she feared they might
give way under her. He was already quite near,
outlined scarcely twenty paces from her, with his
superb figure, his hair curling under his fisherman's
bonnet. She was taken so unawares by this meeting
that really she was afraid of faltering and afraid that
he might see it; she would have died of shame now
if that should happen. . . . And then she imagined
that her coif was untidy, that she looked tired from
having completed her work too quickly; she would
have given she knew not what to be hidden in the
clumps of furze, to disappear into some weasel's
burrow. For that matter, he too had made a movement of recoil, as if in the idea of changing his route.
But it was too late; they met in the narrow lane.

He, so as not to touch her, stood back against
the bank, stepping aside, like a skittish horse which
swerves, and looking at her in a shy and furtive
manner.

She also, for half a second, had raised her eyes,
throwing out to him in spite of herself a prayer and a
yearning. And in this moment when their gaze

met, more rapidly than a rifle shot, her gridelin pupils
had seemed to grow larger, to become bright with some
great flame of thought, to launch a real bluish light,
while her face had grown red to her temples, to the
roots of her fair hair.

He had said as he touched his bonnet:

'How do you do, Mademoiselle Gaud!'

'How do you do, Monsieur Yann,' she replied.

And that was all; he had passed.

She continued on her way, trembling still, but
feeling, little by little, as the distance between them
increased, her blood resuming its normal course and
her strength returning. . . .

In the cottage she found old Yvonne sitting in a
corner, her head between her hands, weeping, and
uttering her little infantine '*Hi, hi, hi!*', all dishevelled, a tail of hair falling from her headband like
a thin skein of grey hemp.

'Ah, my dear Gaud! I met the boy Gaos on the
road to Plouherzel, as I was returning from gathering
wood—and we talked of my poor little one, as you
may guess. They arrived this morning from Iceland,
and in the afternoon, while I was out, he had been to
visit me. Poor lad, there were tears in his eyes, too.
. . . He insisted on returning with me to my door,
to carry my little faggot. . . .'

She heard this, standing, and her heart gradually
contracted: so, then, this visit of Yann, on which
she had counted so much in order to say to him so
many things, had taken place already, and no doubt
would not again be repeated: it was over. . . .

Then the cottage seemed to her more desolate, her
poverty harder, the world more empty—and she
bowed her head with a desire for death.

CHAPTER XIV

WINTER gradually came, extending like a winding sheet which one should let fall very gently. Grey days followed grey days, but Yann did not appear again—and the two women lived on very lonely.

With the cold weather their existence became more expensive and more arduous.

And old Yvonne, too, was becoming difficult to look after. Her poor mind wandered; she was querulous now, and said unkind things and mocking things; once or twice a week the fit took her, as with children, without apparent cause.

Poor old woman! . . . She was still so kindly on her lucid days, that Gaud did not cease to respect her, and to cherish her. To have always been good, and to end by being evil; to disclose, as the end was drawing near, a whole depth of malice, which had lain dormant during life, a whole lore of coarse words which had been concealed, what a mockery of the soul, what a mysterious irony!

She began to sing also, and that was even worse to bear than her choler; whatever came into her head she would sing, the *oremus* of the mass, and even the vile couplets she had heard formerly in the harbour, repeated by the sailors. Sometimes she would intone the *Fillettes de Paimpol*; at other times, nodding her old head and beating time with her foot, she would begin:

My husband has departed,
To Iceland he has gone,
My husband has departed,
And left me ne'er a sou.
But . . . trala, trala la lou . . .
    I 'll make some!
    I 'll make some! . . .

And every time she would stop abruptly, opening
her eyes wide, in a blank, lifeless stare—like a flame
on the point of extinction which flares up suddenly
before it goes out. And, afterwards, she would bow
her head, remain for long inert, her lower jaw dropped
in the manner of those dead.

She was no longer very clean, either, and that was
another kind of trial on which Gaud had not counted.

One day it came about that she no longer remembered her grandson.

'Sylvestre? Sylvestre?' she said to Gaud, with
an air of trying to think who he might be; 'Ah!
goodness, girl, you understand I had so many when
I was young, so many sons, so many daughters, so
many daughters, so many sons, that now, bless
me . . .'

And as she said this she threw her poor wrinkled
hands in the air, with a reckless gesture that was
almost wanton. . . .

And then, the next day, she would remember him
very well; and, citing the hundred and one little
things which he had done or which he had said, she
wept the livelong day.

Oh, these winter evenings, when there were no
faggots to make a fire! To work shivering, to work
for her poor livelihood, to stitch and stitch, with neat,
small stitches, in order to finish, before going to bed,

the work which she brought each evening from Paimpol.

Old Yvonne, sitting by the fire, remained tranquil, her feet close to the dying embers, her hands tucked under her apron. But in the early part of the evening it was always necessary to maintain a conversation with her.

'You are not saying anything to me, my good girl; why is that? In my time I have known girls of your age who knew how to talk. It seems to me we should not be so dull every evening if you only had something to say.'

Then Gaud would recount the odds and ends of news which she had heard in the town, or tell her the names of the people whom she had met on the way, talking of things which to her were quite indifferent, as, for that matter, everything in the world was now; and then would stop in the middle of her tale when she saw the poor old woman was asleep.

Nothing living, nothing young near her, whose fresh youth called for youth. Her beauty bloomed unknown, solitary, and sterile. . . .

The wind of the sea, coming from all sides, made the lamp flicker and the sound of the waves came to her as in a ship; listening to it, she mingled with it the sad and always pleasant remembrance of Yann, of whom these things were the domain; during the wild nights of terror, when everything was let loose, and the darkness outside was filled with a great hurly-burly, she thought of him with an increased anxiety.

And then, alone as she was, always alone with this grand'mère dying in her chair, she was afraid sometimes, and looked apprehensively into the dark corners, thinking of the mariners, her ancestors, who had lived in these shelved cupboards, who had perished

at sea on just such nights as these, and whose souls
might yet return; and she did not feel protected
against the visit of these dead by the presence of this
old, old woman who was already almost one of
them. . . .

Suddenly she would tremble from head to foot, as
she heard, proceeding from the corner by the fire a
thin broken voice, sounding smothered, as if it came
from underground.   In a chirping tone which made
the blood run cold, the voice sang:

> My husband has departed,
> To Iceland he has gone;
> My husband has departed,
> And left me ne'er a sou;
> But . . . trala, trala la lou . . .

And, moreover, she suffered that particular kind of
fear which comes from the company of imbeciles.

The rain fell, fell, with the little incessant noise of
a fountain; one heard it almost without respite
streaming down the walls.   In the old roof of moss
there were leakages which, always in the same
places, indefatigable, monotonous, always made the
same mournful dripping noise; they soaked here and
there the floor of the dwelling which was of rock and
beaten earth mixed with gravel and shells.

One felt that there was water everywhere around;
it enveloped you with its cold, infinite mass; a tormented water, whipping, powdering in the air,
thickening the obscurity, and isolating still more one
from another the lonely cottages scattered over this
district of Ploubazlanec.

Sunday evenings were for Gaud the most sinister,
on account of the gaiety they brought elsewhere:
there were merry evenings of sorts, even in these
forlorn little hamlets of the coast; there was always,

here or there, some close-shut cottage, beaten by the
dark rain, from which came sounds of uncouth song.
Inside, tables aligned for the drinkers; sailors drying
themselves at smoking fires; old men contented over
their glass of brandy; young men courting girls; all
on the road to intoxication and singing to forget their
cares. And, near them, the sea, their tomb of
to-morrow, was singing also, filling the night with
its immense voice. . . .

On some Sundays, groups of young men, who came
out of these taverns or were returning from Paimpol,
passed along the road, close to the door of the Moans;
they were those who lived at the extremity of this
Breton land, in the direction of Pors-Even. They
passed very late, escaping from the arms of the girls,
heedless of the rain, used to squalls and downpours.
Gaud would strain her ears at sound of their songs
and their shouting—very quickly drowned in the noise
of the storm and the breakers—striving to distinguish
the voice of Yann, and trembling then when she
thought she recognized it.

It was not kind on Yann's part not to have come to
see them again: and to lead a merry life, so soon after
Sylvestre's death—all this was not like him!   Clearly
she no longer understood him—and in spite of all she
could not give him up, or believe that he was heartless.

The fact is that, since his return, his life had been
very dissipated.

First of all there had been the usual October journey
to the Bay of Gascony—and for these Icelanders that
is always a period of pleasure, a time when they carry
in their purses a little money to spend without a care
(the small advances for amusement which the captains
give on the share of the proceeds of the fishing, which
is payable only in winter).

They had gone, as every year, to get salt in the islands, and he had fallen in love at Saint Martin-de-Ré with a certain dark-eyed girl, who had been his mistress in the preceding autumn. Together they had wandered in the last light of the warm sun, among the reddening vineyards all filled with the song of larks, all perfumed by the ripe grapes, the marigolds of the sands, and the salty savour of the shore; together they had sung and danced during these evenings of the vintage season, when all the world gets intoxicated, with a lightsome amorous intoxication, from drinking good wine.

Afterwards the *Marie* had pushed on to Bordeaux, and he had found again, in a large café, very much begilt, the fair songstress of the watch, and had good-humouredly allowed himself to be adored for another week.

Returned to Brittany in November he had assisted, as best man, at several marriages of his friends, always in his best holiday clothes, and often drunk after midnight, when the dancing ended. Every week he was mixed up in some new adventure, which the girls eagerly reported to Gaud, not without exaggeration.

Three or four times she had seen him in the distance coming towards her along the Ploubazlanec road, but always in time to avoid him; he, too, for that matter, on these occasions, made off across the barren plain. As by a tacit understanding, they shunned each other now.

CHAPTER XV

At Paimpol there is a large fat woman called Madame Tressoleur. In one of the streets leading to the harbour she keeps a tavern well known among the Icelanders, where captains and shipowners come to engage their crews, to make their choice from among the strongest, as they ply them with liquor.

Good-looking once upon a time, and still on very good terms with the fishermen, she had a moustache now, the shoulders of a man, and an impudent tongue; the air of a camp-follower, under the large white coif of a nun; in her an indefinable something that was religious persisted in spite of all, because she was a Breton. In her head she kept the names of all the sailors of the district as in a register; she knew the good and the bad, knew just what they made, and what they were worth.

One day in January Gaud, having received an order to make her a dress, came to work there, in a room behind the bar.

The entrance to this tavern of Madame Tressoleur is through a door with massive granite pillars, which is set back under the upper storey of the house in the ancient manner; when the door is opened there is nearly always a gust of wind eddying in the street which forces its way in, and customers are wont to make a sudden entry, as if thrown in by an ocean wave. The room is low and long, covered with lime-wash, and ornamented with gilt frames containing pictures of ships, collisions, shipwrecks. In a corner a faïence Virgin stands on a bracket, between bouquets of artificial flowers.

The old walls have heard many a ringing song of sailors, have seen much expansive merriment, uncouth and primitive enough—since the remote days of Paimpol, from the stormy times of the Corsairs, until these present days of the Icelanders, very little different, really, from their ancestors. And many men's lives have been staked and given in pledge there, with both parties drunk, on these oaken tables.

Gaud, as she sewed the dress, overheard a conversation about Iceland matters, which was being carried on behind the partition between Madame Tressoleur and two pensioners who were sitting drinking.

They were discussing, the old men, a certain fine new boat which was in course of being rigged in the harbour: it would never be ready, this *Léopoldine*, to make the next voyage.

'But yes, it will,' replied the hostess, 'you may bet it will be ready! For I can tell you that the crew was engaged yesterday: all those of the old *Marie*, Guermeur's boat, which is going to be sold and broken up; five young fellows came and signed on here, in my presence—at this table.with my pen—so!—and proper men, I can tell you: Laumec, Tugdual Caroff, Yvon Duff, the younger Karaez, of Tréguier—and the big Yann Gaos, of Pors-Even, who is worth any three!'

The *Léopoldine!* . . . the name, barely heard, of this boat which was going to bear Yann away, fixed itself in a moment in Gaud's memory, as if someone had chiselled it there in order to make it more ineffaceable.

In the evening home at Ploubazlanec again, sitting working in the light of her little lamp, this name, the

mere sound of which had for her a mournful ring, still
haunted her mind.   The names of persons, the names
of ships, have a physiognomy of their own, almost a
meaning.   And this *Léopoldine*, a new and unusual
name, pursued her with a persistence that was not
natural, became a kind of sinister oppression.   No,
she had expected to see Yann sail once more on the
Marie, which formerly she had visited, which she
knew, and which the Virgin had protected in its
dangerous vouages for many a long year, and now this
change, this *Léopoldine*, augmented her anxiety.

But presently she began to tell herself that after all
this no longer concerned her; that nothing of what
affected him could any longer touch her.   And, in
point of fact, what did it matter to her whether he
was here or elsewhere, on one ship or on another, at
sea or at home? . . . Would she be more unhappy,
or less, when he was once more in Iceland?   When
the summer was come, bringing warmth to the
deserted villages, to lonely and anxious wives—or
when a new autumn should begin again, bringing
back the fishermen once more? . . . All that to her
was indifferent, alike, equally without joy and
without hope.   There was no longer any link between
the two of them, nothing to bring them together,
since he had even forgotten his poor little friend,
Sylvestre—it was necessary, therefore, to realize
once and for all that this dream was over; that this
sole desire of her life must be put aside; she ought to
give up Yann, to forget him, forget everything that
was connected with his existence, even this name of
Iceland which rang still with so sad a charm on his
account; to drive these thoughts out of her mind, to
sweep them all away; to tell herself that it was ended,
ended for ever. . . .

She looked with tenderness at the poor old woman sleeping there, who still had need of her, but who could have but little longer to live. And then, afterwards, what was the good of living, what was the good of working, and what was there to do? . . .

The west wind had risen outside, and with its distant groaning the leakages of the roof had recommenced their light tranquil noise, as of a child's rattle. And her tears also began to flow, tears of one orphaned and abandoned, passing over her lips with a slight, salt taste, descending silently on her work, like that summer rain which is not brought by the wind, but falls suddenly, thick and fast, from overcharged clouds; then no longer seeing, feeling broken, seized with a kind of vertigo before the emptiness of her life, she folded the ample bodice of this Madame Tressoleur, and prepared to go to bed.

And as she lay down she shivered; every day it became damper and colder—and so, too, did everything in this cottage. Nevertheless, since she was young, even while she went on weeping, she ended by getting warm and going to sleep.

CHAPTER XVI

SEVERAL more gloomy weeks had passed, and they were now in the first days of February. The weather was mild and fairly fine.

Yann had come out of the shipowner's house, where he had been to receive his share of last summer's fishing, some fifteen hundred francs, which he was taking home to his mother, in accordance with the family custom. The year had been a good one, and he was returning well satisfied with himself.

Near Ploubazlanec he saw a crowd at the end of the road: an old woman gesticulating with her stick, and around her a number of excited urchins who were laughing. . . . Old Grand'mère Moan! The kind old grandmother whom Sylvestre adored, all tattered and bedraggled, become now one of those poor old imbeciles who attract a crowd in the street! . . . The sight caused him a horrible pain.

These little rogues of Ploubazlanec had killed her cat, and she was threatening them with her stick, in great anger and distress.

'Oh, if he had been here, if my poor boy had been here, you wouldn't have dared! I know you wouldn't, you wicked boys! . . .'

She had fallen, it appeared, in running after them to beat them; her coif was askew, her dress smothered in mud, and they were saying again that she was drunk (as often happens in Brittany to those old women who have greatly suffered).

Yann knew this was not true, and that she was an

entirely respectable old woman who drank nothing
but water.

'Aren't you ashamed?' he said to the urchins, very
angry himself also, and speaking in a voice and tone
which commanded respect.

And in a twinkling of an eye all the little people slunk
away, shamefaced and confused, before the big Gaos.

Gaud, who at this moment was returning from
Paimpol, bringing home some work for the evening,
had seen this from a distance, had recognized her
grand'mère in the group. Alarmed, she came running up to find out what the matter was, what had
happened, what they had done to her—and seeing
their cat, which they had killed, she understood.

She raised her frank eyes to Yann's, and he did not
turn his away; they had no thought of avoiding each
other this time; they merely became very red both
of them, he as quickly as she, and looked at each other,
a little as if they were startled to find themselves so
near; but without enmity, almost with kindness,
united as they were in a common thought of pity
and protection.

The school children had for long looked with dis-
favour on the poor defunct cat, because it had a black
face and an air of the evil one; but it was a very good
cat and, when you looked at it close, you found, on
the contrary, that it had a peaceful and caressing
mien. They had killed it with stones, and one of its
eyes was hanging out. The poor old woman, still
muttering threats, moved away, tottering in her
distress, and carrying the dead cat, like a rabbit,
by the tail.

'Oh, my poor boy, my poor boy . . . if he was still
alive they would not have dared to do this to me, I
know they would not. . . .'

Tears of a sort were rolling down her cheeks; and her hands, with large blue veins, trembled.

Gaud had straightened her coif, and tried to console her with soothing words, such as one might use to a child; and Yann was indignant; was it possible that children could be so wicked! To do a thing like that to a poor old woman! Tears almost came into his eyes too—not for the cat, needless to say; young men of his rough sort, while they like well enough to play with animals, have little or no sensibility for them; but his heart melted, as he walked behind this grandmother in her dotage, carrying her poor cat by the tail. He thought of Sylvestre, who had so much loved her; of the dreadful grief he would have felt if any one had foretold him that she would end in this way, in derision and penury.

And Gaud excused herself as being responsible for her appearance:

'She must have fallen to have got so dirty,' she said, quite low; 'her dress is not new, it is true, for we are not rich, Monsieur Yann; but it is only yesterday that I mended it, and this morning when I went out I am sure that it was clean and tidy.'

He gazed at her long then, much more touched perhaps by this simple little explanation than he would have been by clever phrases, by reproaches, or by tears. They continued to walk side by side in the direction of the cottage of the Moans. Pretty she had always been, pretty as a girl could be; he knew that well; but it seemed to him that she was even prettier now in her poverty and mourning.

Her air had become more serious, her grey eyes had a more reserved expression, and yet, in spite of that, they seemed to penetrate you more deeply, to the bottom of your soul. Her figure also had taken on its full shapeliness. She was nearly twenty-three years old; in the bloom of her beauty.

And, moreover, she had now the appearance of a fisherman's daughter, in her simple black dress and her quite plain coif; her ladylike air came one could no longer tell whence; it was something hidden in herself and involuntary, with which it was not possible to reproach her; perhaps it was only her bodice, a little more carefully fitted than those of others, by habit learned of old, outlining better her rounded bosom and the upper part of her arms. . . . But, no, it lay rather in her even voice and in her gaze.

CHAPTER XVII

It was clear that he was going to accompany them—
to their door, no doubt.

The three of them walked on, as if for the burial
of the unfortunate cat, and it became almost a little
comical now to see them passing thus in a sort of
procession; and some of the good folk standing at
their doors smiled. The old Yvonne in the middle
carrying the cat; Gaud on her right, distressed and
still very red; big Yann on her left, very tall and
thoughtful.

However, the poor old woman became almost
suddenly pacified on the way; of her own accord she
had straightened her coif, and without saying anything more she began to observe the two of them
alternately, from the corner of her eye, which had
become clear again. Gaud did not speak either for
fear of giving Yann an excuse for taking leave of
them; she wanted to rest on that kindly glance which
she had received from him, to walk with eyes closed
so that she might no longer see anything else, to walk
for long by his side thus, in a dream she was weaving,
instead of arriving all too quickly at their empty
and gloomy dwelling where the spell must needs
be broken.

At the door there was one of those moments of
indecision, during which it seems that the heart stops
beating. Grand'mère Yvonne entered without turning round; then Gaud, hesitating, and Yann, behind,
entered also.

He was in their home for the first time in his life; without intention, probably; what was there he could want? As he crossed the threshold he had touched his hat, and then, his eyes having met first of all the portrait of Sylvestre in its little mortuary crown of black beads, he moved towards it slowly as to a tomb.

Gaud had remained standing, leaning with her hands on the table. He looked now all round him, and she followed him in this sort of silent review which he made of their poverty. It was poor, indeed, despite its clean and ordered air, the lodging of these two forlorn ones who had become united. Perhaps, at least, he would feel for her a little kindly pity, seeing her fallen to this degree of misfortune, to this rough granite and this roof of thatch. There was nothing left of her former riches but the white bed, the pretty modern bed, and involuntarily the eyes of Yann returned to it. . . .

He said nothing. . . . Why did he not go? . . . The old grandmother, who was still so wise in her lucid moments, pretended not to notice him. And so they remained standing, one before the other, mute and anxious, ending by gazing at one another as if for some supreme interrogation.

But the minutes passed, and as each second slipped by the silence between them seemed to become more set. And they looked at each other still more earnestly, as if they were awaiting solemnly some unprecedented thing which was slow in coming.

.   .   .   .   .

'Gaud,' he asked, in a low grave voice, 'if you are still willing. . . .'

What was he going to say? . . . One felt that he had come to some momentous decision, sudden like

all his decisions, taken on the spur of the moment,
and that he scarcely dared to formulate it. . . .

'— If you are still willing. . . . The catch has
fetched a good price this year, and I have a little
money by me. . . .'

If she was still willing! . . . What was he asking
her? Had she heard him right? She was bewildered
before the immensity of what she thought she
understood.

And old Yvonne, from her corner beyond, pricked
up her ears, scenting the approach of happiness. . . .

'We should be able to get married, Mademoiselle
Gaud, if you were still willing. . . .'

And then he awaited her reply, which did not come.
What was it that prevented her from pronouncing
this yes? . . . He was surprised, he was afraid, and
she perceived it well. Leaning with her two hands
on the table, become quite white, with eyes swimming,
she was voiceless, she resembled a beautiful woman
dying. . . .

'Come now, Gaud, answer!' said the old grandmother, who had risen and come towards them.
'You see, Monsieur Yann, this has taken her by
surprise; you must excuse her; she will think it over
and answer you very soon. . . . Sit down, Monsieur
Yann, and take a glass of cider with us. . . .'

But Gaud was not able to reply; no word came to
her in her ecstasy. . . . It was true, then, that he
was good, that he had a heart. She had found him
again, her true Yann, such as she had never ceased
to see him in her dreams, in spite of his rudeness, in
spite of his rough refusal, in spite of all. He had long
disdained her, now he accepted her, now that she
was poor: it was his way, no doubt, he had some
motive which she would know later on; at this moment

she had no thought of asking him to explain, or, any more, of reproaching him for her two years' grieving. All that was so forgotten, all that had been swept so far away, in a second, by the delicious whirlwind which was passing over her life! . . . Still silent, she declared her adoration of him only with her eyes, her flooded eyes, which gazed at him with an intense yearning, while a copious rain of tears began to descend along her cheeks. . . .

'Now then, God bless you, my children!' said Grand'mère Moan. 'As for me I owe Him great gratitude, for I am now content to have become so old, in order to have witnessed this before dying.'

They remained, standing there, one before the other, holding each other's hands, and finding no words to say; knowing no word that was sweet enough, no phrase that could express their feelings, none that seemed to them worthy of breaking their exquisite silence.

'Kiss each other, at least, my children. . . . Bless me, they have nothing to say to each other! What a droll pair of grandchildren I have, to be sure! . . . Now then, Gaud, say something to him, my girl. . . . In my time, it seems to me, people used to kiss when they became engaged. . . .'

Yann took off his hat, as if seized suddenly with an unwonted deep respect, before stooping to kiss Gaud —and it seemed to him that it was the first true kiss he had ever given in his life.

She kissed him also, pressing with all her heart her fresh lips, unskilled in the refinement of caresses, on this cheek of her lover which the sea had bronzed. In the stones of the wall the cricket chirped out happiness to them; this time, by chance, his note was in harmony. And the poor little portrait of Sylvestre

seemed to smile at them, from amid its black crowning.
And everything appeared suddenly vivified and
rejuvenated in the dead cottage. The silence was
filled with a wonderful music; even the pale winter's
twilight, entering by the little window, had become,
as it were, a beautiful enchanted light. . . .

'And when shall it be, my dear children; on the
return from Iceland?'

Gaud hung her head. Iceland, the *Léopoldine*—it
is true she had forgotten these spectres that waylaid
her path. On the return from Iceland! How long
it would be, all this summer of anxious waiting! And
Yann, tapping the ground with his foot with rapid
little beats, become eager in his turn, reckoned up
very quickly in his mind, to see whether, if they made
all possible haste, they would not have time to marry
before the departure: so many days to obtain the
necessary papers, so many days to publish the banns
at the church, that would take them only to the 20th
or 25th of the month, for the wedding and, if nothing
hindered them, they would still have a full week to
remain together as man and wife.

'I must go now and inform my father,' he said,
with as much haste as if the very minutes of their life
were measured and precious. . . .

PART IV

CHAPTER I

LOVERS are always very fond of sitting together on the benches, in front of the doors, when night is falling.

Yann and Gaud were no exceptions in this. Every evening, on the old granite bench, at the door of the cottage of the Moans, they did their courting.

Others have the spring, the shade of the trees, warm evenings the flowering rose-trees. They had nothing but the February twilights descending on a seabound country of furze and stones. No green branches overhead or around them, nothing but the immense heavens, over which the wandering mists passed slowly. And for flowers, brown seaweed which the fishermen, coming from the shore, had trailed in the pathway with their nets.

The winters are not severe in this region, warmed by the currents of the sea; but, for all that, these twilights brought often an icy dampness and an imperceptible fine rain which was deposited on their shoulders.

They did not move, however, being very happy where they were. And this bench, which was more than a hundred years old, was not surprised at their love-making, having seen many love-makings before; it had heard, too, the soft words uttered, always the same, from generation to generation, by the lips of the young, and it had become used to seeing the lovers return later on, changed into tottering old men,

179

and trembling old women, to sit in the same place—
but in the daytime then, to breathe still a little air,
and to warm themselves in their last sunshine. . . .

From time to time Grand'mère Yvonne put her
head out of the door and looked at them. Not that
she was uneasy about what they might do together,
but out of affection merely, for the pleasure of seeing
them, and also to try to make them come in. She said:

'You will get cold, my children, you will make
yourselves ill. Why, gracious me! to remain outside
so late. I should like to ask you, is there any sense
in it?'

Cold! Were they cold? Were they conscious even
of anything except the happiness of sitting side
by side?

The people who passed in the evening along the road
heard a soft murmur of two voices, mingling in the
noise the sea made below, at the foot of the cliffs.
It was a very harmonious music, the pure voice of
Gaud, alternating with that of Yann, the deep note
of which had a tender and caressing resonance. One
could make out also their two silhouettes standing
out against the granite of the wall which was at their
backs: first of all the white of Gaud's coif, then all her
slim black-robed form, and at her side the square
shoulders of her lover. Above them the hunch-
backed dome of their thatched roof, and behind all
this, the twilit infinitude, the colourless emptiness of
the waters and the sky. . . .

But in the end they would come in and sit by the
fire, and old Yvonne, falling asleep at once, her
head nodding, did not much embarrass the two
young people in their love-making. They would
resume their conversation in a low voice, having to
make up for their two years of silence, having need to

hasten in their courtship since it must needs be so short.

It was arranged that they should make their home with Grand'mère Yvonne who, in her will, had bequeathed to them her cottage; for the moment they would attempt no improvement, for want of time, and would postpone until after the return from Iceland their project of beautifying a little this poor and far too desolate nest.

CHAPTER II

ONE evening he amused himself by recounting to her
a thousand little things which she had done or which
had happened to her since their first meeting; he told
her even the dresses she had worn, the fêtes she had
attended.

She heard him with an extreme surprise.   How did
he know all this?   Who would imagine that he had
noticed these things, and was capable of remembering
them?

He smiled, affecting a mysterious air, and continued
to tell her of other little details, even of things which
she had almost forgotten.

Now, interrupting him no more, she let him talk
on, seized with an unlooked-for ravishment which
possessed her wholly; she began to guess, to understand; he had loved her, then, he also, all this time!
. . . She had been his constant preoccupation.   And
this was his simple way of letting her know! . . .

Then, what did it all mean?   Why, in Heaven's
name, had he so long repulsed her, why had he made
her suffer so much?

There remained this mystery, which he had promised to clear up for her, but of which he deferred the
explanation from day to day, with an embarrassed
air, and the ghost of an incomprehensible smile. . . .

CHAPTER III

ONE fine day they went to Paimpol, with Grand'mère
Yvonne, to buy the wedding dress.

Among the pretty modish dresses which remained
to her from her affluent days there were some which
might very well have been adapted for the ceremony,
and there was really no need to buy another. But
Yann had wanted to make her this present, and she
did not press her objection too strongly: to have a
dress given by him, paid for out of the money earned
by his labour and his fishing, it seemed to her that
that would make her already in some slight measure
his wife.

They chose black, for Gaud was still in mourning
for her father. But Yann found nothing good enough
in the stuffs that were shown them. He was rather
haughty with the shopkeepers, and, he who formerly
would not for the world have entered any of these
Paimpol shops, on this day concerned himself with
every detail, even with the way in which the dress
was to be made. He insisted that they should trim it
with broad bands of velvet in order to make it prettier.

CHAPTER IV

ONE evening, when they were sitting on their stone
bench in the solitude of their cliff, as night was falling,
their eyes rested by chance on a blackthorn bush—the
solitary one round about—which grew among the
rocks by the side of the road. In the gloom it
seemed to them that they could distinguish on this
bush little light tufts of white:

'It looks as if it were in bloom,' said Yann.

And, to make sure, they went up to it.

It was in full bloom. As they could not see very
clearly they touched it, verifying with their fingers
the presence of these little flowers which were quite
damp with mist. And then there came to them a
first impression of spring; at the same time they
perceived that the days were lengthening; that there
was something warmer in the air, something more
luminous in the night.

But how forward this blackthorn bush was! Nowhere in the country round by the side of any road
would one have found its like. No doubt it had
blossomed there expressly for them, to celebrate
their love. . . .

'Come, let us gather some!' said Yann.

And, almost gropingly, he made a bouquet in his
big hands; with the large fisherman's knife which he
carried in his belt, he carefully removed the thorns,
and then he put it in Gaud's bodice.

'There, like a bride!' he said, stepping back to see,
despite the darkness, if it became her well.

Below them, the sea, very calm, was breaking on the pebbles of the shore, with a little intermittent soughing, regular as the respiration of sleep; it seemed indifferent, and even favourable, to this courting that was going on there quite near it.

The days seemed long to them in their waiting for the evenings, and afterwards, when they separated on the stroke of ten o'clock, there came to them a curious little sense of dissatisfaction with life, because they were over so soon. . . .

There was need for haste, great haste, in order to get the necessary papers, to arrange this and arrange that, with the risk of not being ready in time and of letting their happiness escape them until the autumn, until the uncertain future. . . .

Their courting, done in the evenings in this mournful spot, to the continual murmur of the sea, and with this rather feverish preoccupation with the march of time, took on from all these circumstances a peculiar and almost mournful character. They were lovers different from other lovers, graver, more anxious in their love.

He still would not tell her what it was that for two long years had set him against her, and when he had left her at night this mystery tormented Gaud. And yet she was sure now that he loved her well.

It was true that he had loved her all along, but not as now. His love was growing in his heart and in his soul like a tide which rises, rises, until it overflows. He had never experienced this kind of love before.

From time to time, on the stone bench, he would sprawl, lie down almost, throwing his head on Gaud's knees, in the coaxing manner of a child that wants to be caressed; and then, very quickly, he would sit up again, from a sense of propriety. He would have loved to lie on the ground at her feet and remain there, his forehead pressed against the hem of her dress. Apart from the brotherly kiss which he gave her on arrival and on departure he did not dare to embrace her. He worshipped an invisible, indefinable something in her, which was her soul, which manifested itself to him in the pure and tranquil sound of her voice, in the expression of her smile, in her brave, clear gaze. . . .

And to think that at the same time she was a woman of flesh and blood, more beautiful and more desirable than any other; that she would soon belong to him in as complete a manner as any of his former mistresses, without ceasing on that account to be *herself*! . . . This idea thrilled him to his very marrow; he did not conceive very clearly the ecstasy of the consummating hour, for he would not let his thought dwell on it, moved by a feeling of respect, asking himself almost whether he would dare to commit this sweet sacrilege. . . .

CHAPTER V

ONE rainy evening they were sitting side by side in the chimney corner, and old Yvonne was nodding opposite them. The flames which leaped among the faggots on the hearth made their magnified shadows dance on the dark ceiling.

They were talking very low, as is the way with lovers. But on this particular evening there were long embarrassed silences in their conversation. He especially said scarcely anything and hung his head with a half smile, seeking to avoid Gaud's gaze.

And the reason was that she had been plying him throughout the evening with questions on this mystery which he found so much difficulty in explaining to her, and this time he saw that he was caught; she was too shrewd and too determined to know; there was no shift now by which he could escape from his predicament.

'Have scandalous tongues been busy on my account? Have wicked things been said about me?' she asked.

He ventured to answer yes. Wicked things, oh! . . . there had been many said in Paimpol and in Ploubazlanec.

She asked him what. He was in difficulties and knew not what to say. And she saw clearly that it must have been something else.

'Was it my clothes, Yann?'

Yes, that, to be sure, had something to do with it: she seemed for a time to be too fond of them to become

the wife of a simple fisherman. But, even so, he was
forced to admit that that was not all.

'Was it because, at that time, we were rich? You
were afraid of being refused?'

'Oh, no! Not that.'

He made this answer with such a naïve confidence
in himself that Gaud was amused. And then a new
silence fell between them, during which they heard
outside the moaning sound of the wind and the sea.

While she was watching him attentively an idea
began to dawn on her, and her expression gradually
changed.

'It was none of these things, Yann; then what was
it?' she asked, gazing suddenly straight into his eyes
with the irresistibly inquiring smile of one who
has guessed.

And he turned his head away, bursting out into
a laugh.

So that was it. She had discovered the secret:
reason he could not give her, because he had none
and never had any. Yes, it was simply his waywardness (as Sylvestre had been used to say), and that was
all. But there was this also, that folk had pestered
him so much about this Gaud! Every one had
pressed her upon him, his parents, Sylvestre, his
Icelander comrades, and finally Gaud herself. And
so he had begun to say no, obstinately no, while all
the time cherishing deep in his heart the idea that
one day, when no one any longer expected it, it would
end surely by being yes.

And it was through this piece of childishness in her
beloved Yann that Gaud had languished, abandoned
for two long years, and had wished to die. . . .

After the first inclination, which had been to laugh
a little, in his confusion at being found out, Yann

looked at Gaud with grave kind eyes which, in their
turn, questioned profoundly; would she forgive him
at least? His remorse to-day was great for having
caused her so much suffering; would she forgive
him? . . .

'It is my character, Gaud, which is like that,' he
said. 'At home, with my parents, it is just the same.
Sometimes, when it comes into my stupid head, I
remain for a week on end as if angry with them,
speaking scarcely to any one. And, for all that, I
love them dearly, you know, and always end by
obeying them in everything they wish, as if I were still
a little boy of ten. . . . Do you think it was in my
mind never to marry? No, that would not have
lasted long in any case, Gaud, you may be sure.'

Oh, would she forgive him? She felt tears come
softly into her eyes; they were the last of her one-time
grief, which vanished utterly at this avowal from her
Yann. Besides, without all her previous suffering
the present hour would not have been so exquisite;
now that it was over she was almost glad she had
known this time of proof.

Now everything was cleared up between them; in
a manner unexpected, it is true, but complete: there
was no longer any veil between their two souls. He
took her in his arms and drew her to him, and they
remained long with heads close together, cheek
pressing against cheek, having no further need of
explanation, no further need of words at all. And,
in this great moment, their embrace was so chaste
that, Grand'mère Yvonne waking up, they continued
to stand before her as they were, without any
embarrassment.

.   .   .   .   .

CHAPTER VI

IT was six days before the departure for Iceland.
The wedding party was returning from Ploubazlanec
Church, pursued by a furious wind, under a dark and
rain-charged sky.

Arm in arm, they made a handsome couple, walking
like kings at the head of their long train, walking as
in a dream.   Calm, thoughtful, serious, they had the
air of seeing nothing, of dominating life, of being
above everything.   Even the wind seemed to respect
them, while, behind, the procession was a joyous
disorder of laughing couples whom the blustering
squalls buffeted.   Many young people were among
them, in whom also was overflowing life; and others,
already grizzled, but smiling still as they recalled the
day of their own wedding and their earlier years.
Grand'mère Yvonne was there, and followed in the
procession, very flustered, but almost happy, on the
arm of an old uncle of Yann's, who was paying her
old-fashioned compliments; she wore a fine new coif
which they had bought for her for the ceremony and,
of course, her little shawl, redyed for the third time
—black for Sylvestre.

And the wind buffeted all these guests without
distinction; one saw skirts uplifted, dresses turned
partly inside out, hats and coifs blown off.

At the door of the church, according to custom, the
bride and bridegroom had bought bunches of artificial
flowers to complete their festive attire.   Yann had
fixed his at hazard on his broad chest, but he was of

those whom everything and anything becomes. As
for Gaud, there was an air of refinement still in the
way, in which these poor common flowers were pinned
to the upper part of her bodice—a bodice close-fitting,
as formerly, to her exquisite figure.

The fiddler, who conducted all these people,
bothered by the wind, played anyhow; his airs reached
the ear in puffs and, in the noise of the squalls, seemed
a comical little music, shriller than the cries of a gull.

All Ploubazlanec had turned out to see them.
This marriage had something about it which keenly
interested the countryside, and people came from far
around; at the crossings of the lanes there were
everywhere groups stationed waiting for them.
Nearly all the Icelanders of Paimpol, Yann's friends,
were there in position. They saluted the newly-
married pair as they passed; Gaud replied by bowing
slightly like a young lady, with her serious grace, and,
all along her route, she was greatly admired.

And the hamlets round about, the most remote,
the most benighted, even those in the woods, had
sent their beggars, their cripples, their half-witted
folk, their idiots on crutches. This tribe was echeloned along the road, with accordions, hurdy-gurdies,
and noise-making instruments of divers sorts; they
held out their hands, their bowls, their hats to receive
the alms which Yann threw to them with his large
lordly air and Gaud with her pretty queenly smile.
Some of these beggars were very old, and the hair
was grey on their empty heads which had never
contained anything; squatting in ditches by the side
of the road, they were of the same colour as the earth
from which they seemed never to have completely
emerged, and back to which they would soon return
without having had a consecutive thought; their

bewildered eyes were as disturbing as the mystery
of their abortive and useless existences. Without
comprehending they watched this festival of full and
superb life. . . .

They continued their walk beyond the hamlet of
Pors-Even and the home of the Gaoses, in order that
they might repair, in accordance with the traditional
custom of newly-married couples in the district of
Ploubazlanec, to the Chapel of the Trinity, which is
as it were on the edge of the Breton world.

At the foot of the last farthermost cliff, it stands on
a ledge of low rocks, quite near the water, and seems
to belong already to the sea.   To reach it you have to
follow a goat's path among blocks of granite.   And
the wedding party spread itself over the slope of this
isolated cape, amid the rocks, their words of merriment
and words of love quite lost in the noise of the wind
and the waves.

It was impossible to reach the chapel; in this rough
weather the passage to it was not safe, the sea broke
thunderously too near it.   You could see the white
spouts rising very high, and, as they fell, spreading
over everything like an inundation.

Yann, who had advanced the farthest, with Gaud
leaning on his arm, was the first to draw back before
the spray.   Behind, his escort stood echeloned on the
rocks, as in an amphitheatre, and he seemed to have
come there to present his wife to the sea; but the sea
showed a very unfriendly face to the new bride.

As they turned back he saw the fiddler, perched
on a grey rock, and trying to resume, between two
gusts, his jig-like air.

'Pack up your music, my man,' he said to him;
'the sea is playing us another tune, which goes better
than yours. . . .'

At the same time a heavy, lashing rain, which had been threatening since the morning, began to fall, and there was a wild stampede with shouting and laughter to climb the cliff and seek shelter in the home of the Gaoses.

CHAPTER VII

THE wedding feast was held in the home of Yann's
parents, on account of the poverty of Gaud's dwelling.

It was in the large new room on the upper floor, a
group of twenty-five people at table with the new-
made man and wife: sisters and brothers; Cousin
Gaos, the pilot; Guermeur, Keraez, Yvon Duff, all
of the old *Marie*, and now of the *Léopoldine*; four
very pretty bridesmaids, their plaited hair wound in
coils above the ears in the fashion adopted long ago
by the Byzantine empresses, and their white coifs
of the new style worn by the young, in the shape of a
sea-shell; four groomsmen, all Icelanders, upstanding
fellows, with fine proud eyes.

And below, too, needless to say, there was eating
and cooking: all the tail-end of the procession had
gathered there in disorder, and the working women,
hired in Paimpol, were at their wit's end before the
assemblage of pots and pans in the fireplace.

Yann's parents, no doubt, would have liked for
their son a wife more richly dowered, but Gaud was
known now to be a brave and sensible girl; and, moreover, to compensate for her lost fortune, she was the
most beautiful in the countryside, and it flattered
them to see so well-matched a couple.

The old man, Yann's father, elated after the meal,
referring to the marriage said:

'This is going to increase the number of Gaoses,
although there's no shortage of them even now in
Ploubazlanec.'

And, reckoning up on his fingers, he explained to an old uncle of the bride how it came about that there were so many of this name: his father, who was the youngest of nine brothers, had had twelve children, who had all married cousins, and that had helped to keep the number up, notwithstanding the lost ones in Iceland.

'For my part,' he said, 'I, too, married a Gaos, a relative, and between us we have added another fourteen to the total.'

And, at the thought of this tribe, he rejoiced and nodded his white head.

The dickens! He had had a struggle to bring up these fourteen little Gaoses; but now they were getting over their difficulties, and, besides, those ten thousand francs got from the derelict had helped greatly to put them in comfort.

Waxing merry also, neighbour Guermeur told of his adventures while in the *service*,[1] stories of China, of the Antilles, of Brazil, making the young people who, later on, would visit these parts, open their eyes wide.

One of his happiest memories was of an occasion when, on board the *Iphigénie*, they were filling the wine vats one evening in the dark, and the leather sleeve, through which the wine is poured had burst. Thereupon, instead of giving warning, one and all had set to work to drink their fill; the feast lasted two hours; and in the end the gun-room ran with wine, and everybody was drunk!

And these old sailors, sitting at table, laughed their honest boyish laugh, which was spiced with just a little malice.

[1] Seafaring men speak thus of their time as sailors in the Navy.

'People decry the service,' they said, 'but how else can one see so much of the world?'

Outside the weather did not improve; on the contrary, the wind and the rain were raging furiously in a thick darkness. In spite of the precautions they had taken some of them became uneasy about their boats moored in the harbour, and talked of going to see that all was well.

Meanwhile, another noise, much more pleasant to hear, came from below, where the young people of the wedding party were feasting together; there were shouts of joy and bursts of merry laughter from the little boy and girl cousins, who were beginning to feel very exhilarated by the cider.

The guests had been served with boiled meats and roast meats, with chickens and several kinds of fish, with omelettes and pancakes.

They had talked of fishing and smuggling, discussed all manner of ways of hoodwinking the good gentlemen of the Customs who are, as every one knows, the enemies of sea-going men.

Above, at the table of honour, they were even beginning to talk of rather doubtful adventures.

This particular vein of conversation was developed with gusto in Breton by these men who all, in their time, had made the round of the world.

'At Hong-Kong, the *houses*, you know, the houses that are there as you go up the little streets. . . .'

'Ah, yes!' from the end of the table replied another who had frequented them—'Yes, turning to the right when you arrive?'

'That's it; the Chinese ladies, what? Well, we had amused ourselves there, three of us. . . . Ugly women, by Jove, ugly, ugly. . . .'

'Aye, ugly, I believe you,' said Yann carelessly, for

he also, in a misguided moment, after a long voyage,
had made the acquaintance of these Chinese ladies.

'Afterwards, when it came to paying, which of us
had any money? . . . Feel, feel in your pockets—not
I, nor you, nor he—not a sou amongst us all. We
made excuses, promising to return'—(here he con-
torted his rugged bronzed face and simpered like a
surprised Chinese woman)—'but the old woman, not
trusting us, began to caterwaul, to play the devil,
and ended by clawing us with her yellow paws'—
(now he mimicked the shrill voices of these ladies and
grimaced like the angry old woman, rolling his eyes
which he had tilted up at the corners with his fingers)
—'and then who should come in but the two Chinamen, the two . . . well, the two proprietors of the
show, you understand?—and they locked the door
with us inside! Naturally we laid hold of them by
their pigtails and prepared to knock their heads
against the wall when, hey presto! a number of
others came out from holes and corners, at least a
dozen, who rolled up their sleeves with the intention
of setting upon us—with airs of misgiving, nevertheless. Fortunately I had my packet of sugar-
sticks, bought as provender for the journey; and a
packet of sugar-sticks is solid, it doesn't break when
it is fresh: so you can imagine it was very useful to
hammer these monkeys with. . . .'

The wind was blowing furiously now. At this
moment the window-panes rattled under a terrible
blast, and the storyteller, cutting short the end of
his tale, got up to go and look after his boat.

Another began:

'When I was a master gunner, acting as corporal
at arms on the *Zénobie*, at Aden, one day some sellers
of ostrich feathers came on board'—(imitating the

accent of the country)—'"Good morning, corporal;
we are not thieves, we are honest merchants." I
sent them down again in double-quick time. "You,
honest merchants," I said, "well, then, bring me first
of all a bunch of feathers for a present; we'll see then
whether we can let you on board with your trumpery
wares." And I might have made a tidy bit of money
over it on my return, if I had not been so stupid!'—
(sadly)—'but you must remember that in those days
I was very young. . . . And a lady friend of mine,
at Toulon, who worked at a milliner's. . . .'

But at this moment one of Yann's little brothers,
a future Icelander, with a comely red face and two
sparkling eyes, was suddenly taken ill from having
drunk too much cider. He had to be carried out
hurriedly, the little Laumec, and this cut short the
recital of the perfidious way in which this little
milliner had secured the ostrich feathers.

The wind howled in the chimney like a soul in
torment; every now and then, with terrifying force,
it shook the whole house on its stone foundations.

'One would think it was angry, because we have
begun to enjoy ourselves,' said the pilot cousin.

'No, it's the sea that is not pleased,' replied Yann,
smiling at Gaud, 'because I had made it a promise
of marriage.'

As the evening wore on a strange kind of languor
came over both of them; they spoke together in a
lower voice, hand holding hand, isolated in the midst
of the others' gaiety. Yann, knowing the effect of
wine on the senses, drank nothing the whole evening.
And he reddened now, this great big boy, when one of
his Icelander comrades made a sailor's jesting remark
on the night which was before them.

At moments, too, he was sad as he thought

suddenly of Sylvestre. . . . It had been agreed that there should be no dancing on account of Gaud's father and on account of him.

They were now at dessert; presently the songs would begin. But, before that, there were prayers to be said for deceased members of the family; at the marriage feasts this duty of religion is never omitted, and when the elder Gaos was seen to stand up and uncover his white head, there was silence everywhere:

'This,' he said, 'is for Guillaume Gaos, my father.'

And, making the sign of the Cross, he began to pray in Latin:

'Pater noster, qui es in coelis, sanctificetur nomen tuum . . .'

A silence as of a church had now spread even to the room below, to the joyous tables of the little ones. All who were in the house repeated in spirit the same eternal words.

'This is for Yves and Jean Gaos, my brothers, lost in the seas of Iceland. . . . This is for Pierre Gaos, my son, shipwrecked on board the *Zélie*. . . .'

Then, when all the Gaoses had had each his prayer, he turned towards Grand'mère Yvonne:

'This,' he said, 'is for Sylvestre Moan.'

And he recited another *pater noster*. Then Yann wept.

> . . . Sed libera nos a malo. Amen.

Afterwards the songs began. Songs learnt in the service, in the forecastle, where there are, as every one knows, many fine singers:

> Un noble corps, pas moins, que celui des zouaves,
> Mais chez nous les braves
>   Narguent le destin,
> Hurrah! hurrah! vive le vrai marin!

The lines were sung by one of the groomsmen, in a very sentimental manner, which went to the heart; and then the chorus was taken up by other deep, resonant voices.

But the newly-married couple seemed to hear all this from the background of a kind of distance; when they looked at each other their eyes shone with a dimmed brightness, like a shaded lamp; they spoke in a more and more subdued way, hand still holding hand, and Gaud often hung her head, seized gradually, before her master, with a greater and more exquisite fear.

Now the pilot cousin went the round of the table to serve a certain wine of his own; he had brought it with many precautions, caressing the recumbent bottle, which must on no account be shaken, he said.

He told them the history of it: one day when they were fishing they saw a cask floating all alone in the sea; they were not able to get it on board—it was too large: so they stove it in in the sea, filling all the pots and mugs they had. Even so it was impossible to empty it. They had made signs to other pilots, other fishermen: all the sails in sight had assembled around the find.

'And I know more than one who was drunk when we got back to Pors-Even that night.'

Still the wind continued its formidable roar.

Below, the children were dancing merrily. Some of them indeed had been put to bed—the quite little Gaoses, these—but the others were playing the very deuce, led by little Fantec and little Laumec, wanting even to go and dance outside, and every now and then opening the door to the furious blasts which blew out the candles.

The pilot cousin continued the story of the wine;

his share had amounted to forty bottles; he begged them not to say a word about it, on account of the superintendent of the Record Óffice who might have something to say to him about this undeclared booty.

'But,' he said, 'it was necessary to take great care of these bottles: if one had been able to filter it the wine would have been a most excellent one; for there was no doubt that in it there was much more of the juice of the grape than in all the cellars of the wine merchants of Paimpol.'

Who can tell where it may have grown, this ship-wrecked vintage? It was strong, rich in colour, with much admixture of sea-water, and retained the bitter taste of salt. It was, nevertheless, voted very good, and many bottles of it were emptied.

Heads began to turn a little. The sound of the voices became less distinct, and the lads began to kiss the girls.

The songs went on gaily, but nevertheless the guests were not altogether easy in their minds, and the men exchanged glances of anxiety on account of the wild weather which grew steadily worse.

Outside, the noise continued, worse than ever. It became, as it were, a single roar, continuous, swelling, threatening, uttered in unison, with full throat and outstretched neck, by thousands of enraged beasts.

And one heard, too, what sounded like the for-midable reports of heavy guns firing in the distance; and that was the sea pounding on the coast of Plou-bazlanec. It was true, indeed, that the sea did not seem to be pleased, and Gaud's heart was wrung by this terrifying music, which had come unbidden to their wedding feast.

Towards midnight, during a temporary lull, Yann,

who had risen quietly, made a sign to his wife to come and speak to him.

It was to ask her to come home. . . . She blushed out of modesty, in confusion at having got up. . . . Then she said that it would not be civil to go away so soon, and leave the others.

'No,' replied Yann; 'it was the old man who suggested it. We can go.'

And he led her away.

They escaped unseen.

Outside they found themselves in the cold, in the sinister wind, in the dark, tormented night. They started to run, holding each other's hand. High up on this cliff road they divined without seeing them the distances of the furious sea, from which came all this noise. They ran together, the rain beating into their faces, with bodies bent forward against the blasts, obliged, sometimes, to turn round with hands before their mouths, in order to recover the breath which the wind had taken away.

To begin with he took her by the waist and almost carried her, in order that she might not trail her dress, might not wet her pretty shoes, in the water that streamed over the ground; and, then, he lifted her bodily in his arms, and continued to run more quickly still. No, he had not believed he could love her so much! And to think that she was twenty-three; and he nearly twenty-eight; and that, for the last two years, they might have been married and happy as they were to-night.

At last they reached their home, their poor little damp-floored dwelling, their roof of thatch and moss; and they lit a candle which the wind twice blew out for them.

Old Grand'mère Moan, who had been taken home

before the songs began, was there, lying, as she had lain for the past two hours, in her press-bed, the shutters of which she had closed; they approached respectfully and looked at her through the open-work of her door in order to wish her good night if by chance she was not yet asleep. But they saw that her venerable face remained motionless and that her eyes were closed; she was asleep, or else pretending to be so, so as not to disturb them.

And they felt then that they were alone together.

They were both trembling, as they held each other's hands. He bent towards her to kiss her lips; but Gaud turned her lips away in ignorance of this form of kissing, and, as chastely as on the night of their betrothal, pressed them against Yann's cheek, which was cold as ice from the wind.

Very poor, very low, was their little cottage, and it was very cold there. Ah, if Gaud had remained rich, as in the olden days, what joy she would have had in arranging a pretty room, very different from this one with its floor of bare earth. . . . She was scarcely used yet to these walls of rough granite, to these primitive surroundings; but her Yann was there with her; and by his presence everything was changed, transfigured, and she saw only him. . . .

Now their lips had met, and Gaud had not turned hers away. Still standing, clasped in each other's arms, they remained there silent, in the ecstasy of a kiss which did not end. Their panting breaths mingled and they both trembled violently, as in a burning fever. They seemed not to have strength to break their embrace, and were conscious of nothing, wanted nothing, but this long kiss.

She freed herself at last, suddenly troubled:

'No, Yann! . . . Grand'mère Yvonne might see us!'

But he, smiling, sought the lips of his wife again, and took them quickly between his own, like a thirsty man from whom one has taken a cup of cool water.

The movement they had made had broken the spell of their exquisite hesitation. Yann who, in his first moments, had been ready to go down on his knees as before the Holy Virgin, felt himself seized with a kind of savagery; he looked furtively in the direction of the old press-beds, annoyed to be so near this old grandmother, seeking some sure means by which they might not be seen; still without letting go her exquisite lips, he stretched out his arm behind him, and with the back of his hand extinguished the light as the wind had done.

Then, suddenly, he seized her in his arms: in his manner of holding her, his mouth still pressed against hers, he was like a wild beast which had fixed its teeth in its prey. She abandoned her body, her soul, to this rape which was imperious and beyond possible resistance, even while it remained sweet as a long enveloping caress; he carried her in the darkness towards the pretty white bed which was to be their nuptial couch.

Around them for their bridal night the same invisible orchestra played continuously.

Hoohoo! Hoohoo! Sometimes the wind gave full rein to its cavernous noise with a trembling of rage; sometimes it repeated its menace more softly to the ear, as in a refinement of malice, with little, long-drawn-out sounds, taking on the piping voice of a sea-gull.

And the great tomb of the mariners was quite near, restless, devouring, hammering the cliffs with its heavy blows. One night—sooner or later—it would be his lot to be caught in it, to struggle in it, amid the frenzy of dark and icy things—they knew it.

What did it matter! For the moment they were on shore, sheltered from all this useless and baffled fury. And, in the poor and gloomy lodging about which the wind made riot, they gave themselves to one another, heedless of everything, even of death, enraptured, exquisitely ensnared by the eternal magic of love.

CHAPTER VIII

THEY were husband and wife for six days.

At this time of departure the things of Iceland occupied everybody. The labouring women were busy loading salt for the brine in the store-rooms of the ships: the men were arranging the rigging, and, at Yann's home, the mother and the sisters were occupied from morning until night in the preparation of the sou'-westers, the oilskins, the whole outfit for the voyage. The weather was overcast and the sea, which felt the approach of the equinox, was restless and agitated.

Gaud submitted to these preparations with anguish, counting the fleeting hours of the day, waiting for the evening when, the day's work done, she had her Yann to herself.

Would he depart thus in years to come? She hoped indeed that she might be able to retain him, but she did not dare, at the present time, to speak to him on the subject. . . . Yet he loved her well; with his mistresses of old, he had never known a love like it. It was something new and different; it was a tenderness so trusting and so fresh, that the same kisses, the same embraces, with her were of another order, and each night their twin raptures of love were increased one by the other, and never knew, when the morning came, a sense of satiety.

What surprised and charmed her was to find him so kind and childlike, this Yann whom she had seen sometimes at Paimpol so off-hand and disdainful with amorous misses. With her, on the contrary, he showed an unvarying courtesy which seemed a thing natural to him, and she adored the ready smile he had for her whenever their eyes met. For, among these simple folk, there is a consciousness of, an innate respect for, the majesty of the wife; a very abysm separates her from the mistress, a thing of pleasure, to whom, in a smile of disdain, one seems to cast back the kisses of the night. Gaud was his wife, and, during the day, he gave no thought to their caresses, which seemed not to count, so much had they two become one flesh, one flesh for ever.

. . . Uneasy, to be sure, she was in her happiness, which seemed to her a thing that passed all hope, a thing unstable as dreams. . . .

Was it possible that with Yann this love should endure? . . . Sometimes she remembered his mistresses, his wildness, his adventures, and then she was afraid; would he retain for her always this infinite tenderness, this gentle respect? . . .

Truly, six days of marriage, for a love like theirs, was nothing; a mere little feverish advance on account of the period of their existence—which they would share for so long together! They had scarcely had time to speak to each other, to see each other, to realize that they belonged to each other. And all their prospects of life together, of tranquil joy, of making a home, had perforce been postponed until his return. . . .

Oh, in future years she must prevent him at all costs from going to Iceland! . . . But how was she to set about it? And how would they manage to live then, seeing they were both so poor? And then he was so fond of his fisherman's calling. . . .

She would try, nevertheless, on future occasions,

to hold him back; she would bend her whole will to it, all her intelligence, all her heart. To be the wife of an Icelander, to see the spring approach with sadness, to pass every summer in grievous anxiety; no, now that she worshipped him beyond anything she had ever imagined, she was seized with dismay at the thought of these years to come. . . .

They had one spring day together, a single one. It was the day before the fishing fleet sailed; the boats were all in readiness, and Yann spent the whole day with her. They rambled arm in arm along the lanes, as lovers do, very close to each other and talking of a thousand things. The good people smiled as they saw them pass.

'It's Gaud, with big Yann of Pors-Even. They were married the other day.'

A real day of spring, this last day; it was noticeable and strange to see suddenly this great calm and no longer a cloud in this usually stormy sky. The wind had completely dropped. The sea had become very kindly. It was everywhere of a pale blue colour, and remained tranquil. The sun shone with a white brilliance, and the rugged Breton country was impregnated with this light as with a thing fine and rare. It seemed to gladden and revive, even in its farthest distances. The air had taken on a delightful warmth, foretasting of summer, and one would have said that the weather was set fair for ever, that there could be no more gloomy days, no more tempests. The capes, the bays, over which no longer passed the changing shadows of the clouds, were revealed in the sunlight in their broad immutable lines; they, too, seemed to be resting, in a peacefulness which should never have an end. . . . All this as if to render more tranquil and more eternal their holiday of love; and, already even, there were flowers, the early spring flowers, primroses in the ditches, and violets, frail and without perfume.

When Gaud asked:

'How long will you love me, Yann?'

He replied, astonished, looking straight into her face, with his handsome, frank eyes:

'Why, Gaud, for ever. . . .'

And these words, said very simply by his unsophisticated lips, seemed to have their true meaning of eternity.

She leaned on his arm. In the enchantment of her dream come true she pressed against him, solicitous still—feeling that he was a fugitive thing like some great sea bird . . . that to-morrow would be soaring over the wide ocean! . . . And this first time it was too late, she could do nothing to prevent his going. . . .

From these cliff paths where they were walking they commanded the whole of this sea-bound country, which seemed to be treeless, carpeted with short furze and sown with stones. The fishermen's houses stood here and there on rocky ground with their old granite walls, their roofs of thatch, very high and hunch-backed, and made green with a new growth of moss; and in the far distance the sea, like a great diaphanous vision, described its immense and eternal circle, which seemed to embrace everything.

She took it into her head to tell him of the surprising and marvellous things of Paris, where she used to live; but he, full of scorn, showed little or no interest in them.

'So far from the coast,' he said, 'so far inland . . . it must be very unhealthy. So many houses, so many people. . . . There must be much disease in these cities; no, I don't want to live there, that's certain.'

And she smiled, surprised to find what a simple child was this great fellow at her side.

Now and then they descended into folds of the ground where real trees were growing, looking as if they were in hiding from the wind of the sea. There the view was shut out; on the ground, heaps of dead leaves and a cold dampness; the sunken lane, bordered with green furze, became gloomy under the branches, and presently squeezed itself between the walls of some dark and lonely hamlet, crumbling from old age, which slumbered in the valley; and there was always a crucifix raised high before them, among the dead branches, with its large wooden Christ eaten away like a corpse, grimacing in endless suffering.

Further on the lane ascended, and once more they dominated the immense horizon. They came back into the vivifying air of the high ground and the sea.

He, in turn, told her of Iceland, of the pale and nightless summers, of the oblique sun which never set. Gaud could not understand this and asked him to explain.

'The sun goes round, goes round,' he said, moving his outstretched arm along the distant circle of the blue waters. 'It stays low always, because, you see, it has not strength to climb; at midnight it dips its rim slightly in the sea, but quickly it rises again and continues its circular promenade. Sometimes the moon also appears at the opposite side of the sky; then they work together, each on its own side, and it is not easy to distinguish one from the other, for they are very much alike in that country.'

To see the sun at midnight! . . .

How far away it must be, this Iceland. And the

fiords? Gaud had read this word inscribed many
times amid the names of the dead in the chapel of the
shipwrecked; it seemed to her to designate a sinister
thing.

'The fiords,' replied Yann; 'they are large bays,
such as this bay of Paimpol, for example, only they
have around them mountains so high, so high that
you can never see the tops, on account of the clouds
which rest on them. A mournful country, Gaud, I
can tell you. Rocks, rocks, nothing but rocks, and
the people of the island don't know what trees are.
In the middle of August, when our fishing is over, it is
high time to leave, for then the nights begin, and
lengthen very quickly; the sun sinks below the earth
and cannot raise itself again, and the night lasts then
all the winter.'

'And then,' he went on, 'there is also a little
cemetery on the coast, in a fiord, just as with us,
for those of the Paimpol district who die during the
fishing season, or who are lost at sea; it is sanctified
ground, even as it is at Pors-Even, and the deceased
have wooden crosses, just as here, with their names
written on them. The two Goazdious, of Ploubazlanec, are there, and also Guillaume Moan, the
grandfather of Sylvestre.'

And she imagined she saw it, this little cemetery,
at the foot of a desolate headland, under the pale
pink light of these days that had never an end. And
then she thought of the dead under the ice, under the
dark shroud of these nights that are as long as the
winter.

'And do you fish all the time . . . all the time?'
she asked, 'without ever resting?'

'All the time. Of course we have also to look after
the boat, for the sea is not always smooth out there.

Jove! one is tired at night; one has an appetite for supper and, sometimes, one is ravenous.'

'And you never grow weary?'

'Never!' he said, with an air of conviction which hurt her; 'on board, at sea, the time never seems long to me, never!'

And she hung her head, feeling sadder, vanquished by the sea.

PART V

CHAPTER I

. . . A⊤ the end of this day of spring which they had
had together the falling night brought back a sensation of winter, and they returned to dine before their
blazing brushwood fire.

Their last repast together! . . . But they had still
a whole night in which to sleep in each other's arms,
and this respite prevented them from being sad
already.

After dinner, when they were outside once more on
the road to Pors-Even, they had again a soft impression of spring; the air was calm, almost warm, and a
remnant of twilight trailed lingeringly over the
countryside.

They went to pay a farewell visit to Yann's parents,
and returned early to go to bed, for it was in their
minds to rise at daybreak.

CHAPTER II

THE quay at Paimpol, on the following morning, was full of people. The departure of the Icelanders had begun two days before and, at every tide, a new group put to sea. On this morning fifteen boats were leaving with the *Léopoldine*, and the wives of the sailors, or the mothers, were all present to see them off. Gaud wondered to find herself mingled with them, become, she too, the wife of an Icelander, and brought thither by the same fatal cause. Her destiny had unfolded so quickly in these last few days that she had scarcely had time to realize what was happening; slipping down an irresistibly steep slope she had arrived at this pass, which was inexorable, and which she must needs suffer, even as the others were doing, those who were used to it.

She had never assisted intimately at these scenes, at these farewells. It was all new and strange to her. Among these women there was none like her and she felt herself isolated, different, and the refinement of her prosperous days, which persisted in spite of all, placed her apart.

The weather had continued fine for this day of separation; but off shore a heavy swell coming from the west was a herald of storm, and in the distance you could see the sea, which was waiting for these people, breaking white.

. . . Around Gaud there were others who, like her, were pretty and very pathetic with their tear-filled eyes; there were some also who were thoughtless, who were laughing, who had no heart or who, for the moment, had no lover. Old women, feeling the shadow of death upon them, wept as they said good-bye to their sons; lovers embraced with long kisses, lips on lips; and drunken sailors sang to keep themselves in cheer, while others went on board with a thoughtful air, departing as to a calvary.

And brutal things happened, too; unfortunate fellows who had signed their engagement unwittingly, one day in a tavern, and who were being embarked now by force; their own wives helped the gendarmes to drive them. Others, again, whose resistance was feared on account of their great strength, had been made drunk by way of precaution; they were carried on board on stretchers, and taken down like dead men into the ship's hold.

Gaud was horrified to see them pass: with what sort of companions was her Yann going to live? And what was the terrible nature of this Iceland calling, that it should announce itself in this manner and inspire in men this manifest dread? . . .

There were, however, some of these sailors who smiled, who, no doubt, like Yann, loved the life at sea and the fishing. These were the best of them; they had a proud and handsome mien; if they were unmarried they went away care-free, throwing a last glance at the girls; if they were married they embraced their wives or their little ones with a tender sadness, and the fond hope that they would return enriched. Gaud felt a little reassured when she saw that they were all of this type on board the *Léopoldine*, which had, in fact, a picked crew.

The boats went off, two by two, four by four, pulled out of the harbour by tugs. And as soon as they began to move, the sailors, uncovering their heads,

intoned at the top of their voices the hymn of the
Virgin, *Hail, Star of the Sea!* On the quay the
hands of the women were waved in the air for a
last adieu, and tears rolled down on the muslin of
the coifs.

As soon as the *Léopoldine* had left Gaud made her
way as fast as she could to the house of the Gaoses.
It was an hour and a half's walk, along the coast, by
the familiar footpaths of Ploubazlanec, before she
arrived at last, at the kind of land's end where her
new family dwelt.

The *Léopoldine* was going to anchor in the open
roadstead before Pors-Even, and would not finally
set sail until the evening; and it was at Pors-Even,
therefore, that they had arranged a last rendezvous.
And, surely enough, he came in the ship's gig; he
came for three hours to bid her a last good-bye.

On shore, where the swell could no longer be seen,
there was still the same fine spring weather, the same
tranquil sky. They went out for a short walk, arm
in arm. It recalled their ramble of the previous day,
only this time the night would not come to reunite
them. They walked without purpose, in the direction
of Paimpol, and presently found themselves near their
home, led thither unconsciously; once again, therefore,
for a last time, they entered the cottage of the Moans,
where old Grand'mère Yvonne was surprised to see
them reappear together.

Yann had many recommendations to make to
Gaud about a number of little things he was leaving
in their cupboard; especially about his fine wedding-
clothes: he wanted them unfolded from time to time
and put in the sun. On board the warships sailors
learn these little ways of carefulness. And Gaud

smiled to see him giving himself this air of knowledge; he might be quite sure that everything that belonged to him would be lovingly preserved and cared for.

In any case, these preoccupations were secondary for them; they talked of them for talking's sake, and in order to beguile themselves. . . .

Yann told her that on the *Léopoldine* they had just drawn lots for their fishing posts, and that he had been lucky enough to secure one of the best. She asked him to explain what this meant, knowing scarcely anything of the things of Iceland.

'It's like this, Gaud,' he said, 'on the gunwale of our boats there are openings made at certain places; we call them Mecca-holes: and in them we fix the little pulleys over which the lines are passed. And before we leave we play for these holes with dice or else with numbers shaken up in the shipboy's bonnet. Each of us gets one, and during the whole of the subsequent voyage he has no right to plant his line anywhere else; there is no changing. Well, my post is in the stern of the boat, which is, as you should know, the place where most fish are caught; and, besides, it is close to the main shrouds to which one can always attach a piece of canvas, an oilskin, in short a little shelter of some sort, to protect the face against the snow and the hail. That is some comfort, you know; your skin does not get so burnt, during the dark heavy squalls; and the eyes can see clear far longer.'

They were talking low, low, as if fearful of scaring the moments that remained to them; of making the time fly faster. Their conversation had the peculiar character of everything that draws inexorably to a close; the most insignificant little things they said seemed to become on this day mysterious and supreme.

In the last minute of the departure Yann took his

wife in his arms, and they clung to each other without
saying any further word, in a long silent embrace.

He embarked; the grey sails were unfurled and
spread themselves to a light wind which rose in the
west. He, whom she recognized still, waved his
bonnet in the time-honoured manner. And she
watched him for long, watched her Yann, in silhouette against the sea, slowly drawing away. It
was still he, that little human figure standing there,
black against the ashy-blue of the waters—and
already indistinct, lost in that distance in which the
eyes, if they seek to pierce it, become dim and cease
to see. . . .

And as the *Léopoldine* drew away Gaud, as if drawn
by a magnet, followed on foot along the cliffs.

She had soon to stop, however, for the land came
to an end; she sat down then at the foot of a last tall
cross, which stands there amid the furze and the
rocks. And as it was an elevated point, the sea seen
from there seemed in the distance to slope upwards,
so that the *Léopoldine*, as it drew away, appeared to
rise gradually, very small, on the slope of an immense
circle. The sea had long slow undulations—like the
last counterstrokes of some tumult which had raged
elsewhere, beyond the horizon; but, in the deep field
of vision where Yann was still, all remained peaceful.

Gaud continued to watch, striving to fix in her
memory the physiognomy of this boat, the silhouette
of its canvas and hull, in order that she might recognize it from afar, when it returned, might look out
for it in this same place.

Enormous uprollings of water continued to come
in from the west, regularly one after the other, without
ceasing, without respite, renewing their futile effort,
breaking on the same rocks, sweeping over the same

places to inundate the same strands. And, in the end, it seemed a strange thing, this weighty movement of the waters with this calmness of air and sky; it was as if the bed of the sea, over-filled, was striving to find an outlet and invade the shore.

Meanwhile, the *Léopoldine* became smaller and smaller, distant, lost. No doubt currents were bearing her away, for she was moving rapidly, although the wind, this evening, was light. Become a little grey spot, almost a point, she would soon reach the extreme edge of the circle of visible things, and enter the infinities beyond, where darkness was beginning to reign.

At seven o'clock, when the night had fallen and the boat had disappeared, Gaud returned to her home, brave enough in the main, despite the tears which still filled her eyes. How different it would have been, after all, and how much more empty and gloomy her life would have seemed if he had departed once more as in the two last years, without even a good-bye! Now everything was changed, sweetened; this Yann so much belonged to her, she felt herself so much beloved notwithstanding this departure, that, in returning all alone to her dwelling, she had at least the consolation and the delicious expectancy of that *au revoir* which they had said to each other for the autumn. . . .

CHAPTER III

THE summer passed, melancholy, warm, tranquil
——she waiting for the first yellowing of the leaves,
the first gatherings of the swallows, the sprouting of
the chrysanthemums.

She had written to him many times, by the Reikiavik packet and by the *Chasers*; but she was not sure
that these letters had reached him.

At the end of July she received one from him.   He
informed her that he was in good health on the 10th
of that month, that the prospects for the fishing
season were excellent, and that he had already some
fifteen hundred fish to his credit.   From beginning
to end it was written in the simple style and copied
from the uniform model of all the letters from these
Icelanders to their family.   Men brought up as Yann
was are absolutely ignorant of how to write of
the things they think and feel and dream.   Better
educated than he, she was able to make allowance for
that and to read between the lines the deep tenderness
which was not expressed.   On many occasions in the
course of these four pages he addressed her by the
name of wife, as if he took pleasure in repeating it,
and, moreover, the address itself: *To Madame Marguerite Gaos, Maison Moan, Ploubazlanec*, was a
thing she read over and over again with happiness.
She had yet had so little time to be called Madame
Marguerite Gaos! . . .

CHAPTER IV

SHE worked hard during these summer months.
The ladies of Paimpol, who at first were distrustful
of her talent as an improvised worker, saying that
her hands were too soft and white, had discovered,
on the contrary, that she excelled in making dresses
which set off their figures to advantage; so that she
had become almost a dressmaker of renown.

What she earned went to embellish the home—for
his return. The wardrobe, the old press-beds, were
repaired, waxed, and their ironwork shone; she had
had the window looking on the sea glazed and had
hung it with curtains; bought a new quilt for the
winter, a table, and some chairs.

All this, without touching the money which her
Yann had left with her on departing, which she kept
intact in a little Chinese box, to show him on his
arrival.

During the summer evenings, in the fading light,
sitting in front of the door with Grand'mère Yvonne,
whose head and ideas were sensibly better during the
warm weather, she knitted for Yann a handsome
fisherman's jersey of blue wool; on the borders of the
collar and the cuffs there were marvels of complicated
and open-work stitches; Grand'mère Yvonne who, in
her day, had been a skilful knitter had recalled little
by little the processes of her youth, and had taught
them to her. And it was a work which had taken a
great deal of wool, for it needed a big jersey for Yann.

And presently, especially in the evening, she began

to be aware of the shortening of the days; certain plants, which had given all their growth in July, had already taken on a yellow, withered look, and the violet scabious, flowering again on the roadside, were smaller, and longer in the stalk; and finally the last days of August came and the first of the Iceland boats appeared one evening, off the headland of Pors-Even. The festival of the return had begun.

A crowd gathered on the cliff to welcome it—which was it?

It was the *Samuel-Azénide*—always the first to return.

'Depend upon it,' said Yann's old father, 'the *Léopoldine* will not be long now; out there, I know it well, when one begins to leave, the others are not long in following.'

CHAPTER V

THEY were coming back, the Icelanders.   Two the second day, four the day after, and twelve in the following week.   And, in the countryside, happiness came back with them; there was rejoicing among the wives, among the mothers; rejoicing also in the taverns where the fair damsels of Paimpol filled the glasses of the fishermen.

The *Léopoldine* remained one of the tardy ones; there were still ten missing.   She could not be much longer, and Gaud, reckoning that in another week at the outside, which she allowed to avoid disappointment, Yann would be home again—Gaud was in a fever of eager expectancy, keeping the house in apple-pie order, very clean and very neat, for his reception.   All arranged as it was there was nothing left to do, and, in any case, she was beginning to be too impatient to give much thought to anything.

Three more of the stragglers arrived, and then five. There were now only two missing.

'Well,' they said to her, laughing, 'this year it is the *Léopoldine* or the *Marie-Jeanne* that will bring up the rear of the return.'

And Gaud laughed also, very animated and very pretty, in the joy of her expectancy.

CHAPTER VI

MEANWHILE, the days went by.

She continued to dress herself up, to assume a cheerful air, to go down to the harbour to talk with the others. She said it was quite natural, this delay. Did it not happen every year? And then they were such good sailors, and the boats were two such good boats!

Afterwards, when she was back in her home, there came to her in the evening the first little tremors of fear, of anguish.

Was it really possible that she should begin to fear so soon? Was there any reason for it?

And she became alarmed, she was really afraid. . . .

CHAPTER VII

THE tenth of September! . . . How the days sped!

One morning when there was already a cold mist over the land, a real autumn morning, the rising sun found her sitting very early beneath the porch of the chapel of the shipwrecked, in the place where the bereaved go to pray—sitting with fixed eyes and temples compressed as in a ring of iron.

Two days before, these melancholy morning mists had begun, and on this morning Gaud had awakened with an uneasiness made more poignant by this impression of winter. . . . What was there about this day, this hour, this minute, that made it different from those that had gone before? . . . One often sees boats delayed a fortnight, even a month.

Yet there must, no doubt, have been something special about this morning, since she had come for the first time to sit under this chapel porch, and to read again the names of young men dead.

In memory of
GAOS, YVON, lost at sea,
In the neighbourhood of Norden-Fiord. . . .

.   .   .   .   .

With what seemed like a great shudder a gust of wind rose from the sea, and, at the same time, came the sound of something falling, like rain, on the vault above; dead leaves! . . . A flight of them entered the porch; the old beruffled trees of the chapel yard

were defoliating, shaken by the ocean wind.   Winter
was at hand!

                . . . lost at sea,
        In the neighbourhood of Norden-Fiord,
in the hurricane of the 4th and 5th of August 1880.

    .   .   .   .   .

She read mechanically, and, through the ogive of
the door, her eyes sought the distant sea; this morning
it was very indistinct, under the grey mist, and a
suspended shag trailed over the distance like an
immense curtain of mourning.

Another gust; more dead leaves which entered in a
mad dance.   A stronger gust, as if this west wind,
which had formerly sown these dead in the sea, wanted
still to torment even these inscriptions which recalled
their names to the living.

Gaud gazed, with an involuntary persistence, at
an empty place on the wall, which seemed to be
waiting with a grim obsession; she was pursued by the
idea of a new plaque, which it would be necessary
perhaps to place there soon, with another name which,
even in spirit, she did not dare to read in such a place.

She was cold, and remained sitting on the granite
bench, her head leaning back against the wall.

    . . . Lost in the neighbourhood of Norden-Fiord,
        in the hurricane of the 4th and 5th of August.

                Aged 23 years.

            May he rest in peace!

Iceland appeared to her, with its little cemetery—
distant Iceland, illumined from below by the midnight sun. . . . And, suddenly, always in this same
empty space on the wall which seemed to be waiting

—she had, with a horrible clearness, the vision of this new plaque of which she was thinking: a freshly-painted plaque, a skull and crossbones and in the middle, amid flourishes, a name, the adored name, 'Yann Gaos'! And she rose abruptly to her feet, and a hoarse cry came from her throat, as if she had gone mad. . . .

Outside, the grey mist of the morning still hung over the land; and the dead leaves still continued to enter in a whirlwind dance.

Footsteps in the lane! . . . Someone was coming?

Then she rose and stood erect; with a deft touch adjusted her coif, composed her features. The footsteps drew near; whoever it was was going to enter. Quickly she assumed an air of being there by chance, unwilling yet, on any account, to assume the guise of a wife of one lost at sea.

As it happened it was Fante Floury, the wife of the mate in the *Léopoldine*. She understood at once what Gaud was doing there; pretence was useless with her. And at first they remained silent, looking at each other, the two women, their fears augmented, angry at meeting thus in the same sentiment of terror, moved almost to a feeling of hate.

'All those from Tréguier and Saint-Brieuc got back a week ago,' Fante said at last, pitilessly, in a harsh and querulous tone.

She was carrying a candle to make a vow.

Ah! Yes. . . . A vow. . . . Gaud had been unwilling, so far, to think of this recourse of those desolate. But she entered the chapel behind Fante, without speaking, and they knelt down side by side like two sisters.

And ardently they prayed, with all their soul, to the Virgin Star-of-the-Sea. And, presently, there was no sound but the sound of sobbing, and their urgent tears began to fall to the ground. . . .

They got up more reconciled, more confident. Fante assisted Gaud who staggered and, taking her in her arms, kissed her.

Having dried their tears, smoothed their hair, brushed the saltpetre and dust of the flagstones from their skirts where they had knelt on them, they went their different ways without saying anything more to each other.

CHAPTER VIII

THIS latter part of September resembled another summer, except that it was a little melancholy. The weather indeed was so fine this year, that had it not been for the dead leaves which fell in a sad rain on the roads, one might have thought it was the merry month of June. The husbands, the fiancés, the lovers had returned, and everywhere there was the joy of a second springtime of love. . . .

One day, at last, one of the two tardy Iceland boats was signalled in the offing. Which? . . .

Quickly the groups of women gathered, silent, anxious, on the cliffs.

Gaud, trembling and pale, was there by the side of the father of her Yann.

'I do believe,' said the old fisherman, 'I do believe it's them! A red sheer-rail, a rolled topsail, that looks very like them; what do you say, Gaud, my girl?'

'And yet no,' he continued, with sudden discouragement; 'no, we are disappointed again, the boom is not like and they have a mizzen-sail. Well, well, not them this time, it's the *Marie-Jeanne*. But it's all right, my girl, they'll not be long now.'

And day followed day; and night came in its turn with an inexorable tranquillity.

She continued to wear her best dress, a little recklessly, impelled still by the fear of resembling the wife of one shipwrecked, getting angry when others assumed towards her an air of compassion and

mystery, turning away her eyes so as not to meet
these glances which chilled her.

She had now made it a habit to go in the morning
to the furthermost point of the land, along the high
cliffs of Pors-Even, passing behind the paternal home
of Yann, so as not to be seen by his mother or his
little sisters. She went alone to the extreme edge of
this district of Ploubazlanec, which stretches out like
a reindeer's horn into the Channel, and sat there all
day long at the foot of a solitary cross which dominates
the immense distances of the water. . . .

These granite crosses rise up everywhere on the
advanced cliffs of this mariners' land, as if beseeching
mercy; as if seeking to appease the great, moving,
mysterious thing, which lures men and does not give
them back, keeping by preference the most valiant,
the most beautiful.

Around this cross of Pors-Even there were plains
eternally green, carpeted with short furze. And, at
this height, the sea air was very pure, filled with the
delicious perfumes of September, and having but a
slight odour of seaweed.

One could see, outlined into the far distance, one
beyond the other, all the indentations of the coast;
the land of Brittany ended in denticulated points
which stretched out into the tranquil emptiness of
the waters.

In the foreground rocks riddled its surface; but
beyond, nothing disturbed its mirror-like polish; it
gave out a scarcely perceptible caressing noise, soft
and immense, which ascended from the depth of all
the bays. And the distances were so calm, the depths
so still! The great blue emptiness, the tomb of the
Gaoses, preserved its impenetrable mystery, while the
breezes, light as zephyrs, carried with them the

perfume of the broom which had flowered again in the last sunshine of autumn.

At certain regular hours the sea receded and large patches appeared as if the Channel were being slowly emptied; afterwards, with the same slowness, the waters rose, continuing their eternal coming and going, without any thought of the dead.

And Gaud, sitting at the foot of her cross, remained there, in the midst of these tranquillities, watching, watching, until darkness fell, until she could see no more.

CHAPTER IX

SEPTEMBER had come to an end.   She no longer took
any nourishment, she no longer slept.

She remained now within her home, sitting dejec-
tedly, her hands in her lap, her head thrown back and
supported against the wall behind.   What was the
good of getting up, what was the good of lying down?
She threw herself on her bed without undressing when
she became too utterly exhausted.   Otherwise she
remained there, sitting always, benumbed; her teeth
chattered with the cold, in her immobility; she still
had that impression of a ring of iron compressing her
temples.   She felt that her cheeks were drooping,
her mouth was dry, with a taste of fever, and from
time to time she uttered a hoarse groan, repeated
spasmodically and continuing for long, while her head
beat against the granite of the wall.

And at times she called him by name, very tenderly,
in a low voice, as if he had been near her, and murmured to him words of love.

It happened sometimes that she thought of other
things than he, of small, insignificant things.   She
beguiled herself, for example, with watching the
shadow of the faïence Virgin and of the holy water
font lengthen slowly, in proportion as the light failed,
on the high woodwork of her bed.   And then her
anguish would begin anew, more horrible, and she
cried out once more, her head beating against the wall.

And all the hours of the day passed, one after
another, and all the hours of the evening, and all those

of the night, and all those of the morning. When she reckoned up how long it was since he should have returned, her terror increased; she wished to know neither the dates nor the names of the days.

Ordinarily there comes news of the shipwrecks of Iceland; those who return have seen the drama from a distance; or perhaps some wreckage has been found, or a body; there is some indication from which the truth may be surmised. But of the *Léopoldine* there was nothing; nothing had been seen, nothing was known. The crew of the *Marie-Jeanne*, the last who had seen her, on the 2nd of August, said that she must have gone to fish farther north; after that all was impenetrable mystery.

To wait and wait, and to know nothing. When would the hour come in which she would finally have to give up hope? She did not know even this, but now she was eager almost that it should be soon.

Oh, if he was dead, would not someone, out of pity, tell her so! . . .

Oh, if she might but see him as he was now—him or what remained of him! . . . If only the Virgin in answer to her prayers, or some other power, would do her the favour, by a kind of second sight, of letting her see her Yann!—see him living, manœuvring to enter the harbour—or else his body rolled about the sea . . . so that she might be sure, so that she might know!

Sometimes the notion suddenly came to her that a sail had appeared, on the edge of the horizon: the *Léopoldine*, approaching, hastening to port! And she made a first unreflecting movement to get up, to run and scan the circle of the waters, to see if it were true. . . .

But she sank back again, hopeless. Alas! Where was she now, this *Léopoldine*? Where could she be? Far away, no doubt, far away, in that awful distance of Iceland, abandoned, crumbling, lost. . . .

And at the end came this haunting vision, always the same: a wreck, broken open and empty; rocked in a silent sea of rosy grey; rocked slowly, noiselessly, with an extreme gentleness, in irony, amid a great calm of dead waters.

CHAPTER X

Two o'clock in the morning.

It was at night especially that she was most attentive to all the footsteps that approached; at the least stir, at the least unaccustomed sound her temples beat violently.

Two o'clock in the morning. On this night, as on others, her hands joined, her eyes open in the darkness, she was listening to the wind making its eternal noise over the barren plain.

A man's footsteps suddenly, hurrying footsteps in the road! At such an hour who could be passing? She got up, stirred to the depths of her being, her heart ceasing to beat. . . .

The sounds stopped before the door; someone was coming up the little stone steps. . . .

Yann! Oh! Heaven be praised. Yann! There came a knock. Was it possible it should be someone else? She was standing, her feet bare; she who had been so weak for so many days had leapt up nimbly like a cat, her arms open to enfold the loved one. The *Léopoldine*, no doubt, had arrived in the night and anchored opposite in the bay of Pors-Even—and her Yann had hastened to her; she had arranged all this in her head with the swiftness of lightning. And now she lacerated her fingers on the nails of the door in her impatience to draw back the bolt which was stiff. . . .

Ah! And then she recoiled slowly, collapsing, her

head falling on her breast. Her beautiful, mad-brained dream was over. It was only Fantec, their neighbour. And as soon as she realized that it was only he, that nothing of her Yann had passed in the air, she felt herself sinking by degrees into her same dark gulf, even to the very bottom of her same hideous despair.

He begged her pardon, poor Fantec: his wife, as they knew, was very ill, and now their child was choking in his cradle, seized with some affection of the throat; and so he had come to ask for assistance, while he went straightaway to fetch the doctor from Paimpol. . . .

What had all that to do with her? Become wild in her grief, she had no longer anything to give to the sufferings of others. Sunk down on a bench, she remained before him with staring eyes, like one dead, without answering him, not listening to him, not even looking at him. What had they to do with her, the things this man was talking about?

He understood then . . . he realized why the door had been opened to him so quickly, and he was sorry for the suffering he had been the means of causing.

He stuttered out an apology.

It was true that he ought not to have disturbed her . . . her! . . .

'Me!' replied Gaud quickly, 'and why not *me*, Fantec?'

Life came back to her suddenly, for she did not want yet to be regarded by others as one bereaved, emphatically she did not want that. And then in her turn she was sorry for him; she dressed herself in order to follow him, and found strength to go and look after his child.

When she returned to throw herself on her bed, sleep came to her for a brief time so great was her weariness.

But that moment of immense joy had left an imprint in her mind which, in spite of all, was persistent. She woke up presently with a shock, and half rose, with a memory of something. . . . There had been some news concerning Yann. . . . Amid the confusion of ideas which came to her she tried to remember, she tried to remember what it was. . . .

'Oh, nothing, alas! . . . Nothing but Fantec.'

And, a second time, she sank to the deep depths of her same abysm. No, in reality, nothing was changed in her mournful, hopeless waiting.

Nevertheless, the fact of having felt that he was so near made it seem as if something emanated from him was hovering about her; it was what is called in Brittany an omen; and she listened more attentively to the footsteps outside, having a presentiment that someone perhaps might enter who would speak of him.

And, in fact, when day came, Yann's father entered. He took off his bonnet, brushed back his handsome white hair, which curled like that of his son, and sat down near Gaud's bed.

He, too, was sore at heart, for his Yann, his handsome Yann, was his eldest, his best-beloved, his glory. But he did not despair, really he did not, he did not despair yet. He began to reassure Gaud very gently; first of all the last arrivals from Iceland had all spoken of the very dense fog which might well have delayed the boat: and secondly, and he laid much stress on this, an idea had come to him: they might have called at the Faroë Islands, which are distant islands on the way, and letters from there take a long time to come; that had happened to him, some forty years ago, and his poor dead mother had even had masses said for

his soul. . . . A fine boat like the *Léopoldine*, with
such fine sailors as they all were on board . . .

Old Yvonne hovered round them, shaking her head;
the distress of her adopted granddaughter had restored
to her something of strength and intelligence. She
busied herself about the room, looking from time to
time at the little faded portrait of her Sylvestre,
hanging on the granite of the wall with his sailor's
anchors and his memorial crown of black beads. No,
since the calling of the sea had bereft her of her own
grandson, she believed no longer in the return of
sailors; if she prayed to the Virgin it was out of fear
—a lip service rendered by her poor withered old lips;
in her heart there was a deep rancour.

But Gaud listened greedily to these consoling
things, her large, dark-ringed eyes gazed with a deep
tenderness at this old man who was so like her beloved
one; merely to have him there was a protection against
death, and she felt reassured, nearer to her Yann. Her
tears fell, silent and comforting, and she said once
more to herself her ardent prayers to the Virgin Star-
of-the-Sea.

They had put in to these islands, for repairs,
perhaps; it was a thing quite possible. She got up,
smoothed her hair, dressed herself, as if he might yet
return. No doubt all was not lost, since he, his father,
did not despair. And, for some days still, she
continued to wait.

It was autumn now, the late autumn, and the night
fell mournfully at an early hour, making all dark in
the old cottage, all dark also in the old Breton countryside round.

The very days seemed to be only twilights; immense
clouds, passing slowly, would suddenly bring obscurity
at midday. The wind moaned constantly, with a

noise like the distant sound of a great church organ, playing an angry and disconsolate air; and there were times when it seemed to come close to the door, roaring there like a wild beast.

She had become very pale, and carried herself in a dejected way, as if age had already brushed her with its bald wing. Very frequently she went to Yann's clothes, unfolding and refolding them like a mad-woman—especially one of his blue woollen jerseys which had preserved the shape of his body; when it was laid gently on the table, it outlined of itself, as if automatically, the shape of his shoulders and his chest; so that in the end she had placed it alone, on a shelf of their wardrobe, unwilling to disturb it any more lest it should lose the loved impress.

Every evening now a cold mist rose from the ground; and she looked out from her window on the mournful plain, where here and there little tails of white smoke commenced to issue from the cottages of her neighbours; everywhere the men had come home, wandering birds brought back by the cold. And before many of these fires the evenings must have been very happy; for the renewal of love had begun with the winter in this country of the Icelanders. . . .

Clinging to the idea of the call at those remote islands, hoping still with a kind of hope, she waited, waited. . . .

· · · · ·

CHAPTER XI

HE never returned.

One night in August, in the waters of sombre Iceland, amid a great fury of sound, his wedding with the sea had been celebrated.

With the sea which formerly had also been his nurse; she it was who had rocked him, who had reared him tall and strong—and in the end she had taken him, in the glory of his manhood, for her own. Dark clouds moved overhead, shifting, tormented curtains, spread to conceal the nuptial feast, and the bride roared with a mighty horrible voice to drown his cries. He, mindful of Gaud, his wife of the flesh, had resisted, in a gigantic struggle, this wife of the tomb. Until the moment came when he surrendered, his arms open to receive her, with a great cry like the dying roar of a bull, his mouth already filled with water; his arms open, outspread and rigid for ever.

And at his wedding they were all there, those whom long before he had invited. All, except Sylvestre, who had fallen asleep in an enchanted garden—far away, on the other side of the earth. . . .

EVERYMAN'S LIBRARY: A Selected List

BIOGRAPHY

CLASSICAL

ESSAYS AND BELLES-LETTRES

FICTION

ROMANCE

SCIENCE

THEOLOGY AND PHILOSOPHY

TRAVEL AND TOPOGRAPHY

FRANÇOIS MAURIAC

FRANÇOIS MAURIAC

THE WEAKLING

and

THE ENEMY

TRANSLATED BY GERARD HOPKINS

NEW YORK
PELLEGRINI & CUDAHY

THE WEAKLING was published in French under the title LE SAGOUIN Copyright 1951 by Librairie Plon

THE ENEMY was published in French under the title LE MAL Copyright 1935 by Editions Bernard Grasset

Library of Congress Catalog Card Number: 52-5923

Copyright 1952 by Pellegrini & Cudahy

THE WEAKLING

1

"WHY go on saying that you know your lesson, when it's quite obvious that you don't? . . . . You just learned it off by heart, didn't you now?"

There was the sound of a slap.

"Go to your room, and don't let me set eyes on you till dinner-time!"

The child raised his hand to his face and felt it gingerly, as though his jaw had been broken.

"Ooh! that did hurt!" (he might as well make the most of his advantage) "I'll tell Mamie, you see if I don't! . . ."

In an access of fury, Paula grabbed her son's skinny arm, and administered a second slap.

"Mamie, eh? . . . well, here's something for you to go whining to your father about! . . . . what are you waiting for? . . . get out of my sight!"

She pushed him into the passage, shut the door, then opened it again to fling lesson books and notebooks after the retreating Guillaume. Still snivelling, he squatted down on his heels and picked them up. There was a sudden silence; not so much as the sound of a snuffle in the darkness. At last she had got rid of him!

She listened to his departing footsteps. It was pretty certain that he would not seek refuge with his father, and, since his grandmother, his "Mamie," was out, pleading his cause with the schoolmaster, it would be the kitchen he'd make for, to get a little sympathy from Fraülein. He was probably at it already, taking a surreptitious lick at the cooking food under the sentimental eyes of the Austrian woman. "I can as good as see him doing it. . . ." What Paula saw, when she thought about her son, was a picture of knock-knees, skinny legs, and socks festooned untidily over his shoes. This little scrap of humanity, this flesh of her flesh, had eyes the color of ripe blackberries, but of them she took no account. On the other hand, she was horribly conscious, with bitter loathing, of the sagging, adenoidal mouth and the drooling lower lip. It was less prominent than his father's, but it was enough for Paula that it reminded her of a mouth she hated.

Rage flooded her mind—rage?—or was it just exasperation? It is no easy thing to tell where exasperation ends and hate begins. She went back into the room, and paused for a moment in front of the wardrobe looking-glass. Each year, when autumn came round, she put on the same old knitted jersey of greenish wool which had grown too big for her round the neck. No amount of cleaning could keep the stains from reappearing. The brown skirt, spattered with mud, stuck out in front as though she were with child—though, thank God, there was no fear of that!

"Baronne de Cernès"—she muttered to herself—"the Baronne Galéas de Cernès. Paula de Cernès." Her lips parted in a smile which brought no gaiety to the bilious cheeks with their thick growth of down (the Cernès urchins made a great joke of Madame Galéas' whiskers!). She stood there, laughing to her-

4

self, and thinking of the girl she once had been who, thirteen years earlier, before another mirror, had stood nerving herself to take the plunge with repetition of the selfsame words: "The Baron and the Baronne Galéas de Cernès. . . . *M. Constant Meulière, sometime Mayor of Bordeaux, and Madame Meulière, take pleasure in announcing the marriage of their niece, Paula Meulière, to the Baron Galéas de Cernès.*"

Neither uncle nor aunt, eager though they were to be rid of her, had urged the taking of that lunatic step. They had even warned her against it. What school influence was it that had bred in her a weakness for titles?—to what pressure had she yielded? Today she could find no answer to that question. Perhaps mere curiosity had been the reason, or the longing to force an entry into a forbidden world. . . . She had never forgotten the groups of aristocratic children in the City Park—the Curzays, the Pichon-Longuevilles—in whose games there could never have been a question of her joining. The Mayor's niece had circled in vain about those arrogant scions of a nobler race. . . . "Mamma says we mustn't play with you. . . ." The grown girl had, no doubt, sought to avenge the snubbed child. Her marriage, she had thought, would open a way for her into the unknown, would be the harbor from which she could set sail for unimagined splendors. She knew all right today what people meant when they spoke of "closed circles": only too well she knew! To enter this one had seemed hard enough, almost impossible—but not so hard, not so impossible, as getting out of it again!

And for that she had thrown away her life! To have said she felt at moments a regret, would have been to indulge in understatement! Even obsession was too weak a word! Her hideous fate had only too real a body. Never a moment passed but she was conscious of it. It was there to be seen, the embodiment of idiotic vanity, of criminal stupidity, the sign and symbol of an ineluctable destiny. To make matters worse, she was not even "Madame la Baronne." There was only one Madame la Baronne, her ancient mother-in-law. Paula would never be anything but Madame Galéas. Her imbecile husband's outlandish name had become her own, so that she was bound still closer, if that were possible, to the ruin she had married and made her own forever.

At night, the mockery of her life, the horror that came with the thought that she had sold herself for a golden vanity of which she could not enjoy even the shadow, filled her mind and kept her sleepless until morning. If she sought distraction in imagined fantasies—not seldom filthy—the rock-bottom of her thought remained immovable. All night long she lay in the darkness, struggling to clamber from the pit into which she had fallen of her own free will, knowing there was no escape. Whatever the season of year, night for her was always the same. In the Carolina poplars near the window the owls in autumn hooted to the moon like baying dogs, but they were infinitely less hateful than the implacable nightingales of spring. The sense of rage, of desperation at having been duped was always waiting for her when she woke, especially in winter, to the sound of Fraülein's heavy-handed drawing of the curtains. Emerging from the mists of sleep, she saw through the windows a few ghosts of trees, still hung with tattered leaves, waving their blackened branches in the eddying fog.

And yet, those were the best times of her day, those morning

6

moments when she could lie torpid in the snug warmth of the half-deserted bed. Little Guillaume was only too glad to forget the duty of the day's first kiss. Quite often Paula could hear, beyond the door, the voice of the old Baronne, urging the boy to go in and say good morning to his mother. Though she detested her daughter-in-law, she would make no compromise with principle. Then Guillaume would slip into the room and stand for a moment on the threshold, all eyes for the terrifying head upon the pillows with its hair drawn tightly back upon the temples to reveal a narrow, vaguely defined forehead, and a yellow cheek (with the mole nestling in a tuft of black hair) to which he would hastily press his lips. He knew in advance that his mother would wipe away the hasty salutation, and say, with disgust sounding in her voice, "You always make me so wet. . . ."

She no longer struggled against her feeling of disgust. Was it her fault that she could get nothing from the wretched creature? What could she do with a sly and backward child who always knew that his grandmother and old Fraülein would back him up? But now even the Baronne was growing sensible. She had agreed to see what she could do with the schoolmaster—an irreligious schoolmaster, to be sure, but that couldn't be helped. The curé had three parishes to serve, and lived over a mile away. On two separate occasions, once in 1917, and again in 1918, they had tried the experiment of boarding Guillaume away from home, first with the Jesuits at Sarlat, then at a small Seminary in the Lower Pyrenees. But he had been sent back after a term. The nasty little creature soiled his sheets. Neither the Jesuits, nor the Seminarists, were equipped, especially not just then, to deal with backward, or with sickly, boys.

How would this schoolmaster, with his curly hair and laughing eyes, a veteran of Verdun, welcome the old Baronne? Would he feel flattered that she had put herself out for him? Paula had managed to get herself excused. She lacked the courage now to face strangers, least of all this brilliant teacher. She was terrified of him. The Cernès bailiff, Arthur Lousteau, though a strong adherent of the *Action française,* was full of admiration for him, was convinced that he would go far. . . . The old Baronne, like all the country gentry, thought Paula, had a way with the "natives." She knew the subtleties of local patois. One of the few things about her which still had power to charm was the outworn elegance with which she spoke that ancient tongue. . . . Yes, but this socialist schoolmaster had other origins, and the Baronne's excessive affability might seem to him insulting. The affected pretense of seeming not to notice social differences no longer appealed to young men of his type. Still, after all, he had been wounded at Verdun, and that would create a bond with the old lady, whose younger son, Georges de Cernès had been reported "missing" in Champagne.

Paula opened the window, and saw, at the far end of the avenue, the Baronne's bent, emaciated figure. She was leaning heavily on her stick. A black straw hat was perched high on her piled hair. She moved between the elms which seemed ablaze, herself all glowing in the light of the setting sun. Paula could see that she was talking and gesturing. That she should be so agitated was no good sign. The young woman went down the great double staircase which was the glory of Cernès, and met her in the hall.

"A boor, my dear, as was only to be expected."

"Did he refuse? Are you sure you didn't rub him the wrong way? I do hope you didn't put on your grand manner . . . I told you . . ."

The elder lady shook her head, but her denial was only the automatic protest of the very old, which seems to be saying "No" to death. An artificial white flower trembled ludicrously on her straw hat. Her eyes were dim with tears which would not flow.

"What excuse did he make?"

"He said that he was too busy . . . that his work as the Mayor's secretary left him no leisure. . . ."

"He must have cooked up a better story than that. . . ."

"I assure you that he did not. He spoke only of his work. He didn't, he said, want anything to 'interfere with it'. . . ."

The Baronne de Cernès clung heavily to the banisters, and kept stopping for breath. Her daughter-in-law followed slowly, climbing the stairs behind her, questioning her all the time with that nagging obstinacy of which she was so little aware. She noticed, however, that she was frightening the old lady, and made an effort to lower her voice. But the words still hissed between her clenched teeth.

"Why did you say at first that he behaved like a boor?"

The Baronne sat down on the landing sofa. She was still shaking her head, and a grimace, which might have been a smile, was agitating her lips. Paula raised her voice again: had she or had she not accused the schoolmaster of boorishness?

"No, my dear, no . . . I was guilty of exaggeration. Maybe I misunderstood . . . Quite possibly the young man was innocent of intentional offense . . . I may have read meanings into his words which were not there."

But Paula would not desist. What meanings? What had he said?

"It was when he asked me why we had not applied to the curé. I told him that the curé does not live here, that he has three parishes on his hands. Do you know what that wretched schoolteacher had the effrontery to say? . . . but, no, it'll only make you angry . . ."

"What did he say? I won't give you a moment's peace until you tell me exactly what he said."

"Well, he told me with a snigger that on one point, it seemed, he saw eye to eye with the curé. Neither of them liked entanglements, and he certainly had no intention of getting himself mixed up with the great house. Oh, *I* knew well enough what he meant, and I would have you know that if he hadn't been wounded at Verdun, I would have made him explain himself more explicitly. *I'd* have known how to defend you!"

Paula's rage fell suddenly to silence. She hung her head, and, without another word, hurried downstairs, and took her cloak which was hanging in the hall.

The Baronne waited until the front door had closed behind her. This time there was no doubt about the smile which disclosed her discolored dentures. Leaning over the stair-rail, she spat out the three words—"*That* got you!", and then, in a cracked but piercing voice, cried out suddenly—"Galéas! Guillou!—darlings!"

She was not kept long waiting for an answer. It came from the remote depths of the service wing, from the kitchen: "Mamie! Maminette!" Father and son came dashing up the stairs, making no noise in their stockinged feet. Her call had meant that, for a time at least, the enemy had gone. They could get together now and sit round the lamp in Mamie's room.

Galéas took his mother's arm. He was wearing an old brown woolly. His shoulders were narrow and sloping, his disproportionately large head was covered with a great mat of hair. There was a childlike charm about his eyes, but the drooling, open mouth and thick tongue were horrible. His trousers hung loose above his feet, and sagged in great folds about his skeleton legs.

Guillaume had taken Mamie's other hand, and was rubbing his cheek against it. Of her words he retained only those that concerned him nearly. The schoolmaster didn't want to be bothered with him; he wouldn't have to stand trembling under those appraising eyes. The shadow of that particular monster was growing less. All else that Mamie had said was incomprehensible. "I got a good one in on your mother!"—A good one? What was that? The three of them entered the beloved room. Guillaume made for his corner between the *prie-Dieu* and the bed. In the back of the *prie-Dieu* there was a tiny cupboard filled with broken rosaries. One of them, with mother-of-pearl beads, had been blessed by the Pope: another, of olive stones, had been brought back by Mamie from Jerusalem. There was a metal box made in the shape of St. Peter's at Rome. It had been one of Galéas' christening presents, and bore his name in silver letters. There were prayer-books crammed with pictures showing the smiling features of the dead. Mamie and papa were whispering together under the lamp. A fire of logs threw vivid gleams into the corners of the room. Mamie took from the drawer in the pedestal table a greasy pack of tiny cards.

"We shan't be disturbed until dinner-time, Galéas: you can play the piano."

She was soon absorbed in her game of Patience. The piano had been brought into this room, filled though it was to bursting with assorted furniture, because Paula could not bear to listen to her husband's strumming. Guillaume knew in advance what the tunes would be. His father would play them in exactly the same order. First, the *Turkish Patrol*. Every evening Guillou waited for the same wrong note in the same place. Sometimes Galéas would talk while he was playing. His toneless voice sounded as though it were still at the breaking stage.

"This schoolmaster's a red, isn't he, mamma? As red as red —at least, that's what Lousteau says."

The *Turkish Patrol* resumed its uncertain course. A picture rose before Guillaume's eyes of the red man all smeared with ox blood. Not that he didn't know him well by sight—a limping figure, always bareheaded, and leaning on a handsome ebony cane. The red must be hidden by his clothes. Red like a fish. The last of the daylight still showed between the drawn curtains. Mamma would go wandering about the country till dinner-time, as she always did when she was in a particularly bad temper. She would come back, hatless, with mud on the bottom of her dress. She would smell of sweat. As soon as dinner was over, she would go to bed. They would be able to have a good hour together in front of Mamie's fire. Fraülein came in, tall and fat and flabby. She always found some excuse to join them when the enemy was out tramping the roads. Would they like their chestnuts boiled or roasted? Had she better do an egg for Guillou? She brought with her into grandmamma's room a mixed smell of onions and washing-up. This asking of her employers' wishes was a pure formality. Guillou would have his egg . . . (he had been so called since the war on account of his being unlucky enough to have the same name as the Kaiser—or "késer" as the Baronne pronounced it).

Already they were talking of "her." "She told me my kitchen was dirty . . . so I said that I was mistress in my own kitchen. . . ." Guillaume could see Mamie and papa stretching their skinny necks, the better to hear what Fraülein was saying. To him it was of no interest whatever, since for other people he felt neither hate nor love. His grandmother, his father, Fraülein provided that climate of security which he found so necessary, from which his mother fought tooth and nail to drive him, like a ferret attacking a rabbit deep in its warren. At no matter what cost, he had got to come out, and, dazed, bewildered, submit to her furious rages. When that happened he just rolled himself into a ball and waited for the storm to pass. Thanks, however, to the state of warfare that was forever smoldering between the grown-ups, he could, to some extent, live his life in peace. He hid behind Fraülein. The Austrian woman spread over him a bulky shadow of protection. Mamie's bedroom might be a safer refuge than the kitchen, but he knew better than to trust Mamie, or to rely upon the kindness of her words and gestures. Fraülein was somebody apart. With a love that was half a passion of the flesh, she brooded over her chick, her duckling. She it was who gave him his bath, and soaped him with her old hands, which were so chapped and dirty.

Meanwhile, Paula had turned into the path which led off to the left from the front steps. She reached, unseen, a narrow lane behind the stableyard. It was almost always deserted. She strode along it like a man. As a rule she went nowhere, but this evening her progress was marked by a strange air of haste. Walking, she could the more easily chew over the words spoken by the schoolmaster, and told her by her mother-in-law, those veiled references to the gossip about her and the late curé. The knowledge that she, and none but she, had built the prison in which she now lived, was ever a horror with her. It might have been tolerable—or so she thought—but for the shame that had fallen upon her during the first year of her married life. Inevitably she was a branded criminal in the eyes of all who saw her. She had been made to bear the burden of a fault which she had not committed, of a fault that was not so much shameful as ridiculous. For once it was not her husband, or his mother, who was responsible for the ill-natured gossip. Her real enemies lived in a world where vengeance could not reach them. Only at an occasional religious ceremony had she so much as seen them at a distance—those Vicar-Generals, those Canons of the Church in whose eyes the daughter-in-law of the Baronne de Cernès was a walking danger to the spiritual health of all anointed priests. The scandal was a matter of common knowledge throughout the diocese. It was bandied from mouth to mouth. Already there had been three successive chaplains at Cernès, and each had been reminded by the diocesan authorities that permission to say Mass in the private chapel had been rescinded; that, though there must be no open scandal, they must be careful to avoid familiar discourse with the family (for all its great name) "because of a scandal that is only too well known to all of us."

For several years now, because of Paula, the Chapel at Cernès had been left unconsecrated. That in itself was a matter of complete indifference to the young woman (the distance of the Parish Church had provided her with a blessed excuse for never setting foot in it). But there was not a person within ten miles who did not know why that interdict had been laid upon the family. It was because of the old lady's daughter-in-law—"her as had been caught with the curé." The more indulgent gossipers would add that, actually, no one knew precisely how far things had gone. Probably they had not done anything really *wrong* . . . all the same . . . well, the priest had been sent away, hadn't he?

The tree trunks were in shadow, but a streak of red still lay low against the sky. It was long since Paula had noticed such things—trees, the sky, the wide stretches of the countryside, though, at times, like any peasant, she would read the signs in nature of a coming storm, of a change in the temperature. Once she had found pleasure in the visible world, but all that part of her had died on the day when, at this very hour, and on this selfsame road, she had walked beside an overgrown innocent, a young, half-famished priest. He had been pushing his bicycle and talking to her in a low voice. The peasants who had seen them pass had had no doubt that love was the burden of their words. But all that had ever happened had been the meeting, in their persons, of two solitary sufferers whose loneliness had never mingled.

Paula had heard the laughter of a group of girls and boys behind a turning in the road. In a moment they would be in sight. She had pressed into the bank so as not to see them, so as not to be seen. She had led her companion into a track which branched off from the lane. It had been a foolish thing to do, because it had at once given rise to suspicion.

This evening, though a damp mist was rising, she sat down among the dead leaves of a chestnut copse, drew her knees up to her chin, and clasped her hands about her legs. Where was he now, that poor young priest? Where was he hiding his suffering? She did not know, but only that, wherever he might be, he would be suffering if he were still alive. No, there had never been anything between them. It was not the thought of *that* which worried her. Brought up in the horror of the priestly habit, such an intrigue would have been for her impossible. Yet, the poor imbeciles who lived about had classed her—and with authority to back them—among those mad and sex-starved women who make themselves a burden to the clergy. Nothing she could do would ever tear that label from her neck. But what of him? Had he in any way been guilty? He had responded to the confidences of a young, despairing woman, not with the grave words of a spiritual director, but with confidences returned. That had been the sum-total of his wrongdoing. She had sought help from him, as she had had a perfect right to do—and he had welcomed her like some shipwrecked mariner seeing a companion in misfortune land upon his desert isle.

The poor young priest, still little more than a rather backward boy, had been the prey of some secret despair, though what its nature was she had never really known. So far as she could judge (she took very little interest in such matters) he had believed himself to be a useless soul rejected of God. A species of hatred had taken possession of him, hatred of the loutish, unresponsive countryfolk, to whom he could not talk, whose thoughts were bounded by the land they lived by, who had no need of him. Solitude had sent him nearly mad. Yes, quite literally, he was well on the way to going mad through loneliness. No help had come to him from God. He had told Paula that, as a result of emotional transports and a fleeting visitation of grace, he had believed himself to have a vocation. Once caught in the trap, however, he had never experienced those feelings again. . . . It was as though somebody had laid a baited snare, and then had lost all interest once he was tangled in the net. That, at least, was what Paula had thought he had said. But for her all such concerns belonged to an absurd, an "unthinkable" world. She had listened to his outburst of self-pity with but half an ear, only waiting until he paused for breath to take up the story of her own unhappiness. "And I . . ." she had said, and straight embarked upon the narrative of her marriage. There had been nothing between them but this alternation of monologues. Once only, in the Presbytery garden, and then because he was at the end of his tether, he had, for the space of a few seconds, rested his head upon her shoulder. Almost at once she had slipped away, but not before a neighbor's eye had seen them. That had been the start of the whole business. Because of that single gesture (and it might have changed his whole life) the little lamp was never more to burn before the altar in the family Chapel. The old Baronne had scarcely even protested against the interdict. It was as though she found it natural that the presence of God at Cernès should be thought incompatible with that of the daughter-in-law who had been born a Meulière.

Paula was beginning to feel cold. It was growing dark under the chestnuts. She got up, shook out her skirt, and went back to the path. One of the towers of the great house, dating from the fourteenth century, could be seen from here between the pines. But by now the night was so dark that even this descendant of a race of muleteers could no longer make it out.

For twelve years she had borne upon her back the burden of this calumny, knowing it to be in everybody's mouths. But suddenly the thought that it had reached the ears of a schoolmaster to whom she had never so much as spoken, seemed to her to be beyond all bearing. She knew every man by sight for miles around. There was scarcely one of them she would have failed to recognize at a distance. But the picture of that curly head must have forced its way, almost without her knowledge, into her consciousness—the picture of a schoolmaster whose name was still unknown to her. For schoolmasters and priests have neither of them any need of names. Their function is enough to give them an identity. She could not endure the thought that he should go on believing in this story about her even for one day longer. She would tell him what had really happened. The same imperious need to confess, to lighten herself of a load she could no longer carry, which, twelve years earlier, had led her to confide imprudently in a priest who had been too young and too weak, was nagging at her again. She must fight down her shyness. She must take up the cudgels once again for Guillaume. Perhaps the schoolmaster would yield. In any case, she would have made contact with him. A bond might form between them.

She hung up her cloak in the hall. By force of habit she washed her hands at the scullery sink, then went into the servants' sitting-room, where the family, since the death of Georges, the younger son, had taken to having their meals. The official dining-room, a vast and icy cold apartment, was never used except during the Christmas holidays, and in September, when the Baronne's eldest daughter, the Comtesse d'Arbis, came from Paris with her children and Georges' little daughter, Danièle. On the occasion of those visits, the two garden-boys were put into livery; a cook was engaged; a pair of saddle horses was hired.

This evening, Paula did not go straight to the smaller dining-room. Eager to reopen as soon as possible the argument about the schoolmaster, she made her way instead to her mother-in-law's room. She entered it, perhaps, ten times in the year. She stood now behind the closed door listening to the gay babble of the four conspirators within, to the sound of a tune which Galéas was playing with one finger. Something that Fraülein had just said produced a burst of laughter from the old Baronne. How Paula hated that forced, affected titter! She opened the door without knocking. Like the wooden figures on a public clock those in the room were smitten into sudden immobility. The Baronne sat for a moment with one hand raised, holding a card. Galéas slammed the cover of the piano and swung round on his stool. Fraülein turned toward the enemy, looking for all the world like a cat confronted by a dog, its face flattened in a snarl, its ears laid back, its body arched, and just about to spit. Guillou, surrounded by newspapers from which he had been cutting photographs of airplanes, put his scissors on the table, and curled up once again between the *prie-Dieu* and the bed, drawing in his legs, and playing "possum."

Never before had Paula realized so clearly—accustomed though she was to such scenes—how baleful an influence she exercised on those with whom she had to live. Almost at once, her mother-in-law recovered from the shock of the surprise, and gave her a twisted smile, exhibiting the same slightly excessive amiability that she would have shown to a stranger of inferior social status. She started fussing about the younger woman's damp feet, and told her to come to the fire. Fraülein grumblingly muttered something about its not being worth while because she was just going to serve dinner. She made for the door with Galéas and Guillaume hard at her heels. "As usual," thought the Baronne, "they're unloading her on me."

"Have I your permission, my dear, to put on the fireguard?"

She effaced herself in Paula's presence, and, not for the world would she ever have left a room in front of her daughter-in-law. All the way in to dinner she talked incessantly, making it impossible, until they were all at table, for Paula to get a word in edgeways. Galéas and Guillaume were standing by their chairs. As soon as they were seated, they started noisily lapping their soup. The Baronne asked whether they didn't all think it was very mild today, adding that it was scarcely ever cold at Cernès in November. She had started making her melon jam that very afternoon. This time she was going to try the experiment of mixing it with apricots.

"The sort my poor, dear Adhémar always called, so amusingly, old women's ears—do you remember, Galéas?"

She was talking for the sake of talking. All that mattered

was that Paula should not be allowed to start arguing again. But watching her, she saw signs of impending trouble on the hateful face. Guillaume sat with hunched shoulders, uneasy under his mother's watchful eyes. He, too, felt that there was danger in the air, and that it had something to do with him. Try though he might to make himself one with the table and the chair, he knew only too well that Mamie's talk would not fill the silence, and could offer only a feeble barrier to the storm already piling up behind the tight lips of the adversary.

Galéas ate and drank without looking up, bending so low over his food that the graying thicket of hair on the enormous head was at Paula's eye-level. He was hungry, having worked all day in the churchyard, which it was his self-imposed task to keep tidy. Thanks to him there were no neglected graves at Cernès. At the moment he was untroubled, since it was not at him that his wife was looking. He was in luck's way. She had banished him from her mind, which meant that he was the only one of the company who could bask at ease and indulge such whims as pouring wine into his soup, and, as he put it, "trying a little of everything." He mashed and munched, piling his plate with everything on the table, and the Baronne was hard put to it to keep Guillaume from imitating his father without undermining the respect due to him. Papa could do as he liked, she said: but Guillou must sit at table like a well-brought-up little boy. It didn't, in fact, ever occur to him to criticize his father, finding it impossible to imagine him as different from what he was. Papa belonged to a species of grown-ups which threatened no danger. That would have been Guillaume's verdict had he been capable of forming one. Papa never made a noise, never interrupted the

21

stories which Guillaume was forever telling to himself. Indeed, he became part of them, and was no more intrusive than the dogs and oxen on the farm. His mother, on the other hand, broke in upon them with violence, and stuck there like some foreign body. He was not always conscious of her presence, but he knew that she was there. . . . Suddenly, he heard her speak his name. That had torn it!—they were going to talk about him! She mentioned the schoolmaster. He tried to understand what she was saying. He had been dragged by the ears from his earth, and now lay exposed to the glare of the grown-up world.

"But what do you suggest that we should do with Guillaume, then? Have you any alternative to suggest? Oh, I know he can read and write and just about manage to count . . . but that's not saying much for a twelve-year-old. . . ."

According to the Baronne there was no hurry. They must take their time about thinking what would be best to do.

"But he's already been sent away from two schools. You say that this schoolmaster won't do anything about him. In that case, we must have a tutor for him, at home—or a governess."

The old lady protested loudly at such an idea. She would not dream of having a stranger in the house . . . she trembled at the mere thought of exposing their life at Cernès to alien eyes—their life as it had become since the day when Galéas had given his name to this Fury!

"Perhaps *you* can think of something else, my dear?"

Paula emptied her glass at a gulp and refilled it. Both the Baronne and Fraülein had noticed that, since the first year of her marriage, Paula had shown a fondness for the bottle. Fraülein had tried making a pencil mark on the bottles of liqueur so as to check her consumption, but Paula, noticing this, had accumulated in her wardrobe a secret supply of anisette and cherry-brandy, of curaçao and apricot cordial. But this the Austrian woman had discovered. One day, the Baronne had felt it to be her duty to put the dear girl on her guard against strong drink, but her words had led to such an outburst that she had never again dared to refer to the subject.

"In my opinion we have no choice but to try again with the schoolmaster. . . ."

At that, the Baronne raised her hands, declaring that not for any consideration in the world would she expose herself again to the insolence of that Communist. Paula reassured her. There was no question of that, she said. She herself would make the approach, and do her best to succeed where her mother-in-law had failed. She refused to discuss the matter, but said, over and over again, that her mind was quite made up, and that, after all, Guillaume's education was her concern.

"It seems to me that my son might have something to say in the matter!"

"You know that his 'say' will be precisely nothing!"

"If that is how you feel, I have at least the right to insist that you speak to this creature in your own name only. You can, if you like, tell him that I know nothing of your intentions. Should you, however, object to soiling your lips with so white a lie, then I must ask you to make it clear that you are acting contrary to my judgment, and in direct opposition to my wishes."

Paula mockingly suggested that it was the old lady's Christian duty to suffer humiliation for her grandson's sake.

"My dear girl, whatever you have done, or still may do, I

wish it to be fully understood that I am in no way involved. I don't wish to be offensive, but no one could well be less a member of the family than you."

Her tone was perfectly polite, and her long upper lip curled in a smile which revealed her fine and rather too regular teeth.

Paula's nerves were frayed and she found it difficult to contain herself.

"If you wish to imply that I have never shown the slightest wish to resemble the Cernès—you are perfectly right."

"In that case, my dear, there is nothing for you to worry about. No one, I feel sure, has ever done you the wrong of taking you for what you are not."

Guillaume would have liked to slip from the room, but did not dare. Besides, he found this rumbling battle of the gods above his head rather thrilling, though the point of their acid exchanges escaped him.

Galéas got up, leaving the sweets untouched, as he always did when there was cream. The adversaries faced one another.

"It would be a bad day for me if I was to be considered as one of the family when you find the house burning over your head. . . ."

"Are you, by any chance, trying to frighten me? For more than four hundred years the Cernès have always treated their people well, and set a good example. They have been, and are, thank God, loved and respected . . ."

Indignation had set the old voice trembling.

"Loved? . . . Respected? . . . why, you're hated by the whole village. Your obstinacy in keeping Fraülein here during the war. . . ."

"Forgive me for smiling . . . An Austrian of sixty-four, who has lived with us ever since she was a girl! . . . The military authorities thought it wise to shut their eyes—and they were right."

"But the people here are only too glad to have so good an excuse. It is quite incredible that anyone should be so wilfully blind! . . . You have always been detested . . . Do you really think that the tenant-farmers and the tradespeople are taken in by the soft-soap you give them? Because of you, they hate everything you love . . . priests and all. Just you wait and see! . . . Unfortunately, I shall be lumped in with the rest of you. Still, I think I shall die happy!"

She finished by muttering a vulgar phrase which the Baronne had never heard before. "How revealing language can be," thought the old lady, her anger suddenly abated. It sometimes happened that her daughter from Paris, and particularly her grandchildren, would risk using a slang expression in her hearing, but never would they have said anything so common! What, precisely, had it been? "You're going to get it in the neck!"—yes, that was it. As always, Paula's displays of temper had a calming effect on the old lady. She recovered the advantage which self-control always enjoys when at odds with hysteria.

"I would not have you think for a moment that your hatred of the aristocracy surprises me. No matter what may be your opinion, the countryfolk have always loved their masters. Both they and we have a proper self-respect and know our places. It is in the ranks of the lower middle class that you find social hatred, and it springs from envy. It was the middle classes that did most of the butchering during the Terror. . . ."

Her daughter-in-law declared in self-complacent tones that,

owing to the treachery of the emigrés, the Terror had been "just and necessary." At that, the Baronne drew herself majestically to her full height.

"My great-grandfather, and two of my great-uncles perished on the scaffold, and I forbid you . . ."

Paula suddenly found herself thinking of the schoolmaster. Her words would have pleased him. He would have approved her attitude. Paula's views had been inherited from her Meulière uncle, a narrowly fanatical Radical and Free-Mason. But her expression of them took on a special value for her now that she was offering them on the altar of the man she was to see tomorrow. It was a Thursday, and he would be free. What she had said, had been said as a result of *his* influence (uncle Meulière had had nothing to do with it), the influence of someone to whom she had never spoken, whom she had passed occasionally in the street, who never so much as said "Good morning" if she happened to pass when he was working in his garden (though he would pause in his digging to look at her).

"Do you know what you are, my dear?—an incendiary: nothing more nor less than an incendiary. . . ."

Guillaume raised his head. He knew what an incendiary was. Hundreds of times he had looked at a picture in the 1871 volume of *Le Monde Illustré,* which showed two women squatting in the darkness by a cellar door, making some sort of a fire. Locks of untidy hair straggled from underneath their proletarian caps. . . . He gazed at his mother with his mouth open . . . an incendiary?—why, of course she was! . . .

She grabbed him by the arm.

"Upstairs with you—quick now!"

The Baronne made the sign of the cross upon his forehead with her thumb: but she did not kiss him. As soon as he had left the room, she said:

"We ought at least to spare him . . ."

"You needn't worry, he doesn't hear, and if he did hear, he wouldn't understand."

"That is where you are wrong. Poor little mite! He understands a great deal more than we think. . . . And, talking of him brings me back to the subject of our discussion. We seem to have strayed a long way from it, and for that we are equally to blame. If, as I have very little doubt, and, as I hope will be the case, this man persists in his refusal . . ."

"In that case, there'll be nothing for it but to let Guillaume grow up like a little country lout. . . . It's nothing short of a shame to see rich people's children enjoying all the benefits of an education from which they are incapable of profiting, while those of the poor . . ."

Once again, the commonplaces which had been constantly in uncle Meulière's mouth went suddenly to her head. No doubt her views would be shared by the schoolmaster, whom she credited with every kind of advanced theory. It never occurred to her that he might not be built to the official pattern.

The old lady, determined to avoid a fresh outburst, got up without saying a word. Paula followed her to the stairs.

"Why should not you and I join forces and teach him what little we know?"

"If you've got sufficient patience, well and good. I confess that I've had about as much as I can stand."

"A good night's sleep will work wonders, my dear. Please

forget anything I have said that may have wounded you, as I, for my part, freely forgive you."

Her daughter-in-law indulged in a shrug. "That's just so much talk, and doesn't really alter what we feel. We can no longer have any illusions. . . ."

They stood facing one another in the bedroom corridor, candle in hand. Of the two faces thus brightly illuminated, that of the younger woman looked by far the more formidable.

"Please believe, Paula, that I am a great deal less unfair in my attitude toward you than you quite naturally think. You have much to excuse you . . . the burden you have been called upon to bear is heavy for a young woman . . ."

"I was twenty-six," broke in Paula sharply. "I blame nobody. My fate was of my own choosing. If it comes to that, you poor thing . . ."

The meaning behind her words was—my wretched husband is your wretched son. She found some consolation for the hell in which she lived in the knowledge that she shared it with her old enemy. But the Baronne refused the proffered sympathy.

"With me it is quite different," she replied in a voice shaken by emotion. "I, after all, had my Adhémar. For twenty-five years I was the happiest of women. . . ."

"Perhaps . . . but not the happiest of mothers."

"It is five years since my Georges died a hero's death. I do not weep for him. I still have his little Danièle, I still have Galéas. . . ."

"Yes, you most certainly have Galéas!"

"I have my children in Paris," went on the other obstinately.

"But they just sponge on you. For them you have never been

anything but a cow to be milked. You may shake your head as much as you like, but you know it as well as I do. Fraülein throws it in your teeth often enough when the two of you are alone and think that I am out of hearing. . . . No, let me go on . . . I *will* raise my voice if I want to. . . ."

The words, echoing down the corridor, woke Guillaume with a start. He sat up in bed. The gods were still hard at it up there in the sky. He snuggled down again, a pillow pressed against one ear, his finger stuck in the other. While he lay there waiting for sleep to come again, he took up the thread of the story he had been telling himself, about the island and the cave—like in *Un Robinson de Douze Ans*. The night light peopled the linen closet in which he slept with familiar shadows and with monsters tamed.

"We live here deprived of everything so that your Arbis daughter may keep her state in Paris, and weave what she calls her marriage plots. What does it matter if we starve so long as Yolande marries a Duke with Jewish blood, and Stanislas an American nobody. . . ."

Thus did Paula nag away at the old lady who, eager for silence, retreated hurriedly and bolted her door. But through the panels the implacable voice still sounded.

"The fewer hopes you have of Stanislas, the better. *He'll* never marry anybody, that little . . ."

She finished up with a word the meaning of which the Baronne would not have grasped even if she had heard it, even if she had not been kneeling at her *prie-Dieu* with her head buried in her arms.

No sooner had Paula shut herself into her own room than her anger fell dead. There were still a few embers glowing in the grate. She threw on a fresh log, lit the oil lamp on the table by the sofa, undressed in front of the fire, and put on an old quilted dressing gown.

We speak of "making love": we should be able, too, to speak of "making hate." To make hate is comforting. It rests the mind and relaxes the nerves. Paula opened the wardrobe. Her hands hovered, momentarily hesitating. Then she chose the curaçao, pitched the sofa cushions onto the floor, as near the fire as possible, and stretched herself out at full length with a glass and a bottle within easy reach of her hand. She started to smoke and to drink, thinking the while of the man, of the schoolmaster, who was the enemy of all aristocrats and rich folk, a "red," maybe, a Communist. He was despised as she was despised, and by the same type of person. Before him she would humble herself, and, in the end, would force her way into his life. He was married . . . what was his wife like? She did not even know her by sight. For the time being she kept her strictly out of the story she was imagining, burrowing into her fantasy, prodigal of more invention than ever professional story-teller showed. Before her inner eye visions arose beyond the power of language to express. Now and again she got to her feet to put another log upon the fire and fill her glass. Then she lay down again. The occasional flicker of a flame played on her face, revealing alternately the mask of a criminal—or of a martyr.

EARLY next afternoon, wearing a mackintosh, heavy shoes, and a beret pulled down over her eyes, she made her way to the village. The rain beating on her face, she thought, would wash away the telltale signs of last night's orgy. She no longer felt exalted. Only determination kept her going. Any other woman would have spent hours choosing what clothes she should put on for so important a mission, or, if not that, would at least have tried to look her best. It never so much as occurred to Paula to powder her face, or to do anything that would make the hirsute appearance of her cheeks less noticeable. If only she had washed her hair it might have looked less greasy. It should have entered her mind that the schoolmaster might, like most other men, be susceptible to scent. . . . But no: without paying any more attention than usual to her person, and looking as bedraggled as always, she set out to try her luck for the last time.

The man, the schoolmaster, was sitting in the kitchen, facing his wife. He was shelling kidney-beans, and chatting as he worked. . . . It was Thursday, the best day of the whole week. The schoolhouse faced the street, like all the other houses of the ugly village of Cernès. The smithy, the butcher's shop, the Inn, and the post office were not, as elsewhere, grouped about the Church, which, set in solitude among its huddle of graves, stood upon a promontory, dominating the valley of the Ciron. . . . Cernès had only one street, and even that was not a street proper, but only the main road. The schoolhouse stood a little way back from it. The children used the front door, and the schoolmaster's kitchen opened off to the right of the narrow passage which led to the playground, and, beyond it, to the kitchen-garden. Robert and Léone Bordas, untouched by any presentiment of the fate which was approaching their home, were once again hard at it, discussing their strange visitor of the day before.

"It's all very well your talking," his wife was saying with no little eagerness, "but a hundred and fifty, perhaps two hundred francs extra each month, just for seeing that the kid from the great house keeps his nose to the grindstone, are not to be sneezed at. Anyway, it's worth thinking about."

"We haven't sunk that far. There's nothing, so far as I can see, that we have to do without. I'm getting practically all the books I want now. . . ." (he did the reviewing of poetry and fiction for the *Teachers' Journal*).

"You never think about anybody but yourself. After all, there's Jean-Pierre to be considered. . . ."

"Jean-Pierre's got all he needs. You're not suggesting, I suppose, that he should have a coach?"

Her smile expressed satisfaction. No, certainly, their boy didn't need anything of that kind. He was always top of his class in every subject. Though he was only thirteen, he had just got into the upper school a good two years ahead of the normal time, and would almost certainly have to stay in it an extra three terms, because it was very unlikely that his age would be taken into account. He was already being picked for a winner at the Lycée, and his masters had very little doubt that he would pass the school certificate at the first attempt, both in science and the humanities.

"That's where you're wrong: I do want him to take private lessons."

As Léone made this announcement there was nothing in the expression of her face to indicate either that she had any doubts of her own wisdom, or that she felt she was asking a favor. She was a thin, pale woman with reddish hair and small features. Though not in her first youth, she was still pretty. Her voice was rather sharp and penetrating as a result of having to keep a roomful of youngsters in order.

"He must learn riding."

Robert Bordas went on with his task of shelling beans. He affected to believe that she was joking.

"Of course he must, and dancing too, I suppose, if you want him *to*."

Laughter creased his long and rather narrow eyes. He was wearing no collar and was unshaven. Nevertheless, there was something still of the charm of youth about him. It was easy to see what he must have been like as a boy. He got up and moved round the table, leaning on a cane with a rubber ferrule. He limped, but only very little. His long, supple cat's back was that of an adolescent. He lit a cigarette and said:

"I know somebody who longs for the Revolution—but wants a racing-stable for her son!"

She shrugged her shoulders.

"Why do you want to turn Jean-Pierre into a horseman"— he would not let the subject drop—"So he can serve in the

33

Dragoons with a lot of rotters who'll send the schoolmaster's son to Coventry?"

"Don't get excited. You'd better take care of your voice. You'll need it at the November 11th Meeting. . . ."

She saw from his face that she had gone too far, emptied her apronful of beans into a dish, and gave her husband a kiss. "Listen to me, Robert. . . ." She wanted the same things that he wanted. He knew that. She followed him blindly and with utter confidence. Politics were not for her. She found it difficult to imagine how the world would go once the Revolution was an accomplished fact. The only thing she knew for certain was that there would always be an élite who would rule the country. It would be drawn, of course, from the most intelligent and the best educated, but also from those with the gift of leadership.

"All right then, I do want Jean-Pierre to know how to ride a horse, and, more than anything, I want him to acquire those virtues of initiative, courage and enterprise in which he is rather lacking. He's got everything else, but not them."

Robert Bordas looked at the absent expression on his wife's face. She was completely unaware of him. Her heart, at that moment, was far away.

"The Ecole Normale trains an élite of University teachers," he observed with a touch of dryness. "That is the sole purpose of its existence."

"But think of all the Ministers, all the great writers, all the Party chiefs, who have passed through it: Jaurès, first and foremost, Léon Blum . . ."

He broke in on her. "Personally speaking, I should be quite proud enough if Jean-Pierre could produce a first-rate thesis, and end up as a Professor in the Faculty of Letters. I ask nothing better for him . . . or even, perhaps, at the Sorbonne, or, who knows . . . at the Collège de France!"

There was a touch of bitterness in her laughter.

"It's my turn now to point out what a fine revolutionary *you* make! Do you really imagine that all those antiques will be left standing?"

"Of course they will! The University will be transformed, no doubt, and injected with new blood. But in France, higher education will always be higher education . . . You don't know what you're talking about. . . ."

Suddenly he stopped speaking. He had just seen, through the glazed panel of the door, the figure of a woman emerging from the mist.

"Who on earth is that?"

"Some mother, I expect, who has come to complain that her darling is being treated unfairly."

Paula took a long time scraping her shoes and ridding them of mud before she entered the house. They did not recognize her. They had no idea who this strange woman could be, with a beret pulled down over dark, black-circled eyes, and a face which had as thick a growth of down as a youth's. She carefully avoided mentioning her name. All she said to Robert was that she was the mother of the boy about whom the Baronne de Cernès had spoken to him on the previous day. It took him a few seconds to grasp the significance of her words, but Léone had already guessed.

She led the way into a freezingly cold room and threw open the shutters. Everything was bright and shining, the floor, the sideboard and the table in department-store style. A coarse lace blind masked the window. There was a wide frieze with a design of giant hydrangeas just below the ceiling. The wallpaper was dark red.

"I will leave you with my husband. . . ."

Paula protested that she had no secrets to discuss. It was just a question of clearing up a slight misunderstanding. Robert Bordas' cheeks had flushed a bright red. They had always done that ever since he was a child. His ears were aflame. Was this woman with the evil gleam in her eye going to make him give an account of his yesterday's half-joking behavior? Indeed she was! She had the brazen effrontery to embark at once on the subject, without the slightest show of embarrassment. She was afraid, she said, that her mother-in-law had misunderstood some perfectly innocent remark of his, and had gone off in a huff. She had no intention of asking Monsieur Bordas to withdraw his refusal, but she would hate to think that the incident had created a new enemy for herself in the village. She was so defenseless, and he was one of the few persons from whom she had the right to expect some measure of understanding.

She turned her blazing eyes from Robert to Léone. The slightly drooping corners of her mouth gave the look of a tragic mask to the great hairy face. Robert stammered that he was deeply shocked, that there had been no intention of offense in what he had said. Paula cut him short, and, turning to Léone:

"I never thought there had been," she said. "You have only too good reason to know, both of you, what the people round here are like, and how they gossip."

Had they understood the veiled allusion? Had they heard

the story which was going round to the effect that the school-master had been wounded while holding a cushy job in one of the back-areas? Some went so far as to hint that he had let off his own rifle . . . pure clumsiness, of course, but . . .

They showed no sign of embarrassment. Paula had no idea whether she had touched them on the raw or not.

She went on: "I know, madame, that you come of an old Cadillac family . . ."

It was, indeed, true that Léone's parents were peasant-proprietors in a small way, and belonged to an honorable and ancient line. But they had been looked at askance because of their advanced views. Their daughter had not had a church wedding, and there seemed to be some doubt as to whether Jean-Pierre had been baptized. In order to stay near the family, the Bordas' had given up a chance of rapid promotion.

"Cernès," said Paula, "has a better schoolmaster than it deserves."

Once again the young face opposite flushed crimson. But there was no stopping her. She knew, she said, that Robert Bordas had only to raise a finger to be a Deputy tomorrow if he chose. His color deepened, but he merely shrugged his shoulders: "You're pulling my leg!" Léone laughed: "You'll be turning my poor Robert's head, madame!"

The young man's face creased in a smile.

"I'm not expressing my own views. It was Monsieur Lousteau, our bailiff, who said that. He's a friend of yours, I believe? Of course, he's a Royalist, but he can be fair to his enemies. With a husband like yours, madame, a woman can afford to be ambitious."

In a low voice, she added: "If I were in your shoes! . . ." The tone in which she said this was exactly right. There was no undue stressing of the allusion to her own wretched husband.

"Jean-Pierre will be the first great man in *our* family," said the schoolmaster with a laugh, "isn't that so, Léone?"

Their son? The visitor's smile expressed understanding. His fame had reached even her ears. Monsieur Lousteau had often spoken of him. How happy they must be, and how proud! Again she sighed, again she showed that her own misfortune was uppermost in her mind. But this time she made no bones about talking of it.

"Speaking of infant prodigies reminds me. It was to discuss the future of my own son that I came here today. I think it not unlikely that my mother-in-law may have slightly exaggerated the position. He *is* backward, I know, and I realize that the suggestion she made may rather have frightened you!"

Robert protested vigorously that lack of leisure, and the dread of not being able to devote enough time to an additional job, had alone prompted his refusal. His duties as Mayor's secretary, and his own private work, took up every moment he could spare from his teaching.

"Oh, I know what a worker you are!" she said, adding in a sly tone of flattery: "a little bird has been whispering that certain unsigned articles in *la France du Sud-Ouest* . . ."

Once again, the schoolmaster's cheeks and ears glowed scarlet. In order to cut the interview short, he began to put a few questions to her about Guillaume. Could the boy read and write fluently? He actually read sometimes for pleasure, did he?— well, then, he certainly was not a hopeless case.

Paula felt a little uncertain how to proceed. It was important not to put this man off at the start. All the same, it was only wise to make him realize what a little half-wit his future pupil was. Yes, she said, there were two or three books which he read over and over again, and he was forever browsing over bound numbers of the *Saint-Nicholas Annual* dating from the 'nineties, though there was no reason to think that he took anything in. She was afraid her little brat was not very attractive, not very winning. One had to be his mother before one could put up with him at all, and there were times when even she . . . The schoolmaster felt his heart bleed for her. The best thing, he suggested, would be for him to have the boy round after five o'clock one evening, when school was over, just to see what he was like. He would not make any definite promise until he had had an opportunity to study him.

Paula took both his hands in hers. Emotion, only half feigned, made her voice tremble as she said: "I can't help thinking of the difference you will find between my poor, unhappy boy and your own son!"

She turned away her face as though to keep him from seeing how ashamed she felt. . . . Her behavior, this afternoon, had been nothing short of inspired! Something undreamed of had happened to this teacher and his schoolmarm wife. They had grown used to living in an atmosphere of perpetual hostility, of being objects of suspicion to countryfolk and gentry alike, of being treated by the clergy as public enemies—and now, someone from the great house had come to ask a favor of them! Just fancy what it must mean to them to know that she not only admired, but actually envied, them! In how humble a tone had she referred to her own husband and her degenerate son! . . . The adventure had quite gone to Robert's head. He could not forget that this beret and this mackintosh concealed a genuine lady of title! He could not resist a little mild badinage.

"I find it a little surprising, madame, that you should not be afraid of my influence on the boy. . . . My views, you know, are not at all what is usually called respectable."

Again the creases appeared in his face. His eyes almost vanished, so that only their glitter showed between the half-closed lids.

"You don't know me," replied Paula with a serious air—"or what I am really like."

If she told them that nothing would please her more than to think her poor boy capable of feeling that influence, they would not believe her.

"The world in which I live is not my world. I am just as much a fish out of water as you would be . . . one of these days I'll tell you . . ."

In this way did she prepare the way for future confidences. No need to say more: no need to break down barriers. She would say good-bye now, for the time being, leaving them quite overwhelmed by what she had just said about her "views." . . . It was agreed that she should bring Guillaume to the schoolhouse next afternoon, about four. Then, all of a sudden, she became the great lady, the replica of her mother-in-law, of the Comtesse d'Arbis.

"So many thanks! You have no idea how relieved I feel. Yes, really, I mean it. Our little chat has meant *so* much to me."

"It's pretty obvious she's fallen for you," said Léone.

She had cleared the table, and now, with a sigh, took up a number of exercises which she had to correct.

"She's not a bad sort, you know."

"There you are! She was very careful to treat you with respect, but, if you want my opinion, you'd better watch your step!"

"She's a bit touched, I should say . . . or, to put it mildly, rather hysterical."

"She knows what she wants all right, touched or not. Don't forget that story about her and the curé! I think you ought to go very carefully."

He got up, stretched his long arms, and said: "I don't like bearded ladies."

"She wouldn't be bad looking," said Léone, "if she took more care of herself."

"I remember now what Lousteau told me. She's not an aristocrat by birth, but the daughter, or niece, of Meulière who was once Mayor of Bordeaux. . . . Why are you laughing?"

"Her not being a genuine aristocrat seems to depress you!"

While his mother was making ready to hand him over to the tender mercies of the red schoolmaster, the poor little hare, hunted from his form, was wondering whether he would ever get back to it. The bright light of the grown-up world into which he had been chased made him blink. During his mother's absence, a difference of opinion had developed between his three beneficent deities—papa, Mamie and Fraülein. Mamie and Fraülein, it is true, were frequently at loggerheads, but almost always about things which didn't much matter. The Austrian woman would sometimes employ language which seemed the cruder for being couched in the respectful third person. But today Guillaume had an uncomfortable feeling that even Fraülein was in favor of his being entrusted to the schoolmaster.

"Why should he not have a proper education? He's as good as anybody else!"

Then, turning to him: "Run away and play, my duckie, my chickabiddy. . . ."

He left the house, but, a moment later, came back and slipped into the kitchen. Wasn't it the general view that he never listened, and that, even if he did, he couldn't understand?

The Baronne, without condescending to answer Fraülein, was haranguing her son, who was lolling in his favorite wicker armchair in front of the kitchen fire. He spent almost every rainy afternoon of winter there, making paper spills, or polishing his father's guns, which he never used.

"Do exert a little authority, for once in your life, Galéas!" the old lady was saying. "You've only got to say, 'No, I won't have my son handed over to this Communist!' . . . There'll be a storm, of course, but it'll blow over."

Fraülein entered a protest: "Don't you listen to Madame la Baronne. Why should not Guillou be as well educated as the Arbis children?"

"You leave the Arbis children alone, Fraülein. This has got nothing to do with them. I don't wish my grandson to be inculcated with this man's ideas—that's the long and the short of it."

"Poor chick! As though anyone was going to talk politics to him!"

"It is not a question of politics. . . . There is religion to be considered. The boy's not so strong in his catechism as he might be. . . ."

Guillaume watched his father sitting there without stirring a finger. He was staring at the smoldering logs, and showed no sign of inclining to one side or other of the argument. Guillou, his mouth half open, was trying hard to understand.

"Madame la Baronne does not really mind him living like a clodhopper when he's grown up . . . for all I know, she may prefer to have it that way!"

"The idea of you setting yourself up against me and pleading my grandson's cause! That really is too much!" The Baronne tried to sound indignant, but it was clear that she did not feel very sure of herself.

"Oh, I know that Madame la Baronne is very fond of Guillou, and likes having him with her here; but it is not him she has in mind when she thinks about the future of the family."

The Baronne professed to regard Fraülein as a bull in a china shop. But the Austrian's shrill voice easily drowned her mistress's.

"And the proof of that, if proof were needed, is that after Georges' death, it was agreed that Stanislas, the eldest Arbis boy, should add the name Cernès to his own, as though there were no other Cernès left, as though Guillou wasn't really Guillaume de Cernès."

"The boy's listening," said Galéas suddenly, and then relapsed once more into silence. Fraülein took Guillou by the shoulders and gently pushed him through the door. But he went no further than the pantry, where Fraülein's loud tones reached him easily.

"I know somebody who wasn't called 'Desiré' when he turned up. Madame la Baronne will doubtless remember her own words—that it couldn't be a very common occurrence for an invalid to get a child on his sicknurse. . . ."

43

"I never said any such thing, Fraülein! . . . Galéas was perfectly well and strong. . . . Besides, it is not my custom to make coarse remarks of that kind."

"Madame la Baronne will surely recollect that a child was no part of the bargain. I, who knew my Galéas, was well aware that he was as good as the next man—as the event proved. . . ."

A dangerous glitter showed between the Austrian's reddish, lashless lids—"pig's eyes"—Madame Galéas had once called them. The Baronne, shocked by what had just been said, turned away.

Guillaume, his nose pressed to the pantry window, was watching the splashing raindrops. They looked like little dancing figures. The grown-ups seemed to be forever going on about him, and quarrelling, too. No one had found it possible to call him "Desiré." He wanted to go on telling himself the stories which only he knew. But this time there would be no excuse, unless the schoolmaster went on refusing. If he did that, Guillou would be so happy that he wouldn't a bit mind not being called "Desiré." All he asked was not to have to be with a lot of other children who would make his life a misery to him, not to have anything to do with schoolmasters with their loud voices, their bad temper, their stern looks, and the way they had of producing a lot of words which didn't mean anything.

Mamie hadn't wanted him, nor his own mother either. He knew that all right. Had they foreseen that he wouldn't be like other boys? How about poor papa?—had *he* wanted him? He didn't know, but he did know that papa wouldn't be any good at getting him out of the schoolmaster's clutches.

The Baronne was keeping on at that very subject, until she was sick of the sound of her own voice.

"You've only got to say 'no'—surely it's not all that difficult! Listen to me, it's just a question of saying 'no' . . . Since you've only got to say 'no' . . ."

But all he did was to sit there shaking his great mop of grizzled hair, and saying nothing. Finally, however, he did speak:

"I haven't the right . . ."

"Haven't the right? What do you mean, Galéas? Who, then, has a right if not the father of a family, where his children's education is concerned?"

But he kept on shaking his head, looking mulish, and repeating:

"I haven't the right . . ."

It was then that Guillaume ran back into the room in tears, and flung himself into Fraülein's lap.

"Here's mummy!—and she's laughing to herself. Oh! I know it means that the schoolmaster's going to . . ."

"What of it, you little silly? He won't eat you! Wipe his nose, Fraülein, he's a disgusting sight."

He vanished into the scullery, just as his mother entered the kitchen with a look of triumph on her face.

"It's all arranged," she said. "I'm to take Guillaume along there tomorrow afternoon at four."

"If your husband is agreeable."

"Oh naturally; but he'll be agreeable all right, won't you, Galéas?"

"You're going to have your work cut out with that boy, whatever you do. . . ."

"That reminds me—where is he?" asked Paula. "I thought I heard him snuffling."

They caught sight of Guillaume sneaking out of the scullery.

45

He was looking his very worst, with tears and dribble and snot all over his face.

"I won't go!" he whined, without looking at his mother. "I won't go to the schoolmaster!"

Paula had always been ashamed of him, but now, behind the boy's puckered face was the image of the father in his chair. The child's drooling mouth was the very replica of that other mouth, moist, and without warmth.

With an effort she controlled her temper. In a voice that was almost gentle she said: "Of course, I can't drag you there by force. But, if you won't go, you'll have to be sent away to board at the Lycée."

The Baronne shrugged her shoulders. "You know perfectly well that no school would keep such a little misery."

"Then I see nothing for it but a Reformatory . . ."

She had uttered this particular threat so often that Guillaume had ended by conjuring up a vague but terrifying image of those disciplinary establishments. He began to tremble. "No! mummy, no!" he blubbered, and, hurling himself into Fraülein's arms, hid his face against her flabby bosom.

"Don't you believe a word she says, my chick. You don't think I'd let her do a thing like that, do you?"

"Fraülein has no say in the matter. And this time I'm not joking. I have made inquiries, and have several addresses," said Paula, and there was a note of gay excitement in her voice.

What finally brought him to the breaking point was the sound of old Mamie's laughter.

"Why not just put him in a sack, my dear, and have done with it? Why not throw him into the river like a kitten?"

Mad with terror, he began scrubbing away at his face with a filthy handkerchief.

"Oh, no, Mamie, no!—not in a sack!" Irony meant nothing to him. Everything he heard he took quite literally.

"Little silly!" said the Baronne, and drew him to her, but only to push him away again, quite gently.

"Really, it is difficult to know what to do for the best. Such a grubby little urchin—take him, Fraülein . . . run away, my boy, and clean yourself."

His teeth were chattering. "I *will* go to the schoolmaster, mummy; I *will* be good! . . ."

"Ah, now you're seeing sense at last!"

Fraülein took him along to the scullery and washed his face at the tap.

"They only want to frighten you, my chick. They don't mean what they say; just you laugh at them!"

At this point Galéas got out of his chair, and, without a glance at any of them, said:

"It's quite fine now. You coming along to the churchyard, son?"

Guillou dreaded going for walks with his father, but this time, he gladly took the proffered hand, and started off, still snuffling.

It had stopped raining, and the drenched grass was sparkling in the warm sunlight. They walked along a field-path which skirted the village. Ordinarily, Guillaume was afraid of cows, of the way they raised their heads and stared, as though they were making up their minds to charge. His father had tight hold of his hand, and said nothing. They could have walked for hours without exchanging a word. Guillou could not know that these long silences were his father's despair, that the poor man was trying, all the while, to concentrate his mind. But he could not think of anything to say to a small boy.

They entered the churchyard through a hole in the wall, choked with nettles. It lay at the east end of the building.

The graves were still covered with the faded remnants of flowers laid there on All Saints' Day. Galéas dropped his son's hand, and went in search of a barrow. Guillou watched him walk away. That was his father—that darned brown jersey, those trouser legs which looked as though there were nothing inside them, that tousled head under the tiny beret. He waited for him, seated on a gravestone which was half buried in the grass. The late sun had warmed it slightly. All the same, he felt cold. The thought came to him that he might catch a chill, that he might not be able to leave the house tomorrow. To die . . . to become like the people he tried to imagine lying under this rich soil—the dead, those human moles, marking their presence with little heaps of earth.

Beyond the wall he could see the countryside already emptied of life by the approach of winter: the shivering vines, the greasy, sticky soil—the elements at odds with man, to which it would be as mad to trust oneself as to the waves of the sea. At the bottom of the slope the Ciron flowed on toward the river, a small stream, swollen by the rains, moving through mysterious marshlands and a tangled wilderness of water plants. Guillou had heard the villagers say that sometimes they had put up woodcook there. Like one of them, the boy, driven from his hiding-place, sat trembling with cold and fear, with nothing to protect him from a hostile world and nature's cruelty. On the hillside, the industrial red of brand-new roofs shone harshly. Instinctively, his eyes sought the rain-worn pink of old and round-backed tiles. Close at hand, the church wall showed dishonorable cracks. One of the colored windows had been broken. He knew that "the Good God was not there," that the curé would not leave God in such a place for fear of sacrilege. Nor was the Good God in their Chapel at home, which Fraülein used now as a room in which to keep brooms and packing-cases and broken chairs. Where in this harsh world had God set up His dwelling? Where was a trace of Him to be found?

Guillou felt cold. A nettle had stung him on the calf. He got up and walked the few paces which lay between him and the War Memorial, unveiled the year before. There were thirteen names for this one small village: De Cernès, Georges; Laclotte, Jean; Lapeyre, Joseph; Lapeyre, Ernest; Lartigue, René. . . . Guillaume saw between the gravestones his father's brown jersey bend down, then straighten, and heard the squeaking of the barrow wheels. Tomorrow he was to be handed over to the red schoolmaster. Perhaps the schoolmaster would die suddenly in the night. Something might happen—a hurricane, an earthquake . . . But nothing would ever silence his mother's terrible voice, nothing would ever put out the terrible gleam in her eyes which, when they rested on him, made him conscious, all at once, of his skinniness, of his dirty knees, of his wrinkled and untidy socks. On those occasions, Guillaume would swallow his saliva, and, in the hope of pacifying the enemy, shut his mouth. . . . But the exasperated voice shattered the silence (it was as though it had pursued him into the tiny graveyard where he stood shivering). "Oh, go away, do; anywhere you like, so long as I don't see you!"

About the same time, Paula had lit the fire in her bedroom, and was giving free play to her thoughts. No one can make themselves beloved at will, or attract another merely by wishing to. But no power in Heaven, or in the earth beneath can keep a woman from picking out one man from the crowd, and choosing him to be her god. It does not matter to him, since he is not asked to give anything in return. It is she who decides to make him the idol at the center of her life. There is nothing she can do but raise an altar in the desert, and consecrate it to her curly-headed divinity.

Others, in the end, always ask favors of their god, but she was determined to ask nothing of hers. She would rob him only of what can be taken from another without his knowledge. . . . How miraculous a power dwells in the furtive glance, in the undisciplined thought! A day might come perhaps when she would dare to make some gesture of approach, and then— who knows?—her god might bear, without flinching, the touch of lips upon his hand.

HURRIEDLY, his mother dragged him along the road. The ruts were filled with rain-water. They passed the children going home from school, who spoke no word, nor laughed. The satchels on their backs were only to be guessed at from the way they showed as humps beneath the capes. Dark eyes and light from all these little hunchbacks gleamed from the shadow of their hoods. Guillou thought how soon they would have grown to be tormentors had he been forced to work and play with them. But he was to be delivered, sole and unaccompanied, to the schoolmaster who would have no one else to occupy his mind, who would concentrate upon his single person that terrifying power all grown-ups had to crush him with their questions, to weigh upon him with their arguments and explanations. No longer would that power be spread over a whole classroom of children. Guillou, and Guillou alone, would have to stand up to this monster of knowledge, who would be exasperated, irritated, by the presence of a boy who could not even understand the words with which his ears were being deafened.

He was going to school at a time when the other pupils were on their way home. The thought that that was so made a deep impression on him. He felt different, he felt lonely. The dry, warm hand which held his own tightened its grip. A force that was indifferent, if not actually hostile, to his feelings, was dragging him along. Shut away in a secret world of passions and of thoughts, his mother spoke not a single word. Already they had reached the first houses of the village. The lamps and the firelight shining behind the clouded window panes, cast a radiance on the dusk. The smoke of chimneys filled the night air with a smell of burning. From the Hotel Dupuy there streamed a brighter glow. Two wagons were standing in front of the door. The broad backs of their drivers were jostling before the bar. Still a minute to go. The light over there —*that* was it. He remembered the gruff voice his grandmother put on when she told him the tale of *Tom Thumb—"It was the ogre's house!"* Through the glass panes of the front door he could see the ogre's wife on the lookout for her prey.

"What are you trembling for, you little fool? Monsieur Bordas won't eat you."

"Perhaps he's cold?"

Paula shrugged and said irritably: "No, it's just nerves. It always takes him like that, for no apparent reason. He suffered from convulsions when he was eighteen months old."

Guillou's teeth were chattering. The only sound to be heard was the noise they made, and the ticking of the grandfather clock.

"Take off his boots, Léone," said the ogre, "and give him Jean-Pierre's slippers."

"Oh, please," protested Paula, "don't go to all that trouble."

But already Léone was coming back into the room with a pair of slippers. She perched Guillou on her knee, took off his cape, and moved close to the fire.

"Aren't you ashamed, a great big boy like you?" said his mother. "I haven't brought any of his schoolbooks or notebooks with me," she added.

The ogre assured her that he did not need them. This evening they would just talk and get to know each other.

"I'll come back in two hours," said Paula. Guillou could not hear what his mother and the schoolmaster were whispering in the entry. He knew that she had gone because he no longer felt cold. The front door had been shut.

"Would you like to help us shell kidney-beans?" Léone asked. "But perhaps you don't know how?"

He laughed and said that he always helped Fraülein. This talk of beans gave him a sense of security. He plucked up courage to add:

"Ours have been picked for a long time."

"These," said the schoolmaster's wife, "are the late kind. A lot of them are bad; you'll have to sort them out."

Guillou drew up to the table and started on the work. The Bordas' kitchen was like every other kitchen. It had a wide hearth with a pot hanging from a hook, a long table, copper saucepans on a dresser, a row of jam jars on another, and two hams in sacks suspended from the beams. . . . But Guillou felt that he had come into a strange, delicious world. Was it the smell of the pipe which was always in Monsieur Bordas' mouth, even when it wasn't alight? What most struck him were the books everywhere, and the piles of magazines on the sideboard and on a small table which stood within easy reach of the schoolmaster's hand. He sat there now, with his legs stretched out, paying no attention to Guillou, but engaged in cutting the pages of a Review which had a white cover with the title printed in red.

Above the chimney-piece was the portrait of a big, bearded man with folded arms. There was a word printed beneath it which the boy tried to spell out in a low voice from where he was sitting: "Jaur . . . Jaur. . . ."

"Jaurès," said the ogre suddenly. "Do you know who Jaurès was?"

Guillou shook his head. Léone broke in: "Surely you're not going to start by talking to him about Jaurès?"

"He began it," said Monsieur Bordas. He laughed. Guillou liked his eyes when they were all squinnied up with laughter. He would have liked to know who Jaurès was. He didn't at all mind shelling kidney-beans. He made a separate pile of the bad ones. He was being left to himself. He could think his own thoughts and take in the ogre, the ogre's wife and their house.

"Had enough of it?" Monsieur Bordas asked suddenly.

He was not reading his Review. He glanced through the table of contents, cut the pages, paused now and again at the names of the various contributors, held the paper close to his face, sniffing at it greedily. A magazine straight from Paris. He thought how unbelievably happy must be the lives of the men who worked on it. He tried to picture their faces, the editor's room where they met to exchange views . . . men, all of them, who knew everything, who had made the "circuit of the human mind." . . . Léone did not know that he had sent in an essay he had written on Romain Rolland. It had been refused, though the letter that told him so had been extremely polite. His approach had been too markedly political.

The rain was now splashing on the roof and gurgling in the gutters. One has only one life, and Robert Bordas would never know what it was like to live in Paris. Monsieur Lousteau was forever telling him that he could write a book about his experiences at Cernès, and advising him to keep a Journal. But he wasn't interested in himself. He wasn't, if it came to that, very much interested in other people either. He would have liked to persuade them, impose his ideas on them, but as individuals they did not appeal to him. . . . He had the gift of words, of writing articles at short notice. Monsieur Lousteau thought his contributions to *la France du Sud-Ouest* better than anything published in Paris, except in *l'Action française*. There was no one on the staff of *l'Humanité,* so Lousteau said, to hold a candle to him. . . . Paris . . . He had promised Léone never to leave Cernès, not even when Jean-Pierre went to the Ecole Normale . . . not even later, when their son should have made his mark and was occupying a high position. He mustn't be an old man of the sea, mustn't get in the lad's way. "Everyone's got his own place in life," said Léone. Robert got up and stood for a while with his face pressed to the glass panel of the front door. Coming back into the room, he saw Guillou's moist and gentle eyes fixed upon him. The boy looked away as he approached, and the schoolmaster remembered that he liked reading.

"Had enough of shelling beans, old man? Like me to lend you a picture-book?"

Guillou replied that it wouldn't matter if there weren't any pictures.

"Show him Jean-Pierre's library," said Léone, "then he can choose for himself."

Monsieur Bordas, carrying a paraffin lamp, led the way into the family bedroom. To the boy, following him, it seemed magnificent. The huge carved bedstead was dominated by a cherry-colored eiderdown. It was as though red-currant syrup had been spilled all over the counterpane. A number of enlarged photographs hung on the walls, close to the ceiling. Monsieur Bordas introduced him into a smaller room which had a slightly stuffy smell. It seemed to have been shut up for some time. The schoolmaster proudly raised the lamp, and, at once, Guillou was lost in admiration of Bordas Junior's room.

"Not so fine as up at the big house, of course," said his guide. "Still," he added, with a self-satisfied air, "it's not too bad. . . ."

The boy could scarcely believe his eyes. For the first time this little scion of a noble line found himself thinking of the hole in which he spent his nights. It was impregnated with the smell of Mademoiselle Adrienne who was in charge of the household linen, and spent all her afternoons there. A dressmaker's dummy, now out of use, stood beside a sewing machine, and there was a truckle bed covered with a dustsheet, which Fraülein occupied when Guillou was ill. He had a sudden vision of the shabby piece of rug on which he had so often upset his chamber pot. This room was all Jean-Pierre's own, with its painted bed in blue and white, and its glass-fronted, well-stocked bookcase.

"Almost all the volumes are prizes," said Monsieur Bordas. "He's always top of his form."

Guillou touched each separate book with loving fingers.

"Take what you'd like."

"Oh! . . . *The Mysterious Island!* . . . have you read that?"

56

he asked, looking at Monsieur Bordas with shining eyes.

"Yes, I read it when I was your age," said the schoolmaster, "but, d'you know, I've forgotten every word . . . it's a sort of Robinson Crusoe story, isn't it?"

"It's ever so much better than Robinson Crusoe!" said Guillou with enthusiasm.

"In what way is it better?"

This direct question sent the boy back into his shell. The vague, almost vacant, look reappeared on his face.

"I always thought it was a sequel to something else," went on Monsieur Bordas, after a pause.

"It is. You ought to have read *Twenty Thousand Leagues Under the Sea,* first, and *Captain Grant's Children*. . . . I haven't read *Twenty Thousand Leagues Under the Sea,* but it doesn't really make any difference. You can understand *The Mysterious Island* just the same . . . except where Cyrus Smith makes things like dynamite . . . I always skip those parts."

"Isn't there a shipwrecked man on one of the neighboring islands whom the engineer's companions discover?"

"Yes, he's called Ayrton, you know. There's a lovely bit when Cyrus Smith says to him, 'If you can cry that means you are a man.'"

Without looking at the boy, Monsieur Bordas took the fat, red-bound book and held it out.

"Try and find the place . . . I seem to remember; there's a picture, I think."

"It's at the end of chapter fifteen," said Guillou.

"Read that page to me . . . it'll take me back to my childhood."

He lit an oil lamp and settled Guillou at a table covered with Jean-Pierre's ink-stains. The boy began to read in a muffled voice. At first the schoolmaster could catch only one or two words. He was sitting far back in the shadows, scarcely daring to breathe. It was as though he were afraid of startling a wild bird. Gradually, the reader's voice grew stronger and more distinct. He had forgotten now that anyone was listening.

". . . When they reached the spot where the first tall trees of the forest grew, their leaves faintly stirring in the breeze, the stranger began greedily sniffing the smell which filled the air. He sighed deeply. The planters kept well behind, ready to seize him should he make any attempt to escape. And indeed, the poor wretch was about to plunge into the creek which lay between him and the forest. For a brief moment his legs were like two springs at the moment of release. . . . But almost at once he fell back, half collapsing, and a large tear welled up in his eye. 'Ah,' exclaimed Cyrus Smith: 'If you can cry, it means that you have once more become a man!' "

"How fine that is!" said Monsieur Bordas. "It all comes back to me now. Isn't the island attacked by convicts?"

"Yes, and it's Ayrton who first catches sight of the black flag. . . . Would you like me to go on reading?"

The schoolmaster pushed his chair still further back. He could, he should, have been lost in wonder at sound of the ardent voice coming from this boy who was generally regarded as an idiot. He could, he should, have rejoiced in the task that had been laid upon him, at the power that was his to save this trembling scrap of humanity. But he heard the boy only through the tumult of his own thoughts. . . . Here he was, a man of forty, burning with desires, bursting with ideas, yet fated never to escape from a schoolhouse in an empty village street. He could understand and appraise all that was printed in the magazine. The smell of its ink and gum was in his nostrils. All the questions of which it treated were familiar to him, though he could talk of them to nobody but Monsieur Lousteau. There was a lot, too, that Léone could have grasped, but she preferred her daily chores. Her mind was growing indolent as her physical activities increased. It had become a matter of pride to her that she could scarcely keep her eyes open when evening came, so tired did she feel. Sometimes she was filled with pity for her husband, for she was too intelligent not to realize that he was suffering. But in Jean-Pierre they would find their compensation. It was her opinion that when a man has reached her husband's age he is willing enough to shift the burden of ambition to the shoulders of his son . . . that was her opinion.

He noticed that the boy, having reached the end of the chapter, had stopped.

"Shall I go on?"

"No," said Monsieur Bordas, "take a rest. You read very well. Would you like me to lend you one of Jean-Pierre's books?"

Guillou jumped up and once again began to examine all the volumes, one by one, spelling out their titles in a low voice.

"*Sans famille* . . . is that a nice one?"

"Jean-Pierre used to be very fond of it. But he reads more serious books now."

"D'you think I should understand it?"

"Of course you would! My school work doesn't give me much time for reading nowadays. . . . You shall tell me what it's about, a bit each day. I shall enjoy that."

"That's what you say! . . . but I know you're laughing at me, really. . . ."

Guillou walked over to the fireplace. He looked at a photograph leaning against the mirror. It showed schoolboys grouped round two masters wearing pince-nez. Their trousers were stretched tight over their large knees. He asked whether Jean-Pierre was there.

"Yes, in the front row—to the right of the master."

He would have recognized him, thought Guillou, even if he had not been pointed out. Among all the other dim and meaningless faces, this one face glowed. Was it because of all he had been hearing about Jean-Pierre that he thought that? For the first time in his life, he was realizing what a human face could be like. He had often looked long and fondly at pictures, in love with the features of some figure of fiction. But now it suddenly came to him that this boy with the high forehead, the close curls, and the frown between his eyes, was the boy who had actually read these books, worked at this table, slept in this bed.

"Is this room really his very own? Can't anyone come into it if he doesn't want them to?"

He, himself, was never alone except in the lavatory. . . .

The rain was splashing on the roof. How lovely it must be to live all shut away among all these books . . . beyond the reach of other people. But Jean-Pierre needed no defenses. He

was top of his form in every subject. He had even won a prize
for gymnastics, Monsieur Bordas had said.

Léone pushed the door open. "Your mother has come for
you, young man."

Once more he followed on behind the schoolmaster carrying
the lamp. Once more he crossed the family bedroom. Paula de
Cernès was drying her shoes at the fire. She must have come
by dirty field-paths. . . .

"No need for me to ask whether you got anything out of
him. Of course you didn't!"

Monsieur Bordas protested that things hadn't gone badly at
all. The boy stood with hanging head while Léone buttoned
his cape.

"Would you mind coming outside with me for a moment?"
said Paula. "It has left off raining, and I should like to know
what you really think."

The schoolmaster took down his mackintosh. His wife followed him into their bedroom. He wasn't going to go stump-
ing the roads at night with that madwoman, was he? He'd
be getting himself talked about. . . . All this she asked, but
only got a snub for her pains. Paula, who could guess the subject of their whispered conversation, pretended that she had
heard nothing. At the front door she once again overwhelmed
Léone with protestations of gratitude. Then, with the schoolmaster at her side, she plunged into the damp darkness. She
said to Guillou:

"You run along ahead, and don't keep getting under our
feet."

Her voice, when she turned to her companion, was firm and
determined.

"I want to know the truth, no matter how painful the truth may be to a mother's ears."

He had slowed his pace. Might not Léone be right after all? Whatever happened, they mustn't be seen together crossing the path of light which came from the Hotel Dupuy. But even had he been certain that they would not be seen, he would still have been on the defensive. He had never been anything else with women, since the days of his boyhood. It had always been they who sought him out, always he who had run away —and not that he might be the more urgently pursued.

As they approached the Hotel Dupuy, he halted.

"We had better postpone this conversation till tomorrow. Come to my house toward the end of the morning. I finish at the *Mairie* just before noon."

She knew perfectly well why he did not want to walk further with her. The thought that there was something very like the beginning of a plot between them filled her with joy.

"Yes," she murmured; "that will be much better."

"Till tomorrow evening then, Guillaume, my boy. You shall read *Sans famille* to me."

Monsieur Bordas did no more than raise one finger to his beret. Almost at once he was lost to sight, but Paula could still hear, from time to time, the noise made by his stick striking a stone. The boy too remained for a few moments motionless in the middle of the road, gazing back at the light which came from Jean-Pierre's home.

His mother took him by the arm. She asked him no questions. There was nothing to be got out of him. Besides, what did she care? Tomorrow they were to have their first meeting, their first intimate talk. She gripped Guillou's little hand more tightly than she need have done. The cold of the rain-drenched road struck through her shoes.

"Come to the fire," said Fraülein; "you're soaked to the skin."

Every eye was fixed on him. He would have to answer all their questions.

"Well, so your schoolmaster didn't gobble you up after all?"

He shook his head.

"What did you do for those two hours?"

He did not know what to say. What *had* he done? His mother pinched his arm.

"Didn't you hear? What did you do for those two hours?"

"I shelled beans."

The Baronne raised her hands.

"So he shelled beans for them! A nice thing, I must say!" she said, unconsciously imitating her Arbis grandchildren. "Do you hear that, Paula? The schoolmaster and his wife sit there gloating, while *my* grandson shells their beans for them! Just what I might have expected. Perhaps they asked you to sweep out the kitchen?"

"No, Mamie. I only shelled beans. A lot had gone bad, and I had to sort them out."

"It didn't take them long to size him up!" said Paula.

Fraülein protested: "I think it was only that they didn't want to scare him the first day."

But the Baronne knew what was to be expected from people like that once they had got anyone in their clutches.

"No doubt it gives them a great deal of pleasure to play a trick like that on us. But if they think they've got the better

63

of me, they're very much mistaken. I don't mind in the least."

"If they treated Guillou badly . . ." broke in Fraülein sharply, "I am very sure that Madame la Baronne would not tolerate it . . . after all, he is her own grandson. . . ."

Guillou's voice rose shrill: "The schoolmaster isn't a bad man!"

"Because he made you shell beans? . . . you like doing servant's work . . . you like being a good-for-nothing. . . . But he's going to make you read, and write and do sums . . . and with him," went on Paula, "you'll have to watch how you go. Don't forget that he's a schoolmaster!"

In a low, trembling voice Guillou stuck to his point. "He isn't a bad man . . . he's made me read already . . . and he says I read well."

But his mother, Mamie and Fraülein had begun bickering again, and were not listening.

All right, then, what did he care? He'd *keep* his secret. The schoolmaster had made him read *The Mysterious Island*. To-morrow he was going to start on *Sans famille*. Every evening now he would go to Monsieur Bordas' house. He could look at Jean-Pierre's photograph for as long as he liked. Already he adored Jean-Pierre madly. They would become friends during the summer holidays. He would turn the pages of all Jean-Pierre's books, one by one, the books which Jean-Pierre's hands had touched. It was not because of Monsieur Bordas that his heart was overflowing with happiness, but because of an unknown boy. The sense of delight never left him for the whole evening. It was with him during the interminable meal, at which the irascible gods sat, separated by deserts of silence, during which Guillou could hear Galéas chewing and swal-

lowing. It stayed with him while he groped his way out of
his clothes between the dressmaker's dummy and the sewing
machine, while he lay shivering between his stained sheets,
when he began his prayers all over again because he had not
paid attention to the meaning of the words, and when he had
to struggle against the temptation of lying on his stomach. . . .
Long after sleep had come, a smile still lit the child's face, that
was like the face of an old man, with moist and pendulous
lips. It was a smile which might have filled his mother with
surprise had she been one of those women who tuck their
children up in bed, and leave a blessing with them for the
night.

About the same time, Léone broke in on her husband's reading.

"Look!" she exclaimed, "what that filthy little creature has
done to Jean-Pierre's book! There are finger marks all over
it, and even traces of nose-dirt! What can have come over us
to lend him Jean-Pierre's books!"

"There's nothing particularly sacrosanct about them . . .
You're not the mother of the Messiah!"

Léone, now thoroughly put out, raised her voice:

"I won't have the little horror here again! You can give him
his lessons in the schoolroom, in the stables, anywhere you
like, but not here!"

Robert shut his book, got up, went across, and sat down
beside his wife in front of the fire.

"You're not exactly a model of consistency, are you? Only
a little while ago you were blaming me because I showed the
old Baronne the door, and now you've got a grievance because

I behaved decently to her daughter-in-law. . . . It's the bearded lady that's the trouble . . . it's no use your denying it . . . poor bearded lady!"

"And don't *you* deny that it'd be a fine feather in your cap!" said Léone, giving him a kiss. "I know you. What a scalp to hang at your belt—the lady from the great house!"

"I really don't think I could bring it off, not even if I wanted to."

"Oh I know all about what differentiates men," said Léone; "you've explained it to me often enough. There are those who are always ready for it, and those who aren't . . ."

"Yes, and those who are always ready, don't, really, live for anything else, because, whatever people may say, it's about the pleasantest thing in life."

"And those who aren't," said Léone, continuing with the litany (there were several "gags," dating from the days when they were first engaged, which they were always trotting out, because they could always be relied upon to bring every argument to a happy end), "devote themselves to God, to Science, or to Literature. . . ."

"Or to their own sex," wound up Robert. She laughed and went into the bathroom, leaving the door open. As he was undressing, he called out to her:

"You know, I wouldn't have minded taking on the little wretch . . . might have been interesting."

She came back looking pleased with herself and rather appealing in her faded red flannel nightgown, with her rather lifeless hair braided in a plait.

"Then you've given up the idea?"

"If I have, it's not because of the bearded lady! But I've

been thinking . . . I'll have to go back on my promise. I ought never to have given it in the first place. We mustn't have anything to do with the great house. The class-war isn't just something in a textbook. It's part of our daily life, and it ought to control our every action."

He broke off. She was squatting on her heels, cutting her toenails. She was quite determined not to listen.

". . . One can't talk to women . . ."

The mattress creaked under the weight of his large body. She snuggled up against him and blew out the candle. The room was filled with the smell of burned wick. It was a smell they both of them loved, because it was the precursor of love-making and sleep.

"No, not tonight," said Léone.

They whispered for a while.

"Stop talking now, I'm going to sleep."

"Just one more thing: how on earth am I going to get that urchin off my hands?"

"All you've got to do is write a note to the bearded lady, explaining all about the class-war. She'll understand all right . . . after all, she *was* a Mademoiselle Meulière! . . . We'll send one of the kids round with it tomorrow. . . . Look, it's hardly dark at all!"

Cocks were crowing to one another. In the linen closet of the great house, where Fraülein had forgotten to draw the curtains, the moon shone down on Guillou, a pale little ghost perched on his chamber-pot. Behind him, armless, headless, stood the dummy which no one ever used.

4

THE note delivered by one of the schoolchildren had brought his mother and Mamie much earlier than usual from their rooms. They had the terrible appearance of old people early in the morning, before they had washed, and while their discolored teeth, embedded in pink, are still reposing in tumblers of water by their bedsides. Mamie's scalp looked smooth and polished between her thin strands of faded hair, and her empty mouth made it seem as though she were sucking in her cheeks. They were both talking at the same time. Galéas, seated at table, between his two hounds—whose jaws snapped every time he threw them a scrap of food—was drinking his coffee as though it hurt him. To see him, one would think that every mouthful was an agony. It was Guillaume's firm conviction that the enormous Adam's apple prevented the food from going down. He kept his mind concentrated on his father. He did not want to understand the meaning of the heated words now passing between his mother and Mamie on the subject of the note. But he knew already that he would never again enter Jean-Pierre's room.

"That wretched little Communist teacher's nothing to do with me!" exclaimed Mamie. "It's *you* he's written to. This snub is aimed at you, my dear."

"What do you mean—snub? He is reading me a lesson. It

is a lesson I needed, and I'm glad of it. I believe in the class-war just as much as he does. I didn't mean him any harm. Still, I did urge him to betray his own people."

"What on earth you're getting at, my poor dear, I do *not* know!"

"Here's a young man with all his life before him, and every reason to hope for a brilliant future. And what do I do? I try to compromise him in the eyes of his comrades and his Party leaders . . . And for what, I ask you? . . . For the sake of a little backward degenerate. . . ."

"I am present, Paula."

She guessed at, rather than heard, her husband's protest. He was still sitting crouched over his bowl of bread and milk. When he grew excited, his thick tongue gave passage only to a confused muddle of sound. Raising his voice, he added: "Guillaume happens to be present too."

"The things one's got to listen to!" exclaimed Fraülein, and vanished into the scullery.

By this time, the old Baronne had recovered her breath.

"So far as I know, Guillaume is your son too!"

Hatred had quickened the senile jerking of the aged head which was bare and bald and prepared already for the noth-ingness of death.

Paula whispered in her ear: "Just look at them both—the original and the copy. It's extraordinary how alike they are!"

The Baronne straightened her back, looked her daughter-in-law up and down without replying, and then, with not a word to Guillou, got up and left the kitchen. The child's gray little face expressed nothing at all. There was a fog outside, and, since Fraülein never washed the one and only window, almost the only light in the room came from the flickering logs in the grate. . . . The two hounds with their muzzles on their paws, and the rough-hewn legs of the enormous table, looked for a moment almost as though they were on fire.

Not another word was spoken. Paula had gone too far, as she fully realized, had affronted the great army of her husband's race, his thousand sleeping ancestors. Galéas uncurled his long legs, scrambled to his feet, wiped his mouth with the back of his hand, and asked the boy whether he had got his cape. He fastened it round the scrawny, birdlike neck, and took Guillou's hand in his. He kicked the two dogs awake. They leaped, fawning on him, all eagerness to follow. Fraülein asked where they were off to. Paula took the words out of his mouth:

"Oh, to the churchyard, of course!"

Yes, that was where they were going. A red sun was struggling with the fog which might lift later, or dissolve in rain. Guillou clung to his father's hand, but very soon had to let it go because it was so damp. Not a word did they exchange until they reached the Church. The family tomb of the Cernès stood against the churchyard wall from which the eye could look across the Ciron valley. Galéas went off to fetch a spade from the sacristy. The boy sat down on a gravestone at some little distance from the tomb. He pulled the hood of his cape over his head, then moved no more. . . . Monsieur Bordas didn't want to have anything more to do with him. The fog was acting like a sounding-board. He could hear a distant wagon, a crowing cock, the monotonous drone of a motor car, above the unbroken threshing of the mill-wheel, and the roar

of the weir, near which, in summer time, the village boys
bathed naked. A robin sang quite close to him. The migrant
birds he loved had flown. Monsieur Bordas didn't want to have
anything more to do with him. Not a soul, anywhere, wanted
him. "I don't care," he said in a low voice, and then, again,
as though in challenge to some unseen enemy—"I don't care!"
What a noise the weir was making—it was less than a kilometer
away as the crow flies. A sparrow winged its way out of the
Church through the broken window. "The Good God isn't
there"—that was what Mamie said: "They have taken the Good
God away. . . ." He was nowhere else, only up in the sky.
Dead children are like angels, with pure and shining faces.
Guillou's tears, said Mamie, were dirty tears. The more he cried,
the filthier his face became, because his grubby hands smeared
it with earth. When he got home, his mother would say . . .
Mamie would say . . . Fraülein would say . . .

Monsieur Bordas wasn't going to have anything more to do
with him. He would never again go into Jean-Pierre's room.
Jean-Pierre. Jean-Pierre Bordas. How strange to love a boy
whom one has never seen, and never will see. "If he had met
me, he would have thought me ugly, dirty, stupid." That was
what his mother told him every day: "You're ugly, dirty, stupid." Jean-Pierre Bordas would never know that Guillaume de
Cernès was ugly, dirty, stupid—a ragamuffin. And he was
something else, too. What was the word his mother had used
just now?—a word which had struck his father like a stone?
He tried to remember, and could think only of "regenerate."
It was some word like "regenerate."

Tonight he would fall asleep, but not at once. He would have
to wait for sleep, wait through a whole night like last night

when he had been trembling with happiness. He had fallen asleep thinking that when he woke he would see Monsieur Bordas again, that when evening came, he would sit in Jean-Pierre's room and start to read *Sans famille.* . . . If only he could believe that tonight everything would be as it had been then! . . . He got to his feet, made his way round the Cernès tomb, clambered over the wall, and took the path which went steeply downhill toward the Ciron.

Galéas turned his head and saw that the boy was no longer there. He went to the wall and looked over it. The little hood was moving among the vine rows, getting further and further away. He threw his spade aside and started off down the same path. When he was no more than a few yards from the boy, he slowed his pace. Guillou had thrown back his hood. He was not wearing a beret. Between his large, projecting ears his cropped head looked very small. His legs were like two twigs ending in enormous boots. His chicken neck stuck out above the cape. With his eyes Galéas devoured the little shambling creature, the tiny shrewmouse with marks of blood upon it of the trap from which it had escaped. It was his own son, his image in the flesh, with a whole life to live, yet now, already, burdened with a long-borne weight of suffering. But the torment had only just begun. The torturers would gain new strength. Those of childhood are different from those of youth; and there would be still others when he had become a man full grown. Could he learn to be numb and sottish? Would he have to defend himself, at every moment of his life, against the woman who would be always there, the woman with the Gorgon's face blotched with bilious yellow? Hatred caught at his breath, but, more than hatred, shame, because it was he who had been that woman's torturer. Only once had he taken her in his arms, only once. She was, now, like a bitch confined—not for a few days only. Through all her youth it had gone on, and for years and years she would go howling for the absent male. . . . With what fantasies . . . what actions . . . had he, Galéas, cheated hunger . . . Every night, yes, every night, and in the morning, too. . . . Such would be the lot of this abortion born of their one embrace, and now running, now hurrying—to what? Did he know? Though the child had not once turned his head, perhaps he was conscious of his father's presence. Galéas was persuaded that it was so! He knows I am behind him. He takes no pains to hide himself from me, no, nor to cover his tracks. He is as a guide, leading me to where he wants me to be with him! Galéas could not bring himself to face the issue to which these last two of the Cernès line were hastening. A tremble of alder leaves spoke of the nearby river. Not now was it the King of the Alders who, in a final gallop, was pursuing the boy, but the boy now who was leading his uncrowned and insulted father toward the sleeping waters of the weir, the pool in which the village boys, in summer, bathed naked. They were close now to the watery confines of that kingdom where never more would they be harassed by wife or mother. They would be delivered from the Gorgon; they would sleep.

They had reached the shade of the tall pines on the river bank. The still living bracken fronds were almost as high as Guillou, whose cropped head Galéas could scarcely see emerging from their tangled wilderness. At a turning of the sandy path the boy once more vanished from sight. They might have met some resin-gatherer, the muleteer from the mill, a sportsman out after woodcock. But every witness had withdrawn from this small corner of the world that the act might be accomplished which these two were fated to perform—one leading the other? or urging him forward unwillingly?—who would ever know? There was none to see them, but only the giant pines crowding about the weir. They burned during the following August, left too long untapped. For a long while they spread their calcined limbs above the sleeping water; for a long while they reared against the sky their blackened faces.

The accepted view was that Galéas had jumped into the water to save his son, that the boy had clung about his neck and pulled him down. Such vague rumors as had at first been current were soon silenced by the touching story of a father done to death by his small son's clutching hands. Some might shake their heads and say . . . "Well, I don't feel sure that it happened like that" . . . but the true explanation no one could well imagine. How should anyone suspect a father who loved his boy, and took him every day when he went to the churchyard? . . . "Monsieur Galéas may have been a bit simple, but he had his wits about him all the same and there never was a sweeter-natured man."

No one grudged Fraülein the cape which she had taken, sodden with water, from Guillou's body. . . . The old Baronne was happy to think that Cernès would descend to the Arbis children, and that she would be quit, once and for all, of Paula, to whom the Meulières had offered a home. She was, as they put it, back on their hands. But she had a malignant tumor. On the glossy walls, in the stifling atmosphere of the hospital (the nurse forever coming in with the basin whether she wanted it or not, and even if she was too tired to open her eyes—and the morphine which was so bad for her liver—and the visits of her aunt always worrying over the terrible expense, which was quite useless anyhow, because the end was a foregone conclusion)—on the glossy walls she sometimes saw, as on a screen, Galéas' shaggy head, and the brat looking up from a torn book, an ink-stained exercise, with his dirty, anxious face. Perhaps she imagined these things? She saw, in fancy, the boy creeping close to the bank, shivering because he was afraid, not of death, but of the cold—and his father tiptoeing behind him. . . . At that point she hesitated. Had he pushed him, or plunged after him?—or had he taken the small boy in his arms, saying, "Hold tight to me, and don't look." . . . Paula did not know, nor ever would. She was happy to think that her own death was close at hand. She kept on telling the nurse that the morphine made her feel ill, that her liver could not stand any more injections. She wanted to drain her cup to the dregs—not that she believed in an unseen world whither our victims precede us, where we can fall at the knees of those who were confided to our care, and have, through our fault, been lost. It never occurred to her that she might be judged. She stood at no bar save that of her own conscience. She was absolved in her own sight from the horror she had felt for a son who was the image of a hated father. She had spewed up the Cernès family, because nausea is something that one cannot control. But it was of her own free will that she had consented to share the bed of a half-impotent monster. She had allowed him to take her in his arms, and that, in her eyes, was the crime for which there was no pardon.

Sometimes the pain was so acute that she could not resist the morphine's promise of a moment's respite. In those lucid intervals she thought of all the lives she might have had. In fancy she was Robert Bordas' wife, surrounded by a brood of healthy boys, whose lower lips did not hang down, who did not slaver. Each night he took her in his arms, and she slept pressed close to his body. She dreamed of men's hairy pelts, and of their smell. She never knew what time of day or night it was. Pain knocked at the door; pain entered in and took its lodgement, and started slowly to eat her life away.

That a mother should be ashamed of her son, or of her grandson, should not, thought Fraülein, be permitted. She could not forgive her mistress for having shed so few tears over Galéas and Guillou having gone, for having, perhaps, been happy at their going. But Madame la Baronne would pay a heavy price. The Arbis family would never let her die in peace at Cernès. "Suppose I told Madame la Baronne what I heard their chauffeur say after the funeral—about how could anyone think that a woman of her age could possibly need a gardener, an assistant gardener, and two indoor servants, and all the expenses of a house? That is how their minds are working. I know that they have been inquiring about terms for aged pensioners of the Ladies of the Presentation at Verdelais." . . . The Baronne kept turning and twisting her bald vulture's head among the pillows. She would refuse to go to the Ladies of the Presentation . . . If the Arbis have decided, Madame la Baronne will go, and I with her. Madame la Baronne has never been able to say "no" to the Arbis. They frighten her; and, I confess, they frighten me.

Thursday: a respite from the children. But the schoolmaster had his work to do at the *Mairie*. Hurriedly he passed a washing glove over his face which was puffy with sleep. What point was there in shaving? Nobody who mattered would see him. He did not put on walking shoes. In weather like this a pair of socks would keep his feet warm, and with clogs on, he need not fear getting them wet. Léone had gone to the butcher's. He could hear the rain upon the roof. There was a puddle right across the road. When Léone got back, she would say, "What are you thinking about?" and he would answer "nothing." They had not so much as mentioned Guillou's name since the day when the two bodies had been fished out of the mill-pond. Then, for the first and only time, he had said: "The lad killed himself, or else his father . . ." and Léone with a shrug had muttered, "Do you really think so?" From then on, they had never mentioned the boy's name. But Léone knew that the little skeleton in cape and hood was forever wandering through the school, and creeping about the playground, not joining in the games. Robert Bordas went into Jean-Pierre's room, and took up *The Mysterious Island*. The book opened of itself. ". . . the poor wretch was about to plunge into the creek which lay between him and the forest. For a brief moment, his legs were like two springs at the moment of release . . . But almost at once he fell back, half collapsing, and a large tear welled up in his eye. 'Ah,' exclaimed Cyrus Smith: 'if you can cry, it means that you have once more become a man!'" . . . Monsieur Bordas sat down on Jean-Pierre's bed. The thick red book with its golden titling lay open on his knee. . . . Guillou . . . In that suffering body a human spirit had lain unawakened. How wonderful to have helped it into consciousness. That, maybe, was the task which Robert Bordas had been born into this world to accomplish. At the Ecole Normale, one of the professors had taught Etymology—*Instituteur*—schoolmaster—from *Institutor*—one who builds, one who instructs, one who sets the human spirit in a man. A fine word. He might meet other Guillous on his road. For the sake of the child whom he had left to die, he would never again refuse to give of his utmost to those who came to him. But none of them would be that same small boy who now was dead because Monsieur Bordas had one day taken him in, and the next, had thrown him out like a stray puppy that he had warmed a moment at his fire. He had sent him into the darkness forever. But was it really darkness? He strained his eyes in an effort to see beyond material things, beyond the walls and the furniture of this, his house, beyond the tiled roof, beyond the star-pointed night, beyond the winter constellations. He sat there, seeking the kingdom of the spirit where, rapt away into eternity, the boy could see him still, and on his cheek, stubbly with unshaven beard, a tear he had not thought to wipe away.

The spring grass strayed into the churchyard at Cernès. Roots took hold upon the untended graves; moss made the epitaphs unreadable. Since the day when Galéas had taken his small son by the hand, choosing that they should sleep together, there had been nobody at Cernès to concern himself about the dead.

THE ENEMY

1

IT WAS the habit of Madame Dézaymeries to get up at daybreak and, after Mass, to waken Fabien with a kiss. The kiss tasted of church and smelt of fog. The child loved the light, as of some unknown land, that showed in his mother's eyes. Each afternoon, when he got back from the park, she took him to the Cathedral for the Holy Hour. He watched her lips, convinced that she must be seeing God because she never stopped talking to Him. Fabien was conscious of the boredom of the passing moments, but there was in them, too, a quality of pleasure. He pretended that his right hand was a woman whom he was loading with necklaces. These necklaces were a rosary. A priest passed under a canopy, preceded by a small boy. A bell tinkled. The figures of the faithful turned, with a noise of scraping chairs, toward this manifestation of the Presence. When the Monstrance gleamed in the middle of its six candles, Madame Dézaymeries did not kneel, but stood, head up, looking God straight in the face.

When evening came, she walked up and down the passage, her rosary twined about her fingers. She held it stretched between her two hands, like a skein of wool, the better to see the point she had reached in her "telling." Fabien followed behind, holding up her dress, which he liked to imagine was of silk brocade. Night began for him with the evening prayer.

His mother put him to bed, made the sign of the Cross on
his forehead with her thumb, crossed his hands on his breast
and listened while he repeated the ritual sentences that should
guard him against the threat of sudden death. She did not
scruple to let him see the possibility that sleep might open
straight into the endless vistas of eternity. His life followed
the rhythm of the liturgical year. When the candles were lit
round the Manger, he became a shepherd. On Holy Thursday
he kneeled before the stripped altar, hearing with mingled terror and delight the lamentations of Jeremiah, and watching
the candles of yellow wax go out one by one. The bells on
Resurrection Morning danced with the gaiety of life reborn.
The air of the Month of Mary filled his nostrils with the scent
of white roses. No somber weight lay upon his life. Austerity
wreathed it like a mist shot through with sunlight. No fears
of hell-fire troubled him, nor yet of purgatory, since no Indulgence was neglected, and he drew with method on the treasures
of the Faith.

Joseph, his fifteen-year-old elder brother, took delight in
games that foreshadowed his vocation, games in which altars,
processions and sermons played the principal parts. He was at
boarding school, and came home only on Sundays after Ves-
pers. The prevalent view was that, thin and overgrown though
he was, he had a constitution of iron because he had escaped
whooping cough, mumps, measles and all the childish ailments
to which Fabien owed many periods of dreamy happiness during which he lived the life of a lazy and pampered Prince.
But sickness of quite another kind was laying in wait for
Joseph. It was, indeed, already at work in his system, though,
for the time being, the only sign of its presence was what

Madame Dézaymeries called a "shocking cold" which the local nursing Sister treated with a daily spoonful of "Tolu" syrup. Fabien sought his company but rarely, and as a rule only when, after making his confession and tortured by scruples lest he might not have described certain of his faults in sufficient detail, he went to him for comfort. Quite often he would deliberately munch a blade of grass before Mass, or swallow a mouthful of water when he cleaned his teeth, so as to avoid having to take Communion, so fearful was he of committing sacrilege. Joseph was always very indignant at such tricks.

Madame Dézaymeries' Spiritual Director had a little talk with Fabien every day. He did not wear his stole on these occasions, and was careful to smile throughout the interview. With nothing of aggressiveness in his manner, but with an air of determination which was never oppressive, he had so worked on Madame Dézaymeries that she had grown to regard her widowhood as a species of religious vocation. He had set before this family of three the goal of perfection, and kept them isolated in a hedged and cloistered life. They visited none but the poor, and limited their social existence to official contacts with the clergy of the parish, about whom, Madame Dézaymeries sometimes went so far as to maintain, there was nothing supernatural. As President of the Christian Mothers, and Vice-President of the Ladies of Charity, she lent her drawing room for meetings so little worldly that the dust-sheets were never taken off the chairs, and the chandelier in its protective envelope hung like Montgolfier's balloon, motionless beneath a ceiling that prevented it from rising.

This pious routine had such a hold on Fabien that even at school, whither he went when he was about thirteen, he was completely untroubled by the prickings of the flesh. Hints and murmured revelations fell dead on the threshold of his heart and penetrated no further. He was entirely without interest in the things of the body, and was blessed with a divine stupidity in all matters that had to do with the vice of sensual indulgence. A saintly woman kept her hand in front of his eyes and shut him away from any vision of the world. He was wholly without knowledge of the powers that lurk within us, of the strident clamor of desire, of the storm that rages about the ship of humanity when God slumbers in the stern. But no woman can, unaided, make a man. Madame Dézaymeries, happy in her contemplation of the innocent and tranquil face that Fabien bent about his books, was blind to the fact that his arms were not so weak as Joseph's, nor his chest so hollow. At fifteen his boy's head with its brown hair sat ill upon his sturdy frame. She forgot that another than herself had had a share in the forming of this young creature whose expression was so pure though he was over-given to dreaming; who was so scornful of bodily activities though built for physical prowess; who was content to live in ignorance of a body which stood already on the threshold of manhood.

She never spoke to her sons of their father, who had died shortly before Fabien was born. Yet the boy had only to look at his strong peasant bones, at his large, well-formed hands and wrists, at the muscles that were so tough for all their lack of exercise, to get some inkling of the nature of the unknown man who had given him life. Though the two boys had been brought up entirely by their mother, their movements were those of "poor papa," and the thick tones and country intonations of their voices belonged to him. Like him they were slow of step and seemingly docile to all external authority. But, deep down, they were reserved and inaccessible. Up to the age of twenty they knew nothing of the denizens of this world—with one exception. As the result of some curious aberration, their mother had given the freedom of the family circle to a stranger. Twice in each year, between Christmas and the New Year, and again in the middle of July, she shot across their night-sky, like one of those stars whose trajectory can be plotted in advance, leaving a trail of brilliance.

She had only to ring the front-door bell for the boys to go scampering from the fireside. "It's Fanny Barrett! It's Fanny!" they would cry in the hall. A distillation of perfume hung about her furs. For a moment she pressed her veiled face to Madame Dézaymeries' shoulder. A pastry cook and a waiter always came with her, because she feared that the dinner prepared for her might be insufficient. Fabien long remembered the labels on her bags, "Wanted on Voyage." It seemed to him as though the salt of all the oceans of the world had eaten into them. Toys, sweets and books made their appearance to a wonderful and rustling accompaniment of tissue paper. Octavie got the green room ready—that spare room that was spared only for Fanny.

The children knew that Fanny Barrett had been left an orphan, had moved from Dublin, her native city, and had come to the great port on the southwest coast of France where her uncle, on whom the duty of bringing her up had devolved, was associated in business with their Dupouy grandfather. At that time, Madame Dézaymeries, or, as she then was, Thérèse Dupouy, had the reputation of being a gawky girl of devout tendencies. Her father and mother, though rich, lived in self-imposed poverty. The only pleasure they would countenance, whether for themselves or for others, was that of "putting money aside." This they regarded as being the highest of all virtues. Old Dupouy had trained his wife in the ethics of economy so successfully that their house, filled with old trunks, disused bottles and empty packing-cases, had at first the dusty, overcrowded appearance of one of those dwellings where nothing is ever lost or thrown away. An elder and detestable sister had succeeded in casting a blight on Thérèse's youth. The Dupouys were one of those "good families" the members of which can endure one another only by behaving as miracles of virtue, who put up with this present life simply and solely because they believe in a better life to come. On each first Thursday in the month, Monsieur Maggie, Dupouy's partner, who was held in horror by the family because of his dissolute life (he kept a *première danseuse* called Mademoiselle Lovati, who cost him a hundred louis a month), was always at his wits' end to know what to do with his niece Fanny during her twelve hours' exeat from the Convent. He handed her over, therefore, to the tender mercies of the gloomy Thérèse, much as he might have given her a tame bird, and very soon a passionate devotion grew up between the two girls. The Dupouy parents dared not object to a charge of such manifest piety, but they grew to dread those recurring Thursdays which filled their melancholy abode with gusts of laughter and the sound of young feet racing up and down the passages. Much later, when Fanny, now of age and her own mistress, returned from Ireland after a long period of eclipse, to visit her great friend who was already a widow and the mother of two sons, living in what had once been the Dupouy, but was now the Dézaymeries' house, Thérèse blamed

86

herself for having been too indulgent toward the faults of her junior, whose coquetry, petulance and excessive fondness for caresses she had, in the past, gone so far as to encourage. Particularly was she conscious of a sense of guilt in that she had taken so little heed of her companion's neglect of everything that touched upon religion. But this early love had left deep traces in her character, as was proved by the fact that she still remained loyal to it and shut her eyes to what, in anybody else, she would have regarded as an abomination.

The Irish girl had married an officer of the Royal Navy, but spoke of him as little as possible. She wandered about the world as freely as though she had been a widow. The Dézaymeries' knew nothing of her vagabond existence, and were completely unaware that she had been, for some time, separated from her husband, that she busied herself with selling curios in every capital of Europe, and that for many years she had lived comfortably off the proceeds of a trip to the Far East from which she had returned with a quantity of lacquer.

Her independence worried Madame Dézaymeries far less than did her lack of religion. It was not so much that she was actively hostile as utterly indifferent. For her the problem of religion just had no existence. On one occasion she interrupted a lecture from Thérèse on the subject with a "But, darling, it's all so *improbable*!" Thérèse found it convenient to lay the blame on Fanny's husband—an Anglican by birth but an atheist by temperament—and persuaded herself that it was her duty not to scare her friend away, but, by giving her a warm welcome, to lead her all unsuspecting to the Manger. The truth of the matter was that the widow clung to the younger woman because she represented the only tenderness of feeling she had ever known. When, after their mother's death, the family estate had been broken up, there had been a breach between Thérèse and her sister, since when no one had ever dreamed of giving her a kiss except her children and this same Fanny whose lack of all religious feeling she chose to regard as a natural infirmity. Fabien, already clearer-sighted than his mother, found this characteristic of her childhood friend at once attractive and terrifying. He hung about the alluring visitor whose error was, to all seeming, invincible. No argument had the slightest effect on her. It was as though she had no part nor lot in the sin of Adam, as though her tiny, isolated destiny were moving to its predestined end in a world that knew nothing of redemption. God could appeal neither to her heart nor to her reason; not but what she was a philosopher and prided herself on a liking for abstract ideas.

She had, all the same, when she was staying with the Dézaymeries, to acquiesce in Friday fasts and Sunday observances. "But why," she would say, half joking, half in earnest, "but why make life gloomier than it is already?" To such remarks Thérèse would reply by pointing out how useless it was to shut one's eyes to the fact that the world is a place full of suffering, to which Christ alone can give meaning and value. The Irish girl merely laughed and gave her dear friend a kiss.

She was fonder of Fabien than of Joseph and marked her preference by constant fondlings. Only a superstitious, a morbid, craving for contrast could explain the attraction which, twice every year, brought this lover of beauty into a cribbed and Jansenist provincial home. She would descend upon it with a flapping of weary wings. No doubt an emotional loyalty which nothing could altogether destroy had something to do with her behavior. She might be the slave of her desires, but it so happened that some of her desires were good. Her first and perhaps her only really pure passion had found its object in a young girl. Each year she wandered back to this clear source of refreshment, known only to herself, and bathed her hot hands and painted face in its icy waters.

But a year came when, unknown to herself, a change of emphasis took place in that love which had the power to bring her back from the far places of Europe. Was it for Thérèse Dézaymeries that she came, or for the boy who once, on a July afternoon, in the shuttered drawing room which the two lads believed to be sacred to the spirit of their dead father, had roughly broken from the two bare arms so fondly twined about his neck? Though not fully aware of the peril, Madame Dézaymeries was conscious of a vague feeling of alarm. She felt its presence deep within her, could *smell* the spiritual threat. Fabien, in a mood of childish fun not wholly innocent, would creep away and smoke the butt-ends of Fanny's drugged and scented cigarettes. His mother, always scrupulous in her judgments, was careful to avoid any suspicion that might incriminate her friend. To her she was still the unsophisticated little companion who had clung to her in the old days, nor would she let anything disturb that happy memory. But it was not altogether easy to maintain such an attitude, and again and again she would say to herself, though with dwindling conviction, "There's no evil in her . . . it's just that we're not used to her ways." Another of her self-deceiving phrases was: "She's such an oddity." Experience had never taught her that vice may often hide behind eccentricity, and lurk in the shadow of quiddities and affectations. Loyalty to this affection, in which God had no

share, was her secret weakness. Trained though she was to examine her conscience with meticulous care, accustomed though
she might be to explore with morbid and meticulous intensity the
motives of her every thought, she always averted her eyes from
the special corner of her heart where her tender affection for
Fanny dwelt. Had their visitor ever been guilty of carelessness,
the Dézaymeries might have been warned to be on their guard.
But it amused her to adapt herself to the exigencies of their
cloistered life. She chose her dresses and disciplined her tongue
with the sole object of charming her Christian hosts.

She did not know that her spirit gave off a smell. When she
went away she left behind her a troubled odor which hung
about the very air that Madame Dézaymeries breathed. As,
when the shot bird has vanished, a scrap of fluff among the
dead leaves will show the sportsman where it is lying, so Fabien's melancholy languors were full of meaning to her. She
noted his silences. Where the lovely bird had fallen, the boy's
heart bore, as it were, a physical mark. On the pretext of wanting to be undisturbed, he insisted on doing his lessons in the
green room, which was never heated and had a northerly aspect.
He rummaged in the dressing-table drawers and hoarded as
treasure-trove forgotten ribbons and a tortoiseshell comb.

At last, when Fabien was sixteen, Madame Dézaymeries had
her eyes opened. That year Fanny Barrett did not pay her accustomed visit. Each evening between Christmas and the New
Year Fabien was on the watch, his face pressed to the window,
or lurking on the landing, his ears pricked for the sound of a
footstep. Joseph, who had always instinctively avoided Fanny,
poked gentle fun at him. Of the three of them, he, already a
priest at heart, already a sworn enemy of those lost women who

have it in their power to bring damnation into unfledged lives, was by far the most sensitively alive to the corruption which she carried about with her. One evening, when the two brothers were deep in an argument, Joseph maintaining that to paint one's face was a deadly sin, their mother had had to silence them. After the New Year, Fabien begged her to write to Fanny at the various addresses she had left. The boy's general taciturnity, the prolonged silences into which he fell, were a sign that all was not as it should be, and she became alarmed. Finally, she confided in her Spiritual Director. The good Father continued to smile as usual, because his smile was a permanent feature of his face which nothing would ever erase, but his words expressed a deep displeasure. She had, he said, locked in the wolf with the sheep. Her care for the young soul in her charge had been of no avail, because the Evil One had been able to sow his seed at leisure. So shaken did she seem to be by his reproof that he felt bound to soften the hard words he had spoken, and to this end added that, since it was Fabien's destiny to live in the world, it might be no bad thing that he should learn the nature of its illusory charms. The mother's imprudence might, God willing, serve, after all, to insure the boy's salvation. All the same, he warned her to turn this temporary separation to good account, and to see to it that the friendship should be permanently discontinued.

The priest had little difficulty in bringing Fabien to a calmer state of mind. But the only effect of this was that the boy showed less confidence than ever in his mother, avoiding her questions, and, though he appeared to have lowered his defenses, was in fact more wary than ever. During the Easter holidays, which were spent as usual on the Dézaymeries' country estate some twenty miles from the city, he developed a strong liking for solitary walks. He would set off alone through the pine woods and spend long days out on the heath which, though it formed part of his father's property, was, with its sandy distances, its straight, tall tree trunks gashed with resin-oozing scars, a visible symbol of his mother's teaching. Nothing more arid than this countryside could well be imagined, nothing more featureless, more uniform. Yet, for all that, it is a land of hidden springs with waters stained red by the stony soil. Ice-cold, they bubble up beneath the overshadowing alders and in the thickets of wild mint. Just so is the human heart, trained by the will to woo austerity, but thrilling to the call of love and informed by grace. When evening fell the silence was so complete that the ear could catch the movement of the hidden streams on the surface of which lay long trails of slowly moving weed that looked like the hair of drowned and vanquished nymphs held prisoner by depths of stainless sand and washed by freshets. Giant pines made a circle of gloom about the house. As straitly as by the high walls of the Catholic faith, by its unbreached and solid doctrine, the Dézaymeries' lived hemmed about by the endless army of the pines which stood in serried ranks for forty miles. Only in that far distance did an ultimate ridge of sand lie as a barrier against the ocean surge. No austere heart is less responsive to the lure of passion than is this countryside to the magic of spring. The stunted oaks greet the winds of April with a rustle of dead leaves, and only the song of birds is eloquent of love.

Madame Dézaymeries felt a deep concern at these lonely expeditions from which Fabien would return with bleeding hands, and sometimes with dead leaves in his hair. She was alarmed to find that she felt lost when he was not with her, and that the companionship of Joseph brought her no comfort. Joseph, at this time, was a thin, tall youth who walked with a stoop, knew the names of all the curés of all the parishes of the diocese, and found his chief pleasure in playing on a miniature harmonium.

It was in the course of these holidays that, realizing her preference for Fabien, she sternly sat in judgment on her feelings and decided that her much-loved son must be sent away from home. She saw only too well what joy it would be for her to grow old with him beside her, and indulged herself with the thought that she might suffer the more by rejecting the sweet temptation. She began to speak to him of the École des Chartes, which was the obvious goal of anyone who had so strong a taste for the history of the Middle Ages. In this way her passion for self-sacrifice led her to plan the establishment of her son in that city where every passion can be gratified.

No incident came to disturb the family circle, where Fanny Barrett's name was no longer mentioned. In July Fabien took his baccalaureate, and the family removed once again to the country. There, in Les Landes, the sand concentrates the heat of heaven, and the crowding trees present a barrier that stops and turns aside the promise of cool breezes. All three were so consumed by inner heat as to be insensible to the torrid weather. Joseph, when daylight ebbed, rehearsed the reading of his breviary with the aid of a black-bound book crammed with sacred pictures. Fabien avoided his brother, but could not escape the rigor of the dog-days. In the pitiless blaze of noon he would lie with a book by Père Gratry on the bank of the stream where the warm moisture of the spongy moss brought refreshment to his body. The heathy wastes were filled with the tumult of cicadas. Blue or tawny dragonflies hovered above the bracken fronds. Now and again the play of squirrels would set the motionless tree-tops momentarily swaying. Imprisoned among the gashed, tormented trunks, where his dreaming mind could find no outlet from the constricting sand, Fabien knew that nothing would come to shatter the drowsy peace of the afternoon save possibly the breathless sound of tocsin bells warning of heath fires. The merciless season of late summer makes the promise of autumn seem like a breath of deliverance. The first shower brings respite alike to earth and human flesh. The rain patters on the branches with a sound of happy tears. The drops, caught in their fall and absorbed by all the sickly leaves, never reach the sandy, burned-up surface of the earth. Westward, the pine trunks stand in black array, whipped by brief squalls borne on the bitter wind.

But in Fabien's heart it was August still, and he burned with a passion that he did not understand.

In October Joseph was received into the Seminary at Issy-les-Moulineaux. A little later it was Fabien's turn to depart. One November evening, his mother, stern in her resolve not to see him off on the Paris train, touched his forehead with the kiss which was her habitual talisman for the perilous passage of the hours of darkness. So successfully did she disguise her emotion that he dared not exhibit his own. But when at last, among the noises of the city, she could no longer hear the sound of the fly that was taking him from her, she let her widowed glance play about the vacant room. The lamp shone only on an empty chair. Octavie had already made her bed ready for the night. The hideous curtains of deep purple that masked the windows looked black.

2

EVEN when Fabien, in the early hours, stood shivering on the platform of the d'Orsay station, his suitcase in his hand, the climate of his mind remained unaltered. He was imprisoned at the center of a cocoon spun by his mother and by his Spiritual Director. How, then, was it possible that he should feel the impact of Paris? In the hotel where he was lodged, close to the Catholic Institute, he was forever passing bishops on the stairs, tottering old men leaning on the arms of discreetly dressed valets. There was a prevailing smell of vegetables which reminded him of school, nor in these musty odors of the kitchen was there any admixture of those scents that, in hotels of a different sort, fill the passages when the rooms are being "done." Such time as he did not spend at the École des Chartes, at the Record Office or the National Library he gave to a small group which existed for the study of social problems. But the theories and the formulæ which he read in various learned journals and glibly repeated, had no real hold on his secret self. They were merely an element of the mental atmosphere which kept him from the outside world. As a river may flow through a lake without becoming part of it, so did Fabien move through Paris. Of the ardors burning in the secret lives of men, ardors that may be glimpsed in the tense expressions of certain faces lit by the candle-light of Montmartre or of Notre-Dame-des-Victoires, he knew nothing. Never was a scrupulous Christian so empty of enthusiasm. He went so far as to take positive satisfaction in the sense of spiritual aridity which beset him, imagining that his feet were set upon that path of purification so well known to the mystics as desolate and comfortless. Strong in his Jansenist heritage, he held aloof from all contact with his fellow-students, never relaxing his hold upon his feelings, never seeking the intimacies of friendship, but meeting all advances with the cold detachment of his Dézaymeries training. He did not even make an effort to pay a visit to his brother at Issy. By sheer will-power he kept himself within the bleak rigidity of duty. But even so, he would often, of an evening, close his books and let his attention wander. The silence of the room spread till it held his very mind enveloped. He went to the window and drew the curtains aside. A frozen moon sailed above the city where millions of hearts were beating. The glass of the pane was cold to his forehead. He did not even try to pray, conscious that no words of love other than those contained in his prescribed evening devotions would rise to his lips. He was like a dry desert that is fully aware of its dryness. But, deep within himself he could catch, as from the distance of a torrid summer day, the echo of a muted rumbling. Fearful, yet with a stirring of hope, the listener says, "A storm is brewing"—a storm that will bruise the vine-shoots with its hail, but will bring, as well, relief to the dried and gaping earth, to the leaves drooping with the heat. Sometimes, so lonely was his state, he would fall so far as to listen to the confidences of the chambermaid who implored him to protect her from the unwelcome attentions of the "master," an uncouth and pasty sacristan, and of his sixteen-year-old son who had a flat head, looked like a louse, and was always lying in wait for her in the passage.

During Lent, Madame Dézaymeries paid a visit to Paris. He went with her to Issy, where Joseph, already suffering from his lungs and behindhand in his studies, sat coughing in the dark parlor under the painted stare of Sulpician worthies. He showed them the theatrical chapel—a sumptuous antechamber to the throne-room of the King of Kings. Fabien envied Joseph his life in this holy mountain, this tabernacle. It never occurred to him that, left to himself, he would have felt no wish to go and see him there. Madame Dézaymeries was filled with admiration of his virtue, of his active response to the charms of the perfect life even in the very heart of Paris. An experienced priest would have seen in it the ultimate rictus of a will absurdly stretched to breaking-point, and quite untouched by the spirit of love.

When he returned after the Easter holidays, Fabien began to take stock of his loneliness. The old stones of palaces and bridges lay basking in the soft radiance of a misty sun. The city was full of young bodies responsive to the call of spring, meeting at every corner, sitting on the terrace of every café. The air was full of stale romance. It was the time of year when the enemy within us finds a ready ally in the outward scene. To the moaning of desire repressed and stifled, nature replies with an invitation to escape, with a proffered gift of satisfaction. At the school even the most studious leaned gazing from the windows, their hands and their foreheads moist. A thousand strident posters called temptingly from sun-baked walls. It was that season when the streets are full of faces that no longer try to hide their secret yearnings, when parted lips and seeking eyes take no account of the dangerous abyss.

The threat of an approaching examination at first saved Fabien from himself. He tired his eyes with poring over facsimiles of ancient documents. In his brief snatches of leisure he dreamed of the moment, now close at hand, when his weariness would find rest in country air. Among all those motionless and wounded trees whose tops alone swayed gently, he would be but one wounded thing the more. Soon he would take his way to that land of scented heat. . . .

But, two days before he was due to start, a letter from his mother filled him with consternation. She told him to fetch Joseph from the Seminary, and to travel home with him. The boy had sent word that he was very ill, and his superiors had made no attempt to hide from Madame Dézaymeries the fact that there was very little hope indeed of saving the stripling priest. Fabien was overcome with terror when he saw the tall, emaciated body standing at the top of the main staircase at Issy, supported by two fellow-seminarists. If only he had kept a watchful eye on him, had not left him so utterly alone! The night that followed was horrible. Fabien lay in the upper bunk of their sleeper, hearing through the noises of the train his brother's paroxysms of coughing, and the sound of the spittoon rattling on the shelf.

For a day or two it seemed as though the air of the country would check the progress of the disease. But one night a sudden haemorrhage showed that it had returned with redoubled strength. The summer became a nightmare. The noise of coughing tore the siesta hours to shreds, and even the scent of the pines could not overpower the stench of iodoform, though the windows were always kept wide open. Madame Dézaymeries insisted on Fabien spending his days in the air, at the mercy of the hot sun. She stood at the door of the room where her other son lay dying, intent on keeping the young and healthy life from coming near. As he wandered through the damp heat that hung above the stream, Fabien fancied that he could still hear the sound of coughing.

A night came when he was awakened by the noise of ominous retchings. He heard a door creak, voices whispering, and the clink of china. He got up. The pitchpine of the stairs was cool to his bare feet. He crept to the closed door and caught from within the low murmur of frightened words: "Is it hopeless? Am I going to die?" and the voice of Madame Dézaymeries replying, "Yes, my boy, it is quite hopeless." "Have I still a month or two to live?" "No, Joseph, no." "A few weeks, then? . . ." Fabien put his hands over his ears, went back to his room, and stood leaning on the wooden balcony. The sound of living waters reached him. A dark blur of tree-tops half concealed the stars. A bird's note sounded like a sob.

During the days that followed, Madame Dézaymeries, as she ate her hurried meals, took note of Fabien's pallor. More than once she seemed to be on the point of issuing an order, but hesitated. At last she spoke. The doctors had said that he ought to go away at once. Joseph might linger on for months. It would be better for Fabien to return to Paris before the end of the holidays. He put up a show of resistance, but hoped that it would be overcome. At the end of August, since Joseph continued to enjoy an unhoped-for respite, he let himself be persuaded. He made use of his impending departure as an excuse for encouraging the dying boy. "D'you think I should be going away if there was really any danger?" But just as he was closing the door, the look of the lie fading from his face, he noticed in the glass of the wardrobe two eyes fixed upon him with lucid awareness, two agonized and dilated eyes that could read only too well the message of a face from which the mask had fallen. At that moment, though he had never been particularly fond of his brother, he recalled the games they had played together, and was assailed by a swarm of all the shared memories of their common childhood, of the pill-box in which they had kept their collection of pebbles, of the pine cone they had buried and dug up again when the next holidays came round. He wept because never again would he see this witness of his earliest years, this boy-priest with a heart devoured by love, who was more chaste than a young girl; this child who had been starved of all affection but had never uttered a word of complaint except to God.

3

JOSEPH DÉZAYMERIES died in the odor of sanctity on a day of early December. As soon as the funeral was over Fabien decided that he would stay with his mother until after the New Year holidays. Madame Dézaymeries allowed nothing, during those winter evenings, to distract her attention from the pale face of her surviving son. She noticed how, as Advent progressed, and already the appearance of Christmas trees and cradles kept the children's faces glued to the sweet-shop windows, he seemed to grow more tense and worried. She sat knitting garments for the poor. The sirens of ships leaving harbor, the rattle of cabs, the rustle made by the turning of a page, the chiming of clocks, some close at hand and others distant, the crackling of the fire—all these familiar, comfortable sounds had the effect of keeping Fabien uneasily on the alert. She looked at the young man facing her. Only in the dark, soft depths of his eyes could she still trace some remnant of the pious child he once had been. She prayed for Joseph, reciting in French the Canticle prescribed by the Church for use when interceding for the dead—"If Thou, Lord, shouldest mark iniquities, O Lord, who shall stand?" A deep despairing note crept into her voice which reminded Fabien of those days in his childhood when he had been taken to visit his father's grave in the country cemetery. On those occasions she had always told

him to take off his cap. He had noticed the pathetic efforts
made by the living to prevent the wild riot of nature, which
crept up to the cemetery's very walls, from choking with grass
and roots the space where the bodies which had given them life
lay rotting in the ground. A damp wind was usually rattling the
bleached and colorless beads of the funeral wreaths. . . . At
other moments he saw again in memory the waxen mummy of
his brother Joseph as it had lain upon the bed, the scalp showing
white between the strands of hair, the bony structure of the face
looking as though it were thrusting upward and about to pierce
the skin's dry parchment. He sighed, and murmured: "Well, he
is out of pain, now," to which she replied with relentless hon-
esty, "Let us pray that he be out of pain."

On December 24th mother and son were sitting up preparatory
to going to Midnight Mass. Between stars and roofs the chimes
held sway.

Then Fanny came in.

They heard nothing, neither the sound of her cab, the
ringing of the bell, nor the closing of the front door. She stood
there, saying nothing, swathed in furs, a veil over her face. Only
her painted mouth struck a vivid note. It was not smiling. For
a moment or two she stayed where she was, not coming near
them.

"Let me just look at you. . . . How you've grown, Fabien,
how tall you are. . . ."

She stared at him as he moved away from the lamp. Then she
said again: "Why, you're a man now!"

How was it that these perfectly ordinary and harmless words
should sound so shameless? While she was speaking she had
taken off her travelling hat, and now at last a smile showed in

her rather shortsighted eyes. Nevertheless she seemed to diffuse an atmosphere of unease, of secretiveness. She talked of Joseph, mention of whose death she had seen in some newspaper. Fabien, struck dumb by emotion, kept his eyes fixed upon her. It was as though she had suddenly swum up from the depths of the last two years to the surface. He no longer recognized her. It was not that she looked older or more worn, but that she seemed to have become smaller, to have fallen away. The color of her hair was more violent than it used to be, her make-up cruder. Her body had thickened, and there was about it a sweet and heavy scent. Yes, her words were true. He had become a man, and that was why she frightened him.

All the same, he ran to the kitchen to make sure that Octavie was getting the green room ready. While he was gone, Fanny rather nervously explained the reason for her long silence.

"You look so stern, so hard!—much sterner and much harder than in the old days. I don't know how I'm going to be able to tell you. . . ."

Then, without any further beating about the bush, she announced that she was no longer living with her husband. They had been apart now for some considerable time.

"You've no idea, darling, what awful habits these sailors pick up!"

Thérèse never knew that Fanny had almost died of drug-poisoning when she was twenty. The wretched man she had married had turned her into an addict. She had to go into a home for treatment. . . . She stood, now, waiting for some word of compassion, some movement expressive of pity. But Madame Dézaymeries, rigid and silent, listened to her like a judge upon the bench. She was wearing a knitted cap of black wool, and her neck was enclosed in a tight tulle collar with a white edging. Her thick eyebrows were twisted in a frown that gave her a hard expression. Her gray hair, drawn tightly back from the temples, gave the effect of having been flattened by the constant wearing of a nun's coif. Perhaps at that very moment Fanny may have been remembering the hot-tempered girl who, years ago, used to lecture her, and how the blood would suddenly rush into her colorless cheeks and flush them red: was seeing again the young rose-tree whose every bud had been cut and hoarded for the harvest of the Lord.

"I've divorced him," stammered Fanny. "I had every right to do so. I really think, Thérèse, that you are the only person in the whole world who would feel like this about it. Don't look so relentless. . . ."

Madame Dézaymeries remained icily aloof. The Irish woman, by this time thoroughly ill at ease, stood tidying her hair. She dared not look at her hostess, but almost in a whisper continued:

"What will you think when I tell you that I have married again? Is it a sin to want to be happy?"

Madame Dézaymeries silenced her with a gesture:

"That's enough! Say no more! I am not sitting in judgment on you, Fanny, but you must leave this house. For years I weakly listened to the promptings of my heart. I realize now the enormity of my crime. If I turn my back upon you it is not because of anything *I* feel. Another's safety is at stake, and for him I shall be held responsible through all eternity. . . . May mine be the guilt, and mine alone! . . . I beg you to forgive me. I shall never cease to pray for you, to suffer for you . . . but you *must* leave this house, Fanny!"

She opened the door, summoned Octavie, and told her to get the concierge to carry down the bags and call a cab.

"Are you really turning me out, Thérèse—*me*?" She began to sob, and Thérèse, looking at the features on which time had already left its traces, was reminded of the puckered face of a little girl in tears whom once she had comforted. She, too, was weeping, and could only repeat:

"I will pray for you: I will suffer for you!" She took the lamp, opened the door again, and stood waiting with lowered eyes.

It was at this moment that Fabien returned. He heard two voices speaking at the same time:

"You must say good-bye to her, my boy."

"Fabien, are you going to let her turn me out?"

Both women had expected the young man to show signs of amazement and despair. But he was perfectly calm. Nothing of the torment in his heart showed upon his face.

"What's the matter?" he asked.

"Would you believe it!" exclaimed Fanny, and her voice was hoarse. "Your poor mother's got to the point where she can't bear to have a divorced woman under her roof! . . . Really, that *is* a bit much!"

Madame Dézaymeries put a finger to her lips. Octavie had just come into the room to say that the bags had been brought down. Devoured by curiosity, alert to all that was going on, the old servant had left the door open and was hanging about the hall. Fabien, overcome by shyness, held out his hand to Fanny and withdrew it again rather too quickly. His eyes were dry. The traveller hurriedly fastened her coat and tied her veil. All she wanted now was to get away as soon as she could, away from Thérèse's pitiless face—away, especially, from the boy. What had his expression meant? Stupefaction or merely indifference? Indifference? Later that night, alone in her hotel bedroom, listening to the Christmas bells, she was to convince herself that his features, incapable of deception, had been eloquent, maybe of desire, but of repulsion, too, of disgust. At the moment of parting she could only blurt out:

"How I hate this religion of yours for coming between us. I would hate Him for coming between us—if He existed!"

She paused in the middle of her violent tirade, stretched her hands toward the door, and saw that Fabien was no longer there. His mother had told him to leave them, adding in a low voice:

"We shall not be going to Midnight Mass. We couldn't be in a proper state of mind after the horrible things that have been going on. Go to bed and forget what has happened."

Kneeling at her *prie-Dieu* with her face buried in her hands, she thrust her two thumbs into her ears that she might not hear the echo of that final blasphemy. Fanny gave one glance at the bent figure. Then, with one more insult, turned and left the room. For a moment she hesitated and sank down on the wood-chest in the hall. Within a cracked and frosted globe a gas-flame flickered. Then she got up and, without knocking, went into Fabien's room. A candle was burning on the night-table. The boy had sunk upon the bed, his face pressed into the pillow. At the sound of the door opening he turned his head and looked at her with sleepy eyes. Before he could do anything to defend himself, two hands had seized his face. He was conscious of a hesitating flutter of warm breath close to his lips, then, for a brief moment, his mouth was caught and held before, with a sudden burst of laughter, she left him.

Standing by the rumpled bed he listened to that wild sound of mirth receding, but did not hear the slamming of the front door, nor yet the clatter of the departing cab, because the deep chime of the Cathedral bell was filling all the holy night.

He looked at his lips in the glass. He could taste on them the saltiness of blood.

4

HALF-NAKED though he was, he flung the window wide and breathed in the misty air. It was as though he took pleasure in feeling the sharp teeth and relentless violence of the December night. Leaning out above the street filled with its hubbub of footsteps and laughter, he shivered. He made, as might be, a sporting bet with himself to endure as long as he possibly could the death-grip of the winter darkness. Only these gulps of icy fog, he felt, could wash him clean again. He scrubbed at his lips with his bare arm. But even while he was conscious of a sense of disgust, of a longing to wipe away a stain, he felt that the beasts and gods patterned by the stars were the only worthy witnesses of a revelation the memory of which burned him more fiercely than the night air froze. He strained his body toward the sky. It was a vessel still stoppered and inviolate, but the kiss that had caught him on the brink of sleep had, though almost imperceptibly, cracked the seal.

Illness followed hard upon that night—an attack of pleurisy which made him free to partake of the glorious privileges accorded to those who are seriously sick, privileges that gave him the right to make no answer when he was spoken to; the right to sleep, or to pretend to sleep. He was blistered, and the pain revealed to him just how much agony the human body could endure. His mother being unable to stand the strain, a nun took over the nursing—a woman who was ageless, almost faceless, voiceless and anonymous. He revelled in the negative quality of her presence, in the crackling of her snow-white coif, in the sound made by her beads as she told them in the dark. One morning he looked in his mirror and saw the boyish fluff of beard, the large dark eyes such as the son raised from the dead must have fixed upon the widow of Nain. So rapid was his process of resurrection that in April he was passed fit for military service. It was not worth while to return to the École des Chartes for three months only, so he stayed with his mother, who was oppressed with a feeling of guilt in giving herself so completely to the pleasure of having him there.

To all appearances no memory of Fanny remained. All the same, neither mother nor son could any longer live as though a storm had not threshed the gray waters of their quiet existence. Thérèse Dézaymeries imposed upon herself a more exacting penance. As soon as she had heard early Mass she went to the hospital and tended the aged cancer patients—because only children appealed to her, and because no form of disease caused her such acute disgust as cancer. Their only visitors were the occasional begging Sisters who rang at the door of this dwelling which was always dark on the hottest days, because the blinds were kept carefully drawn in order to exclude the perilous gaiety of the light. Fabien would watch the play of dusty sunbeams on the moist surface of his hand and sit dreaming of the shrill cry of swifts or the throaty cooing of doves on hot tiles.

In July the Dézaymeries went back to the country, to a country buried in sand as in penitential ashes, with the stripped pines standing up like so many living examples of martyrdom humbly endured. Fabien, who wanted to do his service in the cavalry, spent his time riding over the sandy roads. A patch of fog would hide a stretch of grassland from view. Sheep would be indistinguishable from the mist. The night smell of the fens lasted on into the dawn. He made no effort to struggle against the torpor of his mind and heart. He surrendered to it. Wherever he went he carried with him the climate of his soul. As, when a child tormented by evil thoughts, he had closed his eyes and driven them away with a shake of the head, so now he forbad himself to look for Fanny in his heart. Later, thinking back to this period of his life, he was to feel amazement that he had been served so well by this curious mood of apathy. At the age when passions riot and flourish, he had been caught up into regions where the atmosphere was so rarefied that his desires, unable to breathe, had died. He scarcely fought against them at all, for there was no need for him to fight. His stainless life was no fruit of hard-won victory. He abandoned himself to a routine of piety which touched his sensibilities not at all, but was wholly mechanical. With childlike obedience he followed the path marked out for him.

So reassuring was his behavior that Madame Dézaymeries grew less watchful. She trusted him implicitly, and did not doubt that he had been signed, once for all, for salvation—that he was incorruptible. Perhaps, too, she was conscious of her powerlessness to break down the barrier of his silence and penetrate to the mind within. There was an unbridgeable gulf between them, each being of a different species, since each was of a different sex. But no matter how secret and puzzling the growth of the tree might be, she could see that it was beautiful. She could judge it by its fruit, and to her Christian heart the fruit was cause for rejoicing—for of what did it consist if not

of spiritual humility, chastity, a willingness to work, and withdrawal from the world? How should she have realized that no
love informed his attitude of submission? The spring of his
nature had been coiled tight ever since his childhood days. It
was to be expected that it should now show signs of slackening.
But would not a day come when the solemn moments of the
liturgical calendar would no longer find an echo in his heart?
He might believe that he had banished Fanny from his mind,
but in his flesh still lingered the memory of her fragrance, of
the warmth of her breath. The expenditure of energy which he
sought in his long rides through the woods was but the flight
of Hippolytus wounded. The flies rose in a shimmer of sunlight
from the peaty earth. They swarmed in a deadly cloud about
his horse, making it sweat and bleed. He had to hurry home,
and there, with his books, in the shuttered drawing room, wait
for evening to bring respite. At dusk the smoke from the farm-
steads and the burned-up grass spread over the fields of rye. He
loved the fields when they were stitched with shadow. There
had been, for as long as he could remember, a shortage of labor
on the estate, and each year the forest had encroached a little
further on the plow. The spaces of sky and open land grew
ever narrower, and the dark ring drew tighter round the
meadows. Perhaps, too, within himself the area of purity was
insensibly contracting. But of this he was unaware, even during
the years that he spent with the Dragoons at L. . . . The coarse-
ness of his comrades alienated him by its very excess. He found
nothing to attract him in the hotel bedrooms smelling of bees-
wax, leather and sweat, where a crowd of men and two women
of the town sat pouring absinthe into the toilet jug. And, if his
landlord's eldest daughter kept the vases in his room filled with

flowers, if she rose at dawn so that he might have a cup of steaming coffee before going on parade, if, one evening, wearing an imperfectly fastened dressing gown, she hung about tidying his cupboard, if on the day he left the town for good, her face showed red with crying as she said good-bye—these symptoms of desire and sorrow had no effect on him. He did not so much as turn his head as he rode away, did not so much as spare a glance for the heart which burned for love of him.

He returned to the heath country at the season when all work ceases, when the pines are left ungashed and no resin is collected because the wood pigeons are on the wing. Even the shepherds drive their flocks from their accustomed pastures lest the bleating and the trampling and the sound of sheep bells keep the shy birds from settling in the oaks.

On the first evening, Thérèse Dézaymeries took the bronzed face between her hands and looked long and hard into the eyes that made a show of smiling. But they quickly turned away. Dreams that she knew not of fought for concealment: desires lay hidden there like fish that darken the waters so that they may escape unseen. They took a turn together round the park. She did not ask him about his life in barracks, nor had he anything to tell her. They walked with their heads thrown back. Dreamily she murmured words that she loved to speak on their country strolls: "Pine forests—the only forests in which one can see the sky!" . . . and, indeed, above their heads the tree-tops formed a vast tattered and swaying curtain through the holes in which they could catch sight of small patches of dark and shimmering blue. Mist rose from the stream and eddied about the fields through which it ambled lovingly, and the scent of wild mint struck through the wreathing vapor more powerfully than the smell of briars and resin and bruised leaves.

Thérèse Dézaymeries thought that Fabien's melancholy was but the brooding of a mind which finds God in the onset of the night. Next day he refused to go pigeon-shooting. He grumbled because the presence of the guns made riding impossible. Perhaps because he was unaided now by the terrific physical fatigue which had been his constant companion when in barracks, he turned in on himself, seeking an identity he could not find. The gestures and the prayers of former days seemed like the gestures and the prayers of someone else. The habits of body and mind which belonged to a youth that was his no longer he strove to force upon the stranger who now lived within him, a stranger to be dreaded, on whom he gazed with fear. He began to be conscious of an inner emptiness, or rather, of a feeling that he had been abandoned. And that, in itself, was a form of faith, because one cannot be abandoned except by somebody.

His mother hung about him continually, scanning his face, repressing certain thoughts that rose in her about his life at L. . . .

She wrote to her Spiritual Director:

"When he was a small boy I had only to take him on my knee. Not that he at once revealed the reason for his melancholy, but he was willing that I should probe his heart. He helped me in my search, and, when I had found the hidden thorn that irked him, ran away comforted. But he no longer believes that the old woman who bore him and nourished him, and gave him a second birth into the life of grace, can any longer supply the healing balm. Should I, do you think, ask more people to the house? There are several families in the neighborhood of more or less our own social standing, families with young girls. I don't want to, but I will if you say so. I remember reading in Pascal that marriage is the lowest of all Christian states, vile and unpleasing to God. How strongly I feel the truth of that! How convinced I am that the traffic of the flesh is a grim and filthy business. I long to say so to my child, who as yet, I am ready to swear, knows nothing of it. I sometimes wonder whether the passage through his life of that woman whose name I never mention has not, perhaps, left traces of trouble in his heart. His silence on the subject is far from reassuring. . . ."

The good Father advised that she should wait and watch: that she should be in no hurry to point the way to marriage (though it was very reprehensible on her part to espouse the derogatory views of a heretic on that great Sacrament). It was important to make quite certain, first of all, that Fabien had not been called to a higher destiny. "It might, perhaps, be no bad thing if the dear lad travelled for a while. Let him go to Umbria, to Rome especially. Those places will divert his thoughts, but piously. They may even bring him back by pleasant by-ways to that state of mind in which you, no less than I, desire to see him anchored."

When first she made the suggestion, and as she uttered the one word "Italy," Fabien felt the stranger lurking within him tremble with joy. With the same determination she had shown when formerly she had insisted on his settling in Paris, the good woman now pushed open the double door of this mysterious room. Pious hands drew him from the darkness and thrust him sharply into the arena where the fierce sun beats, and ever hungry beasts prowl up and down.

5

UMBRIA disappointed Fabian. The Christ of St. Damian
who spoke to Il Poverello had no message for him. The sleeping face of St. Clare, and the veiled member of her Sisterhood
who watched over her, did not stir his sleeping heart. Joyless,
he tramped the road from Perugia to Spoleto by way of Assisi
and Foligno, deaf to the fiery Canticle addressed by Umbria to
her brother the Sun. For him the dust of these highways held
no trace of Francis, nor yet of Brother Leo, the little lamb of
God. Why did he decide to make his way, not to Rome where
he longed to be, but to Venice? Not chance, he thought, decides
these things. Someone there must be who sets in motion the
impulse buried deep within us. Another climate beckoned him.
Until the moment of this journey the young man, unresponsive
though he might be to the Holy Spirit, had at least been aware
of Its presence. For years no inner tide had carried Fabien on its
bosom: but he knew that He who did not draw him to Himself
existed. In Venice this child of the Christian tradition was made
for the first time aware of his lack of grace. He was alone. The
sense of an infinite emptiness was revealed to him. His heart
swelled. He knew the treacherous delights that are the mark of
that terrible withdrawal. Abandoning his books and notes he
wandered, unseeing, from museum to museum. He had no eyes
for the sleeping St. Ursula as painted by Carpaccio, for the un-

sullied breeze that fills her room of slumber, for the day open on the darkness, for the angel who leaves untouched the things of every day—slippers, lamp, crown and the half-read page. He preferred the network of evil-smelling lanes, and, at dusk, those districts where languid voices whispered of proffered pleasures. The shoddy music of gay orchestras floating at night upon the Grand Canal in a mist of lanterns brought tears to his eyes. God had departed from him, though not yet did he know the true meaning of solitude. He was like a frightened child whose father has let go his hand. He was fearful at being thus abandoned, yet revelled in his fear. A sense of pleasure caught him by the throat because, for the first time, he knew that he was vulnerable. To see himself exposed, like a virgin to the ravening beasts, was already a delight. He knew that sin, mortal sin, might pounce upon him now from the concealing thickets, and drive straight to his undefended heart. He turned his eyes upon the stranger that was himself, this new, this unsuspected being, whom Evil might possess. His defenses were down. Nothing now stood between his fainting spirit and the vast abyss. He had a feeling of giddiness, and found in his awareness of it ecstatic pleasure. He would not go out of his way to provoke attack, he would take no chances. It was enough for him—a proffered victim, a willing prey—to taste the joy of expectation long drawn out. On the ferry-boats, at Florian's, in his hotel that looked on the Salute, the facile fumes of Asti kept the charm alive. Formerly, like all those whose thoughts are centered on the dialectic of the soul, he had been incapable of seeing anything save through mists engendered by a ceaseless meditation. Venice had the effect of dispelling the cloud. She laid her hand upon him, and his eyes were opened. For the first time faces stood out from the featureless mass around him. He saw them and he loved them. He was conscious, too, that his own face had become the focus for passing glances.

One evening, in the dining-room of his hotel, he felt irked by the fact that someone he did not know was staring at him. The importunate stranger was a big, sturdily-built man with prominent eyes of china-blue. He had the sparse fair hair and ruddy complexion of the north, the full-blooded cheeks produced by mists and alcohol. Facing him, with her back to Fabien, was a woman, and on his right sat a very young man who talked a lot and waved his arms. So high-pitched was his voice that, but for the gipsy band, Fabien could easily have heard what he was saying. He was not addressing his remarks to the woman at his side, who, with back bent, shoulders hunched, and her elbows on the table, gave the effect of someone loosely sprawling. His thick black hair fitted close above his eyebrows like a cap. He had thick lips, and the blueness of his jowl was evidence of an exuberant growth of beard with which his razor fought a losing battle. He had quite forgotten to eat, and the gravy on his plate was fast congealing. He took some paper and a fountain pen from his pocket and started to draw, making some remark as he did so that brought a smile to the lips of his red-faced companion. At that moment the waiter made as though to clear the table, and at once the young man flung himself upon the food before him and cleared his plate with the swiftness of a famished dog.

At length the three of them rose. The elder man, as soon as he got up, was seen to be a veritable giant. He might have been a Prince of some Scandinavian Royal House. The youth, whose length of body from shoulder to waist had, while he was sitting, given the impression that he was of about the same height, reached scarcely to his shoulder. Fabien had never seen anyone quite like him. He wore very tight trousers of light-colored cloth which accentuated the abnormal development of his thighs, which might have been those of an acrobat. He made no attempt to give the woman precedence, but, with an air of cool insolence and a toothpick jutting from his mouth, made for the door, followed by the rubicund giant who once more stared at Fabien as he passed his table. Their companion stayed behind to drink a glass of water, and Fabien, who ever since the beginning of the meal had been eager to see her face, watched her intently. At last she turned round, and he recognized Fanny.

Only a paradox can express his feelings at that moment. He recognized her *although* she had not changed. The modern miracle which has given to women the seeming boon of eternal youth produces in some people, of whom Fabien Dézaymeries was one, a sense of terror and disgust. In these young women of fifty, preserved by some supernatural agency, the eyes alone are eloquent of age. Only in them can be read the secret of a flabbiness that has its origin in the soul; only through them is made visible the wear and tear of the spirit. Fanny had remained so much the same that the effect was frightening. She looked as she had always looked, though the flood of time had swept her on, and each passing moment had marked her as with fire: five years of exigent desires and glutted senses, of lovers lost and lovers found, of passionate abandonments and bleak awakenings: five years of late nights, of endless cigarettes, of rich food, strong drink, narcotics and drugs. Yet there she stood her young body apparently untouched by the passing of the years, strong as steel, tempered and hardened and possessed

Sin, in its way, is a form of life. There is such a thing as *infernal* grace, and it can galvanize, just for as long as may be necessary, that adorable shape of molded flesh which, according to St. Catherine of Siena, stinks in all its parts.

She filled her glass with water, sipped slowly until she had emptied it, took her bag which was hanging on the chair, and brushed by the young man without seeing him. She was wearing a dress of rose-colored brocade cut in the prevailing Poiret fashion, and Turkish slippers slightly turned up at the toes. Her fragrance struck at Fabien, nor could he be sure whether it came from her body or from the long dead days that she had made to live again. He followed her into the hall. She was engaged in a lively discussion—though she kept her voice low—with the elder of the two men (no doubt, her second husband), whose ham-like face was distended in a grin. Meanwhile, the strange-looking youth, now wearing a felt hat and carrying a light overcoat on his arm and an ivory-knobbed cane in his hand, was giving instructions to the porter about forwarding his letters. He lit a cigarette, and then, presumably because the discussion was going on longer than he liked, said:

"Are your bags ready, Donald?"

The other man kissed Fanny's hand and went over to his companion. She remained standing where she was, struck rigid, it seemed, with amazement, and with her eyes fixed on the revolving door. Fabien was gently swaying in a rocking chair, but he finished his cigarette in a couple of minutes. He felt, from the way in which Fanny's two partners were casting sidelong glances at him, that he had been the subject of the recent conversation. He had no doubt at all that they had been talking of him. The younger of the two appeared to be countering some angry remark made to him by the red-faced man, who finally went up to Fanny again and asked her to go with him, for a moment, to his room. Without saying a word, she followed him to the lift. The youth called after them:

"Don't forget, Donald: we ought to leave here not later than a quarter past ten. The train goes at twenty to."

Donald nodded. His smile of assumed candor was horrible. He made a furtive movement of the hand in Fabien's direction.

Scarcely had the couple vanished from sight than the young man approached Fabien in a rather secretive manner and asked him for a light. As a cockchafer agitates its wing-cases preparatory to taking flight, he showed in a number of ways that he wanted to begin a conversation.

"It's really very hard, terrible, actually," he began at last, "to have to leave Venice in the autumn" (he spoke in a singsong, and his r's rattled like a fall of pebbles). "No one ever *leave* Venice, you know: they *tear* themselves away. To be in Venice is to live in an *embrace*."

Fabien smiled but said nothing. The other went on: "Don't you think so, *actually*? It certainly is so in my case, but perhaps you are here alone?"

Fabien felt obliged to nod. The creature before him assumed an air of disapproval and pity.

"Oh, but how *imprudent*! Alone in Venice! The Goddess of Love will punish you! To be alone in Venice is like—if you will excuse the simile—indulging in solitary vice!"

Fabien condescended neither to smile nor to make the slightest gesture. But the stranger obviously interpreted his silence as evidence of interest, for he pointed with his cane at the revolving door.

"Over there stands the witness of many quite *terribly* sad deaths—I mean the Salute. *Actually,* no one could *possibly* reckon up all the young people who have drowned themselves from its steps. One of them was a *great* friend of mine—perhaps you have read some of his poetry?—just a *leetle* bit old-fashioned in manner, perhaps one might almost say *passé,* but then he was only seventeen, you see, and was quite unacquainted with modern art—all the same, he was a god, *actually*. It was the year I was dancing at the Fenice. . . ."

Fabien stared with amazement at this youth with the over-developed thighs. So that was it: he was a dancer! But still he said nothing. The stranger, after a quick glance at his wrist watch, hurried on:

"I'm afraid my mind was wandering. You see, before I go I want to ask you whether you would take on a little mission—actually, that is just the word for it—something that will add a charming note of romance, a delightful *soupçon* of sentiment to your stay here. I won't ask whether you know me: I have, alas! to forego the pleasures of anonymity. They have become quite impossible since the magazines of two hemispheres have taken to printing my portraits. . . ."

Fabien replied dryly that he never looked at magazines.

"But my dear sir, do you mean, *actually,* that you have never seen a picture of Cyrus Bargues?"

Fabien remembered that he had seen the name on some poster or other advertising a season of exotic ballets. The dancer was staring at the imbecile who did not even know who he was!

"If you are not interested in art I very much doubt whether you will consent to undertake this mission which, on the strength of a first favorable impression, I had quite made up my mind to offer you. Your eyes, as you must often have been told, are quite *unique*."

Clearly, he must be a specialist in the matter of eyes, and probably knew all about them as a collector knows all about, say, medals. The fire that glowed deep down in Fabien's held his attention so completely that he looked at least ten times at his wrist watch without seeming to take in at all what its message was. But it was true that he was in a hurry. How could he manage, in the space of a few minutes, to convince this handsome, silent barbarian? Awkwardly, in a torrent of words, he delivered himself of the errand with which he had been entrusted.

"Donald Larsen, my impresario—yes, the tall man with the fair hair—has to go to Switzerland to make final arrangements about Leda Southers' engagement. . . ."

"Leda Southers?"

So, actually, he'd never heard of Leda Southers! Why, with Leda and Cyrus Bargues what more could Larsen possibly ask for? He would have the finest ballet company in the world

"Don't you understand, it will be *immense,* there's no other word for it. . . . But, unfortunately, there is a woman in Donald's life—his wife, yes, the woman who was here a moment ago. . . ."

Again he looked at his wrist watch, hesitated for a brief moment, looked at Fabien, saw that he was now eagerly listening, and grew bolder:

"D'you know, she followed us to Venice—we couldn't stop her—*actually* on the ground that Leda Southers had once been Donald's mistress!"

The trouble, he said, about Donald was that he wasn't ruth

less enough. One couldn't cure him of being *sorry* for people.

"She keeps her hold on him by threatening to commit suicide. But I *did* get him to promise that he wouldn't take her to Switzerland with us. She keeps on saying that she'll kill herself —and he says she's quite capable of doing it. Personally, I make a point of pretending not to believe her. What *I* happen to know, though Donald doesn't, is that Fanny had arranged to meet a gigolo here—but he hasn't turned up. If only he'd come she'd be willing enough to leave us alone. . . . I think, perhaps, I ought to explain that she *did* try to kill herself once, in Paris, but she didn't bring it off. . . ."

"Why are you telling me all these excessively grubby details?"

"You don't appear to be altogether indifferent to them."

Fabien got up, threw away the cigarette which he had only just lighted, took a few paces, and came back to his companion. He muttered, as though talking to himself, "So she tried to kill herself, did she?" So upset was he by what he had just heard that he was no longer listening to the dancer who seemed to be completely overcome by the rapid success that had attended his efforts.

"If I were the *patron*," he went on, "there wouldn't be all this shilly-shallying. After all, what *is* a woman, actually, I mean? One woman more or less in the world can't *really* matter, can it? I wish I could make you see how tremendously important this Swiss trip is. A ballet—how shall I put it?—a sort of cosmic, a sort of *geological*, ballet—which will express the awakening of primeval forces, the primitive *spark*, the first *distension* of matter by the impact of life."

His large nose twitched, his thick lips parted, so that his mouth looked like a bleeding gash in the rind of a ripe fruit.

But Fabien had thoughts only for the great wind that had transported him far from the remote corner of heath and pine, from the desert in which he had been born, to this coast where Fanny old now and soiled by life, had looked for death—for eternal death. . . . Surely it could be no chance meeting? Must he, then, risk damnation that she might be saved? No . . . no. . . . It was no longer a matter of flesh and grace in conflict. The two all-powerful forces would work, now, in close alliance for the salvation of a woman's body, a woman's soul.

"So now, my dear sir, you know that there is in this hotel a lonely woman whom I may, perhaps, be allowed to describe as a professional suicide. Let me repeat what I have told you once already—that she has made one attempt, and failed. It is madness on our part to throw her at your head like this, but we have no alternative—you do realize that, don't you? Maybe you like women of her peculiar type? You can save her at very small cost to yourself. All you have to do is to hand her back to Donald when he returns. He doesn't *want* to lose her, you know. She's got—how shall I put it—a wonderful nose for picking up a good thing, for finding budding geniuses. You should see the pictures and the lacquer she's got in Paris."

He took Fabien's arm and gave it a farewell squeeze. But Fabien stood perfectly still, gazing at the lift.

"There she is . . . promise me . . ."

With the faintest flicker of his eyelids Fabien conveyed consent. The bellboy emerged with the bags, followed by Larsen who, in his travelling ulster with its fur collar, looked larger than ever. Fanny brought up the rear. While Cyrus Bargues was speaking in a low voice to the impresario, the latter kept his eye fixed on Fabien. The giant paused for a moment in the door of the hotel, turned once more to Fanny and wagged his finger, as one might do to a child when conveying a parting "Be good." For the last time he shot a brooding look at Fabien; for the last time the little dancer grinned. . . . Then Fabien, conscious that there was nothing now to restrain him, went across to the woman who was still standing motionless, gazing at the door, touched her on the shoulder, and said quite simply:

"Fanny!"

FOR a second or two she failed to recognize him; then she uttered a faint cry:

"You! . . . here in Venice, you, Fabien!"

She raised her face to his, careless of the danger she ran in thus displaying its mask of paint and powder in the harsh light of the hotel hall. But tears had seamed the mask and broken its surface. Suddenly her gaze expressed nothing but the dull amazement of a woman brought in an instant face to face with a miracle, not believing what she sees before her, denying the evidence of her own eyes.

"You here . . . You here!"

Hurriedly he began to speak of his mother, of Joseph, striving to build up a façade of meaningless detail. She only said again, "You here!" She had been on the point of dying from starvation, and here, suddenly, was this large, warm loaf within reach of her hand, within reach of her mouth. Just as the anchor had been raised, the last mooring-rope loosened; just as the ship was beginning to move out to the dim, dark distance, he who was the furthest from her in space and time, he, this great archangel, had turned up beside her.

She glanced round the hall. Yes, she was really awake. Two porters were quarrelling over a tip. Some Americans were talking with a nasal twang that made them sound like gramophone records.

"Come with me . . . away from this light . . . come!"

She had thrown a coat over her shoulders and now moved away, drawing Fabien after her. The grip of her hand on his arm was that of a drowning woman. The mingled smell of ooze and musk, the confused odors of scented cigarettes and marshland, the wavering reflections of green and red cast by the lanterns in the dark water—all these things that, but a moment before, had seemed the forerunners of death, now suddenly and forever became part and parcel of her frantic joy. This harbor whence ships sailed out into the great nothingness had, in a moment, taken on the appearance of some brightly lit scene set for the action of her happiness. She understood nothing of the broken, stammered phrases in which Fabien was taking terrified refuge from the threat of silence. She had ears only for his voice, for the fresh, male voice of this child-man, and hugged it to her heart.

They crossed the Piazzetta and walked along the quays. They had to take very short steps because of the narrow skirt of her brocaded dress. And what of him? He knew that now at last he had stepped across the forbidden threshold. After all these years, here he was on the other side—but whether dead or alive he did not know. What was this happiness the mere approach of which set his heart swelling and transfigured all the world around him?

"Fanny, what has happened to you?"

Such was the first tiny phrase he uttered in the language of this unknown land into which he was striding so incautiously. It was Fanny now who was talking, he who, without understanding what he heard, was listening to her rather throaty voice. She was confessing that someone she had thought to be her friend, someone to whom she had cried aloud in her distress, had not come. But how sweet now seemed that treachery, how sincerely she rejoiced in the thought of that abandonment! Now and again she stopped in the middle of her flow of words.

"How can I dare to say all this to you who are so innocent?"

He was still for her the Fabien Dézaymeries whom she had known of old—the simple, unspoiled schoolboy. She had opened the lovely book at the page she had been reading when she closed it. The old frank laugh rang out again for a moment as she said:

"Are you still as religious as ever? This meeting has altered my views of Providence."

Unknown to her the fruit had been ripening just when the pangs of thirst were most intense. Something told her that this soul was utterly defenseless—that at the very first assault she could possess it. The young victim lay trembling beneath her hand, unarmed, with no power to resist, already drunk with the fumes of defeat. Time, in her absence, had brought to maturity the seed that she had sown within his heart, and now she had returned at the very moment of harvest.

Standing beneath a street lamp, she opened her black silk bag. Fabien saw the glint of a tiny revolver.

"You are the only person in the world who could have held me back from the last fatal leap—the only one, and you were so far away. And now you're here, you're here!"

Her hand touched his hair, stroked the rough surface of his cheeks. Using a shop window as a mirror, she powdered her face and reddened her lips, like an actress putting a few finishing touches to her make-up before going back upon the stage. Then, in the narrow entry of a deserted café, she clung to Fabien, burying her face in his shoulder as might a child who has found sudden respite from its misery. He noticed then that the cheeks of women who have been crying have the smell of wet earth.

She laughed, and her voice was bruised by the violence of the sobs she had been choking back. Once more she took him in her arms. Thus did she wreak her vengeance on Thérèse Dézaymeries! Driven from her friend's house, she had crept back by way of Fabien's heart. Soon she would dominate his body, too. If only Thérèse could have seen them! She laughed through her tears. Not yet was she quite ripe for death. Once more she would see the morning sun drench with flame the tumbled bed. The fledgling she had hatched, the young creature who for her alone had grown to manhood, trembled.

To them, snared in the enchantments of the body, the echoes of the city's life reached as a medley of mere sound, void and meaningless: music and the sound of laughter, footsteps on the flagstones of the quay, the plash of wavelets and the susurration of ships' prows cleaving the waters of the lagoon. Deeper and deeper did Fabien drive his way into the revealing night—from evening until dawn, and through the day that followed it, a day of rain when the hotel was filled with the whisper of steps in every corridor and the muted playing of an orchestra. Beneath the stirring of his breath a woman was coming back to life. She said to him:

"I hang upon your breath. . . ."

Tomorrow, doubtless, the time would come to make a reckoning. Tomorrow he must descend into the arena and count the bodies of the slain. He must measure the extent of harvest fields flattened by this storm of hail, calculate the miles of virgin forest burned to ashes by this fire.

At length, but half alive, they left the room, and Atilio, the gondolier, steered them, as the whim took him, by the rioting green of walls from which the autumn leaves were falling. At the hour of the siesta they landed on the island of San Francesco-del-Deserto. A friar, his eyes puffy with sleep, half opened the wicket gate, and they caught a glimpse of cloisters, of a well-head, and, against the dazzling blue, of a single cypress. Then the door was closed against the guilty couple. The clack of sandals died away and was lost in the silence of drowsiness and prayer. On another occasion a flicker of flames lit up for them the golden glints within the dark basilica of Padua, where, to a murmured hymn, the monks were bearing in procession a great bleeding Christ. On the empty Lido sands innumerable bathing huts drawn up in rows told more surely of approaching winter than did the arrow-shaped flight of birds migrating. From all the campaniles sounded the evening prayer for grace, and from an acquiescent sky there fell an absolution on the fleet of gondolas and all their loads of sin. Fabien, erect at the center of this burning, fiery furnace, knew that behind them a threat of storm was mounting, accumulating all the arrears of a fearful debt. Without a halt, without so much as pausing to take breath, he was descending an endless flight of stairs in a giddiness of lusts repeatedly renewed, of rending sensations, of the gloomy stupor of satiety. But had he ever imagined, for a moment, what he would find at the bottom of that long descent? Suddenly the rain had come, transforming Venice to a great mist of moisture. The radiators gurgled and gave out a smell of hot painted metal that filled the room's disorder of woman's clothes and books and bottles. Watchful and experienced, Fanny looked for the first signs of weariness upon the thin-drawn face, beneath the mournful eyes. She began to talk about going home. Fabien was like a man waking from a heavy sleep. The course of the descent was broken, and, on the landing where he rested, he knew that Someone waited. For years he had lived a life of chastity and religious devotion, feeling that presence only as something still far off. But now, after a strange and errant course, after treading the winding ways of an exquisite guilt, he felt upon his face the very breeze and breath of condemnation.

But it was on the journey home, especially, imprisoned in their sleeper where he had to submit to the experience of feeling shut in, of knowing that he could not get away, that he realized with astonishment how strangely his long fall had ended. The pleasures of the flesh that blunt so many hearts, had restored to his a mystic sensibility. His mistress was there with him in all the vulnerable intimacy of proximity. Never had they spent so long a time together, never had they seen one another so clearly, as during those long and gloomy hours between Venice and Paris. For hitherto their love had been a bird of darkness. Deep in himself, but very far removed, he felt the presence of that Being whom he had betrayed—while here, within touching distance of his hand, within the very radius of his breathing, was, all the while, this aging partner of his sin. The further the train travelled from the sun, the heavier lay the autumn's wounding hand upon the forests. Great flocks of crows swooped down upon the stubble fields. Fanny was smiling at the thought of winter now close at hand—of that season when lovers in the languor of their satisfied desires hear the patter of drops upon the windows, the sighing of the wind, when, deep in a room drowned in the Paris rain, the clock ticks on its empty reckoning of a life where time means nothing.

In the dining-car she discussed practical details. Fabien must move from his hotel. She knew of a ground-floor flat in the rue Visconti. Would he let her furnish it for him? Everyone in Paris admitted that she had a "gift" for that sort of thing. And it would really be doing her a service; she had a perfect mania for picking up bargains.

"I don't know where to put all the stuff I've got."

Her dear, scatter-brained darling, for whom the outside world scarcely existed, wouldn't, would he—she asked—mind if now and then a chair was spirited away? There are some things one keeps for years, others that one gets rid of in a week.

But Fabien was not listening. His whole mind was bent on the idea of escape.

"You'll come and see me often, won't you? What a sensation you'll be, my tiger-cat! You care so little about art, and certainly Thérèse was the last person in the world capable of teaching you to appreciate beautiful things. She's always had an instinctive love of the ugly. But then, of course, ugliness is a matter of principle with her. I know you're intelligent, but not in matters of that kind."

He broke in on her talk with a harsh gesture, furious that she should have dared to speak of Madame Dézaymeries. She fell silent, quick to notice the dark mood that cast a shadow on her loved one's face. She was no longer intent on changing Fabien. Her knowledge of men made her realize that he would be quite unresponsive to any such attempt. It was simply a question for her of taking him as he was, of drawing him to her with all his heavy load of torment, credulity and remorse. In their early days together she had tried to win him by pretending to be attracted by his metaphysical dreaming. But he had eluded her

every attempt to broach the subject. It was as though he had a
horror of hearing words he held sacred spoken by lips like hers.
Within the little mahogany box of their sleeper Fanny set herself to read the formidable language of his face, to interpret the
meaning of his every silence. She guessed that he was longing
to escape, and trembled when she heard his somewhat theatrical
reply to what she had just been saying:

"There will be no place for me in your house. Do you really
think that I am prepared to accept every extreme of marital
forbearance?"

With his mind on Donald Larsen he added: "From now on
he is a co-conspirator with us."

With a gesture that she knew well, of the meaning of which
she was only too conscious, he buried his face in his hands. She
was caught by sudden panic. Tomorrow morning, in the shoddy
dawn of the Gare de Lyons, would she not see him vanish, disappear forever? Had the time come to play her last card, that
threat of suicide which still worked with her wretched husband? She had no idea how a young Christian would react to
it, so unfamiliar was she with the type. Might it not be that he
would accept his mistress' damnation with a light heart?

A railway official entered to prepare their beds and dim the
light. Fabien sought the solitude of the corridor, where he stood
with his forehead pressed to the rain-drenched window. A few
paces off, Fanny watched him. Tonight the noise made by the
train as it rushed through unknown stations struck a note of
torment to the very heart of their love-making. It was as though,
in a desperate heroism, they had mingled their bodies on the
edge of an eternal nothingness.

FANNY had to play her hand, at first, very carefully. The young man, ever ready to take fright, refused absolutely to live anywhere but in the hotel in the rue de Vaugirard to which he had grown accustomed. Every other day he met his mistress in a ground-floor flat in the rue Visconti, where the only permanent piece of furniture seemed to be the divan bed, where the chairs and screens that stood about the room changed continually. From each of these trysts he emerged so exhausted, so melancholy and so resentful, that she was left with a feeling that she would never see him again. But always he was the first to arrive, impatient to perform the act for which he had come. From this she drew no favorable omen: "He enjoys it, that's perfectly clear . . . but the chief reason is that he fears I will kill myself if he plays me false." She was forever alluding to the possibility of her death: the subject, in fact, had become a perfect mania with her, and the glint of the revolver still showed whenever she opened her bag. It wasn't that she wanted to exert any kind of emotional blackmail on him, but that, as she confessed, nothing gave her such a thrill as the feeling that she was all the time playing a dangerous game with fate.

"I used to be a terrible gambler, darling; but what's money, after all? What I need today is the knowledge that the stake is living flesh and blood, that I'm playing for *you*! I've put everything on you, and, when all's said and done, it's only my own life that's in the balance."

She had as yet ventured to invite him to the Quai Debilly, though she would never really be at rest until he was breathing the air that she habitually breathed, until she could feel that he was continually within her reach. How happy, therefore, it made her to discover that the thought of her unknown life apart from him caused him acute suffering—that he was actually jealous of the woman from whom he longed to be delivered. To his first clumsy questionings she replied quite simply that her life was an open book:

"When you see the kind of people, my dear, among whom I spend my time, you'll stop worrying. Artists are all very well for casual conversation or business deals, but when it comes to love! . . ."

Fabien emitted one of those bursts of frank laughter which he never, except on rare occasions, succeeded in controlling. They always gave the impression that some vast reserve of youth and happiness within him had come suddenly to the boil.

At first he hovered uncertainly upon the frontiers of her strange kingdom, fearful, as in his native heaths, of venturing on to squelching bogs. Nothing that he now did showed any eagerness to escape. The trapped animal, after his first violent struggles, has a way of staying motionless for so long that he produces the illusion of death. Knowledgeable and patient, she had finally succeeded in enveloping him completely. In his moments of satiety he thought: "I'll run away from all this grubby playing ground, from all this filth of mind and body"; but then desire would stir in him again. At Fanny's parties he was most commonly to be seen leaning against a doorway and say-

135

ing nothing. The other guests were as strange to him as the members of some savage tribe. He wandered among them, a melancholy Gulliver, the prisoner of an unknown race. The talk was all of the impending return of Donald Larsen and of Cyrus Bargues, who was at present dancing in London. He was bewildered by the incomprehensible pictures on the walls, and by the music, which sounded to him like recurrent blows with a fist. There was no sign of servants, and at supper-time the guests helped themselves. Under the influence of drink masks did, to some extent fall, but there was always one still clamped to each face. Had he been able to tear it away what raw wound would have been revealed? What was this leprosy he could not see though it stank in his nostrils? At first he felt humiliated when he heard for the first time the name of some musician who was, according to Fanny, the most renowned in Europe, of some poet, of some collector. He suffered agonies when his was the only solemn face while all around the company was doubled up with mirth. . . . But the jokes were all about people he did not know, and the jargon, with its indirect references and implications, was like a foreign language to him. This was a world of which his intelligence had not the freedom. He stood in it like a blind man at a fireworks display. He could hear the "Ah's" of the crowd, the banging of the rockets, but not a glimmer of light reached him through the darkness.

These Philistines had begun by laughing at him, as at some Samson cropped and weaponless. In confidential whispers and at a safe distance (for he looked a tough customer) they exchanged pleasantries on the subject of his presence there among them. But of all this he seemed to be completely unaware, seemed not even to notice how the women sniffed round his body. In the noisy din of the supper table he had ears only for the soughing of his native forests under an autumn rain. The air might be shrill with the voices of ageless women in backless dresses, but what he heard was the sound of pigeons swooping to roost among the oaks. He could catch the wildness of the wind driving the rain against the windows of the nursery where his brother had breathed his last. From far back (and herein lay the secret of his taciturnity) he had, though he did not know it, been oppressed by a grievance against his mother caused by her inflexible austerity, and unconsciously he accused her of painting the world black and showing life in nothing but gloomy colors. But he knew now that the world is a place of leprosy, that life is the home of death. He could see, he could feel, the canker at the hearts of all these people. He was terrified by the stench of his own rottenness. It was true, perhaps, that his mother, under the influence of her own Jansenist upbringing and of a slightly warped vision, had been guilty of distorting the doctrines of her faith: yet, compared with what he saw about him, how right she had been! Though he might entirely fail to understand the poetry, the painting, the music which those around him seemed to admire so much, he could not help feeling that the men responsible for these things had, maybe, employed their art in the creation of a universe of monsters with the object of being able to move among them unnoticed. Was it not true to say, he thought, that their art was the visible form of their despair?

Why, then, did he not profit from the violent shock administered to him by this backfiring of sin? Why, then, wakened by the thud of his fall, did he not take to his heels? If only he could turn to account the sense of horror that pressed so close upon satiety. . . . But Fanny would kill herself. He alone it was who stood between her and the abyss: he was her sole defense against that will to death which kept on coming to the surface of her mind. There were moments when he felt ashamed of his secret wish that she would act upon it. If only she would get out of his life, if only she would vanish forever, if only this torment of his existence would cease, leaving him like a garden with a fresh patina of green after the hail had passed! Why should the weary be refused the boon of sleep? But he did not believe that death was sleep. He believed only in an eternity of rest or punishment—in an ineffable Presence forever there, or forever absent. He believed that absence and presence are the two contrasted aspects of eternity—that there is no third possibility, no refuge for those who, having been the enemies of God and man alike, long only for the dark and nothingness.

8

IN THE rainy dawn, as he stood waiting for the door to be opened, Fabien saw, on the pavement opposite, a number of shadowy figures pass one by one through the half-opened wicket of the Carmelite Chapel where the bell was calling to early Mass. He dreaded lest one of them should turn its head and, with face suddenly displayed, smile with his mother's eyes and lips. He climbed his staircase, which was misted with the stale smell of yesterday's food. The shoes standing outside the doors told mute stories of laborious lives. A telegram was lying on his table. Just as he was about to open it, he remembered that it was the anniversary of Joseph's death.

Memorial service for Joseph Thursday ten o'clock. Expecting you.

He must get off at once, before he might have to fight his way through Fanny's entreaties! Hurriedly he packed a bag and scribbled a note for his mistress. Might not this be the prelude to final and permanent escape? Here was one of those chances that he could not possibly have engineered. His own choice, his own will, had had nothing whatever to do with it. Someone was taking a hand in his life. Someone, perhaps, was concerned about his destiny. It was beyond his power *not* to take the train, *not* to feel his mother's arms about him, *not* to press with his knees the oblong of sand under which his brother slept, *not* to plunge into that atmosphere which death creates, with which he had always tended, since the days of his childhood, to saturate his mind. He began to suffer when, with nothing left to do, he sat waiting in his room until it should be time to start for the station. Suddenly he felt that he would like to say a prayer for the dead boy. Between his brother and himself there lay a solid block of sin—no life-giving corn crop but a foul, luxuriant weed. He could, of course, still pray, but of what avail were prayers uttered from such unholy depths? With the tears streaming down his face, he could do no more than speak the first verse of the *De Profundis: Out of the depths have I cried unto Thee, O Lord!* . . . Shivering, he repeated the words: out of the depths! out of the depths!—and seemed to catch the muffled, despairing notes of his mother's voice far away in the country cemetery. . . . Polluted as he was, what could he do for his dead brother?

A cab took him on the first stage of his journey, then the train, in which he sat shut in with himself. Later, just as darkness was falling, in the city where he had been born, he took another train that would carry him on to the heaths and forests. He had to change once more, this time in a deserted station where he waited for two hours under the stars. The country of his earliest years came out to meet him. Dense walls of pine were already closing in on him, and in his nostrils was the familiar smell of marshy fields and turpentine. Not only in space had he left Fanny far behind: he had travelled back through time to the lost innocence of the dead years.

He was surprised to find how much younger his mother looked, as a result of living alone. She seemed thinner, gentler, less shut away on the barren heights of authority. At first they talked of Joseph.

"The poor boy offered up to God each moment of his final agony," she said. "His faith was without blemish, and so, too, was his innocence. But which of us can stand without fear before the Judgment Seat? Which of us can be sure that he is justified in the eyes of the Almighty?"

Fabien recognized her old familiar tones—but it seemed now as though she were speaking the words from force of habit, merely. They were no longer in accord with a heart that was now like earth which has been softened by the rain.

When they got back from the cemetery he found a letter from Fanny. She had disguised her handwriting on account of Thérèse. The envelope felt heavy, and he dreaded to find within pages and pages filled with supplication. He walked down alone to the little stream. The frosty grass wet his shoes. He could hear the sucking sound of mud beneath his feet. From the letter came the smell that impregnated everything that Fanny touched. He was amazed that her scent should reach even into this country solitude, forcing its presence on the grassy void. The icy current, exposed now to the full light of day, flowed on beneath bare alders and between dead briars. A woodcock flew from a thicket, swift and heavy on the wing. The water had seeped into the holes made by rooting wild-boar. He heard the screaming of a sawmill, and it seemed to him as though the pine trunks were crying aloud in their agony. Without even opening the letter, he tore it into tiny scraps which soon the streamlet mingled with its frothy scum.

He went back to his mother and had, at once, a feeling that

she was about to wield the probe. She said that the curé would be celebrating Mass at seven o'clock.

"Tomorrow morning we shall be able to take Communion together in Joseph's memory. I have told the curé that you may wish to make your confession first."

She was arranging his inner life for him with that artless determination which she had shown when he was twelve years old. In his reply, he was moved less by anger than by the desire to start a quarrel (thereby making it possible to escape without rousing her suspicions).

"You forget how old I am, mother. It was no part of my intention to take Communion here."

She could not understand him, was voluble in protest. How could he not wish to do as she had suggested? He knew what value the intentions of the living have for the dead. . . . She could hardly believe that he would wish to deprive his brother of such aid. She spoke just as she had always done. It did not seem to occur to her that he might be different from the little pious boy he once had been, from the youth so strong in chastity. Suddenly worried, she turned her face to him, all drawn and tear-stained with the day's emotions. She was a million miles away from suspecting anything wrong in her son's conduct. What she dreaded much more was that his faith might be passing through a crisis. She had heard priests talking about new intellectual theories, about forms of heresy against which even the sacerdotal mind might not be wholly proof. Dryly, he cut her short.

"At least, my boy, set my mind at rest by telling me that your faith is unshaken?"

He begged her not to worry. She could be easy, he said, on

that score. If he possessed any certainty in the world it was the one that she had given him as a child. Now that he was grown up he had received ample confirmation of it.

She embraced him with a fervor that was unusual in her. But all that evening there was silence between them, and he, sitting with a book and pretending to read, could feel her eyes upon him. Nevertheless, they prayed together, and he felt as though he were no more than twelve and that his brother was close beside him, kneeling by the bed, his face buried in the counter-pane. As of old, the words sounded muffled because Madame Dézaymeries kept her hands over her face. He found himself remembering a certain evening when, while his mother prayed, he had heard the sound made by Fanny as she turned the pages of a book, sitting by the fire, an exile from this act of family worship. He had, he recollected, twisted his head round and watched the young woman dangling a heelless velvet slipper from her toe. She had been stroking her cheek with an ivory paper knife, and smiled at the pious boy with a look of tender mockery.

He made no attempt to persuade his mother to join him in Paris. "It would be yielding to a weakness," she said . . . but she spoke in the tone of one whose dearest wish it is to yield. "It is just because," she went on, "I want it so much that I must give up the idea of such a trip." In the old days, when she had refused to take a proffered chance of happiness she had wasted no words on the matter. But now, in her softened, unfamiliar mood of loneliness, she added: "I don't seem, now-adays, to be able to live without you."

Fabien could think of nothing to say except "You must do what seems most sensible to you." The words were deceptive, but she would not let herself believe that they contained a hidden meaning. More than once she directed the conversation in such a way that he might return to the charge and spirit her off to Paris in spite of herself—but he said nothing. Until the very last evening she hoped that he would force her to go against her will, would take pity on her overpowering desire, would play an active hand in the sweet plot.

He left before dawn. His mother, with her hair down, and wearing a black dressing gown, stood by the kitchen range and watched him eat. "You're still here," she said, "but this evening you'll be in Paris," and she stroked his forehead and his cheeks as she never would have done when he was small. A farm hand came to carry down the bags. He had a lighted lantern, but put it out. The sky showed white in the puddles of the road. Factory sirens were calling men to work. The pines, with their branches spread wide like crosses, stood drowned in mist. The dawn sky looked as though it had been dragged down to meet their upward thrust and now engulfed their crests so that they were invisible to the resin-drawers busy at their work of enlarging the gashes in the trunks.

That evening, at the d'Orsay station, lost in the anonymous crowd lining the barrier, Fanny scrutinized the grubby faces of the travellers as they came up the stairs. Fabien always took his time. What message would she read in his eyes? His running away without seeing her again, his failure to answer her letter, had inclined her to expect the worst. The dead brother, she had felt, the gloomy heaths, the remorseless mother, would all have been in league against her. Then, that morning, a telegram had come telling her that he was on his way back, and she had begun to hope again. She felt the agonizing thrill of the gambler as she told herself that at any moment now she would know whether what lay before her was death—or life. Suddenly he appeared—the youngest member of all this dusty crowd, and, while he was still some distance from her, smiled. They did not even touch hands, but beneath his gaze she felt herself trembling with happiness. In the car it was he who first kissed her in the hollow of her neck. She said that she would go with him only as far as the door of his hotel. She must hurry back because of the girl.

"What girl?"

"Why, the girl I wrote about in the letter which you never answered. Donald brought her back with him from Brussels, where he's staying on for a few days. He'll be back this evening . . . you'll meet him. It'll all go off splendidly, you see if it doesn't."

He was afraid she might notice the wave of hot color that suddenly flooded his cheeks. He saw in imagination the torn scraps of the letter he had not read mingling with the scum of a moorland stream. He was prudent enough to let Fanny do the talking.

"I explained that it was Donald's darling daughter. I've found out since that he had a boy, too, by Leda Southers—think of it, he's ten years old! Naturally, he's his favorite. But he seems very proud of this Colombe of his. . . . What an idea, giving a girl a name like that—Colombe!"

"There was a parish of Sainte-Colombe quite close to where we used to live."

"Listen, darling. I've got to take the child to a concert this evening in the Champs-Élysées. Why not join us?"

He said that it wouldn't be quite the thing for him to go

to a public entertainment so soon after the anniversary of his brother's death. She burst out laughing. That must be another of Thérèse's ideas!

"My dear, only fools regard music as an entertainment. It's when I'm suffering most that I find I can't do without it. . . ."

She broke off, surprised that he did not protest, as he usually did whenever she brought Thérèse Dézaymeries into the conversation. Instead, he snuggled up against her like a little boy.

"You've no idea how *beastly* I was to mamma. . . . She was longing for me to bring her back. She just waited and waited for a word or a sign . . . and I was so frightened! It's horrible of me, because I do really love her. It's awful to think that now, when we've got such a short time in which we might be together, I can't bear the thought of having her with me. It's as though I were wishing she were dead. . . ."

"What big words! Don't be a little silly, my dear. All it means is that you're twenty and that you don't want your years of youth to be buried alive. . . ."

She followed him up the hotel's evil-smelling stairs. She loved, even more than the flat in the rue Visconti, this squalid room into which Fabien so seldom let her come. It was rich with the day-to-day animal smell of his presence. It was a constant joy to her to wash her hands with his used cake of soap, and dry them on the towel dirtied by his razor. Ever since the day when she had laid her cheek on the rough surface of his bolster and he had violently pulled her away, she loved to sit on the iron bedstead, the student's bedstead, the bedstead that, for her, was forbidden ground.

"Your youth does not wish to be buried alive. As somebody— I forget who—once said: Let the dead bury their dead."

"You're right, my sweet, it is better for the dead to stay with the dead. . . ."

The tone of his voice had changed. She dared not switch on the light, imagining the sudden look of desperation that had come to his face in the darkness.

"You know how fond I was of your poor mother. She drove me from the house, I know . . . but she's only got to hold out her arms. . . . All the same, darling, look at the existence she leads—her attitude of refusal to life."

"And how, may I ask, do you define life?"

"Life is love, my love. At least, that's the only thing I've ever expected of it, and I certainly have found it."

"More than once?"

Momentarily abashed, she took his hand:

"Often it was the shadow only. But even when you were little more than a child, I loved you. Once one has found the real thing, it doesn't matter, does it, how often one has been deceived? Your mother has never had anything. I wish you could know what her attitude to your father was—quite, quite too extraordinary! . . . Anyone looking at her now would take her for an old maid, don't you think so? I don't mean that as an insult, Fabien, but really no one would ever think that she had had children. That hard face of hers . . ."

She was afraid that he might turn on her in anger, but he gave no sign that he had taken her words in ill part. He merely said:

"You've never seen her face, have you, when she thinks no one is looking? There are days when she comes back after Mass, from the Calvary."

"What's the Calvary?"

"A hospital where she goes twice a week to look after the cancer patients. She looks positively radiant, then, I swear she does. . . . I think her face on those occasions is the only face in which I have ever seen real joy. . . ."

"When I am in your arms, Fabien, what do you see in *my* face?"

He replied that he had never dared to look at it.

"That, dear love, is because my joy is so terrible that it frightens you. I, too, know what joy means, *I* have had experience of it . . . of joy . . . of joy . . . of joy! . . ."

Her voice as she repeated the word grew harsh. Her face looked ugly because she was puckering up her eyes in an effort to keep back the tears. Fabien sat down on the bed and took her in his arms like a child. She lay sobbing against his shoulder.

As he was being driven to the theater, he thought: "Yes, let the dead bury their dead." He was surprised to find that he was feeling happy, perhaps because he had forced Fanny to confess her wretchedness, perhaps because at last he had made his choice, and had not consented to be numbered among the dead.

In Fanny's box there was one other woman. He ought to have known her but had to be freshly introduced. He never recognized women. He was fond of saying that every new dress is a disguise, and that there is no end to this playing of variations on the theme of clothes.

"And this is little Colombe, about whom I was speaking to you."

A young, decidedly tall girl rose awkwardly from her seat and held out a gloved hand (she had on the only pair of long gloves to be seen in the theater). Fabien thought her ugly but odd. His seat was behind hers. She must have scrubbed her neck with a rough towel, because the delicate skin showed red. Her hair had been dragged back so that it left, fully exposed, two tiny ears, the lobes of which looked flushed and swollen.

"They taught her to wear her hair like that at the convent," Fanny said to the strange woman. "Of course, it looks very ridiculous to us, but we should think it rather attractive if it happened to be the fashion, as it may well be, soon."

Fabien addressed himself to the girl: "Have you been living in a convent?"

Without looking at the young man, she said that she had been brought up by the Ladies of X . . . in Belgium—and then pretended to read her program, wrinkling her nose and letting a little frown of concentration appear between her rather Chinese-looking eyebrows, which Fabien decided were distinctly comic. Her voice, too, was comic. Suddenly she raised her face, threw a quick glance at Fabien, blushed a deep scarlet, and then looked down into the auditorium, where the orchestra was "tuning up." Finally she inquired whether the concert had begun. He replied, meaning to make her laugh, that with "this sort of music" one could never be sure. But she did not laugh. Instead, she examined the conductor with great care, after which she turned to Fabien and said with extreme seriousness:

"No, they've not begun yet."

This childlike simplicity made him feel very happy. He found in it a satisfaction at once poignant and tender. He had the whole evening before him in which to look at her neck. It was long, and reminded him of a pouter pigeon—which exactly suited her name, for was she not called Colombe, Dove, Pigeon? Fanny had mentioned her in the letter which, at this very moment, must be eddying to and fro on the weedy surface of the stream. It pleased him to think that he had mingled the name and the image of this unknown child with the fresh flow of water which must now be shimmering beneath the moon, and, swaddled in mist, filling the darkness with its chaste murmurings.

"It's over!"

She had turned to him with an expression of infantile relief. She moved her arms and legs. A couple of sweets produced sudden bulges in her cheeks. She thought it wise of Fabien not to take any because "they stick to one's teeth so."

Fanny was staring through her opera glasses. "Look at Coco and the Princess down there in the stalls," she said to the strange lady. "They don't see us, but they can feel they're being looked at. We really must go down and say 'hullo.' . . . You won't mind, Fabien, will you?"

They pressed past him, plump and powdered. He breathed in their scent. He exchanged smiles with the young girl, wondered what he could find to say to her, and finally asked whether she was enjoying Paris.

"I'm frightened of people."

Her answer delighted him. He said he could see that she was still a *wild* pigeon, and that she ought really to have been called *Pal*ombe.

"It was mamma who wanted to call me Colombe, because in the town where she was born there was a parish where they used to have a procession in honor of Sainte-Colombe, and she played the part of the saint. I've seen a photograph of her holding a palm. . . ."

Fabien exclaimed that he too had been born in that same

town. Very soon they decided that they had probably met in the park, might even have played together.

"I was born in Paris," Colombe told him; "but mamma went back to B . . . because my guardian was director of the theater at that time and put her on the free list. Was it on Thursdays and Sundays that you went to the park, and what part of it, the duck pond or the terrace?"

"Oh, we used to run all over the place."

She gave him a long look and said that she was trying to remember whether she had ever known a dark-complexioned little boy.

"But I was much older than you, probably as much as five years older!"

"And then, of course, almost all the little boys in B . . . are dark-complexioned."

There had been only one fair boy in Fabien's form at school, and he had been nicknamed the "English kid."

"If that had been you I should have remembered."

He said in reply:

"My brother was really quite fair when he was a baby, but later on his hair turned chestnut. He was going to be a priest, but he died."

"Oh, I'm so terribly sorry, because it always makes me unhappy, not having any brothers or sisters, and I used to think how nice it would be if mamma would ask God whether she couldn't have some more children. But to have had a brother and then to have lost him! He must have been sweet and gentle to want to be a priest. Perhaps you teased him, because I expect you weren't always good-natured. . . . Oh, they're going to start again."

Fanny and her friend came back into the box. Fabien shut his eyes. What did it matter to him what they were playing? He imposed the rhythm of his own heart on the din made by the orchestra. Not for anything in the world would he have kept his eyes on his mistress' really lovely back. He infinitely preferred the fresh, frail reed before him, the mists of childhood just dispersing, the angular shoulders of his budding Eve.

"I can't find the sleeve," laughed Fanny as Fabien helped her, rather awkwardly, into her evening coat. Someone took it from him with an air of authority. Looking round he saw Donald Larsen.

"I think we've met before, haven't we, Monsieur Dézay-meries? At Venice, if I'm not wrong?"

They exchanged a few more words and shook hands. The giant himself wrapped the young girl up very carefully, and with a strange show of haste propelled her toward the exit. Fanny whispered to Fabien:

"Tomorrow, at our house. . . . Didn't you notice how polite he was to you?"

He made no reply. His whole mind was concentrated for the moment on how to get himself into a position where the girl would see him. She had already moved some distance away, but turned her head to look for him. At last she picked him out and smiled a good-night.

He felt wildly happy striding through the darkness—though what had caused his happiness he did not know. There was nothing to warn him that it was as though an angel had passed through his life, an angel who would not return. It did not occur to him that his mood was due to his meeting this young girl, because he had been conscious of it before he had even seen her, when the train, that morning, had carried him away from the burned-up land of melancholy, away from his mother. It had reached its apogee after his talk with Fanny when she had cried and talked of joy.

He followed the pavement that runs beside the Seine. The river lay swathed in mist. Just so, at this very moment, must the stream look in that remote countryside of his. A wreathing smoke was rising from the water as it must have done in the days when the present stone embankments were a wilderness of trees and rushes. It smelled of the days before history had begun.

Suddenly, with his elbows pressed to his side, and his bare head thrown back, the young man broke into a long, loping run. He did not stop until he had reached the Alexander Bridge. There he crossed to the further bank, with no more idea of where he was going than a homing pigeon. If only there was someone he could talk to! He did not know a soul. Could it be that he had not a single friend? By this time he had started down the Boulevard Raspail. Shortly after passing the Croix-Rouge he recognized the house where Jacques Maïnz lived, a colleague of his at the École des Chartes, with whom his work had sometimes brought him in contact. Maïnz was the best man of his year. He was a Jew, and on one occasion had said to Fabien: "You've the luck to be a believing Catholic, and yet you don't become a Benedictine. I can't think why not." The young man smiled at the recollection. He saw that his friend was burning the midnight oil, and, without stopping to think, called Maïnz's name to the concierge, and, though it was nearer to one o'clock than to midnight, knocked at his fellow-student's door.

A voice asked suspiciously who was there.

"It's me, Dézaymeries."

"My dear chap! at this time of night? What's the matter?"

Sobered by this welcome, Fabien looked at his host. The man might have been any age. Weak eyes peered out from behind a pair of circular spectacles. Suddenly it struck him what a gulf separated his own burning heart from this other heart of ice. He excused his presence by saying that he wanted to copy out some notes of a lecture which he had missed.

"Yes, I know. You *are* getting a bit slack, Dézaymeries, and you could pass so high if only you'd do a little work. Why, I used to look on you as a rival."

Jacques Maïnz gazed at the tall, bareheaded young man whose open overcoat revealed his evening dress. Fabien had followed him into his workroom.

"Here you are, but I must have that notebook back the day after tomorrow without fail. . . . Just a moment, I'll show you where the automatic switch is."

On the landing he added, in a tone in which contempt, affection and envy were strangely mixed:

"You're far too good-looking, you know, to make a scholar."

These farewell words served to rekindle the young man's flickering flame of happiness. He was walking slowly now, weighed down by a load of delicious heaviness. So people thought him handsome, did they? and little Colombe had liked looking at him this evening! He thought of her, at first confusedly, then with a visual precision that embarrassed him—of her shoulder, of the narrow expanse of arm where her long glove ended. . . . He closed his eyes and shook his head in the comical way he had had as a child when he wanted to get rid of a "wicked" thought. But why, now that he had tasted of the fruit of the tree, should he fight against his sense of gushing happiness? He remembered how once, when he was with Fanny at a circus, he had seen a sudden jet of dirty water squirted over the tan, lifting odds and ends of straw and dust, and making a muddy lake, the level of which slowly rose. He wanted to save little Colombe from his own unclean and detailed thoughts—but could not resist the temptation to dirty her with that knowingness which he had learned from another.

In his shabby room he went to bed without a light.

9

FANNY was delighted, next day, to find that he was more ardent, more restlessly expectant, than she ever remembered having seen him. What she did not know was that his mood of desire was linked with the feeling of disgust that always oppressed him, but had now been carried to such an unusual degree of intensity that it resulted in a hatred of which he was ashamed and fearful, because he could not understand the reason for it. When he thanked her because none of the furniture had been moved during his absence, she told him not to infer that her business was doing badly. All it meant was that she had gone into partnership with the Comte de X . . . and thought it better to house her stuff with him. In that way prospective customers would think that the bits and pieces were old family heirlooms, and would be prepared to pay a high price for their mistake. . . . She laughed so loudly that she did not see his sudden flush, his expression of loathing, the furtive look which he turned toward the door. While she was tidying her hair in front of a triple mirror she was able to study him without turning her head. All she realized was that she had torn the old wound open again. She tried to soft-pedal what she had just said, explaining that she had merely wanted him to "see things as they were." But the wound was open and bleeding. She was afraid that he might refuse to dine at her house that evening; but he agreed to do so with a gay alacrity which brought her some degree of reassurance.

Had he not been seated some distance away on her left, Fanny would have realized to what it was she owed his seeming impatience and happiness. He paid no attention to the other guests (English people whose language he did not understand). He spent his whole time staring at the young girl who sat at the far end of the table, her head leaning slightly to one side, her bare arms looking decidedly cold. Her hair, dressed in the Chinese fashion which left her rather bulbous forehead uncovered, gave her the air of belonging to another period. She was wearing round her neck a child's necklace adorned with sacred medals, and each time she caught his eye she replied, as best she could, with a narrowing of the lids, a melancholy smile, a pout of her rather full lips—all intended to express her annoyance at being so far away, but also, though she did not know it, conveying the impression of a kiss. So long as she was there Fabien felt no need to close his eyes or shake his head in an effort to drive away evil thoughts. He could see in the young body, lit, as it were, from within, all the signs of a sensitive conscience, of uncertainty and confused scruples—of some imperfectly understood mood of renunciation. But before their glances could meet they had to cross a danger zone. Donald Larsen, seated opposite Fanny, may have had a suspicion of their unspoken colloquy. He was eating greedily, drinking more greedily still, and talking hardly at all. His complexion passed through all the stages from pink to brick-red, and, finally, to purple. Several times Fabien was conscious that the china-blue eyes were fixed on him as they had been in Venice.

As soon as the ice had been served, Donald made a sign to the girl, and she disappeared. Fanny said with a laugh, "The sandman's coming." Fabien remembered how she used to say that each evening at nine o'clock in Madame Dézaymeries' room, and how she had drawn him to her for a good-night kiss.

He did not see his wild pigeon again that evening, but was happy in the thought that she must be feeling sad.

He took the same way home as on the previous night, but his mood was melancholy and he walked more slowly. No longer did he leap like a chamois in the mist. It was his first evening of tender reverie. He felt absolutely safe, knowing that among all these ravaged hearts his was the only one on which his wild pigeon would choose to alight, because corruption, in his case, had not progressed beyond the initial stage. Only twenty-two years had elapsed since his coming into the world. Who can corrupt the spring? Where his mother had made a mistake was in not realizing that the body, too, can be sanctified. A young man and a young girl blaze in the face of God like two high, clear flames. Drawn into one another, they show the brighter. He understood many things of which his mother was ignorant. He found a glory in realizing that he had no need to protect his love from his muddied thoughts of yesterday. He revelled in that knowledge, quite forgetting that, thanks to physical ecstasies still recent, the demon in him was temporarily sated.

Two nights later, seated at the same table between a couple of Englishmen, it was he who sought a pretext for silence. In the first place, he had been in an agony of apprehension because his wild pigeon had not been in the drawing room. But she slipped into the dining-room with the guests, and, since there were no other women present, Donald made her sit on his right. She smiled at Fabien, but as though through prison bars. The whole situation should have warned him that somebody was doing his best to keep them apart. But if he had any suspicions they were directed solely at Fanny. He felt reassured when he saw that she was deeply involved with her English neighbor in one of those doubtless æsthetic discussions which she pursued so enthusiastically that at moments she seemed almost to be losing her temper. Fabien told himself that he would not look at the girl before the second course. But, though he did not see his wild pigeon, he could hear her fluttering in her invisible cage. She was worried by his feigned indifference. Unable any longer to keep the promise he had made to himself, he directed at her a long and ardent gaze, and saw the little face with its prominent forehead redden with a mixture of love and shame. At the same moment he was aware that Donald Larsen was staring at him in a quite intolerable manner. He pretended to be occupied with a piece of mural decoration, but the china-blue eyes were insistent. As in Venice, this man, without uttering a single word, had voiced an entreaty with a look, so, this evening, he managed to convey by the same means a clear-cut prohibition, an obvious threat. Fabien, who had just drunk a glass of Johannisberger, felt annoyed because of the sense of embarrassment and fear that was oppressing him. He made up his mind to defy the man with the pink cheeks, whose manners, so he told himself, were those of a drunkard. It was a matter of general knowledge that, from five o'clock on, Donald Larsen was never fully under control, though he was skilful at disguising the fact. It was an understood thing that no one should ever talk to him at meals, but this evening, the young Englishman on Fabien's right, was making a polite effort to say something to him in French. He was explaining that he was an army officer, and that none of his comrades ever suspected him of writing poetry or of contributing to magazines. He never talked literature in the mess: to have done so would have more or less disgraced him. Only once had he been able to refer to a poem, because it happened to deal with fox-hunting. Fabien slowly raised his eyes and steeled himself briefly to endure the stare of the giant who, for the last ten minutes, had been drinking nothing. Then he sought the eyes of the girl, who was leaning forward in his direction, feeling his attraction as a sunflower might the sun.

It was only because Fanny's argument had become strident and because everyone else at the table was joining in that nobody noticed the terrible expression in Donald Larsen's face—the white, expressionless stare, the trembling upper lip, the glass shaking in his fingers. "He can't do anything to you," said Fabien to himself; "it doesn't matter to you what *he* wants. What is he, anyhow, if it comes to that?" No one in Paris was more looked down upon. Besides, hadn't he trafficked in his own wife? But what the young country-bred man most strongly felt was the peasant's distrust and hatred of the man of uncertain origins, of the nomad, the mountebank. "No one knows where this Larsen comes from: a Dane fathered by a German Jew!" Fabien out-stared the loathsome jailer with a feeling of delight. Slowly the girl turned her head away. One hand was raised to her rather exposed throat. What would the giant do? The veins were standing out on his temples, and fury was making him sway like a beech-tree. Fabien expected an outburst. If only he too could give his anger rein! He would not mince words! If necessary, he would go for this Goliath physically. But suddenly Goliath grew calm. He leaned toward Colombe and his purple lips began to move close to her flushed little ear. At his first words she stared stupidly at Fabien, then, seemingly, voiced a protest. But the man interrupted her, and she listened in silence. "Look at the old man making up to his daughter!" Colombe directed a quick, terrified glance at Fabien while the purple lips went on muttering. With the whole table between them, what could Fabien do to counter the deadly things the swine was saying? She asked Larsen a question, to which he replied with a melancholy seriousness. Fabien saw her suddenly flush scarlet. He knew that the blow had come!— could feel it strike home in his own flesh. He had no idea what, precisely, had been the blow the man had aimed, but he felt as though he had received a mortal wound. His neighbor asked him whether he was feeling unwell. Fabien gave him a terrified stare, but said nothing. He saw Donald Larsen pass his napkin over his face, which had suddenly become convulsed by a fit of coughing which set his scarlet jowl quivering. Of what nature was the secret with which he had overpowered the innocent girl? Her narrow, childish face had hardened. She was crushing a rosebud in her hand and picking off its petals one by one. Fabien wanted to cry aloud: "Whatever he has been saying about me, don't believe it!"—but he had to sit there motionless, correct, a silent witness of his own death. If only he could have caught her eye!—but she seemed no longer to be aware of his presence. He had ceased to exist for her; he had just been murdered. At last Fanny got up. Another minute and Fabien would no longer have been able to contain himself. In the drawing room the girl handed round the coffee. He waited for the moment when she would approach him.

But, having served all the other guests, she gave him a look of contempt which left him in no doubt of her deliberate avoidance, and passed on. He followed her into the passage, heard a door shut and the sound of a key turning in the lock.

He made for his usual refuge, a small empty drawing room, now completely deserted. It was filled with lacquer furniture, and a single lamp gave light to its equivocal intimacy. Stretched on a divan, he began to smoke Turkish cigarettes, lighting them one after the other, endlessly. On a low table, within reach of his hand, glittered a decanter of sweet wine. Several times he filled and emptied a long-stemmed glass, striving to attain to a state of besotted insensibility, sleep, a death that should be eternal. If only he could get rid of the obsessive thought that Donald Larsen had not even had to lie about him! "In order to pass sentence of death upon me in the girl's eyes, he had only to explain the meaning of my presence in this house. . . . I expect he implied that I was a kept man. I'm twenty-two, and Fanny is almost an old woman. . . . Would it do any good to write to her? I bet he keeps a careful eye on the letters she gets. . . . What bliss it would be never to see Fanny again . . . and if she dies of it, well, let her. . . . No, no, I mustn't say that. Besides, if I were separated from Fanny it would mean that I should be separated from the girl as well. . . . Nothing to do but drink.· . . . " He longed to sleep, and when, finally, sleep overcame him, lay with his head thrown back against the cushions. His arm slipped limply from the divan. His hand lay like a dead thing on the carpet.

He had a confused feeling that someone else was in the room, but did not immediately open his eyes. He could hear the sound of breathing. A young man was standing by him. Where had he seen him already? The frail torso above the over-developed thighs looked as though it had been poured into the short jacket. The clean-shaven face showed blue round the thick lips. Fabien recognized the voice as Cyrus Bargues'.

"Did I wake you up?—how *beastly* of me! There's something so *mysterious,* don't you think, when people are asleep—*young* people, I mean, of course. To see an *old* man asleep is like watching a dress-rehearsal of the stroke that's going to carry him off! *Actually,* my dear, I don't expect you to thank me. . . . All the same . . . in Venice. . . ."

He broke off because Fabien, his hair tousled, his fists clenched and a glowering expression on his face, looked as though he might be about to attack him. But the mingled fumes of sweet wine and Turkish cigarettes made him fall back again on the cushions. He was already half drunk, and there was no longer room in his mind for anything so clear-cut as hatred, disgust or distress. As though he were imparting some profound secret, he said:

"There are, you know, such things as legitimate caresses."

Cyrus broke into a guffaw of strident laughter. He declared that he knew of no caresses that were not legitimate. Fabien replied in tones of the deepest gravity:

"There are such things: of that there can be no doubt—no doubt at all. But we men are so naturally responsive to caresses that they give us a wonderful illusion of infinity—and therein lies danger."

"Therein lies their charm, is what you mean, my dear. You really are the most *delicious* of creatures, quite *entrancing* . . . but to be avoided when you're sober. What you need is another drink. We'd better go by the passage and down the back stairs, so as to avoid our hosts."

At a bar in the rue Duphot they started in on whisky. Fabien achieved a mood of exaltation which brought him relief and peace of mind. Everything was turning out exactly as he wanted it to. He would discard Fanny like a bundle of old rags. Either she would kill herself or she wouldn't. The choice was hers! The only thing he cared about was to get back to his wild pigeon. It needed only a word from him and she would understand and forgive. They would go away somewhere and live far from the haunts of men with the pine trees of his childhood for company. . . . Who was this young man whispering in his ear and pressing him to drink? Seemed a good sort—was saying the dance must be purged of all ornament, made hieratic and expressive of ecstasy. But why should Cyrus want to leave this warm, cosy bar where women sat perched on stools looking like ibises? (he had never seen an ibis). . . . In the cloakroom they all used the same lipstick. . . . Cyrus led him outside. The street was as moist and as warm as a mouth. In the next bar, in spite of the frantic din made by the band, Fabien no longer felt happy. He took a cocktail and it made him sad. With the second his feeling of joy became slowly immersed in a dark flood. He kept on repeating like an imbecile, "Colombe—Sainte-Colombe—little Sainte-Colombe." Cyrus said that, personally, he found her too old for a little girl and too young for a woman.

"You have turned up either too soon or too late. Besides, make no mistake about it, the old man's got ambitions for that child of his. He has suddenly noticed that there beats within his breast a father's heart. He is aiming to find a husband for her from the very tip-top drawer—some superannuated peer or glittering maharajah—they *are* to be found, you know, if only one looks in the right places. . . . Hullo, now you're crying! You look so *funny,* my dear, just like a small boy!"

No woman, he went on, had ever made *him* cry. He loved nothing but his art. Women always needed so much reassuring. One had got to be forever stroking and petting them like animals.

By this time Fabien was quite incapable of controlling his movements. In an effort to blow his nose he upset both their glasses, after which he sank into a doze. When he emerged from it, Cyrus was saying that he had tried cocaine once, when he had been going through hell because of somebody whose name he wouldn't mention.

"But it doesn't soothe one as much as they say it does. The only effect it had on me was to make me *terribly* irritable. A curtain in my room had only to be crooked. . . . It was dancing that saved me."

Somewhat later he said:

"Don't cry, you little silly. The only thing in life that matters is to be twenty-two. . . . A time will come when one will no longer be an object of desire to anyone. There is only one form of perfect happiness—to know that one is surrounded by a thousand fierce desires, to hear about one the crackling of branches. . . . "

Fanny was tolerant of Fabien's escapade; was even pleased to think that he had gone on the loose. She had her own ingenious methods of getting rid of the effects of his night out. Long experience had taught her how to deal with the morning after. But she did say: "What on earth have you done to Donald to make him so mad at you? The moment I try to put in a good word for you he jumps down my throat. You've no idea what coarse language he uses in front of the child, too. It won't be long before the bloom's rubbed off *her*! Why are you making such a face? Are you in pain, my pet?"

She thoroughly enjoyed arranging his pillows, laying cool hands on his forehead, behaving like a young mother comforting her big son. With his haggard cheeks and mournful expression he looked so like the little Fabien whom once she had taken on her knees! She even ventured to mention Thérèse Dézaymeries, and grew slightly sentimental. The only gentleness she had known in her life, she said, was associated in her mind with evenings spent in Thérèse's room. Did Fabien remember the gray wallpaper and the enlarged Nadar photograph of his father? The lamp had had a shade of pink ribbed glass, and they had loved running their fingers up and down the grooves when they were small boys.

"You used to sit on a stool at our feet, and, when you looked at me, your eyes were full of innocence, uncertainty and dreams. You played silent games in the dark corner between your little white bed and your mother's *prie-Dieu*."

Fanny was remembering the whisper of the rain, the crackling of the fire and the boy's low muttering. She had come to that room from very far away, dropping to rest in the quiet lamp-light like a tired bird. She had made one with those innocent hearts and simple things. One evening, Fabien, his face pressed to the crossbars of the window, had been playing a game which consisted in trying to follow the movements of one

single swallow among all the bewildering dartings of its fellows.
She had thought that he looked like the imprisoned Dauphin.
She could never, afterwards, hear the cries of swifts on country
roofs without seeing again, in imagination, the stuffy room,
and Thérèse, all anxiety lest she miss the devotions of the
Month of Mary in the Cathedral. . . .

She stopped talking, realizing that he was asleep. Never before had she been so deeply impressed by the look of chastity
on his virile face, by that nobility which marks the faces of
young men whom it is a woman's mission to corrupt, but which
no soiling can destroy: the last trace of childhood, hovering like
a patch of mist impervious to the midday sun. She touched the
smooth forehead with her lips as she had seen his mother do,
straightened his blankets, and was still at her post when night
fell, lost in dreams beside the sleeping youth.

1 0

FANNY had asked the young man not to come again to the Quai Debilly until after Donald Larsen had left on his next trip to London.

"I just don't know what's biting him. Are you sure you've said nothing to annoy him? And the child's playing up to him! He's putting her against me, against both of us. What on earth can he be up to? I just pretend not to understand all his vulgar hints and innuendos. . . . Darling, *don't* look so tragic! Donald Larsen's scarcely in a position to spread scandal about anyone. I wouldn't say it except to you, but mark my words, it's a good deal more dangerous to have him as a friend than as an enemy. . . . The only thing that matters is that he shan't separate *us*. After all, he's utterly dependent on me, and he knows perfectly well that my whole life is wrapped up in you."

With her head on Fabien's shoulders she begged him in vain to show her a little affection. It was a dark afternoon in the gloomy depth of winter. Fortunately, the low lamp shone only on the young man's hands and knees. His face, with its expression of hatred and repulsion, was invisible. . . . Until Donald Larsen's next trip to London . . . could he hold out so long? He brought himself, nowadays, to endure Fanny's presence only because he knew that if he gave her up he would lose all hope of winning his wild pigeon. But now that he could not see the girl, he found it agony to play the lover with a woman whom he detested. But his performance, alas! was too bad to deceive his former mistress, though she still believed that it **was** because of his religious scruples that he had turned from her. She never dreamed of looking for any other reason to explain his bitterness and lack of ardor. But it was not God who stood between her and Fabien. The wretched youth had certainly not ceased to believe in what once had been the whole of life for him, but he *had* accepted the fact that he was now dead to that life. He had consented to leave the ship, had landed on a coast of dust and ashes. There was no hope that the vessel would ever return to rescue his wrecked soul. He was prepared to envisage what once would have filled him with horror. If it was Fanny's destiny to kill herself, then kill herself she must. He could no longer bring himself to put his arms protectingly about that worn and used-up body. Often, in the course of the sunless winter, sitting on the iron bedstead in his hotel room with its low ceiling and its mingled smell of soap and tobacco, when he ought to have been at his class, or working in one of the libraries, he surrendered himself to the desire of a sleep from which there should be no awakening. The idea fascinated him. But he had no belief in the possibility of such a sleep, and he was afraid of God.

Since the night he had spent with the dancer making the rounds of the bars, though he had not again got drunk, he had taken to drinking rather more at his meals than good sense allowed, and just enough to produce a temporary feeling of exaltation. At such moments he imagined himself sitting outside a café looking on to an unfamiliar landscape, with Colombe at his side gazing at him. He felt like a man armed and vigorous, vigorous enough to fight his way to her through all difficulties, to calm her fears, to overcome her resistance. . . . But later, back once more in his low-ceilinged room, poisoning himself with tobacco, he would wander from bed to window, from window to bed, a prey to uncertainty. "If I did carry you off, my poor little pigeon, what should I do with you? Would my mother welcome a girl born out of wedlock, and with such a father? And could *I* ever feel love for a son of mine who had in his veins the blood of a Larsen? My own children would be objects of horror to me."

It was on these lines that his thoughts were running when Fanny took his face in her two hands, bent above his eyes with their absent look, and said:

"What are you thinking about?"

He replied ill-temperedly: "Not about you."

He broke from her. Wearily, Fanny tied her veil, not even bothering to look at herself in the glass. She was now in a mood of violent self-pity.

"You won't have much longer to wait: you'll be rid of me a good deal sooner than you think. But won't you just give me *one* look? You haven't looked at me since I came in. When I'm in your arms I seek in vain to read your baffled eyes. It is as though something in you were running away from me, were trying to put an infinite distance between us. But take care! . . ."

"Isn't what I leave behind enough to satisfy you?"

"Your body, you mean? . . . The body is everything and nothing. It is of value only because of *that*—I don't know what—that something which you take from it before you hand it over. . . . *You're* the one who gives yourself like a . . ."

The word was crude. He opened the door and, without looking at her, said:

"Get out! Get out!"

She stopped for a moment on the threshold. "It will have been your doing, Fabien." A moment later she was in the street. For all his earlier mood, the threat had its effect upon him. He hurried after her and caught her up at the corner of the rue Bonaparte. She was walking fast, like a woman pursued. Some of the people she passed turned to look at her. When she reached the river she had to slow down. They were side by side now, moving through the mist. A young street urchin followed them with his eyes: perhaps they had roused a sense of envy in him. Fabien said that he was suffering, and that when he was suffering he was an impossible companion. She thought that he was alluding to what she called his mystical day-dreaming. Would he never rid himself of all that nonsense? How dared *he* talk of suffering—a young man of twenty-two who had someone to love him? Had he any idea what she, after this unspeakable afternoon, was going to find when she got home? A girl to whom she was devoted, but who was now turned against her, a girl whose air of contempt was utterly exasperating; a man who put up with her merely because he found her necessary. No good mincing words: at bottom Donald detested her, but he knew that on her depended the bulk of his fortune. If she hadn't a positive genius for picking up old furniture, if she hadn't learned all about the picture racket, what would become of Larsen with all his grandiose but ruinous schemes?

She was at the end of her tether and stopped dead. They hailed a taxi. She continued with the tale of her woes.

"Never any let-up for me! This evening I've got to go to the Cirque Médrano with the pair of them, because Donald, who's got some supper engagement or other, insists on my being there to take the child home. Can't you imagine what fun that drive back will be for me in the company of a self-righteous and hostile little miss!"

Fabien asked her why she didn't leave Larsen. She replied that she no longer felt strong enough or brave enough to live alone.

"And who would have me now, Fabien?"

He turned away without replying. Having dropped her at her door, he went home on foot. He, too, would go to the circus that evening. The thought helped him to bear the burden of existence. He must learn how to get what enjoyment he could out of small, brief pleasures. Walking in Paris was, he had found, the best way of escaping from his troubles. Sometimes he would wake from his fits of dreaming in the middle of the road with traffic swirling round him. Tonight he reached his room without having the slightest idea of the route he had taken. He was surprised to see a light shining from under his door. Jacques Maïnz, his fellow-student at the École des Chartes, had been waiting for three-quarters of an hour. This was the first time he had ever paid Fabien a visit. He apologized for intruding on his privacy in this way, but the matter about which he had come was urgent. The Director was thinking of taking disciplinary measures against Dézaymeries on the ground that he absented himself from half his lectures.

"Don't you know any doctor who would give you a bogus certificate? That'd do the trick. There's a friend of mine; I'd gladly give you an introduction."

Fabien looked at the mass of untidy hair, at the pimply face, at the eyes which would have been fine if they had not grown dim from poring over manuscripts. The whole man was a product of laborious days spent in a library. He said:

"Don't worry your head about me. I'm sending in my resignation tomorrow."

Until this moment such an idea had never even entered his head, but he knew now, beyond all possibility of doubt, that his decision was irrevocable. It had been maturing in his mind without his being aware of it.

"D'you mean to say that you're leaving, Dézaymeries?"

"Why should you care?"

Maïnz, without moving from his chair, raised his lashless eyes and looked at Fabien.

"I shall miss you. True, we've never been friends, and I never really believed we could be. All the same, I liked to see you enjoying life. You brought—how shall I put it?—romance and color into the place. . . . Don't shrug your shoulders and look sullen. As a matter of fact, I think you're perfectly right to clear out. You never really belonged to us. I had a pretty good idea of the way your mind was working. . . . I suppose it surprises you to hear a 'dirty Jew' talking like this?"

"I've never confided in you."

"Yes you have, often, though you didn't know it. For instance, one day when we were talking about Saint Catherine of Siena you trotted out a whole theory of the nature of love. You described the frantic appetite that can never be strangled, the appetite that only we ourselves can divert God-wards. You told me that no human being can remain stationary, that the Infinite is a river and that we've got to go either upstream or down—up to God our source, or down to the desperation of a nameless bitterness. There is, you said, such a thing as a sort of reversed perfection, the possibility of becoming always more and more criminal. . . . You see, you can't get away from your Catholic heritage. And all the time you were talking—we were leaning together over the same facsimile—I was conscious of a sort of fragrance. You're not the kind of chap who uses scent. . . . Now don't get mad. You see, I admire and envy you. Had I been of your faith, I should have been precisely the same sort of person I am now, doing exactly the same work, the only difference being that I should be wearing a monk's habit and living in some abbey or other. But in a chap like you the Catholic religion produces a whole crop of conflicts and private dramas. . . ."

The man was wholly devoid of tact. There was a heavy quality about his laughter. But Fabien, as a rule so quick to take offense, hung his head. It was with an air of humility that he replied:

"There's something I want to beg of you, Maïnz, and that is that you won't judge the tree by its rotten fruit—which is what I am . . . promise me."

"It seems to me very curious and interesting, Dézaymeries, that you should say a thing like that, that you should be obsessed by a scruple of that kind. The rest of us will just turn into archivists. Like everyone else in the world, we have found our particular mill, and we shall spend our lives turning it (in my case, it might just as well have been a lawyer's practice, an office or a factory). Rimbaud was perfectly right when he said, '*La main à plume vaut la main à charrue. Quel siècle à mains.*'' Fundamentally, all a man cares about is stupefying himself. Intensity of life can be found equally well in business or drink.

Work, too, is a narcotic, and action, after all, is a form of sleep. Well, you have chosen life. Who was it said that the inner life is the only reality? My dear fellow, there are only two types of person that I admire: those, like you, who, instead of dissipating their energies in action, are self-creators, achieving self-mastery and enduring self-loss only to find themselves again triumphantly in an emotional struggle for a stake which is God—and those wise men of the East who also find their way to the divine, but by a different and perhaps a surer route; those for whom sanctity is detachment, who say of themselves that they have been 'delivered from the prison of life.' . . . Forgive me if I say that I think they have chosen the better part. I have a feeling that Buddha was, on the whole, the supreme example of human greatness. . . ."

"That's because you have no knowledge of Christ."

Maïnz, who was striding up and down the room, which was so small that the smoke from their two cigarettes shrouded the whole of its contents in mist, stopped in front of the tall, bitter young man whose tormented expression he guessed rather than saw.

"I know something of him, Dézaymeries, because I know you. . . ."

Fabien shook his head:

"He is in me no longer," he said, and repeated the words—"He is in me no longer."

"My poor young Christian, how wrong you are. Why, he possesses you entirely, rends you in twain, tears you from every foothold, detaches you from life at every moment of every day. . . ."

"I say again—don't judge the tree by its rotten fruit. There *are* Christians who can be joyful."

"I know that, my friend. I have made notes on the joys of Christians according to Pascal (you remember his letter to Mademoiselle de Roannez?). I have read the wildly joyful Odes of your poet Claudel."

In a low voice, Fabien said: "I am in torment!"

It was the first time in his life that he had ever confided in a friend, and the experience brought him a secret sweetness. This evening he had met the Jew who was called Simon of Cyrene.

He forgot all about dinner and turned up punctually at the circus. The place smelled of tan and clean stables. He remembered the Thursday long ago when he had gone with Joseph to the circus at Bordeaux. It was the one and only time that their mother had consented to take them. What mingled feelings of wonder and terror he had known on that occasion! . . . They had left before the end because there was to be a ballet. The fag-end of daylight had been hanging about the Place des Quin-conces. The fair was emptying. The damp evening breeze was rapidly dissipating the smell of hot coffee and waffles. He had a headache as the result of laughing so much. He felt detached from all the trivial daily round. His mother said they must hurry. There would be only just time to get their homework finished before dinner.

With a trembling hand he snatched up his opera glasses. The "wild pigeon" was sitting in the front of a box. Fanny looked gross and heavy. She was wearing a frock cut too low in the neck for such an occasion. Larsen's shirt-front glinted. Suddenly Fabien noticed that his wild pigeon had changed. She had lit a cigarette, and looked comic because she smoked it as though she were sucking a stick of barley sugar. She laughed with a great deal of grimacing, and turned to Larsen. She was probably saying that she felt "positively *drunk*" and that she was "laughing herself *sick*." What innocence could stand out for long against the poisonous atmosphere diffused by Fanny? Evil is as infectious as any disease.

Somewhat later he saw her reddening her lips. She was laughing loudly, and a young man in a neighboring box leaned forward to look at her. Fabien told himself that if he could bring himself to renew his visits to the Quai Debilly there might still be time to save her from sinking altogether into the mire.

There was no need for him to pull his hat down over his eyes. These thousands of laughing faces were concentrated on the antics of the Fratellini Brothers. Colombe would never notice him in this dark, surging crowd which rippled with mirth like water under a stiff breeze. There was still time to rescue her. Might he not, by doing so, find his own way back to a state of grace? What else was there for him to do with his life? Fanny, in any case, was lost utterly. No man can save a corpse. He would sacrifice her in the cause of his wild pigeon. . . . Larsen, by failing to acknowledge his paternity, had no legal hold over her. Madame Dézaymeries would give her consent provided he could persuade her that his marriage was a duty, an obligation and not a pleasure. They would live the whole year round in the country—*his* country. . . .

There was a sudden blare of music, and the laughter of the audience was drowned by the din of the brass. A number of trick riders were dashing round the ring lightly poised on the shining cruppers of their horses. . . .

What sort of life would they lead in that remote countryside? He trembled with anticipated pleasure, thinking of the nights they would spend together in the sparsely furnished room smelling of pitch pine. In imagination he could hear the cocks crowing from farm to farm, and the hooting of owls, sounds that would make a background to young love with nothing in it of sin. Unconsciously, his mind took the direction of what Maïnz had said. The thought of an existence that should be all a conquest of the spirit, a process of interior mastery, enchanted him. Deep in the happiness of his home he would again find God. . . . The passages would echo to the noise of children's feet. . . . The lamp would shine upon their faces as they sat nodding sleepily over books. He would saunter with his pigeon through the dark garden. She would say: "I can't see the path." . . . Light would show red in the windows, or perhaps cut hearts of fire in the shutters.

He felt hungry and decided to leave during the interval. It is easier to think when one is walking. How many plans for a life in the country are brought to a head in the streets of Paris! . . . One last look at Colombe in her box and he was off, striding through the night, a tireless child of the heathlands, striving, without success, to deaden with physical fatigue the clamors of his lusty blood. Solitude! solitude! He would have liked to take up his conversation with Maïnz where it had been left. And then, suddenly, he began to think again of Fanny. Could one go on living if there was always with one the memory of a woman whom one had driven to her death? But perhaps she would *not* kill herself. "The main thing is not to go on com-

mitting adultery. That's where my strict duty lies." Any priest
would tell him that. Besides, there was always the fact of grace,
the reality of prayer, to be taken into account. Fanny would *not*
be abandoned. He bit his lower lip and murmured to himself:
"Hypocrite! filthy hypocrite!" . . . He had something cold to
eat at Weber's, and drank champagne. Alone at his table he
felt cut off from the rest of mankind. All of a sudden he was
swept by a gust of happiness. Would he have liked to have
Colombe there beside him at the moment? No. . . . Suppose
she had gone from him forever, suppose she were dead, suppose he were handed a letter which she had written and
addressed to him before she died? He composed its contents
in imagination, and the tears welled into his eyes so that he
had to hide his face. Oh, yes, he loved her, of that there could
be no doubt at all; he loved her. But, in that future time,
when they should be married and living remotely in the
country, the thought of love would not be always, as it was
with Fanny, in the forefront of their minds, a sickening obsession, an idiotic futility. Life, real life, has something better
to bother about. The first thing for him to do was to get some
order into the chaos of his thoughts. Now that the appalling
hurricane had roared through him and passed on, he must
settle down and write, live for the service of truth, be at once
famous and alone, inaccessible to the crowd, yet known to
all the world.

1 1

NEXT day Fabien was prodigal of so much unaccustomed tenderness that Fanny's suspicions were at once awakened. In his clumsy fashion he thought it a master stroke to tell her that he had gone to the circus on the previous evening for the sole pleasure of looking at his mistress from a distance. He entirely ignored all those proofs of weariness which he had far too often given Fanny in the past, and was ready to convince himself that a woman in love can have the wool pulled over her eyes in the crudest fashion. But his kindness worried his mistress far more than the rebuffs to which she had grown used. His clumsiness at times verged on the ridiculous. Much of his charm was due to his attitude of complete indifference where love was concerned. The apathy with which he could take without even pretending to give in return could be actually attractive. It was apt to be shot through with an occasional access of violent passion which made up for all that had gone before, making it possible for her to endure the rapidly ensuing mood of bitterness, and the sight of his face suddenly withdrawn behind a curtain of self-disgust.

How false his voice sounded when he allowed himself to go so far as to say that he was "*longing*" for the Quai Debilly! The stupid creature really believed that it was impossible for love to be clear-sighted. He forgot (if he had ever known) that though the one who is loved may know nothing of the other who loves, the reverse is never true. Fanny knew the youth on whom her whole happiness, her very life, depended, far better than she knew herself. She was too weather-wise a sailor, had too often studied, when they met, her lover's every gesture and every look, not immediately to smell out deception when it came her way. In his case absence of love meant absence of knowledge. Indifference is blind. Why should he want to start coming again to the Quai Debilly? The thought of Colombe as a possible explanation had not yet entered her mind, either because it did not occur to her that so young a girl could please a man in that way (not to mention the fact that she found her gawky and plain), or because the idea of Fabien really in love would have been intolerable to her. She must, however, have been getting "warm" when she said to him:

"You can come to the house quite safely on Saturday. Donald won't be back until late. He's dining at Versailles with the Princess . . . and the next day he's off again."

Instinctively she avoided saying anything more about this projected trip of her husband, which in point of fact closely concerned Colombe. A more attentive lover would have noticed how she was lighting cigarette after cigarette and throwing each away almost unsmoked: the way in which she kept on flicking the ash off with her finger. As a rule she took "a perfect age"—as Fabien said—"to get out of the room," but tonight she seemed all eagerness to be alone. Far from letting this worry him, he found in it a reason for rejoicing. He could not go on much longer aping a tenderness he did not feel, and found himself caddishly blaming her—poor thing!—for the necessity he was under to play a part.

He let her leave first. Only when she had got a good start on him did he emerge from the house in the rue Visconti. Instead of going straight back to his hotel, he crossed the Seine at a brisk pace and walked for a while along the railings of the Tuileries gardens. The gates at this hour had been already closed, so that he was shut out from communion with the trees which lent a note of beauty to the misty emptiness within. That very morning he had sent in his resignation to the Director of the École des Chartes. In two days' time he would be seeing Colombe again. Thus he had taken the first step to freedom and happiness. To gauge the extent of his love he no longer had to imagine that Colombe was dead, nor yet to conjure up the image of that last letter she might have written to him. After every tryst in the rue Visconti his passion for the girl increased, drawing strength from the feelings of disgust which Fanny woke in him. In what way did the young fool imagine that marriage would differ from what he had known already? What sort of a dream was it that he entertained of a sensuality made one with chastity? It was not yet quite dark, and he felt a little shock of surprise to find that the sky above the Place de la Concorde could be so beautiful, brushed in, as it were, for the express purpose of serving as a background to it. He felt no need of companionship. If, at that moment, he had run across Maïnz, he would have avoided him. The fullness of his heart sufficed. In the rue de la Paix he was conscious of the silent invitation lurking in the faces of shopgirls disgorged from the various buildings. His wild pigeon, he thought, would put up scarcely any resistance. He had only to beckon and she would come.

At last the day dawned when he was to see the girl. He

started the afternoon by having his hair cut, after which he returned to his hotel and ran up the stairs, whistling. Fanny was waiting for him in his room. She was sitting on the bed. Her furs gave her a thick and padded appearance, and she was wearing a veil. He tried in vain to keep his temper. He had not been expecting her, and this sort of thing was not playing the game. There was nothing he so much disliked as meeting her at times other than those of their prearranged trysts in the rue Visconti. . . . There would be trouble with the manager.

"And I'd planned it as such a pleasant surprise for you! You were so sweet to me last time!"

He heard the ache in her words, but not the irony. It was just like women all over, he grumbled: the more one gives, the more they want. He walked up and down the tiny room, the ceiling of which he could have touched by stretching his hand. He began gesticulating in a sudden burst of southern exuberance. She, meanwhile, remained motionless on the bed, watching him. Her passivity got on his nerves. He told her that she must go.

"Come on, get out!"

What he meant was, "Leave this room," but she made a pretense of believing that he intended this to be a final break, and began to whine.

"But where am I to go, Fabien?"

She was at the end of her tether, within measurable distance of complete collapse.

"You no longer believe a word I say. No one ever does believe people who say they wish they were dead."

"We're dead already," he replied.

She tried to turn the whole thing into a joke.

"I must say, my dear, you've got a very odd idea of love!

Those who tried to make love a crime were rightly regarded as the enemies of the human race. . . . If only I could convince you that the only way of loving is to avoid all these complicated feelings, these dramas, these metaphysical subtleties. . . ."

"Oh, do for once look at things straight! If you hadn't met me that day in Venice, you would have been dead by this time!"

He had lost all control of himself. He told her, not once but again and again, that, but for him, love would have killed her. None but fools and hypocrites maintained that it was only religion that had given love its power to destroy, that, but for religion, passion would be nothing but unalloyed delight. As though the flesh was not perfectly capable, unaided, of distilling poison! Though, as a rule, he hated any suspicion of rhetoric, he added:

"Go out into the streets, into the promenades of music halls, into the brothels, and see what this beautiful 'love' you're always talking about can make of human beings!"

She protested that what he was referring to wasn't love at all. He agreed, but only to argue that what she called love produced precisely the same fruit. It didn't need God to interfere. Concupiscence alone could set the world in a blaze. He made no attempt to moderate his language, but went on to describe with gloating delight the hideous old age of women who have lived only for the pleasures of the body—Circes made desperate by the realization that they can no longer turn men into swine. It was no arbitrary pronouncement of the Church that had conferred this frightful pre-eminence on the sin of sexual vice and sensual self-indulgence. Once let human beings set their feet upon that slippery slope and there was no stopping their headlong descent.

And so he talked on, pressing his face to the window, not seeing the prostrate figure on the bed, though he could hear her panting breath. Suddenly he was overwhelmed by a sense of shame because he had brought God into this discussion. It was from habit only that he was trotting out these noble sentiments. If he had not wanted Colombe he could have put up with Fanny. It was a young girl—and not the Infinite Majesty—who was estranging him from his former mistress.

Like many women who are quite incapable of putting two and two together, or of arguing rationally, she kept on repeating, either because she had not heard, or had entirely failed to grasp, what Fabien was saying:

"If it wasn't for these morbid scruples of yours, darling, you *would* love me, and there would be joy for you in that love."

"You poor, demented creature, *can't* you see that if I don't wash my hands of you, it's for one reason and one reason only —because I feel that I am responsible for your immortal soul. I wonder whether you've got the slightest idea what it means to be responsible for another person's immortal soul? What binds us together is the sin that we have jointly committed. I can't acquiesce in your eternal damnation. We must sink or swim together. . . . But I don't suppose that a single word of what I'm saying makes sense to you."

Once again he relapsed into silence. He was filled with a sense of self-loathing because if, once upon a time, he really had felt some such scruple, really had believed that he had no right to concentrate upon his own salvation to the exclusion of hers, it was equally true today that he didn't give a hang for Fanny or for the destiny of her immortal soul. Of what had formerly been in him an excessive sensitivity of conscience he retained, now, nothing but the vocabulary. That his sin had been joyless did not alter the fact that, because of it, he had become diminished in moral stature, impoverished and hard.

Fanny got up, went over to him, put her arms round his neck, and moaned in heartbroken accents:

"Oh, *don't* tell me that's the only reason that you have remained faithful to me!"

Because she had been a constant first-nighter, a phrase of modish theatrical jargon came easily to her lips (on anybody else's it would have sounded comic):

"Ah, Fabien, do not be false to our love!"

He gave a mirthless laugh and shrugged his shoulders. She switched on the light, and they gazed at one another with eyes that were eloquent of nothing but violence and death: she, desolate with weeping, old and defeated; he, no whit diminished in his vigor by their acrid argument. His youth seemed actually to have gained something of radiance from the devastation of the storm that had been raging between them, like a tree whose leaves look all the greener and more brilliant for the rain. . . . Fanny was tidying her hair before the mirror, fastening her veil. She must be going because they had a dinner party that evening. In Fabien's mind there was nothing at this moment but the thought of Colombe, and he said with the gayest of gay intonations:

"I'll be round as soon as I've changed."

She turned toward him, utterly dumbfounded. How could he *dream* of dining at the Quai Debilly after such a scene? She noticed his expression of mingled embarrassment and expectation. With assumed indifference she said:

"You'd much better wait a few hours. Donald's going away

tomorrow for a month. He *says* it's because he's got to take Colombe back to her mother, but actually he's going to meet Leda Southers. . . ."

"Is Colombe leaving, then?"

Fabien could not help raising his voice. Fanny appeared to interpret his cry as indicative of joy.

"Yes, you spoiled child: father and daughter are going to leave the coast clear. You'll be able, once more, to treat the Quai Debilly as your home."

He went with her to the door.

"Perhaps," he said uncertainly, "I'll look in for a moment round about ten, just to ask your forgiveness for my ill-temper."

Fanny went down the dark staircase, her face turned toward her lover, who was standing looking over the banisters. In the car she forced herself to gaze straight and firmly at this new uprush of pain, this sudden onset of agonizing jealousy. She was like a newly awakened sleeper who, when the shutters are thrown open, has to accustom his eyes to the blinding sunlight.

12

FABIEN must have realized his danger, because, having dressed with the intention of dining at the Quai Debilly, in spite of Fanny's protest, he dared not take the risk, but wandered about in the mist that hung about between the parapet and the trees of the deserted river bank. He would not go up until he had seen the lights flash on behind the curtains of the drawing-room windows. He had an instinctive awareness of the peril he was running, but could think of nothing but Colombe and her impending departure. Once she had gone he would fall again into the old rut, would find himself face to face with Fanny for ever and ever. From then on his life would be completely empty. But there was still this one evening left, and he had made up his mind to take the chance it offered.

They must have finished dinner by this time. He entered the house, but was terrified by the reflection of his haggard face in the hall mirror, and stopped for a moment to straighten his tie. Fanny was not in the large drawing room, and his entrance passed unnoticed. Colombe was not there either. He hunted for her in vain through all the other rooms, but found no trace of her until he reached the small room furnished with lacquer, where he had got drunk one evening on sweet wine. He came to a dead stop outside the door, his heart beating, because he had recognized the voices of Cyrus Bargues and Colombe.

"*Actually,* in a month's time all the women will have had their hair cut; you see if I'm not right. Do let me cut yours, *dear* Colombe. A balletmaster can turn his hand to anything. I should hate you to go before I had seen you looking like a young and sexless god with a head of cropped curls. . . . It'll be so *screamingly* funny to play a trick on the others. The melancholy stallion will look more melancholy than ever."

Fabien trembled because he heard Colombe say: "Oh, *he* doesn't bother about *me.* We all know why *he's* here, don't we?"

"For you, darling. Why, he just *gobbles* you up with his eyes . . . besides, he has talked to me about you. . . ."

"That's not true, and you only say it because you want to make me angry. You don't believe, do you, that I care what a horrible creature like that thinks? No, please don't tell me what he said. I'm sure it was something beastly."

Fabien could imagine the childish mouth all puckered up to spit out that final word "beastly." But Cyrus was protesting:

"No, really you're wrong. *Actually* he's terribly good-looking."

"I'm not talking about his appearance."

"That's the only thing about him that matters, Colombe, dear. . . ."

"What *did* he say about me? Something awful, I'm sure. Do tell me, Cyrus."

"If you want me to answer your question, go and fetch the scissors. It really will be great fun. You see if it isn't. You will feel them cold against your neck. I can hear the sound of them cutting through that dense young forest of yours . . . cro . . . cro . . . cro. We'll let the melancholy stallion sweep up the fallen locks."

"How silly you are, Cyrus: you're quite the silliest boy I've ever met. You don't honestly think, do you, that I mind what the melancholy stallion said about me? And, by the way, why do you call him a stallion? Isn't a stallion a thoroughbred horse? I don't think *he's* got much breeding . . . he's more like a country lout. . . . Look how thick my hair is, and I've got nothing but embroidery scissors."

"I've seen scissors of all sizes in Fanny's dressing room. Come along, Colombe. Nobody will disturb us there, and we can achieve the transformation at our leisure. I can work miracles. A dancer is possessed of the divine fire. At this moment you're nothing but a little girl—but you're going to be turned into a young Bacchus. You'll enchant not only the melancholy stallion but all those who find delight in ambiguities and uncertainties and the mingling of the sexes."

"There's something awfully odd about you, Cyrus. Do you know what I think when I look into your little burning eyes—that you're possessed by a devil!"

Fabien heard the sound of their mingled laughter, followed by low whispering and the noise of a door being cautiously opened. They were going into the dressing room. Without stopping to think, he followed them, and entered just as Colombe, already seated, was obediently bending her neck. She got up, looking very pale. Turning to Cyrus Bargues, Fabien pointed to the door. Anger made him dumb, but his lower lip was trembling, and he gripped the dancer's arm so tightly that the latter made a face.

"What a *brute* you are, Dézaymeries!"

Fabien pushed him outside, shut the door and mopped his forehead with his handkerchief. The look that he turned on

Colombe was both tender and fearful, so tender that the girl
imparted a tone of gentleness to the insolent words that she had
made up her mind to fling at him.

"What right have you to interfere?"

He answered in a low voice but with the authority of a lover:
"I didn't want him to cut your hair."

She smiled like a schoolgirl remembering her history lesson,
and said:

"You would rather see me dead at your feet than cropped? ..."

Then she stopped short and her eyebrows drew together into
a funny little frown.

"Since you're going away, Colombe, you must forget all the
things that have been said against me in this house. . . . The
people here are just a lot of swine. . . ."

She raised her eyes and looked him straight in the face.

"Doesn't that include you, too?"

He seemed abashed.

"It does," he stammered; "but at least I know it. *They've* no
idea of the depths to which they have fallen. . . ."

"So much the better for them!"

"You *can't* know. Some day I'll tell you. I'm a miserable
sinner, Colombe. Do you hear what I say? A sinner."

With a sad smile, and as though repeating a lesson, she said:
"A miserable sinner."

"Yes, Colombe, a *miserable* sinner, and a bit of a hypocrite
too."

She saw such a look of shame in the dark, virile face that she
made as though to raise her hands—perhaps with the intention
of taking it between them, of drawing it to her—then let them
fall to her sides. Stunned, her arms hanging, the child stood

there, motionless beneath the crude light of the enamelled dressing room which was filled with the untidiness of clothes hurriedly changed. Pots of make-up and various brushes lay all over the table. A bottle of scent with its cork out was slowly evaporating. A thermometer was floating on the soapy water of the bath. The place was so small and so cumbered that they were standing very close together. Colombe, looking as though she had no resistance left in her, said:

"What do you want me to do?"

"Take this sponge and wipe the rouge from your cheeks," he said, as though that were the most pressing need of the moment.

"There!"

"And now the black round your eyes."

"It's done!"

"And the red from your lips."

"What next?"

She obeyed him like someone walking in her sleep. He asked her whether she liked being with her mother in Brussels.

"Mamma is the kind of person you would like," she answered, as though she were familiar with all the tastes of this young man, to whom she had spoken only twice before. "The idea that I'm with my guardian makes her wild! I wish you could read her letters. She's afraid I shall learn bad habits here. She's glad, of course, that my guardian should take an interest in me, but she's worried about my soul. . . ."

"Don't leave her, Colombe—not until I come and fetch you."

"Fetch me?"

She smiled at him, her face transfigured, cleansed, fresh. The only color in her cheeks now came from the young blood flowing in her veins, from the love rising in her heart. Her eyelids fluttered as with a sign of assent. She scarcely more than whispered her address, but Fabien remembered it. They said no more, but stood there looking at one another. They did not know that, at that very moment, Fanny, to whom Cyrus had murmured, "If you want to see two lovebirds, go along to your dressing room," had risen from her chair and was coming toward them. They did not hear the rustling of her dress. She pushed open the door. The two young people were not in one another's arms when she came in, were not even touching, but as they stood facing one another, love blazed in their faces, so that it dazzled her. For a moment she closed her eyes, then, with a smile, turning to Colombe, she said:

"Your guardian's waiting for you, my dear."

She took her by the hand and led her away. Fabien sighed. There would be no dramatics—at the most, perhaps, a scene. It would not be difficult for him to defend himself. Colombe and he had been doing nothing wrong. He avoided going back to the drawing room, but got his overcoat and left the house.

He leaned over the parapet and looked at the river. The surface was popply, and the reflected lights were broken. His eyes took in the bare branches, the sleeping houses, the stars. A clear road was opening through his darkness. He knew now the way he must take, but it would be rough with briars and underbrush and torn roots. Back in his room, he prayed—at long last he could pluck up courage to do that! Then he lay down, not as heretofore, like a corpse, but curled up on one side, with his two hands pressed to his heart, as though they were holding something in, though what he did not know.

In the very early hours of the next morning someone threw the door open very suddenly and turned on the light. Sitting up in bed, he recognized Cyrus Bargues, who was still in evening dress.

"My dear, something *frightful's* happened. You must get up at once! Fanny's gone and swallowed a whole lot of opium and digitalin and heaven knows what else. I gather that there is still hope, but she won't let the doctor touch her unless you come. . . ."

His eyes never left Fabien all the while that the young man was hunting for his clothes.

"Women with a taste for suicide, my dear, are upsetting only if you attach importance to what happens to them. My own view is that it is best to leave them to their fate. Everyone has a right to die if he wants to, don't you agree? *Actually,* death usually *does* simplify matters so much for the survivors. Take your own case. . . ."

"Shut up, for heaven's sake! I don't want to hear another word from you. You give me the horrors! Is the car there?"

"It's waiting. I *adore* you when you're angry. But you can be terribly *rough,* you know. I really felt quite a *worm* yesterday evening. You're nothing but a great brute, really, but then all interesting people are."

The car slipped through the dawn. All the way along the river Fabien felt angry with himself for being so acutely aware of the crisp, sad beauty of the empty city, while Cyrus Bargues sat at his side dreamily quoting:

> *L'aurore grelottante en robe rose et verte*
> *S'avançait lentement sur la Seine déserte.*

The front door was half open. Donald Larsen, his shirt front rumpled, his tie askew, was on the lookout for their arrival. He told them not to make a noise. Colombe, he said, was asleep, and on no account must she know what had happened. At the door of the bedroom he took Fabien by the arm, leaned with his enormous bulk till he was so close that the young man could smell his breath, which reeked of tobacco and spirits, and said:

"She's *got* to live—see?"

He added that he couldn't put off his own or the girl's departure. He made it quite clear that if Fanny were to die he would hold Fabien responsible.

"She's *got* to live!"

Fabien uttered no protest. The man filled him with terror and loathing. He looked like a cat with its ears laid back, and spitting. The sound of Fanny struggling for breath on the other side of the door could not take his mind from another room where Colombe lay sleeping.

1 3

"No, don't draw the curtains, and don't come any closer.
Sit down over there in that beam of sunlight. It's enough for
me if I can just look at you."

Fabien, from the other side of the room, could see the thin
face among the pillows. His thoughts turned to the woman with
whom he had once travelled across Europe. He could feel her
eyes upon him. They affected him like a physical contact. He
begged her, now that she was well again, to get up.

"No," she said; "leave me at least *that* consolation, to lie still,
to doze, to sleep. I'm going to be sensible, Fabien, truly I am.
I was hateful, I was grotesque—that especially; but you don't
have to worry now. I have learned at last to wait patiently
until the end comes . . . but that is all I can do—just wait.
Please realize that. I saw Heinemann, the dealer, this morning:
you know whom I mean, don't you? He's going to sell everything I've got here, bit by bit. It'll be a slow business and will
last as long as I shall. I like to think of ending my days in a
completely empty room. . . . But one thing you must promise
—to come every day and just sit in that chair for a few minutes.
I want to learn again how to love you as I loved you once in
your mother's room. . . . I think it was you, probably, who
made me realize, in those days, how satisfying a refuge a shut
room could be, a bed, with the monotonous ticking of a clock

and the whisper of a dying fire, with shadows moving on the walls and ceiling. Do you remember how you used to revel in your childish ailments? No more games in an icy playground, you used to say, no more masters, no more little school friends."

Fabien remembered the nights when he had kept his mouth tight shut so as not to cough, when he had lain for what seemed an infinity in an uncomfortable position so as to avoid waking his mother and making her anxious. When the doctor had leaned down to listen to his heart his beard had smelled of toilet vinegar. He had been able to see the man's scalp as though through a magnifying glass. The Christmas Annual for '87 had contained *Little Lord Fauntleroy,* and the one for '94, *Moustique.* There had been other stories as well, two of which, he recollected, had been called *Chan-Ook* and *Maltaverne.*

When he found himself once again in the street he felt as though he had returned from some distant land, bringing the old Fanny with him. She seemed emptied now of all desires. She no longer wanted him. How strange that was! So far there had been no answer to the long letter he had written to Colombe. Her long silence should have surprised him, but he had had no time for wondering. He awaited her reply without impatience. His lovely dream was on the point of becoming a rather formidable reality. Should he say anything about Colombe to Madame Dézaymeries? What was the point in telling her that the girl's father was Fanny's second husband, or that she was a natural child? Madame Dézaymeries would consent to no compromise with her standards. Prejudices can be overcome, but not principles, and Fabien knew that in his mother's case, what the world called prejudices were founded in reason and solidly built on foundations which, to her mind, showed no crack. He was amazed to detect within himself no movement of rebellion. Often, now, he let his imagination dwell on the child who would be his son, a child with Larsen's china-blue eyes and Larsen's complexion, which looked as though the blood were oozing through the skin. He must, all the same, make *some* approach to the subject, must indicate, when next he wrote to his mother, that he was contemplating marriage. But his letters were always so short. . . . And, suddenly, he blushed. He who, as a child, had never been guilty of a lie, had not dared to tell his mother that he had left the École des Chartes, had, in fact, quite shamelessly given her details of a purely imaginary success in the quarterly examination. . . . Away with the memory of such cowardice! . . . He must try to concentrate his thoughts on his wild pigeon. . . .

He was obsessed, too, by worry of a different kind, though he did his best to see it only as a rather bizarre oddity. Was Fanny really and truly cured of him? Did she sincerely see him only as the small boy he once had been, or was she playing a deep game? "What does it matter?" he said to himself. "The important thing is that you are free at last. No need, now that you are tied no longer to that aging body, to worry about being a dirty little beast." But there were times, especially at night, as he lay in his lonely bed, when he found his mind dwelling on the thought of the body which once he had so loathed. What is it in our nature that urges us to repeat gestures that used to make us feel physically sick? It is impossible to judge of the damage done until the storm has passed. Now that Fanny had broken loose, had withdrawn into herself and made the great renunciation, the poor young man could turn his eye inward and mark the incurable wound from which the blood still oozed.

Accustomed, ever since the age of seven, to making a meticulous examination of his conscience, to the workings of casuistry in its most subtle forms, he was completely ignorant of the crude mechanism of what the world calls love, of an emotion which can so order matters that an abhorred mistress whom we long to throw overboard can, quite suddenly—if she takes the initiative and, without a word of warning, anticipate our contemplated desertion—become precious in our eyes. When that happens a sudden hunger treads hard upon the heels of our satiety. Fabien believed himself to be precisely as he had been before embarking on a life of sin. He was utterly unaware of the new man within him who lived subject to a new law. That was why, when the existence of this stranger was revealed, the fact of it struck like a thunderbolt.

He had come one day, rather earlier than usual, to the Quai Debilly. The nurse asked him to wait until Fanny should be ready, and he sat in the empty drawing room, a prey to impatience. He thought that he could best rid himself of his obsession by showing Fanny some sign of tenderness, by testing her, by putting temptation in her path.

Consequently it was with considerable nervousness that he approached the bed.

She pushed him away.

"No, Fabien, no: sit down in your usual chair. I like it so much better when you can only guess what I look like."

All the time that she was speaking in her husky voice, he was saying to himself: "She wouldn't be afraid of my seeing her if she had really stopped loving me."

"At least let me hold your hand, Fanny."

She stretched out her small, bare hand, but it no longer

trembled in his own. While he faintly pressed it, she went on talking in that voice that invalids always use when they are interested in nothing but themselves:

"I had a little chicken this morning, and I actually enjoyed it."

He increased the pressure, and she gently withdrew her hand before proceeding:

"How odd it all is. . . . After that other time I tried to kill myself I never really regained the zest of living, but now, when I'm a great deal older, it has suddenly come back!"

"Look at me, Fanny! You haven't once looked at me since I came into the room. . . ."

He remembered how, in the old days, it had been she, always, who had used such words to him.

Very gently she said:

"That was on purpose, my dear. I must get used to not seeing you. . . . I saw enough to tell me how you are. . . . You ought to get away into the country . . . you're not looking at all well."

"I don't want to leave you alone."

"I think the cure is complete, Fabien. But I shan't know for certain until you have been away from me for some time. . . ."

A hint of the old chiding note which had marked their former quarrels crept into his voice as he replied:

"I know why you want to send me away!"

She flashed him a questioning look, and he went on:

"You may as well admit that it's because of Colombe. You want to punish me. . . ."

Once more she stared at him, then struggled into a sitting position and covered her eyes and mouth with her two hands.

Between the splayed fingers there came a sound, but whether it was a laugh or a sob he could not tell.

"You dare mention that name to me. Oh, what a little f-fool you are!" (She stammered slightly over the word.) "And, anyhow, you're entirely wrong, because I don't care *that* for your Colombe, especially now when I realize that you are just like the rest of them. . . . Oh, Fabien, Fabien! there was a time when I thought of you as belonging to a different race. You may be a pious little fanatic on the surface, but underneath you're just the same sort of beast—yes, I mean that—the same sort of beast as all those others who start wanting to get their victim back into their clutches the moment it's stopped yowling!"

How truly had this old purveyor of love summed up love's mechanism! Brooding there over the gawky youth before her, her astute and knowing glance fixed on his thin cheeks and passion-worn face, she said again:

"Just like the rest of them! Just like the rest of them!"

He sat in a species of silent stupor, he who had been used to causing pain, not suffering it. At last he stuttered out:

"All the same, you tried to kill yourself because of me, because of her—you can't deny that!"

She broke in on him:

"That put the lid on it! Yes, I suppose my suicide would have been a feather in your cap. . . . How you'd hate it if I told you it had been just a put-up job! But don't worry; you're perfectly right. The sight of you and her together was more than I could stand. . . . What a fool I was! I wanted at all costs to tear that picture out of my mind, but how thankful, how terribly thankful, I am that I failed! I can be at peace now. I know that I'm stronger than you are. What does it matter now if your Colombe

201

has been sent back to her convent for another two years! What, didn't you know? Then she's not as sharp as I thought her, though of course Donald never leaves anything to chance, and I expect he's taken pretty good care to have a watch kept on her letters. But what does it matter? I said to myself: 'In two years' time he'll have forgotten all about her!' And I thought I knew men! I should have said—in two days!"

She was expecting him to utter some sort of protest, to invoke the absent girl; but he said nothing.

Their eyes met. The young man she saw before her seemed to be a complete stranger, a lover who now, after all these months, was really suffering because of her. There were tears in his eyes, and she almost felt inclined, for the first time in her life, to feel sorry for him. But her pity would not have been quite sincere, for there would have been in it a hint of that satisfaction we all feel when we think, "Well, it's his turn now, poor wretch!"

"Forgive me, my dear, but you really are too ridiculous. I poisoned your existence with my threats of suicide. Then, at last, I actually did something about it. I failed, and suddenly I woke up, free at last, though not of my fondness, if that's any comfort to you. And all through that terrible time, when I really thought that everything was over, life seemed sweeter to me than ever before. You can't have any idea what it is like to see sunlight on a window when one is conscious of it only at a great distance and through gathering shadows. Yes, I was free at last and saved! Lying here in a sort of animal stupor, I took stock of my madness. Thanks to my drowsiness, to the numbness that paralyzed all my physical senses, I could sit in judgment on myself. What a terrible injury I had done you! 'He must go back to his mother,' I said to myself, looking at the misery in your face. 'You must try to have for him the same innocent love as when he was a little boy.' It seemed to me almost easy to do that. I once heard someone say that the wisdom of old age consists in being able to see the difference between pleasure and love."

He listened to her, biting his short mustache, worrying at it with his fingers. At last, in a hard and arrogant tone, he put a question:

"Am I the only person you allow to come and see you?"

"Why do you ask me that?"

"Because I know what you are. You can't live without some man . . . you never have been able to. If you're turning your back on me now, it's because you've found somebody better worth your while!"

She was so taken aback that for a moment she made no answer. To herself she murmured: "It's hardly credible!" She stretched her hand to her bedside lamp and switched it on. Then, tilting back the dark silk shade, she lay silently staring at the stranger in her room, with his tousled hair, his shoes, and the bottoms of his trousers caked with mud, a lunatic look in his eyes. She remembered all those many times when she had praised his looks, and he had said: "I'm just like any mule driver you might meet on the roads round my home." Yes, that was precisely what he *was* like—a young mule driver.

"You really must be going out of your mind, Fabien! Whom else *should* I see? I have given orders that no one else is to be admitted except you and Cyrus Bargues. But his season at Covent Garden begins in a week's time, and he's off on Friday. Besides, Cyrus Bargues, I ask you!"

"Who's your doctor?"

"Why not add, my concierge, my postman! I've had just about as much as I can stand. Go and get some air into your lungs. I'm still pretty weak, you know."

Hesitatingly he went to the door, and stopped. In the light of the lamp he could see her hand fumbling at the sheet. She must have turned away for he caught the glint of her tumbled hair. He used to tell her that it was far too yellow, but at this moment all he wanted was to plunge his face in it.

Suddenly he heard her laugh, and asked her what it was she found so amusing.

"Oh, you're still there, are you?"

"Why are you laughing?"

"Listen to me, Fabien, and don't be angry. I was thinking how you used to reproach me for alienating you from God. I shall be pretty invalidish for the next few weeks, and then it will be Easter. Thérèse is waiting for you. . . . You're not going on playing the part of the prodigal son, are you?"

She heard the door of her room slam, and, a few moments later, the door leading to the stairs. Did she feel sorry that she could not run after him? She took up a hand mirror and looked long at her temples, her neck, her eyelids, her cheeks—stroking them with her fingers.

14

HE WALKED along the street with his overcoat open and his hat pulled down over his eyes, and as he went he said to himself: "She's right: it's never once occurred to you that the road lies open, that there's nothing now to stop you from finding your way back into the life of grace." This forgetfulness showed him, far more clearly than would have done the sense of having committed a fearful crime, how far he had fallen. Had he lost his faith? Of what use is faith if it is not lived? What value has an intellectual system, a theory of the universe, be it ever so perfunctory, if one does not guide one's conduct by its rules? "You're a corpse, you're beginning to stink already: there's not the slightest hint in you of any desire to rise again, nothing but this maniacal craving, this longing to be convinced that you still exercise an abominable influence over Fanny. You loathe her, but you won't give up the power of life and death. You're just like all the other swine—only worse!"

Fabien Dézaymeries did not see that in one essential point he differed from the majority of his fellows, in the fact that he was clear-sighted, lucid, and could gaze without flinching into his own heart. The scrupulous care that he had given, since his childhood days, to the examination of his motives, to the confession of the tiniest impure thought; the readiness he had always shown to blacken himself rather than run the risk of leaving undisclosed the smallest blemish (he had always been terrified of concealing a sin), kept him now from all danger of resting content with deceptive appearances. Most lovers would have gloried in their loyalty to an old mistress, would have waxed sentimental and self-satisfied over the realization that they were more capable than they had ever thought they could be of a love that was deep and sincere. He saw through all such illusions, and plumbed the hateful depths of his own nature where lurked the monstrous feelings that were not even sure of their own identity, such dark regions as those in which two young women may suddenly be forced to realize that what they took for friendship is really passion. He saw now just how much rancorous hatred there was in this suddenly renewed craving for Fanny. How terribly youth can torture itself! It complains because it is fated to drag after itself a huddle of chained slaves whose weight lies heavy on its movements, yet, no sooner is it freed from them than it bewails the absence of those very victims who once gave living proof of its power.

Only when he reached his bedroom door did he awake from this long process of meditation. Among the letters waiting for him he recognized an envelope addressed in his own writing. It contained the letter he had written to Colombe on the very day of her departure, and here it was, returned to him. Although he had been careful to put his address on a corner of the envelope, somebody, who could not have been Colombe, had opened it and read its rather foolish sentiments. How far he felt this evening from all those sugar-sweet protestations! He was not in the least tempted to make even a gesture that might have the effect of averting an obstructive fate. He knew that the battle for

Colombe was lost, but knew too that it was in his own heart that he had been defeated. No external obstacles could have stood against his love, but he could find now, within himself, not the tiniest trace of that small and still-born creature. A girl, still scarcely more than a child, had been the means of revealing to him the existence of carnal delights that might be blessed and sanctified, of caresses from which the shadowy angels would not avert their gaze; but he realized now that this young and charming human being, the only one of her kind whom he had ever known, had been the occasion rather than the object of that great surge of feeling.

The other letter he dared not open, though the neat handwriting was dear to him. It was the same that, in the old days, he had spelled out on the "excuse cards" which had followed hard on the heels of his childhood illnesses, the cards that he would have to hand up to the headmaster: *Madame Dézaymeries begs the Abbé Bernard to be so very kind as to excuse her son Fabien, who has been confined to the house with influenza.* It was the same as that which he had covered with tears and kisses during prep. all through that month of October when he and Joseph had been sent to school as boarders because their mother had stayed on in the country. He had no doubt that this letter which he dared not open had been written, as all her letters to him were, in the belief that it was addressed to a frank and honest boy, to the young Christian who now lay murdered, though she clung obstinately to the conviction that he was still alive. It was true that each time he had gone home she had suffered cruelly because he seemed a stranger, because his voice sounded as though it were reaching her from a distance, because a hot fire glowed in his shifty glances, a fire that was not the sacred flame which she had kindled in his heart. But scarcely had he gone away again than the old lady unconsciously set herself to revivify the ghost of the innocent child who had gone to sleep each night with his two hands, linked by a rosary, crossed upon his breast.

He glanced nervously at the first few lines. No, *this* letter was not addressed to that pious, docile boy. For two months now his own letters had been so short, their tone so dry (especially since he had lied to her about the École des Chartes), that the old lady could not but feel a certain foreboding. "My dear son: I cannot recognize your voice in the words you send me. If your letters were not in your writing I should think they came from a stranger. There was a time when you used to confide in your old mother. I know exactly when that stopped—it was after your first year at school. All the same, up to a month or two ago you did at least tell me about the little events of your life. But now it is only too obvious that you are impatient to get quit of a tiresome duty. Don't you think I can tell that from the shortness of the lines, from their being more widely spaced, from the manifest tricks you've been reduced to in order to cover four pages in the quickest possible time? Someone who knows you said to me the other day: 'When a child no longer confides in his mother, you can be quite sure that there is more on his mind than he wants to tell.' I protested. I reminded the good Father of the notorious Dézaymeries reticence. My poor husband was just the same, and never really unburdened himself. . . . Still, I am not sufficiently convinced myself to be able to reassure our saintly friend. I have never dared to tell him that you refused to communicate on the anniversary of Joseph's death. . . . My dearest boy, I have been thinking a great deal and praying a great deal. I suppose it was partly a mother's pride that led me to think that you are different from other men, that evil is powerless to touch you. . . . If I am wrong, forgive me for making a foolhardy judgment. If my fear is justified, where should you find a surer refuge than in a mother whose love for you is so great that it may well be a cause of offense in the eyes of a jealous God? But Easter is not far off, and on the Thursday in Holy Week we shall, as we always have done every year, kneel together at the Lord's table, and my child in his weakness will take the bread that gives strength. . . ."

Fabien found it impossible to read further. He crumpled the letter in his hand, and began to walk up and down the low, dark room. His eyes were like those of some vicious animal. Could he have seen them in a mirror he would have been terrified. "Oh, why can't she leave me alone!" he muttered. "I'm old enough in all conscience, and my troubles are my own concern. . . . If she really expects to see me at Easter . . ." It was inconceivable that he should go home. What possible excuse could he make for not taking Communion? He would be quite incapable of enduring in silence his mother's searching inquiries. The very thought of the questions she would ask him made him grind his teeth. But what carried most weight with him was the need he felt not to leave Paris without being certain that the other woman was still at his mercy.

"All the same, you don't love her, and you know it." So much the worse, then. There was no use in trying to probe *that* mystery. There was nothing he could do to fight against the urgent demand of his whole being that the former slave should not be allowed to escape him, still less that she should put her neck beneath a new yoke. A new yoke? At that very moment, while he was pacing his room, she was probably laughing at him with some man whom most certainly she would not keep sitting at a safe distance. Who was that unknown for whose sake she had been waiting in Venice, who had failed to turn up? Fabien had never bothered to find out his name. . . .

He took his coat and hat and rushed out into the street. At first he walked, then, mad with impatience, hailed a taxi and had himself driven to the Place de l'Alma. He strode along the dark quay until he reached Fanny's house. A faint light showed behind her bedroom windows—the light of the reading lamp. Perhaps, after all, there was no one with her. She couldn't be asleep at eight o'clock in the evening. Entering, he plucked up courage to question the concierge, who thought, though she couldn't be sure, that Madame was alone. . . .

He hung about for some time between the parapet and the trees of the deserted quay.

Next day he made an immense effort not to ring at her door until three o'clock. He had decided to adopt an attitude of feigned indifference, as though on her alone it depended whether their relationship should remain unchanged, or whether they should draw their lives to a new pattern, see their existences in a new light. Nothing should stand in the way of her finding in him a Fabien drained of all the desire that she no longer felt: nothing should stand in the way of his finding in her the mournful charm of the fugitive from an outworn emotion. From the moment of his arrival he showed a gentle humility toward the woman to whom, in the days of their love, he had been hard and arrogant. He made it clear that he longed to be admitted to every trivial moment in the life of a mistress about whose movements he had formerly shown a lack of curiosity which had driven her almost into the arms of death.

"Who brought you that lilac?"

"I shouldn't have many flowers in this room if I depended on you to bring them. . . . It was Coco and the Princess. They looked in yesterday after you'd gone. The Princess is really kindness itself. Did I tell you that she's taking me with her into the country the day after tomorrow? I'm going to finish my convalescence at Cap Ferrat. She's got one of the loveliest gardens on that part of the coast. . . ."

Not a word did he utter. Whatever he did he must not show what he was feeling. She kept her gaze fixed upon the gawky, carelessly dressed, emaciated and bony youth with the bilious-looking eyes, and to herself she said: "A mule driver." How strange it is to look at a face that we have loved when we love it no longer. Only a short while ago Fanny had been dying for the sake of this same mouth, of these same eyes, which had a glint in them when they smiled. She remembered the Sunday (only a fortnight gone) when she had felt that she would never stop crying, when, on her hands and on her cheeks, there had been the taste and the smell of an almost childlike sense of desolation. She had been quite unable to keep up any pretense, and when people she met and looked at with a haggard and a hunted eye had asked her what was wrong, the mask had fallen from her face as though torn away by the very violence of her feelings. "Please leave me alone," she had groaned; "it's nothing: it will pass"—though not, for a moment, imagining that anything could ever again bring balm to a torment, rather than endure which, she would choose to die.

Fabien went up to her, took her hand, and shyly asked whether the Princess would include him in her invitation.

"You must be mad! She detests you. . . . She thinks of you as my murderer! Besides, I'm going away to get cured, and it's of you I've got to get cured. . . ."

She freed her hand and moved across to the other side of the bed, so as to put a space between them. She remembered the time when the mere proximity of his body had set her trembling, so that her teeth had chattered and her hands grown cold.

"Fabien, I'm going to show you that I'm not such a cat as you think me. I have news of Colombe. . . ."

"Ah!"

"Donald doesn't like the idea of leaving her at the Convent. It seems that she is passing through a highly emotional stage of religiosity, and he's afraid the good Sisters may put ideas into her head."

He said nothing, and she went on:

"As a matter of fact, Thérèse is the only likely obstacle. I think I can persuade Donald without much difficulty. . . . Rather than see his daughter turn nun, as she seems bent on doing . . . after all, it wouldn't be at all a bad match for her, and I'm beginning to think that an affectionate and pious young girl might succeed in making you very happy."

"But what about you, Fanny?"

"Oh, I surrender all claims. I am prepared to go right out of your life. You will have been the last storm that I shall ever suffer. . . . I shall know what real peace means . . . the calm of smooth water after the buffetings of the gale! . . ."

But the flame of his youth refused to burn low, refused to come to terms with such extremities of wisdom. There was a mad look in his eyes as he strode across to the bed and imprisoned her in his arms as in a snare. She dared not struggle, but, inert and clearheaded, lay watching the young man who had once been so spoiled and indolent, and was now embarrassed, awkward in attack, and quelled by her coldness. She laughed, covering her eyes with her arm, and there was a note of uncontrolled hysteria in the sound such as he remembered to have heard when, long ago, on Christmas night, he had been kissed for the first time in the dark old house. . . . At last she grew calmer. Letting fall the arm that covered her face, she breathed out a sigh. She felt numbed but free. She was alone.

Fabien must have spent that night wandering along the deserted river bank near the Champ de Mars and the Magic City. It was not raining, but his clothing was drenched with mist. Just before dawn he found himself at his own door. Fumblingly he undressed, and when morning came was shivering with fever. When the maid arrived to do his room he asked her to put a jug of milk and some aspirin on the table, and leave him to sleep. He had always looked on illness as a soporific drug, a strange world in which he could lose himself, a road beckoning him to a rest without end. Who was it that had said to him that action is but another form of sleep? The restless persons of this world are but sleepers. Real life lies elsewhere. The odd thing was that he felt neither anxiety nor remorse. He kept on repeating to himself a single line of poetry: *Puisque c'est si peu nous qui faisons notre vie.* He felt deep sunk in security because nobody, nobody at all, would come. He had to struggle for his breath. Had he, perhaps, developed congestion of the lungs? He lay struck down by the weight of a deadening slumber, shot through with a sense of something that was almost dreaming, only to sink once more into a sort of burning torpor. Somebody, a man, opened the door. He saw Maïnz taking off his overcoat. He closed his eyes, making believe he slept. A cool hand was laid upon his forehead and fingers pressed his wrist. He heard Maïnz whispering on the landing, telling somebody the address of a doctor.

That night, after the doctor had gone, he opened his eyes and saw in an armchair the figure of the Jew whom he knew so little, watching beside his bed. At dawn it was still there, and came across to lift his head that he might drink. Another day the sick man opened his eyes and saw his mother. She leaned down to kiss him, and he recognized the mingled smell of lavender, naphtha balls and orris root which had always hung about the room where he and Joseph had said their evening prayers. Later, he was conscious of a priest whispering in his ear.

"A woman, my son?"

He made a sign of assent with his eyes.

"Married?"

"Yes. . . ."

The priest said: "I will return . . . offer up your life . . . Our Lord . . . your sufferings. . . ."

They gave him an injection of serum through the pleura,

right into the affected lung. No one knew that he was rejoicing at his sufferings. Maïnz was talking to Madame Dézaymeries at the window. Fabien stirred, moved his lips, and at last was able to articulate:

"Maïnz——"

When the Jew leaned down above the bed, he made a supreme effort and managed to say:

"Don't judge the tree . . . rotten fruit. . . ."

He could say no more, and it occurred to Maïnz that Christ, maybe, had chosen to reveal Himself in the weakest of His vessels.

When he went down to dinner, Madame Dézaymeries put a question:

"Have you sent word to the college authorities?"

"There's no need; he sent in his resignation a month ago."

She showed no sign of amazement. Left to herself she gazed at the man she thought she had known so well. He lay now sleeping peacefully. The doctor had said that injections made directly into the lung can sometimes work miracles. When she had prepared the table for the Last Sacrament (which was to be brought during the night) she kneeled down. Her lips moved, but she could attach no meaning to her words. That morning she had found, tucked away in a drawer, a number of hairpins and a light-colored tortoise-shell comb. *"Third Sorrowful Mystery. . . . Where was I?"* Fabien heard, as once in his childhood's dreaming, the click of the rosary which Madame Dézaymeries was holding like a skein of wool so as to be sure how far she had got in her "telling." But she found it impossible to concentrate on her devotions. She got up and took down from a shelf what she thought was her son's prayer book.

But it turned out to be a small photograph album. She took it to the light, opened it, and turned the pages without making a sound, though she must have read the legends inscribed beneath each picture: *Fanny at the Lido; Fanny on the Piazetta; Fanny at San Francesco-del-Deserto; Our Gondolier; Our Room.*

Quite calmly she put the album back and kneeled down by the bed. She stayed there as motionless as though her body had been turned to stone. Her hollow cheeks had the gray color of stone. At intervals she said, in a low voice, but very distinctly, "On me alone, on me alone. May it all be laid on me." She was remembering the little girl whom she had welcomed, forty years ago, in the old Dupouy house, and how she had loved her frivolity, her impertinent ways, her wild fits of temper. "Was it not for those very vices, then scarcely developed, that she was dear to me, though I did not know it? No, I *did* know it, and later, when I took her in, I did not deceive myself. I refused to see that even then she was prowling around Fabien. Oh, please God let him live, if, by living, he may make atonement. But let him die if death will open the gates of heaven to him. But may Thy justice fall on me alone, miserable sinner that I am."

Fabien still lay dozing. His nose was no longer twitching as it had been earlier, his hand upon the sheet was no longer flushed to a dark red. Thérèse heard a sound of whispering on the stairs, and, thinking it was the Sacrament, lit the two candles on the table that was covered with a cloth. She opened the door and took from the servant a light wicker basket addressed to Fabien Dézaymeries. The name on the card—Madame Donald Larsen —meant nothing to her, but even after all these years she

216

recognized the thin, firm writing of the message that accompanied it: "From the happy land in which I have been born anew, I send to dear Fabien a thought of loyal affection." She tore the card into small pieces and threw them on the fire together with the paper in which the flowers had been wrapped. A flame leapt up. Then she thrust into the blaze great handfuls of gilliflowers, mimosa and carnations, their stalks still wet, that they, too, might be consumed.

At that moment a young priest arrived. There was a devout expression on his face by reason of what he was carrying beneath his cloak. Thérèse dropped to her knees, still holding some flowers in her hand. For a moment she hesitated, then strewed them on the table and the carpet. The priest trod them under his muddy shoes. It was necessary to rouse Fabien. He said that he felt better, and that there was a smell of crushed flowers in the room. His mother wrapped him in a shawl and supported his body while he stretched his waxen face to the Host. The quiet smile never left his lips. God was still in him when he sank once more into sleep. As the priest withdrew he noticed Maïnz standing outside the door, because he had not dared to enter the room.

All that night Madame Dézaymeries watched by her son as he lay sleeping peacefully. She thought that, maybe, the breast that has quivered with the ecstasies of passion had been chosen, as once had been the rim of a well, a publican's table, and that place of sin where the Son of Man had eaten and drunk because he had been sent to call sinners to repentance.

Toward the end of the spring it became possible to move Fabien to the heath country where the sun was already overpowering. From the month of June onward the cicadas made it impossible for anyone to do more than slumber uneasily, and only when with the coming of evening the woods distilled their scent, did sleep come. As darkness deepened the air was filled with the smell of burned heather and brackish water. The Dézaymeries' were expecting a visit from Jacques Maïnz at the end of July. One morning Fabien's mother gave him a letter from Fanny.

He said, averting his eyes: "What ought I to do?"

Perhaps he was thinking that he had in charge a human soul, that sin sometimes binds us to another like a Sacrament.

Madame Dézaymeries thought for a moment before replying: "We are of those who believe that a soul may be influenced at a distance by prayer and sacrifice."

She said no more, but the light of a great joy showed in her face as she watched the young man tear up the letter without so much as opening it. For a while after this frequent letters arrived from Fanny because Fabien made no effort to reply. It became a habit with him to tear them all up unread. For this seeming cruelty he should not be too harshly judged. In order that his mistress might be saved he had refused to open his heart to the call of human happiness, and already he was dead to the world. But for all his resolution the claims of the body could not be altogether stilled. For long months it had been gorged, how then, when it had once more woken to life, could it be kept from craving satisfaction? The real story of Fabien Dézaymeries should, properly speaking, begin at this point, for all that had gone before was in the nature of a prologue. But how is one to describe the secret drama of a man who struggles to subdue his earthy heritage, that drama which finds expression neither in words nor gestures? Where is the artist who may dare to imagine the processes and shifts of the great protagonist —Grace? It is the mark of our slavery and of our wretchedness that we can, without lying, paint a faithful portrait only of the passions.